Vold Book's

OCEANS OF CURTAINS

A NOVEL

SET TO MUSIC

JOHN T. TRAUTMAN

FOR ARKDEMUS

This work is primarily an audiobook set to Vold Book music, written and performed by the author. The author's intent is for the audience to listen to the musical audiobook while they read along. The musical audiobook is available for purchase online.

ISBN: 979-8-9997522-0-8
Published in the USA
December 5, 2025

TABLE OF CONTENTS

A.01 ~ OCEANS OF CURTAINS

< *instrumental* >

A.02 ~ OOC, SIDE A

SIDE A

"I am all that hath been, and is, and shall be;
and my veil no mortal has hitherto raised."

- Plutarch, *On Isis and Osiris*

(2nd century CE)

PLATE I - THE CRUCIFIX TREE

A.03 — CHAPTER 01

A.04 ~ THE CEREMONIAL HALL

The city of Ksevia was all a ruin, and the shifting images that shone through windows of Phalanx were vacant and serene. It appeared that great periods of time had passed, and Ksevia was no longer populated. The vision of their dreams must have been from a distant time, for all that remained of Ksevia was an overgrown extension of the forest that surrounded it. The buildings were seen all around in their desolate state. The courtyard where Koravo and Pandara had shared their first kiss was disordered and dense with wildlife. There were entire ecosystems making a living from where the Ksevians had shared expansive and illustrious memories.

Pandara quietly mourned the ruins of Ksevia, though he maintained emotional control. He thought about the Ksevia he knew and wanted to restore it to its former glory. He hoped that he would have the chance and waited for a sign as to what would come next. Ksevia was also a precious treasure to Koravo. To see it in ruin made her heart sink and belly ache. Like Pandara, she wanted to restore Ksevia to its former glory and hoped to have a chance to do so.

They looked to Hal Fala; off in the distance, the mountain's peak glistened its pearly white crest. Pandara and Koravo wondered as to the state of the Hal Falans. Koravo took a step toward the wreckage, and Pandara followed closely behind.

They went to the Ceremonial Hall and removed some vines that were preventing their entry. Inside the light shone brightly, revealing a dismantled cathedral subject to the erosion of entropy. Most of the pews were intact, though vacant of all but an inaccessible memory.

At the front of the hall, a crucifix tree stood suspended looking over the empty basilica, and behind it were the frescos of scenes from the life of Ksevia, stories which now lived on only in the hearts and minds of Koravo and Pandara. They looked for relics to salvage, but nothing remained from the age in which they had lived in Ksevia. Nothing remained, though they had the book so recently acquired, *Oceans of Curtains*. "Let's leave it here for now," said Koravo. "It looks so natural in this position."

They visited the abandoned water purification tower and went inside. On the wall was the drawing of their idyllic house with horses and the stream, so fondly remembered. Koravo pointed to the necklace on the rock and said, "Look, Pandara!" She held up the talisman and compared it to the little image; it was identical. "How did you know?" asked Koravo.

And Pandara said, "It must just be the power of imagination. Imagination works in mysterious ways."

"That it does," replied Koravo. They rested for a moment and recalled the time they waited here on that day when Ksevia first began to crumble. They were older now and wished for the vitality of youth.

Koravo leaned over and kissed Pandara, who welcomed

the exchange. He leaned in and returned the blessing, accepting her kiss with the longing of thousands of days. As they kissed, the wrinkles on their faces began to recede, and their hair which had lost color began to return to vibrant shades. "We're getting younger!" said Koravo. "Let's continue."

Koravo wrapped her arms around Pandara and pressed her bosom against his chest. He massaged her back and lifted her shirt, feeling there all that he knew and loved. She removed her shirt and asked him to kiss her chest, which he did. She could feel herself reversing time as it were, though in this place time did not proceed on a straight-line course. Age could be manipulated, and the lovers were resetting the clock back to when they were here before.

Pandara and Koravo continued to undress and left the shelter of the purification tower. Out in the open, beneath the hot sun, they made love and celebrated their relationship.

By the time they had finished, the sun was high in the sky. They were youthful and rejuvenated. They knew where they had to go next. It was time to read *Oceans of Curtains*. Koravo said, "You wait here Pandara. I will go fetch the book and return."

He felt for the ring.

When she returned, not only did she carry the fabled book, but she also held in her hand the last two vials of a shimmering Prellian mixture. "I don't know what these are," she said, "but I think we should drink them."

Koravo removed the talisman and placed it on the earth outside in the field. She placed the book, which was indented perfectly, onto the talisman, and Pandara remarked in exclamation. "I remember seeing this book cover in the library," he said. "It was drawn in some of the plates in the book of *Rông*. I believe this book has magical healing properties."

"Well, let's open it!" she said with a smile.

They opened the book, and the pages were blank. She

flipped through and found that none of the pages contained text or image. Then, as she turned a page, an image began to appear. The two watched as lines were laid down by the invisible hand of an unknown author. Ksevia was seen in its current condition. It depicted Pandara and Koravo sitting in the field looking at the book. "That's us!" said Koravo. They turned the page.

A new sight graced the blank page, and Pandara and Koravo watched as the image took shape. They were clearing out the overgrowth, tossing the vines just beyond the threshold where the city met the forest.

They spent many days cleaning up Ksevia, preparing it for some grand event. They turned the page. The city was spotless and restored. Pandara and Koravo had returned it to its previous glory. They turned the page again. A dark storm began to form over Ksevia, according to the image. As the rain poured down, people began to appear from the wood and took shelter under the eaves and inside the buildings of Ksevia.

Just then, Pandara and Koravo looked up. Clouds were forming and they began to feel the slight tinge of raindrops upon their skin. "What?!" said Pandara. "It's not time yet!" He looked to the edge of the city and saw a face looking back at him. The young woman entered Ksevia, and a man was just behind. "It's not time!" shouted Pandara. "We haven't cleaned up the city yet!"

But the storm was gathering, and the people were flooding in as well. The people came slowly toward Pandara and Koravo, forming a circle around them. Pandara and Koravo turned the page; the lines began to show a man sitting at a table writing a book. The surroundings were unfamiliar, but it appeared to be an ancient place from another world. In the blink of an eye, Pandara and Koravo were pulled into the book for a lifetime!

A.05 ~ THE VETRIVAL PARGONIAN

A long time ago, right at the very heart of our galaxy, there existed a beautiful world in the shape of a disc. The supermassive black hole now at the Galactic Center of the Milky Way was an unborn, hidden, and unlikely potentiality. Instead, the Milky Way, or Ελλας as it was then known: the sum of all things in permanent transition, held a bright and eternal future. No one living could have imagined that such a radical transformation to the structure of the cosmos was looming, just below the slow-moving horizon. Yet, so it was.

There were two lands, one on either side of the disc: Tristulle and Phalanx, as they were known to inhabitants. These two worlds were indeed very much aware of each other, as impenetrable windows laced the earthen floor separating the two worlds. Looking down from Tristulle, one could see the world of Phalanx and glimpse its happenings. While on Phalanx, beneath the ground lay the world of Tristulle, displayed with mystical resplendency. These windows into neighboring lands were randomly dispersed, scattered across the natural terrain.

Before this time, another realm existed where the Milky Way now resides. Tristulle and Phalanx were not unified in one land as two sides of a coin. There were two ethereal planes called The Pure Land and Fotoa. The Pure Land was a heavenly place, and in opposition, the hellish cavity of Fotoa was stationed.

Between the floating lands were the Mists of Oblivion. It is said that when The Pure Land and Fotoa collapsed into one world, under immense primordial pressure, this lavender fog formed the crystalline windows that line the boundary between Tristulle and Phalanx.

And yet, there was a third cosmic state prior to our Milky Way. This was the first, nameless land of which little is known. Its origin has been lost to the dark gradient of history. It can be described only as the Realm of Forms, for it is thought that all subsequent lands were conceived of in this place. It was in the Realm of Forms that the architecture, the blueprint for all existent, future lands spontaneously came into being.

Ελλας, the Milky Way, is not necessarily bounded by the reality of time. Time is the substrate through which transformation takes place; however, it is possible to travel between the realms and impact all events as they unfold in their own times. Our people have not discovered the mechanism through which such travel can take place, but we experience the malleability of time every night, in dreams.

Our technology has advanced to the simulation phase. We can construct artificial realities that simulate other dimensions, yet the inventors of old found ways to traverse the actual dimensions that exist in our space. Perhaps, one day we too may discover such methods, and perhaps Ελλας will transform again.

As the various dimensions of reality in our galactic corner can be traversed, i.e. through time travel, it is best to think of all times that have passed as existing here in the present.

Traveling through time is just like traveling through space. All times exist right now, all times except for the future. The future is a constantly gyrating sphere of possibilities; what is now washes up on the shores of the sea that cannot be seen.

Our story spans the realms of the past and the present. A thread of narrative winds between the worlds in the shape of two lovers from the Tristullian city of Ksevia. Their actions determine the outcome of Ελλας and shape the Milky Way into what we know today: a collection of stars and planets spiraling the great and turbulent emptiness of a churning black hole.

However, this story cannot be understood by only looking at the lovers themselves. There is a network of individuals, passing through time, whose choices are inextricably linked to Pandara and

Koravo: the lovers. To see things as they really are, we must fully experience the context of the constellation of which the lovers are a part.

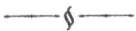

     The spider-like contraption was hung, suspended in front of his face, and anchored to his shoulders like a deep-sea diver's helmet. The arms and apertures revolved with a system of gears, housing the lenses that he used to perceive, with minutiae of detail, the operations that he was performing.

     The Innovator was nearing the summit of his life's work. Elemental forces converged inside the vacuum where his hands shaped the future of all things. It was the rising of a new age. The dawn of transcendent transport was upon him.

     Explosions of angst and anger erupted in a nameless land. A cavern deep inside the essence of thought gave birth to fire and flame. Where there was once nothing, something terrible emerged. Of a nauseated feeling, sparks and smoke manifested directly, culling from the diverse atmospheres of all things possible. The selected forms were twisted and contorted, molten and desperate to consume the environment which contained them.

     From the fiery bowels of hate and illusion, a consciousness coalesced, comprised of vengeance and intelligence beyond anything previously seen. Apep, the white dragon, slithered into being like snakes furiously agitated by an unseen hand. The resultant inferno spread across empty space, generating the territory of Fotoa.

     From Alexander's point of view, a dish of chemicals ignited as expected beneath the palette of his mercurial creation. Suspended inches below the stage where his invention would take on a life of its own, the tiny dish flickered and heated the substance which was being assembled above.

Subtle ingredients were combined from all sources, from all corners of distant locales. Viratus, the black dragon, was emerging from ethereal winds high above a mountainscape. Whisking existence into the air, her delicate fortitude shone forth cutting the vapors which had previously concealed that which was only a vacant dream. Viratus churned the heavens with strength and majesty. She emerged at top speed, flying high above the snow crests where previous lifetimes sank into languid, forgotten memory.

Life is a force of indifference that blows past itself courageously into self-determined destinations that it shall never reach; for once it has arrived, it has already departed onward to the next vision that possesses its prodigious sight!

The Innovator had only fleeting suspicions that his invention was tied to the mystical realms of The Pure Land and Fotoa. They had served as inspiration to be sure, but there was no way to know that the Electron Microstar itself had given rise to the lands of yore and legend!

As Apep smoldered in the cavernous wastelands of Fotoa, Viratus briskly sailed on the exalted jet streams of The Pure Land. All was boundless and stretched beyond the furthest reaches of imagination, yet all could fit in the palm of a hand; and it did! For Alexander manipulated tiny strands of energy that gave birth to entire worlds! He did this in the comfort and seclusion of a tiny workshop. The Vetrival Pargonian now existed in primitive form: a nebulous cloud of tangible air suspended above a glowing burn of chemical flame. What was to come next had only been hypothesized as even theoretically possible.

The Innovator removed his hands from the carbon gloves that reached into the vacuum. He collapsed the spider's web of mechanical lenses into a tiny cylinder with a single, spoken-word command. And finally, he pressed on the top of the glass case in such a way that it transformed into a small cube, four inches on all sides, transparent yet bounded by brass pillars.

Carefully, he lifted the slight cauldron and took it to another working space in his organized, yet humble studio. On a pedestal underneath a spotlight, a larger cube was stationed. This glass box was twelve inches on every side.

The Innovator unlatched the front-facing side, which swung open in such a precise way, to give access to the inner chamber. The embryonic microstar was placed in the center of the larger cube.

Two brass arms affixed vertically, suspended the small compartment which contained the brewing mixture, and connectors from every corner unified the two cubes. When the larger cube door was once again closed, the smaller cube seemed to float in the center of the chamber.

Aubergine mists began to fill unseen channels in the case, and the inner cube began to revolve on its axis, like a gyroscope suspended on a string. The tesseract began to emit light to such a degree that it was no longer possible to stare directly at the mechanistic experiment.

In a blink, dark lenses covered Alexander's eyes, so that he could once again observe the transmutation. Black space surrounded him, and only in the center of his vision could anything be seen at all. There, a shape spun so wildly and with such tact that it could not be identified as one form or another.

The mind played tricks on the viewer who saw a sphere, then a cube, then a series of cubes, then pyramidal forms, and so on. The only thing that was certain was that the shape was incrementally decreasing in total volume. As the form became more and more condensed, the light from within grew in intensity. The Innovator blinked his eyes once again, and an even darker membrane took over his eyes.

Finally, the tesseract began to stabilize, and its light began to fade. There, floating above the pedestal, was an onyx sphere no larger than a centimeter in diameter. The Innovator restored his natural sight, grabbed the pearl with a swift gesture, and placed it in his pocket.

Inside the Electron Microstar these initial moments of gestation had lasted an epoch! All lands that would ever come in and out of existence had transpired. The lifetimes of Viratus and Apep had come and gone, and in their place a natural monument poised with dignity, suspended for all time. The cycle of creation was endless and paradoxical. It was both simultaneously over and just beginning. It was endlessly slow and instantaneous.

Alexander held in his pocket one such manifestation of all things; yet in his mind, there was no inkling of recognition as to the events which had taken place. He was just an artist and a scientist, working in a studio on the remote island of Mount Penglai. But he held in his pocket such a long time ago, the answer to a riddle which would astonish and astound billions of souls over the course of countless millennia. There, in his humble studio, a man carried with him Sagittarius A*: the black hole at the center of our galaxy.

A.06 ~ ONLY IN A NEW MOON

Pandara was ready for adventure. He had grown acclimated to the ring's gravity and longed for the right moment to present it to Koravo. He knew abstractly that there might be danger along the way, but somehow this didn't bother Pandara. He felt invincible to every threat and was secure in the goal of his mission.

They gathered some of the most valuable items in their care, along with packs of food and other supplies. They would follow the description as set forth in Jetir's book: southward to the Tristossa River, eastward to the Liddell Plateau and beyond to the

Lakes of Porselena, where the mountain could be found. But first, somewhere along the way to the Tristossa River, they stopped at Buerroni, a mining village near the Glass Shadow, an enchanted wood.

Pandara knew that they had much greater destinations on the horizon and saw the sleepy town as merely a means to an end. Buerroni was Koravo's first glimpse at the excitement of a trek through Tristulle. Now, in a different space, she recast herself as an adventurous spirit and leaned over to Pandara who smiled.

Walking into town, Pandara and Koravo became a bit nervous. The city was constructed of steel beams rising high into the sky. Beneath those towers at ground level, wooden huts and cabins more familiar, yet still alien to the two, lined the dirt road upon which they tread.

Pandara and Koravo had rarely left the shelter of their natural home, with few exceptions.

"What is the purpose of those iron beams?" Koravo asked of Pandara.

Pandara said, "I'm not sure. They look like the inner structure of our buildings at home in Ksevia, though so much colder and more sterile."

A tiny man with a cane passed them on the left, carrying a bundle of sticks on his back. "Excuse me," signed Pandara. The man didn't seem to understand. "What is the purpose of these metal structures high above?" asked Pandara with words.

"Well," said the man, "not from around here? We don't see many visitors in our city. What brings you to Buerroni?"

Pandara replied. "We are traveling far across the land and stopped here to replenish our supplies."

"Ah," said the working man, who shifted his weight and carefully placed the bundle onto the ground. "They are home to the bureaucracy of Buerroni. Administrators live in those structures, taking account of all of the happenings in our city. I'm afraid you likely won't have much luck procuring supplies here. All of our resources are tightly controlled, but if you are determined, perhaps you can barter for supplies at the tavern just ahead."

"Thank you!" said Koravo, having no idea what the man meant by the word *barter*. She figured it out through context clues, knowing better though than to ask too many questions in a strange land.

"It's my pleasure," said the man. "Name's Orno."

"I'm Koravo, and this is Pandara."

"Nice to meet you both. Now, if you'll excuse me, I must get these sticks to the market while they're still fresh."

"Yes, of course," said Pandara curiously, wondering why Orno had not told them about the market if it was a place where goods were exchanged. Surely, that would be a better place than a tavern to retrieve supplies, but they decided to follow the advice of the little man; perhaps they could at least gather more information at the tavern.

Pandara and Koravo walked ahead under the arching beams of the steel structures. Intimidated, they kept their eyes down as often as possible, trying to feign comfort with a walk into a cavern of framework and scaffolding. It was like walking straight into a mine.

The sun was blocked out, and street lanterns illuminated their passage as though it was night. Several strangers walked by, covered in a fine white powder like the dust of diamonds. The strangers kept their heads down, avoiding eye contact with Pandara and Koravo who made their way to the tavern.

They opened the door and were stunned by what they saw. Gaslights hung above every table, filled to the brim with patrons. For as far as the eye could see, people caroused and celebrated an unknown holiday. *Is it like this all the time?* Pandara wondered, looking at Koravo with a smile.

There was fine music in the air. A jug band performed with tubs, fiddles, drums, and the like. People were dancing in twos: man and woman, elder and child. Everything was on point. The tavern was bustling with life and energy. Pandara was pleasantly surprised and found himself called to dance and have a good time. He would have done so if it wasn't for the items that he was responsible for guarding.

Pandara took the lead and led Koravo to the bar. The bartender was polishing glasses, in between serving carafes of beer to the guests of the establishment. "Excuse me," said Pandara to a woman sitting at the bar. She turned around to face him and sized him up before she spoke.

"What is it, dear?" she asked. Koravo seemed taken aback by her choice of words.

"We're travelers heading far to the south and would like to gather supplies for our journey. What can you tell us about the market?"

"Well dearie, you won't find any supplies there, at least none that you can have. The market is highly regulated by the administrators of Buerroni."

"That's what I understand," said Pandara, faking an understanding. "Can we barter for supplies here at the tavern?"

"It's possible," she said, "but you're likely to have better luck in the Glass Shadow."

"The What?" inquired Koravo. The woman at the bar took a moment to size up Koravo before she spoke. Koravo subtly recoiled with surprise.

"The Glass Shadow, love. It's a forest a few miles to the east. Some artists live out there in the wilderness, and perhaps, if you have something of value, you can trade it for supplies there."

"Oh, I see," said Pandara. "Thank you for your help. We'll

have a look around and head out there in the morning."

The woman at the bar smiled. As soon as Pandara and Koravo had turned their backs, she signaled to the bartender, who in turn signaled to a man standing by the door. He abruptly left the tavern. The mistress picked up her stein and took a drink, enjoying the cool, frothy beverage of wheat and hops.

This time Koravo took the lead and guided Pandara through the tightly knit crowd of rabble rousers in revelry. With his pack on his back, it was difficult to maneuver around the dancers and between the tables, though Pandara managed. They took a seat at an empty booth in the back. A waitress approached them soon enough.

"Welcome to Sapkillo's. What can I bring you?" she asked.

"We're from out of town and don't have any sort of payment."

"Nonsense!" she said. "It's on the house! Everyone who decides to stop at Sapkillo's can have a drink for free!"

Free? thought Koravo, realizing that she and Pandara had a lot to learn.

"Thanks!" said Pandara. "We'll have whatever you recommend." Koravo nodded in agreement, thinking that this was a good idea.

"You see, Koravo? This isn't so bad; we're going to have a great journey." Koravo smiled in agreement, shielding her doubt from her love. Pandara and Koravo watched as the patrons of Sapkillo's danced and lifted their arms in time with the music. A few minutes later, the waitress returned with their drinks.

"Two Breath of the Willows for ya! Now if you would, please fill out these forms." The waitress handed Koravo and Pandara each a packet of paper, filled with personal questions about who they were and where they were going. Koravo looked around and didn't see anyone else filling anything out.

"Does everyone have to fill these out?" she asked as politely as she could.

"Yes hun, but only once. You two are the first travelers we've had in quite some time, so we had to go looking for these documents. Take your time; just leave them behind when you leave."

"Okay thanks," said Pandara, who proceeded to fill out the forms.

Koravo noticed that Pandara seemed to be someone altogether new. The Pandara who first stepped out of Ksevia back in the day would have had more wits about him. *Who were these people, and why did they require so much information?* She wondered what had come over him. She had heard that people could change with time, but was this new version of Pandara someone she would get used to?

Koravo decided to embellish the form in some minor ways, whereas Pandara was forthright, well almost. He decided to not explain the purpose of their quest, as he felt that its nature was too personal.

They drank their drinks, which tasted unfamiliar in a pleasant way. The lightheaded effect it imparted was refreshing, and Pandara began to want for Koravo's attention. An exciting aspect of the journey was that they didn't know when they would have time all to themselves.

Pandara leaned over to the people next to him and said, "Excuse me."

"Yes?" the man said. Koravo took interest in what Pandara was up to.

"What can you tell us about the Glass Shadow?"

"Ah, the Glass Shadow!" said the man, clearly proud to discuss the subject. "Well, the Glass Shadow is interesting indeed. The trees there are made of glass, and as you walk through the forest, a very fine powder of snowlike debris falls upon you, covering your clothes. The effect is quite intriguing, but I wouldn't stay there for too long. Breathing in the fine diamond-like mist is not too good for your health."

"Is that so?" asked Pandara, quite interested in what the man had to say. Koravo was also curious.

"The nomads who pass through the forest frequently have relatively short lives, though it is understood that their lives tend to be quite meaningful from what I've heard."

"How so?" asked Pandara.

"Well, they have a very developed sense of spirituality and can often be found performing various rituals of one kind or another. Are you planning to go there?" he addressed to Koravo.

"Yes!" she said. "We leave in the morning."

"Well, I hope you have a wonderful time. Is the Glass Shadow your final destination?"

"Oh no," said Pandara. "We are heading far to the south and east to a mountain range unlike any other."

"Oh yeah?" he said. "What is the purpose of your travels?"

"Koravo and I are on a mission to save all living beings from suffering. We believe that a clue as to how to accomplish this resides on the summit of the mountain."

"And the two of you will make this journey on your own?" the man inquired.

"That's right," said Koravo, with a subtle hint of indignation in her voice.

"Well," said the man, "that is quite the adventure. I hope that you succeed in your mission, as I'm sure all the people of Buerroni would if they knew about your quest. It is quite interesting."

"Thank you," said Pandara. "We should be leaving now. What was your name?"

"My name is Joei," he said.

"Joei, it was nice to meet you. Perhaps we will cross paths again. Good luck to you."

"I am Koravo, and this is Pandara," Koravo declared calmly.

"I wish you a fine journey, Koravo and Pandara."

And they left for the exit in high spirits.

A.07 ~ A VORTEX OF TIME

One year in Ksevia is 630 days long, comprised of seasons that each contain 126 days over 3 months. Time is demarcated in this way due to the appearance of stehn, which appears exactly once each season, always on the last day. Although there is little communication between Ksevia and the world of Tristulle outside, Tristulle interestingly marks their days in precisely the same way. This is due to the full moon, which occurs once each month, exactly at the midpoint. The full moon and stehn kind of coincide, but we'll get to that later.

Unlike Tristulle, the seasons in Ksevia do not follow a predictable course; however, like Tristulle, there are five of them. Stehn is not considered a season, though it may be best understood by thinking of it as one. What makes stehn remarkable is the way it both anchors and disorients the non-linear perception of time in Ksevia; stehn is a convergence of time. During the rite of stehn, time seems to slow and combine its three distinct phases: the past, the present, and the future. Stehn is like an inverted prism for time. On the day of stehn, all three phases of time are subjectively experienced as though unifying from within the stretched moment.

Although a day on Tristulle lasts for forty hours, the experience of stehn seems to go on for much longer. It can be thought of as a vortex of time. The seasonal occurrence of stehn shakes up time in Ksevia, and the usual, non-linear experience of time in Ksevia feels rooted in stehn.

The Marc-Qey school of thought suggests that it is the moon's influence upon a rare biological formation of microorganisms only found beneath Ksevia that has evolved to produce stehn and all of its subsequent effects unique to Ksevia. Although stehn's exact mechanisms remain unclear, it is interesting to note that it always occurs precisely at the midpoint between full moons. Stehn always happens when the moon appears absent from the sky.

There are many indigenous forms of wildlife in Ksevia, most of which can only be found in Ksevia. There are exactly sixty-five living galochsia trees in Ksevia, and none have ever been found outside its city walls. These are the only examples of the specimen known to exist. The galochsia tree never dies; however, it sheds its sap on a fifty-year cycle in a regenerative process. This process lasts for twelve days at the end of every fifty-year period.

Each galochsia tree supports, on average, one hundred xynipha flowers or so. The xynipha lays dormant most of the time, that is it cannot be seen. However, it is believed that even the dormant xynipha maintains a symbiotic relationship with the galochsia; it is not a parasite.

Once every seven years a xynipha flower blooms, and each flower is on a different schedule. As there are over 6,000 xynipha flowers in Ksevia, if one were to be persistent, one might find a blossom just about every other day. In practice though, seeing a xynipha in bloom is a rare occurrence.

Something unusual happens when the xynipha blooms during stehn. Exactly why this occurs remains a mystery, but it has been theorized that natural qualities of stehn, in particular its electromagnetic effects on moisture in the air, catalyze a chemical reaction within the mature xynipha plant. Its petals radiate a phosphorescent glow about forty-five minutes after stehn begins, and they remain glowing for several hours after stehn has completed. It is, on average, possible to see this phenomenon a few times each year, though it too remains more elusive than one might think.

When the galochsia tree is shedding its sap, once every fifty years, a xynipha blossom on this tree would naturally soak up a degree of the sap. The exact mechanics and purpose of this process remains unknown, but it is believed that the sap of the galochsia tree is what drew the xynipha flowers to the tree in the first place.

A blooming xynipha on a shedding galochsia is quite a rare occurrence, taking place about once every year, given that there are more than sixty galochsia trees in Ksevia. Furthermore, there has not been much study of this process due to:

1) the fact that neither the xynipha nor the galochsia appear to change in any obvious way during the process;

2) the apparent lack of useful byproducts produced by the xynipha as a result of digesting the sap. Perhaps the digestion of sap facilitates other processes in xynipha, but this too is unknown.

On extremely rare occasions, about once every one hundred years, a xynipha in Ksevia would be in bloom during stehn while its galochsia is shedding sap. If, hypothetically, one were to find such a xynipha blossom, not only would it glow phosphorescent, it would be converting the sap into a very special compound at this time.

Pulling the blossom at just the right moment would be the art of maximizing the opportunity, and one citizen of Ksevia deduced that something very special would indeed take place during this confluence of natural wonders. His name was Darnaby Prellius, and Shanti named the resultant extract of the activated xynipha-galochsia sap after him.

Prellius was known to have located three or four Prellian blossoms over the course of his time spent in Ksevia. Seeing the first blossom glow during stehn, dripping a luminescent substance, ignited his passion for this area of study. Perhaps Prellius tasted the liquid that first time; this remains unknown, but he continued to hunt down a second blossom for many years.

He eventually found one! He took care to remove the blossom during the event and used it to derive three vials of the mixture; Prellius had not yet refined his extraction technique.

The third blossom is known to have yielded at least seven additional vials; however, it has been theorized that Prellius in fact captured additional quantities of the extract for his own personal usage.

Moreover, a fourth blossom may have been located to help procure the seven additional vials. All of this remains speculation; however, Prellius left for the wood abruptly during a particularly difficult winter season, leaving his family, friends, and all of the items in his care behind.

The full effect of the Prellian mixture on Ksevian history, and the history of the universe, cannot be overstated.

A.08 ~ OUTSIDE THE TAVERN

Outside of the tavern, Pandara and Koravo regrouped to collect their thoughts. The night was young, and the moon was gone. Koravo was tired and remembered her anxieties about the quest which had been so vivid. Although they had passed into relative subtlety, she had not forgotten her first impressions of the journey. She felt uneasy about its beginning but remembered that she alone built her destiny. It wasn't something predetermined.

Destiny is the summit of her love, will, and choice. Her love was like a lantern that Pandara took with him on his way; she relished in her role and stood by Pandara.

"Let's leave the city, while we can still see in the few remaining shreds of daylight. Perhaps then we can find a good place to camp for the night."

"Sounds good to me," said Koravo. They walked along, hand-in-hand, and made their way towards the fading light. "So that explains the fine, white dust covering their clothes," said Koravo.

"Yeah, I suppose that they've been to the Glass Shadow recently," Pandara said.

"It reminds me of almost extract, though not as powdery as rest." Koravo added. "I hope that we find the artists easily."

Unbeknownst to them, a third member had joined their group. It couldn't be said exactly when she arrived, for she was invisible. Her name was Annie Levine, and she was full of doubts. She had died many years ago while being born. It wasn't her fault, and she didn't know where to go. Though try as she would, nothing had ever seemed to go right. It was a mystery how she ended up on Tristulle, for she was from another planet far away. But as the years strolled into decades, she seemed to slip deep into a rabbit hole.

Following a thread, Annie drifted from land to land until finally she arrived at Tristulle. There she shuffled along, wandering, following some unseen, umbilical cord toward a place where she could hopefully find peace. Like a magnet, she was drawn to Koravo. As in a cocoon or a chrysalis, she waited for deliverance. In what form would it come? Perhaps she would never know. Several paces behind her leaders, Annie floated along feeling that old familiar pull at her petticoat.

Pandara and Koravo found a place to camp for the night. In between some trees, they built a little fire and took out two blankets: one for above and one for below. To their knowledge, Tristulle was an exceptionally peaceful place; they had nothing to worry about.

Koravo, however, laid wide awake thinking about the journey. She didn't know what to expect, and that thought frightened her. She decided to try and appreciate the adventure, but she couldn't sleep. She heard a faint shuffle that night, but it was nothing.

A.09 ~ PARTING WAYS

In the morning, Koravo and Pandara awoke in each other's arms. Paucs was already up; he had built a new fire and was writing in his journal. "Morning, love birds!" he said. Pandara and Koravo smiled, opening their eyes to another day, and failing to not let on certain facts of their engagement from the night before.

"So, today's the big day," Paucs chimed in, changing the subject in doing so.

"Today's the day," Pandara said, trying to not betray his nerves but revealing them instead.

"I don't suppose that you've changed your mind," Paucs inquired.

"Changed my mind?" Pandara asked.

"Yes, about stranding me at the foothills," Paucs remarked, half-jokingly.

Pandara grew serious. "We need to make this journey alone," Pandara said, leaving it at that.

"I understand," said Paucs. "If you don't mind, I've decided to wait for you down here."

"We don't know what will happen," said Pandara. "We may go to the other side."

"That's okay," Paucs replied. "If I don't see you, I can take care of myself."

They split up the food and began to say their goodbyes.

"We've got to get going Paucs. What will you do?"

"Oh, I'll continue to work on my report," he said. "There's much to be done."

Koravo approached Paucs and gave him a big hug. "I don't know what we would've done without you Paucs. You've been a great companion, and we thank you for joining us." Koravo was clearly moved and struggled to hold back the tears.

"It was my pleasure m'lady. Take care of this guy, will ya?"

Pandara stepped forward and shook Paucs' hands. "It's been great Paucs. We'll look you up when we pass back by through Buerroni."

"Okay," said Paucs. "That'll be great!" he paused. "Good luck, you two. Be careful! That's a mountain you're going to climb, you know?"

"Yes, of course," said Pandara. "We will."

"Okay, take care Paucs!" Koravo said, as she stepped back to join Pandara.

"Take care, guys. Good luck and god speed."

"Bye, Paucs."

"Bye."

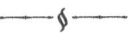

Paucs was sad to say goodbye, but he knew it was for the best; at least, he hoped it was. Their mission seemed unattainable to Paucs, but he wished them nothing but good fortune. Paucs was pleased to receive such warm wishes from Pandara and Koravo. He valued their friendship dearly and set them along their way. And just like that, it was down to two.

Pandara and Koravo surveyed the landscape and discussed their approach. There were cliffs, but there were several passages that looked surmountable. They decided on an avenue of passage and began their ascent.

"You know, Koravo. I've been thinking about Yaronne Jetir. I can't figure out what happened to him. Let's keep a lookout for any signs that he may have passed this way."

"Thanks for reminding me, Pandara," Koravo replied. "I will certainly do just that." There was a brief silence, and then Koravo continued. "Perhaps he made it to the top and couldn't put into words what he found." Koravo was trying to inject their passage with hope and optimism.

Pandara noticed this and replied to the same effect. "I've considered that, and I think it's the most likely scenario," he said. "I truly believe that we will find what we're looking for up there."

Koravo's doubts resurfaced, but she kept them hidden. Pandara stopped. "Koravo?" He looked into her eyes. "I want you again."

She touched her ring and closed her eyes. "We should save our energy, Pandara," and she prayed to the Gods, sensing gold deep within her body. They kept walking.

"What did you learn from Jetir?" Koravo asked.

Pandara placed one foot in front of the other, steps growing steeper by the minute. He looked ahead for slower avenues of ascent. "Jetir was a wise man," Pandara said, and he led them over to more level terrain. "He wrote many passages about love, life, justice, servitude, bliss, peace, humility. I will never forget his final surviving words. He said that he 'had found his home within the shifting tides of time's endless cycle towards its own beginning.' I've thought about that quite a lot, and it doesn't make sense to me; I wonder what he meant by that."

Koravo didn't know if this was the time to reveal her ultimate concern, but she decided to go for it. "Perhaps he meant that settling down and enjoying what life has to offer is a greater quest than seeking out resolution from an unpredictable world."

Pandara hesitated, then spoke. "I understand your meaning, Koravo. I hope that one day we get there."

"We have everything we need right now, Pandara. It's not too late to turn back." She thought about Pandara's premonition, and she thought about how he'd changed, how he'd grown. She realized that now. Pandara wasn't merely changing; he was growing. She felt self-conscious and regretted that she'd placed her desire before his. She mentioned none of this to him. "I just want to be with you and see who you'll become," she said.

Pandara was thinking about her offer. It was appealing, but if he turned back now, he would never be able to forgive himself. "Koravo?" he said. "I wish you'd wait for me with Paucs. I should make this trek alone. I'm the one who has to go, not you." They continued to climb. "I wish you'd seriously consider turning back." He stopped.

Koravo thought about what he said. She wished that there were two of her, one to go with him and one to stay behind. "I don't know what to do," she said.

"Neither do I," said Pandara.

"Perhaps you're right. Perhaps I'll go rejoin Paucs."

With that, Pandara felt a profoundly selfish emptiness. The truth was that he didn't know if he could make it on his own; he felt weak without her. "I'll only be a day or two, and then we can meet up. I'll tell you what's on the other side." He winked.

She smiled. They both knew how his premonition would end, yet neither of them seemed to be able to draw from within the courage to adjust course. They paused and took a seat on rocks nearby.

"Pandara, I want us to return home to Ksevia or find somewhere where we can be free. Don't you want that?"

The thought made Pandara remember his quest in all its detail. "I do," he said. She felt her stomach sink. "But I have to do this. I feel as though I'm failing my destiny if I don't go."

"But what about my destiny, Pandara? I don't want to die!" They were at an impasse.

"What about the countless souls across the universe who don't have a place to sleep tonight? What about the children who cannot eat? We have to think of them, Koravo."

"But are we in any kind of position to do anything about that Pandara?"

"I don't know, Koravo. I don't know." He paused. "I just know I have to try."

"Well, then I can try too. Curse that premonition! I'll take each step carefully. I don't have to die." But little did they know, the dream was not fully understood; they were in the dream. This was the premonition.

"Well then, together then?" he said, still feeling uneasy with the plan.

"Let's hit it," she said and stood up, brushing herself off. Pandara didn't rise.

He honestly didn't know what they should do. He couldn't turn back now, but Koravo's presence on the summit was not essential to a completed mission. The thought of continuing without her, however, made Pandara uneasy and frightened. His secret wish was that she would come along, though that fact made him feel irresponsible and selfish.

"Well, hell!" Koravo shouted. "What is it?" Pandara was frozen in his steps. She walked over to comfort him. She placed her hand on his back and rubbed it smoothly. Koravo knelt and kissed his forehead. "Everything will be alright."

Pandara looked up and addressed her squarely. "Really?" he said. "I'm not so sure. The Yuit never came back and the labyrinth, Koravo. I don't want to lose you again."

"But even if you lose me, you know now that we'll never

really be apart. Isn't that priceless?"

Pandara had to admit that she had a point. Death was an illusion. They couldn't let fear get the best of them. "Okay, Koravo. Let's do it. Just be extremely careful."

"You too, Pandara. You too."

Koravo didn't know what to make of the doubting. She had decided to come along, and Pandara's thick hesitation literally stopped her in her footsteps. On the one hand, Koravo was supportive and believed in the nature of their mission. On the other, she didn't want to die and didn't know what she would do if something happened to Pandara. She couldn't bear to think about those possibilities, and the doubting made her frustrated.

They stood and continued along the path. Koravo was truly a brave soul to embark on the mountain climb. Although Pandara knew that he did not force her to come along, he still felt responsible for her and prayed that everything would go according to plan.

The air was getting frigid and severe, and they had a long way to go. The most difficult part wasn't even near. They knew that they would likely have to scale the side of a cliff or two. It was treacherous, but they were determined.

A.10 ~ THE MILES OF YEARS

Live like you're dying, and you've never lived before. Where did that thought come from? Pandara didn't know, but there it was. "Live like you're dying, and you've never lived before," he spoke aloud.

Koravo turned to him and said, "What Pandara? What was that?"

He repeated the phrase, and she said, "That's incredible. Where did you get that?"

"I don't know," said Pandara. "It just came to me. Perhaps

it was from a dream." He paused for a moment. "Yes, that's it. I was riding the waves of an enormous body of water, and then it came to me. Live like you're dying, and you've never lived before."

"I think we've accomplished that," Koravo said, trying to keep herself from looking down.

Pandara and Koravo had reached the end of level terrain. Pandara stopped and motioned to Koravo to stop as well. "It's about to get tricky," he said.

"Yes, I can see that," Koravo said, who did not feel confident about the path they had chosen.

"We will get through this," Pandara stated, with reassurance in his voice. "There's another easy passage about twenty feet beyond the cliff. All we have to do is walk that narrow ledge, and we will be on the other side."

"Yes, but look Pandara. From there we have to climb." Pandara looked beyond the easy way and saw the dead end up ahead.

"One step at a time," he said. "One step at a time."

Koravo was unsure in her ability to climb. She watched Pandara for suggestions of footing and posture. She learned quickly, and he helped her become more acclimated to the task. Koravo was afraid of the climb, but she put all of that aside and went along anyway. This was Pandara's supreme wish, and she wanted to help him succeed in the mission.

Pandara moved onto the ledge first. "Lean against the rocks, Koravo, and place your steps in parallel, like this." He moved a little out onto the ledge, and Koravo felt a sinking sensation in the bottoms of her feet. Shuffling slowly, he made it halfway to the other side before Koravo began to follow his example.

She treaded lightly on the side of the mountain, doing what Pandara had described but adjusting his movements slightly, as her center of gravity was different from his. Pandara made it across.

"Keep going Koravo, you're almost there."

She leaned into the rocks and alternated her gaze between Pandara and the cliff just in front of her nose. Moments later she was a few steps from the end, and the pathway began to expand. She turned to face Pandara and had safely crossed the chasm.

"That's a relief!" she said.

"Great work, Koravo. I knew you could do it." They continued along their way.

Before long they had reached a section where they would have to climb. They stopped to assess the situation. It looked as though another pathway would be found about thirty feet above their heads. "We just have to climb a little," said Pandara, "then we'll reach an open space." He began to scale the wall.

"Watch where I place my feet," he told her. "If a place seems insecure, don't step there."

She watched as Pandara took deliberate steps to ascertain the firmness of his footholds. It seemed easy enough, though she did not have the upper body strength of Pandara to lift herself up. They climbed.

Slowly they made their way up the side of the mountain. "Patience and focus!" Pandara yelled, careful to not lose track of his attention. If Pandara fell, Koravo was right beneath him. He didn't think about that. He merely gauged his steps and felt for footholds that would support his weight.

"Stay focused!" he offered up to the void. "Stay focused!"

Pandara reached the clearing and took care to not tumble any rocks down below. He crawled on his belly over the ledge and lifted his leg up and over the side of the cliff. Koravo was just behind him, and Pandara reached down to help pull her up to safety.

"We made it!" she exclaimed.

"Well done," Pandara said, as they looked at their surroundings. They were about a quarter of the way up the mountain and, from here, they could see the Lakes of Porselena curl back to meet the Liddell Plateau.

"It's beautiful," Koravo said.

"Just imagine what it will be like from the top," added Pandara.

Neither of them had ever climbed a mountain before, so they were unfamiliar with the rush of pride and exaltation that success brought with it.

"Let's keep going," said Pandara. "There appears to be a little trail just over there." He pointed to an area thirty or so feet to their right, and sure enough, there was a path that winded up and around a corner.

"It's as though that path is laid out for us." Koravo said. "Perhaps this won't be so difficult after all."

"Yes!" said Pandara. "Perhaps it won't!"

"Can we stop and rest here for a few minutes?" Koravo asked. "I'd like a drink of water, and my stomach is empty."

"Sure," said Pandara. "We still have half the day. I just want to be sure that we reach a secure place to stop and rest for the night. I don't know where that will be, but I think that we must go further. Do you agree?"

"I do," she said. They leaned back against the rocks, and Pandara removed rations and water from his pack. They were out of direct sunlight. Though it had been cold earlier, it was getting quite warm.

"I figure it's about lunch time," he said. "I'd like to reach at least the halfway point before tonight, so that in the morning we can make our final ascent." The sun would be blaring on them before long, and Pandara took off his shirt. Koravo looked over at him. "You can do the same if you want," Pandara said with a grin.

"Nice try," Koravo responded. "I think I'll keep my clothes

on." They laughed.

"Suit yourself," he said.

After a short break of silence, Pandara and Koravo stood to carry on. They walked over to the trail which was like a blessing from the Gods. "It almost seems like this path was created by a person!" Koravo exclaimed.

Pandara said, "I was thinking the same thing. Perhaps it was, Jetir?" He asked.

"Maybe," Koravo said, "or perhaps the Lone Spirit."

Pandara thought for a moment about the Lone Spirit, and the thought filled him with wonder and awe. "I can't believe we're actually doing this," he said.

"You can't?" asked Koravo, surprised to hear him say such a thing.

"I mean, the implications are immense."

"I hope you're right," Koravo added, "and I hope you're not." They proceeded in silence for a long way.

The path was perfectly set, unexpectedly so. They were able to cross a great distance in a short period of time, which Pandara found fortuitous and Koravo found relieving. The path climbed the mountain for them, as it was carved at an incline not too great but not too low.

After some distance, Pandara finally said, "I think we're about halfway there." They stopped to take in the view, which was majestic and satisfying.

"Let's keep going," said Koravo.

"If the path cooperates," Pandara said, beginning to step once again, "perhaps we can reach the summit today!"

Koravo was thinking the same thing but didn't want to curse the expedition.

They reached another platform, which extended out on either side of the trail. "Look!" said Pandara, and he pointed at an area not far from where they stood. There, leaning up against the rocks, was a skeleton dressed in the fragments of an ancient garb.

"Yaronne!" he exclaimed, and he rushed to the poor man's side. They hovered over Yaronne Jetir, at first not knowing what to do about the hero and his remains!

The bond which connected Pandara and Jetir was profound and crossed the miles of years. Though they had never met in the flesh, he felt that the bones of Yaronne were like the bones of one from his family. They were brothers, and Pandara began to have closure with the loss.

Seeing Jetir in that state made him realize the universal importance of their mission. *What if they were able to succeed? The end goal was nothing short of the liberation of all living beings from suffering! What if there was a shortcut?* Pandara knew that everything depended upon their success, and he thanked Jetir for the role he had played in the mission. Though the mission had not come to an end, he felt that he and Koravo were reaching the end rapidly.

Koravo had not studied the work of Yaronne Jetir, but she heard much about it from Pandara. She was interested in the nature of the mission and admired Pandara's desire to eradicate suffering. However, she honestly thought it was an insurmountable goal. Suffering would never completely come to an end, and Koravo was careful to keep her true feelings to herself. She didn't want to argue or dampen Pandara's motivation. Maybe she was wrong, and she was curious to see what the journey would bring.

"Do you think?" asked Pandara. "Do you think it'd be alright if I looked in his pack?"

Koravo didn't know what to say, but she knew that Pandara needed resolution. "Yes, I think that'd be fine," she said.

With her permission, he knelt down and removed the skeletal hands from the pack that it clutched. He opened the treasure chest to see what it held inside. The first item that Pandara noticed was a journal. "Gold!" he said. He removed the journal from its place of rest and the two eyed it enviously. "We have to find out what happened!" said Pandara.

Reading Yaronne Jetir's journal was like uncovering one of the mysteries of the cosmos for Pandara. Not only was he eager to understand what had happened to Jetir, but he sought the immediate understanding of what Jetir had encountered at the top of the mountain. Those realizations were finally upon him, and he began to read.

A.11 ~ TRAJECTORY BEGINS

Pandara's experience of waking from his dream was sudden and swift. As white faded to gray, he opened his eyes in an empty stare to the ceiling overhead. Although he was disoriented, just like countless other humans throughout time waking from dreams, he grasped ahold of the day with a grip of speed. And then he calmed.

Resting in bed with eyes open, he allowed himself a moment to brush off the dissolving fantasy. It didn't matter what it was about, for it was assuredly deceptive.

The only thing that mattered was the here and now. Koravo slipped into his passing thoughts. Koravo was always in his thoughts, she who filled the ethereal vignettes of his mind with sublime vision. Pandara embraced this idealized form of his muse and saw through the self-defeating impulse to cage her. She was a play of dynamic poetics in an ever-evolving dance of will that captivated his attention. There was no dream; all was dream. There was nothing but Koravo and her heart of flame.

He leaned forward, his white tunic somewhat creased by one or two movements in the night. His mind became clear, as clear as the sky drifting on a blue summer afternoon.

Ksevia was in a peaceful part of the world. No one knew anything but, except for those who had ventured far beyond its walls perhaps, or just beyond the tree line for all they were concerned. You were either in or out. No one who left had ever returned, though a departure was always a sign of forthcoming birth. The grand cycle continued as it had for so many centuries, and there was no sign of it stopping now.

Having traded his white linens for the gray garb of community, Pandara approached the mirror which was not his. It belonged to everyone. Everything belonged to everyone, and he ran a hand across the bare stubble of his faultless head. *Was it even his own?* It was time for a shave.

With every stroke of the razor, he thought about soft Koravo. She who tended to the river of his soul with the natural grace of elegance. They had known each other since birth; they had known each other forever. Another stroke of the blade.

He wondered if she was awake yet, though he felt her movements and knew that she was. He wondered if she had had another dream, one that she would tell him about. He knew that she valued her dreams, and that her beliefs were very important to her. It's not that there was a lack of expression in Ksevia; it's just that everyone chose to live more or less equally for the benefit of homeostasis.

Koravo was exceptionally intelligent and spoke to him of dreams and desires only in the privacy of their quiet walks. She believed that some part of Pandara longed to break free from the mold, and perhaps she was right. Yet, another part of him resisted; she assumed it was an extension of his protective nature.

Another stroke. Restlessness grew at the thought of her; she was his future. He knew that his thoughts were clouded by indulgences in daydream, but he loved to imagine her. She was right of course. He wouldn't let this on, and the game they played was of the utmost importance. The push and pull were calming; they eased his subtle social restlessness. Sometimes, in the morning, he would imagine living with her for the certain benefits it would afford. *Soon*, he thought.

Pandara finished his shave and bent down to rinse his clean head. In the mirror, symmetrically reflected and hanging on the wall, was a wooden object. It looked somewhat like a crucifix but more so resembled a stylized tree. What this symbol meant at the dawn of its creation was lost in time now, but to the living descendants of those original forebears, the symbol represented balance. Pandara was skeptical of this interpretation but kept such thoughts from himself. He believed that the symbol represented oppression, but to publicly, or even in his own mind, renounce the symbol would be upsetting in the least and potentially treasonous. He was not accustomed to self-sabotage.

He kept the symbol on the wall, where it belonged. Walls were necessary and essential though highly undesirable. Pandara thought about the invisible wall between he and Koravo and how he longed to tear it down. Being confined to his room made him feel somewhat numb. How he wanted to be with Koravo. He lifted his head and supplanted the symbol. It was carefully placed so that he could not see it in this position.

Gazing into the mirror, he thought about her slender body. Though he had never seen it, he had imagined it so many times before: the supple curves and soft crevices of her womanhood. He felt no shame in that. He knew that she would welcome him toward such ends, for it was in her nature to do so with him.

They were destined for one another; they always had been. They were born to be together. All one had to do was wait for the passing of the seasons to permit the flow of nature to take its course. That time had come, and he knew that she felt it as well.

Stepping into the hall, Pandara walked to the cafeteria

with a confident, upright gait, though he had no awareness of this. Turning corners and passing fellow allies, he made his way following the subtle scents of ginger and yeast. Slight running water sounded around, and the joy of the morning greeted all with dignity and mutual respect.

He stepped into the common space, silent in a flurry of hand gestures. Sight was the primary sense, and everything was public, even speech. No one spoke with words; it would be considered so primitive and crass, unthinkable. Everyone welcomed the open communication of sign language, visible for all to see.

His heart rose out from its neutrality at the sight of her, but Pandara suppressed this joy instinctively, knowing that its emergence would destabilize the collective balance. He greeted Koravo with a simple "Hello" sign; she signed back in accord.

Pandara was her sage. He casually knew exactly how to set free her heart and mind. Koravo was uncertain like the wind, but with Pandara her currents became elevated and serene. She derived confidence from his confidence, knowing that everything was exactly as it should be. Her rebellious nature was activated by his subtle acknowledgments of affection: the way he looked at her, the things he'd say. Pandara always knew how to transport her imagination and kindle her feelings.

He asked her how she slept, and she responded, "Quite well, thank you for asking." He knew better than to ask about her dreams, for to do so might embarrass her and upset the balance.

Dreams were meaningless noise, mindless representations of transient change. Though she was of a different nature, Koravo respected and admired his discipline to place Communitas above Sui, or self. She prided herself on knowing his true feelings, and though she did not let it on, she knew his thoughts: all of them.

The tensions and excitement she experienced were tamed only by his lack of acknowledgment. It was cute that he had no idea that she knew he thought about her in that way. She longed for him as well and felt confident that she could indulge such fantasies without letting on the slightest inclination of doing so. They would be together soon; she was certain of that.

They were seated with their meals: porridge and fruit, juice, tea, water and bread. "Did you understand the presentation last night?"

"Yes, I believe so," signed Pandara. "Why? Is there some part of it that you didn't understand?"

"I don't get how the changes being made to Life Sanctuary next year will impact services for those under the age of twelve."

"It won't," responded Pandara. "Credits will be allocated from the Elephant, Feather, and Phoenix funds. Stick will actually increase."

"But that's what I don't understand," she followed. "If Stick increases, but Elephant, Feather and Phoenix are reduced, won't services to youth change as well?"

"Perhaps, but autosum will not change." Pandara slowly and patiently ate his porridge, while Koravo cut a piece of mango. "Anyway, it should be a very subtle shift. No one will be negatively impacted, though trace changes in this generation may be noticed a little down the road. It shouldn't be so dramatic as to cause any significant fluctuation in homeostasis."

"I guess you're right," signed Koravo.

Changes happened, and that couldn't be avoided. Just as it wasn't entirely possible to control the weather, people Koravo knew would be impacted by the evolution of Ksevia. Last year's harvest couldn't be helped, and they had to adapt. Pandara thought about Koravo's interest in individuals over the community. Yet, it did seem like a significant shift was taking place in Ksevia rather abruptly, but he let the thought go.

"So, what would you like to do today?" asked Pandara.

"We could start with a walk and see where that leads us."

She noticed a hint of flirtation in his movements and grinned slightly. "I'd like that," she spoke with signs.

They quietly finished their meal and continued pleasant discourse on things that amused them: music, the Arts, friendship, and trust. The benevolent way had led them to the end of conversation.

Walking a pace behind Koravo, Pandara noticed a minuscule anomaly on the ground, just between two of the trash bins. He put up his tray as Koravo stopped to say hello to Wrobrte. As they chatted, he inconspicuously reached over and picked up the torn piece of paper off of the ground. It was just the torn corner of standard issue journal, yet Pandara knew to trust his instincts. Something about this debris called for him, and he knew better than to doubt synchronicity in the making. He did not, however, immediately feel the need to open it and see what it said. He placed the fragment into his pocket and rejoined Koravo.

"Oh, she is fine thanks," signed Wrob. "It's nothing a little Boragove almost and litmusz won't resolve."

"Always nice to see you, Wrob," Koravo motioned. "Please give Tiyphani and the little one all our best."

"Yes, my friend, please do," signed Pandara.

"See ya at Minard's, and don't get Buttle'd!"

He exited back into the heart of the building.

"Shall we?" asked Koravo. "Let's go get some fresh air."

And as Pandara moved toward the exit, he felt Koravo's hand slip into his. He looked at her innocently, and she smiled. Their restraint was clear as Koravo traced little signs into the palm of Pandara with her finger.

Walking toward the open air, they stepped outside into a glorious summer day. Koravo's right hand bent up to meet the side of Pandara's face; he turned to look at her, and she planted a tender kiss, impassioned yet restrained, beside his lips. There was a momentary pause, then again, a moist embrace this time without restriction. They gained a little separation from the city, and it was clear that someone would soon be leaving for the wood.

A.12 — CHAPTER 02

A.13 ~ HEART OF THE FOREST

The exact origin of Ksevia is lost to obscurity. The world outside remains a mystery. All that is known is that at least fifty centuries have passed in more or less the same fashion. The belief is that people come from mountains far away. Their anthos, or spirit, travels back and forth to a distant land high where the fog meets the clouds. The mountains are a vessel like the womb, and the destiny of one is the destiny of all.

Everything that's needed is right here in Ksevia. There is education, though all share a common knowledge that is born with them. Art is considered the highest form of intelligence, of accomplishment, though all vocations are equally important. Thankfully, there is no need for the law.

There is no immorality in Ksevia, or at least there hasn't been for the longest time. And in fact, the events of today, so outrageous and obscene, will likely be viewed from a medical perspective. Mental illness is not unknown to Ksevia, though citizens have been enhanced out of it for many generations.

Ksevia was built by ancient ancestors, some of whom survived in recent memory. Pa'aan was the oldest living citizen and left for the wood a mere eighty-five years ago. She was around at the time of creation. Music and song would fill the air, in an attempt to communicate with those beyond Hal Fala: the great peak. Artists would commemorate the mountain in portrait and poetry. There are forms of art in Ksevia that combined the senses in ways unknowable. Within the community are circles of friends who practiced arts not shared with the public. Art is considered private and sacred. It is not necessarily for public viewing. It is considered a gift from the artist.

The city of Ksevia has remained at an even population of 17,000 people for all enduring memory: sometimes a few more, sometimes a few less. The oldest documentation suggests that 17,000 lived here at the city's inception. The reason for this exact number remains a mystery, though it has been hypothesized that it is the ideal number to generate and maintain homeostasis.

Ksevians have innate birth control. Pleasure and expression of love have always been seen as separate from childbearing. There is no need to expand the population, and when the time comes for a child to be born, the populace is ready.

Myths are a form of storytelling, which is itself one of the highest and oldest forms of art. Perhaps it is so everywhere an intelligent species comes into being. The most well-known myth in Ksevia involves Braidel, the cursed mountain spirit who gave birth to the world while singing the primordial song. The primordial song is called Hansa, and it is believed that the universe flows on this song like a stream. If you listen carefully, you can learn to truly hear. Only if you truly hear do you have a chance to hear the Hansa. All songs come from Hansa, and all songs are components of Hansa, much in the same way as individual instruments come together to form a song. Individual songs come together to form

Hansa, but Hansa is so much more!

The stars at night are visual representations of the notes of Hansa, which float on an endless river toward the end of the song. It is believed that once Hansa is complete, all ancestors will be united together in Sirrung: the Ende of Illusions. Ksevians do their best to survive and promote balance in all things, waiting for the end of the song, waiting for Sirrung, waiting for the illusion to end!

At times, the allure of the forest has overwhelmed the citizens of Ksevia. The allure can come at any age; there is no common age at which it strikes. When someone steps out into the wilderness, a child is born. And when a child is due, someone is about to heed the call of the wood. The two are inseparable and are celebrated as such.

The birth of a child is no more or less magnificent than the exit of Ksevia. Although one signals the end, the other signals anew. The memory of the departed ones lives on in the collective memory of the tribe. It is in this way that every member of Ksevia intimately knows every other member of Ksevia. They are all one family: those who remain, and those who have left.

Many have claimed to attempt a return from the wood before their departure, but none have ever succeeded. It is believed that although the city appears to remain in one steadfast location, it is actually in a constant state of motion. And once you leave to the forest, it can never be found again. Another theory is that it is the forest which moves, and Ksevia cannot be found because of the motions of the wood. One final story tells that the life of Ksevia is a circle, and the day will come when its population will leave just the same as it arrived. That day is unknown, but it is said that it will be possible to reach Ksevia then.

Whatever the case, it is only known that to heed the call of the forest is a lifelong commitment. Once you leave you cannot return. You are inextricably linked to a bright-eyed child whom you will never meet, that is until the days of Sirrung: the beginning of time, the beginning of everything.

For the most part, citizens of Ksevia do not die, at least not from old age. Aging in Ksevia is a non-linear process that flows in both directions. People tend to get older during the winters and younger during the summers.

It is believed that there are civilizations out there, somewhere, who are first young, get older, and then die. Though this thought turns off the citizens of Ksevia, for it suggests that some are not living in harmony with nature.

Nature in their world, in the city of Ksevia, is neverending! Nothing actually dies but rather goes through endless cycles of change; like dreams at night, our lives are mere fantasies played out in Hansa on the way to Sirrung.

Newborns are of course young in body, and small as they are babies, but their character can be quite old, coming into being with the collective knowledge that Ksevia imparts. They become children who can be as children, or as wise leaders. The child becomes a teenager who can seem middle-aged, childlike, or elderly, and the teen becomes an adult. After this stage, the body's development becomes flexible and not predetermined. There is even some influence that the person's conscious mind has over the process. The body listens to the mind and can be persuaded to fit a desired form.

Although it is most common to live a full and rich life in Ksevia, the beckoning wood can leave its mark, and the mind of any age can be enticed to leave. Perhaps one or two ancient Ksevians paved the road to Hal Fala. If so, it would certainly have to be an interesting story to tell, but this work does not detail such exploits. Perhaps in another place or another time such treks will be made known.

An essential aspect of life in Ksevia is that children are

raised by the community. The significance of biological parents is diminished, in favor of the belief and experience and reality that the tribe is all One: with various individuals comprising the aspects of one singular being. The tribe is one consciousness with many eyes revealing the heart of the forest, that is Ksevia. Ksevia is an extension of the lives of the people who live there. It would be accurate to say that the city walls themselves are alive, especially with the memory of all who came before!

Parents celebrate in the triumphs of their children and mourn the tragedies that befall them, as does the whole community. It is only that the parents do not take sole responsibility for the upbringing of the child. The child is raised communally and sets their own course in life. Who decides whose turn it is to give birth to a newborn? How do the birds know the direction of the south! And how do they decide who travels in the lead? Such occurrences are simply the way they have always been. There is a place for all and for all its place.

When a child reaches the age of five years, he or she begins to set the trajectory for what will become his or her contribution to the community. The education system is like a tree, with branches heading out in all directions. A child decides which way to turn at each intersection, until finally they reach the end of the course. At this point they bloom: bearing fruit, leaves, blossoms! Providing for the overall health of the tree of life itself! There are esoteric branches, and there are common ones. It would take an entire book to map out the entire system, but the overview can be gleaned here within.

At age five, the child must decide among a pursuit of one of the five branches of society: Elephant, Dragonfly, Feather, Stick, and Phoenix. The Elephant School teaches how to provide the necessary essentials to the community, such as food, clothing, and shelter repair. Dragonfly is an elite group of politicians who learn how to reform the communal structure based on the needs of the time. They also are the stewards of Life Sanctuary: the financial institution of Ksevia, for lack of a better term.

The School of the Feather welcomes young ones who commit themselves to becoming a Volunteer; it is a very prestigious undertaking. Stick teaches engineering and Phoenix, medicine. Artistry is considered the highest calling and is open to anyone at any point of their life's journey. Some art is practiced and revealed publicly, while many grand accomplishments have been won in private, unknown to all but who was there at the time.

Teaching is considered a noble stage of life that is typically undertaken after adolescence. Teachers tend to prefer to look young, and as such often blend in with their students in a natural movement towards equality. When visiting a classroom, it can be difficult to tell who the teacher is, but upon a closer look it becomes evident who is steering the course of study.

As mentioned earlier, there are other branches on the tree of life, and there are countless branches that spring forth from the primary ones. About ten percent of the time, a student will create an entirely new branch upon graduation from the traditional routes. Some prefer to adhere to tradition, while others innovate anew.

The Life Sanctuary provides currency to all, in a form commonly referred to as credits; however, the actual term of the social mechanism is autosum. Autosum does not provide for the trading of goods and services; those are freely provided to all by the system. Instead, autosum credits can be returned to the Life Sanctuary in exchange for time. Think about it this way: goods belong to all, services are freely given by those who provide them, and free time is exchanged in the form of currency.

Upon birth, every citizen currently receives forty-three credits. Every century, on the anniversary of the city, each newborn receives an additional credit. At graduation, and at successful completion of a major crossroads of a course of study, the individual receives additional credits on autosum. As a teacher, additional credits are earned. As a politician or artist, there are opportunities to gain additional credits and so on and so forth. These credits return to the Life Sanctuary, and free time is spent.

Credits can also be traded for supplemental luxury, artistic, or magical items, though this is somewhat controversial, as items are generally considered to not have ownership associated with them. One could trade credits for a carved staff to be used in a magical ceremony, for example, but the common understanding is that only the care for the item trades places. The purchaser doesn't maintain ownership of the item but rather becomes the caretaker for the good.

There are historical references to what we would call money dating far back in the annals of Ksevian record. However, upon further study, it is seen that the existence of money generated social unrest and was deemed unfavorable by the Ksevians. Money was outlawed over time, and an egalitarian structure emerged. The antecedent construct to autosum was, however, the construct of money!

Although the stages of life are non-linear, i.e., anyone of a certain age could be a child, adult, or elder, there are certain responsibilities associated with each particular stage. Children have the responsibility, or expectation, of bringing youthful energy to society, and they also must attend classes for the betterment of the future community and its body of knowledge.

Adults must care for the young and the old and engage in the politics of Ksevia. In addition, adults are expected to establish and more often sustain traditional events such as festivals and holidays. Elders impart their wisdom on the community and advance the cause of mythology, storytelling. Elder artists are held in the highest regard and revel in a near god-like stature in society; though this dynamic is a complex nuance, for at once they are held neither above nor below any other citizen.

There is one Ksevian who mysteriously arrived in the city, ushering in an age of change. Initially, she resembled a known youth, but with time it became clear that she had in fact been unknown. Her name is Arkdemus, and she demonstrated significant leadership.

By the time she had arrived in Ksevia, she was far along with her master epic, *Desert Lambda*. This work eventually made a profound impact on the development of Ksevia and ushered in the nexus of its coming of age.

Her father is said to be an artist, credited with advancing, among other things, secret communication and upaya techniques. Her mother is rumored to be a mysterious recluse who lives somewhere in the wood just outside of Ksevia. No one knows exactly where Arkdemus is from, though her influence is felt both far and wide in the Ksevian Yuit.

Legend has it that *The Dawn of Sirrung* itself may be merely the title of an ancient book composed by Arkdemus in the galleries of Hal Fala.

A.14 ~ ON SECRET COMMUNICATION

Shanti peacefully eats her breakfast alone in private quarters. The Senator has everything she needs: a banane, whole grains, water, and the daily communiqué of her most trusted advisors. In it she reads the forecast for next week's proceedings, a summary of last week's events, and current happenings around Ksevia. As usual there is little to mention, and Shanti uses the front of the routine to contemplate what is actually going on. For even when she sits in solitude, she must assume that she is not alone.

Shanti had prepared for these days for more than seventy Ksevian years. Although she hoped that they would never come, she overtly knew that she would have to prepare for instability. The form it was beginning to take, however, was one she hoped she would never encounter. Not because the weight of it was too immense, nor because of how it reflected on her, but rather the disturbance spoke of underlying structural volatility that suggested a threat to the very existence of the community.

She read about the recent flower festival and thought about the nuances of mass psychology. One could likely be reformed, but a group of dissidents posed a greater challenge. It was in the nature of the community to strive to protect and promote equilibrium. She was confident in the teachings of history, showing that the masses would always rally behind the organic rise of a benevolent leader. And one would always come just in time for change to preserve normalcy, at least that's how it always had been. But the recent forecasting of changing weather patterns foretold that what was traditionally predictable was no longer so. The code was transparent enough.

She had studied secret communication for many years after her initiation into the inner circles of leadership. A child holding a picked flower seemed innocent enough on the surface, just in case the daily communiqué was compromised somehow. But beneath the surface, symbols of uprising spoke louder than words: the flower had been uprooted by the hand of an unpredictable force. A child symbol, in this context, was of the most dangerous kind. The caption read, *Sylve innocently contributes flair to the fair.*

Sylve was the child's name to be sure, but only a few would know the reference to Sylvan Lockmire who, many generations earlier, nearly brought catastrophe to Ksevia in a revolt against the popular leadership of the time! Such synchronicities were the bedrock upon which secret communication was formed.

His innocent contribution of flair presaged the possibility of fire, which had not been mentioned in several decades. Shanti knew that she must act quickly if the portending flames were to be put out ahead of time. She prepared to scribe a note to Leisa but was interrupted before she could set pen to paper. Bron, her aide, nervously stood at her side. It was a most unorthodox interruption.

"Arkdemus, I'm afraid I bring unsettling news." He continued. "An alarm in Sector Thirteen has been triggered. Our volunteers have been dispatched to inspect."

"Thank you, Bron," signed Shanti. "Is that all?"

"Yes Shea," he replied. "That is all." And he left.

A public disturbance called for a public response, and the interaction between the two sufficed to appease the Gods' watchful eyes. Shanti drank a cupful of water, took her last bite of banane, and rose to leave her quarters.

Sector Thirteen was in itself unimportant. There were only documents stored there: records of timekeeping, transactions, the usual fare. But the injection of uncertainty was brazen and bold! Her mind found itself insensitively analyzing the intrusion like a player playing a children's game. There was someone else playing, and she knew exactly who it was.

She had known for some time that this would happen, and there was nothing she could do. There was nothing she should do. When trapped in an icy river it is best to go with the flow, waiting to make your move. Her time had not yet come.

She knew that a coup was imminent. Unbelievable that he would jeopardize the balance to such great extent, but what was the cause of this? His actions did not smell of basic human nature. There was something more at play than simple hunger for power. There was something peculiar about these events: it was a group of like-minded individuals with a leader. Did he manage to convert followers to an ideology? This would have been noticed in advance and suggested by the commune.

No! They were acting in hive mind; coordination was not necessary. There was something unified going on here: a chemical reaction.

Shanti walked with an air of confidence toward the remote sector. Bron followed suit in case he was needed for any tangential errand. Upon arriving it was clear that no damage had been done, just a trigger of the alarm nothing more. Volunteers surveyed the scene and collected seemingly irrelevant evidence. Shanti stepped forward and asked to see partially written excerpts of a report. As she reviewed the documents, birds flew outside in a playful dance of hide and seek.

A.15 ~ THE SIGN OF SIGHT

The only thing most Ksevians ever knew of Phalanx was the open sky. The windows were silent and serene. Beneath the surface of Ksevia, an ever-changing sky moved slowly with the tides of the air currents. Together, Koravo and Pandara walked unaware of the cloud hanging above the city walls.

"Tell me, darling, do you ever dream of what lies outside the forest?"

The conversation was borderline, but Pandara proceeded to answer in earnest. "Of course I do. Yes, at times. I wonder if we would survive or thrive in such unknown conditions."

She understood his meaning; it was the response she had hoped to see.

Life in the city of Ksevia was blissful and predictable, but she'd always known that their destiny lay outside the city walls somewhere else. They would leave together. Everything was coming into focus, perhaps a little too quickly, hastily even. By what means or force were they being driven? The suggestions of nature urged slow and constant motion. However, periodic revolution did take place, such as in earthquakes seldom felt below. It was always wise in such moments to act quickly and deliberately.

"What would you bring if you left?" she asked.

He replied with reassuring movements. "My polyflute, some food, and water. You?" He awaited her response that came several moments later.

"I don't think I would bring anything at all," she signed, "just my love for you. The rest I would leave to chance."

Such generosity and candor had always been part of Koravo's nature. Pandara knew that he could never possibly meet anyone else like her. She was an aspect of him and always had been.

"Pandara, there is something else that I need to share with you." The choice of signs was curious, but Pandara believed he understood.

"Let's take a side-route away from the center," he offered. She agreed. They walked casually along together and noted the subtly translucent creatures like squirrels amongst flowers, who played on a preset course. "What's troubling you, Koravo?" he asked once out of range of most citizens.

"It's not troubling me too much," Koravo signed. "It's only a dream." Her words informed a multitude of sentiments, and Pandara scrolled through the rolodex of his thought, adeptly seeking those of most relevance. He combined several threads to ease her worries in a gesture of goodwill meant to soothe and inspire.

"Dreams," he signed, "can be the forebears of truth."

She understood his comment, and the words flew into her mind like a white dove in the advanced path of a setting sun. "How so?" she chimed, with flirtation and curiosity. Pandara never spoke of his dreams.

"Dreams are like a river flowing endlessly from the concealed source of all that we know. Sometimes their movements seem abrasive or senseless, but always they are caused by unseen rocks below."

"Like the passage of time," she added, "reconstructing the fallen fortitude of a civilization." He glimpsed a prescience in her comment, to which she may have been oblivious.

"I believe I can help you analyze your dream," he signed after a moment of reflection, curious of what she might foretell. His indulgences were seldom, though picking up in pace recently. Maybe Pandara was in fact becoming more intuitive as she quietly hoped he might.

"It's not actually a dream," she signed. "It's a recurring vision that I fall into nearly every night in slumber. I've been dreaming the same dream all week."

Two illuminated animals dashed in front of them. Pandara and Koravo studied the movements in unison, like watching rune stones fall into place, divining hidden meaning. They chased each other with only subtle glitches in their programming. The chaotic precision suggested an inventor whose experimental forms might be reproduced en masse.

"There you are Pandara, every night," she signed. "The light of the sun is dull and muted. I can see it, but I cannot feel it. It's as though it isn't there at all. You are utterly alone. Not just that there is no one else around, but you are completely alone in the world." She continued. "It is a courtyard, though no life grows there. Only the desolate skeletons of shrubs open from the earth. There is stone; there is technology, though it remains hidden.

"Benches and walls, covered in the remnants of dead and dried vines, sprawl about. The area is somewhat large, like the lawn of a palace, though there is no palace to be seen." Her gestures shifted downward, somewhere out of sight. "I believe you are in a maze, Pandara, a labyrinthine puzzle."

The chilling signs descended upon him and soaked into his

skin, like cold rain when you've nowhere to go, naked before the elements.

"There is no color, no sound. Only the whispers of wind and sand and dust, beige and haze surround you. You walk the scene in an innocent peace, believing you are safe; but you are not safe, Pandara! How I wish you would realize that!

"There is a sundial that captures your attention. Suspended on a pedestal that is chained to the earth for some unknown reason. You approach it from all sides, noting the lack of shadow as though time is forbidden in this dreadful place. You walk along the perimeter, running your hand along the surface of a stone wall as you go. In an alcove of the wall, you see a curious invention. There is a stick-like protrusion, several bowl-like inclusions, and a tray with three crystal marbles laying dull and flat, as though they'd melted under the immense gravity of this place. You toss them gently in the palm of your hand, but it is already too late.

"A demon appears behind you, and you do not see him. He is not only a beast to the eyes, but a horrendous one to the spirit as well. Hovering one meter above the ground, he is tan and shrouded, like a bean three meters high. The rags he sloughs off do not fall; they are a diseased part of him. He is disease incarnate, though he does not smell. Only the faintest fragrance of stale air surrounds him, air that is too rancid to breathe.

"His face is plain, a caricature of plainness. His eyes are like two rank cauldrons full of black water that open and close. It is the only sign that he is living if that can be said at all. He is in animation; of that I am certain. He has no nose, and his mouth is but a thin slit that extends the width of his head. He is a floating head without need for a body! You sense that you are not alone and slowly turn around to face your overlord. He allows you to but momentarily, before he begins his approach."

Koravo was pale with terror. "That is when the dream

ends," she signed. "Every night I try to help you understand the riddle of the alcove, but every night the dream ends with the same terrible finality." She gasped in horror! "Pandara, I don't believe that you survive this dream, and that is why I cannot bear to see what happens next. I hope that I never, ever see that face in real life."

Pandara sank within nauseous déjà vu. After he collected himself, he stated simply, "Don't worry," using an ancient sign for peace. "It is only a dream." He took a breath and proceeded with a force of will, blocking Koravo's vision out of his awareness. Then, he changed the subject, and she knew that he had been brought to his limit.

"I found this piece of torn paper inside the cafeteria, Koravo. The sign of sight surrounded it." This was all he needed to show her, and her internal composition shifted. He handed Koravo the corner slip, grazing the side of her hand as he did, to comfort her. She took the mysterious scrap and carefully unfolded it to read its contents. Next to a word was a rough sketch, strange and quickly drawn. However, the word was known, and she signed it:

Octave.

As soon as she did, a deafening sound unlike anything heard before resounded nearby. A thundering blast was followed by the deathly cries of a scream! An explosion of extreme magnitude rocked Ksevia to its foundation.

A.16 ~ THE TILTING BALANCE

There was a rebellion! Like a volcano spewing forth the fiery flames of Fotoa itself, the plume of wrath bloomed out of place in the otherwise perfectly serene city. There was shock and disarray. There was panic.

Amidst the rubble and ruin, Pandara did not see any

wounded civilians, any wounded friends. The shock set in on a deeper level, and folk were scattering in all directions, like swans taking to the sky with necks outstretched. In times of such great instability, all civilities are worn down to their most fundamental forces: love shines through and begets no stranger.

People shuffled back to the outskirts of the scene, as though to the cusp of a peripheral space where existence might vanish. On their faces were the sights of attention and instinct. They held to their posts with ready potential, prepared to jump in without notice. There were others, however, who had trained for such unexpected events. They were prepared for the unthinkable. They had disciplined for eventual threats that might appear from any direction. They were the Volunteers.

The Volunteers were a special corps of self-sacrificing Samaritans. They must be counted on, should an unexpected event take place. This was not optional; it was the implicit law, or traditional custom of Ksevia. It was the Ksevian way.

Two women, one man, and one child were being tended to. Pandara could now see two others whom, it appeared, had not survived the onslaught.

There was a spattering of red across the lawn, scorched into the ground with black ash. The destruction of one building told of greater damage inside. In fact, it seemed that the attack must have happened inside, as the wreckage was too complete to have been localized outside.

In a daze, Koravo watched as the Volunteers brought out stretchers and supplies. As though moving of one mind, the Volunteers actively repaired the communal spirit in real time. She noted how their efforts were the focal point of a collected and unified populace. Koravo could perceive the damage to the Yuit, the consciously perceived, collective spirit of the people and structures of Ksevia, and trembled. Like parishioners in prayer, the

Volunteers maintained silence with as much concern for the tilting balance as was possible. They were agents of health, sewing stitches and installing stints in the cell of the commune.

Pandara and Koravo stood by and watched with the others on the periphery. Gradually, crowds were thinning, one at a time, as individuals began to perceive danger to the Yuit. It wasn't danger to themselves that they feared. They must stay alive for the collective.

The Volunteers stopped, connected, and braced themselves, as a second blast was heard nearby. "Let's go," signed Pandara. "It's the best we can do."

He knew exactly where to lead them, and she didn't need a reminder as well. They crossed the primary grid, as much like an entrance to the city as there was. They weaved their way through streams of debris, onward past turbine meadows and beyond the eastern garden. There, in a corner of the city, a tower rose above.

There was new technology that the engineers had developed to purify the river, so the purification tower was no longer in use. In fact, it had never been in use in the lifetimes of Pandara and Koravo, who still thought of the purification technology as new.

In the mind of the community, it had only been a century or two since the advent of the technology. Each individual member of the community shared in a collective memory that spanned the lifetime of the city. In addition, the unorthodox nature of time in Ksevia made it so that things that had just happened seemed like ages ago, and certain events that had passed beyond recent memory seemed like tomorrow.

The loose panel that they would slip through should reveal a space that was all theirs alone. Pandara moved it aside for Koravo, and they crawled into the confined space lit well from high above. Resting near a shadow, the two leaned back against the wall to catch a breath. Neither spoke for several moments, and finally

Pandara signed "What do you think…"

"Tâm," signed Koravo. "Let's engage the artform this minute."

With mention of Tâm, Pandara felt his consciousness become heightened. Tâm was only to be signed in dire times of need, and the signature of the word was itself the initialization of the act.

Tâm was capable of tremendous healing, though proper enactment was costly to short-term energy stores. Koravo knew that she and Pandara would need to rest after attempting to penetrate the dark cloud, but she calculated that it was worth it. Engagement of Tâm in an effort to heal the wounded Yuit, the collective mind of Ksevia, was potentially in violation of Volunteer sovereignty. Though, extreme times called for extreme measures; it seemed to her. Pandara and Koravo went inside the mind cloud of Ksevia, searching for the wall which kept them from the truth. They knew that they would not be welcome; the feat was daring and not without risk.

While their bodies were sitting in meditation pose in the abandoned tower, Pandara and Koravo had actually been transported into the collective Yuit. This was not a metaphor or analogy; Tâm was one of a suite of ancient arts that involved projection of spirit consciousness. However, since the art was only to be used in desperation, neither Pandara nor Koravo knew exactly what to expect.

Tâm was an aspect of the body of knowledge that was inherent to every citizen of Ksevia and therefore did not require practice. It was the equivalent of a fire hose or extinguisher safely stored in a glass case. It was also an alarm.

Mere moments after Koravo engaged stage one of Tâm, she and Pandara could feel others joining in the effort, some of whom were Volunteers. The sensation of entering Tâm was akin to swimming underwater, though the water was the organism of the Yuit itself. There was a blockage or storm up ahead that shouldn't be there; this was the place where the threat had sealed itself off from the rest of the tribe.

The cloud was too thick for any single individual to puncture. Koravo felt that there were at least a dozen or so individuals with them now, all of whom she recognized, though some of whom she knew better than others.

Pandara noticed how the experience of Tâm was dreamlike, and its subjective course felt predetermined. Meaning, once enacted, the reality of Tâm took over and had a mind or will of its own. The feeling of other participants was peripheral, and Pandara didn't know how to communicate with the others. Perhaps Koravo did, but he did not.

Suddenly, their senses became even more pronounced. Several enemies had appeared in the Yuit and were combatting the efforts of the group to dismantle the dark cloud. Matters were worse, however, as it became clear that they were indeed attacking the healers. Koravo felt Pandara shift in front of her, forming a human shield between her and the wall. There wasn't time to think, and the melee was brief but consequential.

In her mind's eye, Koravo perceived the group of healers as forming a black dragon that was on the defensive. The enemies were an aggressive force that was immediately comfortable with being on the offensive. She saw Apep, the white dragon, circling around them and attacking from every possible angle. As quickly as the vision came, it passed, and everything collapsed into pure nothingness.

Although Koravo was cast out of the Nåau field, Pandara and a handful of others were able to reach the cloudy wall. His vision returned, and he saw the threatening leader's life flash before his eyes.

Pandara watched the youth grow into adolescence and beyond. Though he had changed over time, one cynical dimension of his persona remained constant throughout the years. The dream culminated with the bombings, and then the real individual himself appeared before Pandara's eyes in the Yuit, tearing his vision to shreds.

He was seen in a large open room wearing a checkered costume that seemed ceremonial but foreign. He was gesturing a dance with a scepter and an orb. The sight perplexed Pandara just long enough for the foe to turn and direct his ritualistic intentions and movements directly at Pandara. Along with the incantation went a series of utterances that Pandara had never before encountered. The enemy had altered Pandara's life course; soon enough, the changes would root.

Just then, Koravo reappeared in the Nåau field in the form of an eagle. She flew directly at the man and assaulted him with her torrential talons, wings, and blistering beak. Revenge set in, although in hidden ways. The enemy was skillful in retribution. She and Pandara had been cursed!

All of these events took place in the collective mind, and Pandara realized that precious time was short. He focused his attention on the ominous cloud and an incantation of his own sprouted from the purity of spirit. With the utterance of a mysterious sequence of syllables, alongside a series of unknown movements, Pandara connected with the wall and appeared to dissolve it down to its most basic elemental components.

From behind the dissolved wall came flooding in a wave of waters and energy that mixed with the saline substrate of the fledgling Yuit. It was not immediately clear what the event signified as to who may have succeeded in the skirmish, but the Nåau field began to dissolve; and Tâm was drawing toward completion.

Everything went white for Pandara, and Koravo was

nowhere to be felt. After some time had passed, he awoke in the abandoned tower alone. Pandara regained wherewithal, brushed himself off, lifted the metal curtain, and exited the tower.

With sudden insight, he knew exactly what must be done. The details crystallized in his mind, and he knew that Koravo had also received the message, for they were one.

A.17 ~ THE RADICALS OF KSEVIA

In the 28th century of Ksevia, engineer and doctor Raulik Stehn devised a cure for mental disorder for the benefit of the balance of the Yuit, homeostasis of the communal anthos, spirit. It was determined that particular deviations from group mind, those that were deemed immoral by nature, brought about suffering to all in the community. Raulik Stehn uncovered a substance which, in its pure form, brought about frightening or euphoric hallucinations but when refined steered the collective spirit toward balance and harmony.

At the time of his discovery, there were many conspiracy theories that came about among those most reluctant to take the drug, those who displayed the most unethical behavior. These individuals stated their belief that the drug was being promulgated by Dragonfly politicians who sought to establish a fascist authoritarian state and overthrow democracy. They fought hard to make the substance illegal, with the ultimate end of striking its existence from collective memory: in itself a fascist notion, no? But after a few generations had passed, the social norm was that everyone partook of the medicine on a regular basis.

Before long, every citizen of Ksevia was indeed nudged into using the medicine daily, but history would paint a different picture from the one the conspiracy theorists sought to paint. All struggles ended! There was no social strife! People lived in peace and harmony and sought only to better the society in which they lived! If this was authoritarian in nature, the people embraced it wholeheartedly with greater elation than any other event on record. Raulik Stehn Day, the nineteenth day of the fourth month, celebrates such ironies of history and literature.

It is currently believed among certain circles of Dragonfly, that a small faction of the population has developed a sensitivity to this medication, Lohrnum. There are social projections showing that their experience of the medicine is less like the refined substance and more like the pure form: they hallucinate their own sub-collective reality and have even found a way to shield their thoughts and endeavors from the community.

Although their efforts to instigate viral expansion are shielded, such intentions were foreseen in certain artistic works that were commonly held to be more than fiction. As Raulik famously articulated, "If dreams can be the forebears of truth, storytelling is the speech of an oracle."

It is known that a particular group of friends displays iconoclastic tendencies, not for the sake of advancement, but for the sake of destroying what is held in high regard by the community. Although such freedom should arguably exist in a vacuum, when the fabric of society is threatened the group will act. And the actions of the group to purge dissent from its established order threatens the social fabric the most. For all must go together if any are to go at all.

It is theorized that this is their strategy: develop counter-cultural weapons in secret and eventually reveal them to the masses. When the masses see what has been done, some will fight to rid Ksevia of the iconoclasts. This will put them at odds with other Ksevians who embrace the change, and the division will cripple the community. The purpose of this end is total anarchy: the death of the collective Yuit, to control the population of Ksevia.

The death of the Yuit, and thereby the death of the anthos of ancestors would, if anything, prevent Sirrung from possibly coming into existence! It is thought that to prevent Sirrung might actually damage Hansa itself! To damage Hansa should be considered the greatest crime possible. Are the radicals prepared to answer for such a crime? Not to answer to the community they have destroyed, but to answer to the stars: to answer to the mysterious wonder of Hansa.

It is the task of the Senator to inspire action for the benefit of Yuit, homeostasis. Now you can see the burden she carries, silently, each and every morning while reading the daily gazette. Current events shape the future of Hansa, which impacts all creation beyond the sun. Unknowable worlds are affected by the radicals of Ksevia, whose actions inspire the death of inspiration itself. What a dangerous time!

Let us lift the veil and see behind this group which has no name. They actually attribute the movement to a resistance of Lohrnum, and they believe that their so-called immunity is evolution! Mankind is not meant to exist in perfect order and cannot by its very nature; so, nature has found a way to evolve humans beyond the limitations of Lohrnum.

Let us refer to them now as the Post-Lohrnumites whose idea of perfection is anarchy itself. Harmony is enjoyable and utopia desirable, but to the Post-Lohrnumites, they are like painting in the shades of gray.

The world was meant to be experienced in all colors, and the Post-Lohrnumites wish to bring color back to the world at any cost, even at the cost of the death of the Yuit. Is it possible to integrate Post-Lohrnumite philosophy into the Yuit? Such a challenge is open to any citizen of Ksevia, although first the Post-Lohrnumite works must be revealed. This gives them the upper hand as it stands.

Ksevia had been, until this day, only subtly aware of any iconoclastic activities or intents on the surface. Blissfully treading the waters of homeostasis, the average citizen followed the implicit rules as suggested by their connection to the common mind. It is unknown just how long it took homeostasis to come into being, and it is believed that the sustainment of homeostasis provides nourishment to the soul of the universe, Hansa: the song of the stars. It might very well be this homeostasis that provides the non-linear cycle of time and, therefore, the relative immortality of Ksevians.

With that in mind it is understandable how few citizens, if any previously, sought change to the established structure of society in any sweeping manner! Anyone can see that an imperfect civilization requires and demands revolution, but the citizens of Ksevia had attained the ultimate end to which all revolutions aim to achieve: a healthy civilization! Providing nourishment to all who partake! Providing sustenance to the stars and beyond! Now the destruction of the Post-Lohrnumites had been acted out, and their plans were far more devastating than anyone had expected: actual carnage.

It is impossible to cast an accurate picture portraying what violence means to the Ksevians. There had been almost no violent acts in their history since the advent of Lohrnum. Even an argument was to be regarded as completely out of place in all contexts. Such things just simply didn't happen. Those who were aware of the pending threat had expected a rival ideology to be unleashed. Perhaps there would be a new religion to be assimilated into the Yuit, one with controversial ideals. This was something that Dragonfly embraced, although in second order to the continuance of balance and harmony.

But now the rumors of a developing coup were more than just rumors. It appeared that the displacement of power in Ksevia was an actual goal, not simply conjecture. After today's events in the courtyard, it seemed like anything was possible. The Yuit was tarnished, bruised, and suffering! Everyone in Ksevia could feel the loss of life and wounded morale. Behind it all was a cloudy patch, a place in which could not be seen. There was a dark cloud and a wall; behind the wall was simply unknown. This was the place where the Post-Lohrnumites were conspiring! Perhaps there is a way to penetrate the wall. Perhaps there is a way to peer into the dark cloud and reveal the veiled happenings going on there.

Shanti was out surveying the damage. Though she was the leader of the Volunteers by the command of her position, she was looking for clues and pondering her next steps. Nothing was made immediately obvious to her. She saw fragments of rubble and rebar that hadn't been seen in who knows how long! These buildings were not meant to be destroyed. They were strong enough to withstand the elements, generation after generation, yet fragile to the toxic whims of ones set out on destruction.

She reached down to pick up one of the stones and turned it over in her hand. Of course, Hector was behind the attack; that was as clear as day! He was behind the whole Post-Lohrnumite movement! And worse, she knew that he knew that she knew. *Was she even safe at this very moment? How far would Hector go to get what he wanted? Was this simply a warning? Surely, he understood that he needed the sway of the people.* She was mostly confident in her safety yet couldn't be sure.

Shanti had to act. She had prepared for this day in theory, yet it had finally come. Was she truly prepared to do what she knew needed to be done? She reflected back on the book from those years long since passed. She remembered the visual information tables and the descriptions of how cities were built, and how they came to fall.

She had worked out her own theories based on what she

had read; were they enough? They had to be. She knew that everything happened for a reason, and although those lost today could
never be replaced, they had merely traveled off into a different
forest: one of Hector's making, or traveled to Hal Fala.

Her mind went to the 43rd century musings of Goliset and
Perselle. They were considered radical outliers in their time, yet
their ideas had been brought into the Yuit and assimilated. Their
followers were even responsible for a very advantageous revolution
in botany, whereby flowers came back from their wilting state
along with salves and extracts that were used in medicine to this
day. In fact, she began to realize that the Yuit subtly depended
on radical advancement. Without the innovations brought forth,
initially considered disruptive, Yuit might collapse in entropy!
Although this sounds trivial and obvious, it went against the
common philosophy of the day.

Perhaps there was a way to reason with Hector; but no,
that was impossible. For the moment she confronted him as the
terrorist, he would have his checkmate. She couldn't openly reason
with someone responsible for the worst act of violence in memory,
but maybe there was a way to call a secret meeting. In order to do
that, she would have to offer something that he wanted, and there
was only one thing that Hector could possibly want. She could not
reveal the secret or its whereabouts.

A.18 ~ A PANEL IN THE WALL

Sector Eleven was an unsuspecting location, but they were close
on the trail. How had they come to know? The secret was hidden
in a panel in the wall. Only the highest authorities were aware
of something having been hidden, and only Shanti knew exactly
where and what it was. There were nine of them left. What would
happen to the Yuit if she parted with only one? But what was she

thinking? She couldn't offer the most dangerous person in the city the keys to the kingdom! There had to be another way.

Her mind was disrupted from all of this stress. She would implement the plan according to her preparations. All of this thinking had been a part of the Yuit's strategy. She was sorting out the violence actively in the Yuit, and for the Yuit. She knew that the citizens of Ksevia could sense the balance returning. No one could see what was behind the dark cloud, but in the empty space where Hector had blown a hole right out of consciousness, repairs were beginning to be made. All could sense it, and she knew that the citizenry would suspect that she was the reason why. She had to have faith.

Perhaps the events of today were meant to expose the Shea's way before the Post-Lohrnumites. Was she falling directly into their plot? Was she exposed and vulnerable before the Yuit, before Hansa? It didn't matter now, for she had her plan. Now she just had to follow through with its front. Hector would end up with a magical vial; it just wouldn't be to the effect he was expecting. And before that there would be a trial, the first in the modern history of Ksevia. There would be a trial, and the whole future of Ksevia would be at stake!

She would go at once to Hector. She would hold him captive for crimes against Ksevia. This train of thought would be almost incomprehensible to the others! It was so disruptive, but they could handle it. Unfortunately, she realized that this was exactly what Hector would want: to remove all shreds of stability so that the council had no choice but to blindly follow Shea Shanti. Then she was isolated, and they could move in for their final attack. No, she couldn't do it! Of course, she knew all along what she would do. She just had to wrestle with her thoughts for the time being, so that her consciousness did not betray the solution.

Shanti could feel the Yuit rebuilding itself, piece by ethereal piece, while she turned over all possibilities in her mind. The Yuit was like a regenerative organism, reconstructing its way back to homeostasis. She had already begun to walk to where she knew the others would be waiting. She entered the council chambers and took a seat at the front of the room, exactly at the prescribed time to do so. She waited patiently until the focus turned to her.

"Ladies and gentlemen of the council," she signed. "As you all know today has been a devastating and shocking day for our city. The Volunteers are working diligently to help the wounded. As no doubt you have noticed, the Yuit is being repaired thanks to our collective efforts." The room was still.

"But there is so much to tell, and some of it will be difficult to learn. To begin, I accept full responsibility for the attack." There were gasps of shock and outcry! "The attack happened under my watch, and I have reason to believe that I could have prevented it. Nonetheless, I have a plan and will tell you all now."

Hector stood up. "You have a plan? Who are you to say what we shall do!"

A.19 ~ IN PLAIN SIGHT

"I am your humble leader," answered Shanti to Hector and the sign of approval all around. "Hear! Hear!" motioned other members of the council, with great regard for Shea Shanti.

"As you no doubt are aware, there is a faction of our society that is heart set on creating radical change; they do not seek this change for the benefit of our community, but rather, they hope to dismantle our way of life as it is."

Sighs and sobs were heard, as though some had in fact not known this was the case. Shanti knew that some would not have known, but it was time to lay the facts bare for all to see.

"Perhaps you have sensed, or seen, the dark cloud in the

Yuit?" The audience nodded and was silent. "Behind that wall is the faction of Post-Lohrnumites, who have negated the effects of our medication."

"No!" shouted one member of the audience. The verbal outbreak was equally shocking, appropriate it seemed.

"It is so," said Shanti. There were whys and wails of sorrow. Hector abstained from any signs of emotion yet did not seem nervous or agitated in any way. Shanti continued speaking, not signing but speaking to mark the occasion's significance in the history of Ksevia. What was to follow was a long shot, by Shanti's estimation. "There exists a secret in Ksevia, a secret only a few are aware of, and only I know the full extent of its background. I ask the Post-Lohrnumites here in this room to come forward. If they do, I will give them the secret to do with as they please."

There were shouts all around. "Treason!" "Blasphemy!" Shanti's voice rose above the roar of the crowd. "In exchange! I ask that all acts of violence cease from this day forth and the Yuit be preserved." The noise of the crowd died down.

The tension was extreme, and the people waited to see if anyone would come forth. No one did; but then something altogether unexpected happened, unexpected to all but Shanti. Hector stood up and made eye contact with Shanti. After a moment's pause, he turned around as though to leave the room.

"Hector!" shouted Shanti. "I know you are responsible for the bombings today."

Hector turned around and faced Shanti. "Where is your evidence?"

Shanti mournfully frowned and said, "Oh, poor Hector, I will present it before the courts! Guards, arrest that man!"

Only a couple of people knew what she meant by that statement, but two of the younger members of the council, both large and well-built, volunteered to restrain Hector. They grabbed him by the arms, and Hector didn't resist. He merely smiled. They escorted him out of the room and took him somewhere that he would be confined.

"What of this secret, Shanti?" shouted a woman in the room.

"What will you do with Hector?" shouted another.

"The events of the day have been too much," replied Shanti. "Let us compose ourselves and reconvene tomorrow morning promptly at nine o'clock."

The sensible suggestion appeased the council, and Shanti made a motion with her hands.

"That is all," she signed, and with that, the most devastating day in the memory of Ksevia came to an end. People stood up to leave the Senate chambers, and Shanti was following along with the crowd.

She could sense where Hector had been taken and made off toward the observatory at once. She wondered if she had said the right things at the right times and trusted in the revolution at hand. Honestly, she thought of Hector as a partner now and clutched the crucifix tree symbol that hung low around her neck.

She approached the tower and thanked the two men who had volunteered to escort Hector out of the Senate.

"We'll be here all night, Shea Shanti," signed one of the men.

"Just tell us what you need us to do," signed the other.

"It's too late," replied Shanti, to the amazement of the men. "But your assistance will be remembered." She was redirecting traffic in the Yuit, almost manipulating the collective mind to balance out the countless factors and variables at play. Try is all she could do now; all she could do is try.

They opened the doors, and Shanti went inside to where Hector was meditating, cross-legged, on the floor.

"Hector!" she began verbally, and Hector opened his eyes. "I appreciate what you have done."

Hector tried to not betray surprise, but with a little twitch of his eye conveyed hope to Shea Shanti.

"I too have sought ways to reform the Yuit."

"We aim to destroy it," said Hector coldly.

A wave of remorse washed over Shanti, and she knew that he was onto her. "Why destroy the Yuit, when you could control it?" she asked.

"I'm listening," Hector signed spitefully.

"The secret is another medicine that amplifies the connection of the individual to the core of the Yuit. You seem prideful of having transcended Lohrnum," she signed, with a curious inflection on the word *transcended*.

"Are you surprised to hear that another medicine has been kept hidden, directly coinciding with your advance beyond the shackles of the Yuit?"

"I am not surprised," he muttered with only a sprinkling of clues that he was speaking truth.

"Come tomorrow morning, and let us discuss it publicly. The Senate will reconvene at 9:00." With that final statement, she turned to leave.

"Shanti?" said Hector. "There is but one way," and she left.

Shanti reappeared on the Senate floor at precisely 8:45. She cleared her thoughts and maintained her public appearance. She had a lot of heavy lifting to do, and hopefully with the help of Hansa, there would be few diversions from her prepared course of action. But who was she kidding? Certainly not herself. At five till nine, Bron burst into the room looking somewhat embarrassed and disheveled.

He leaned over Shanti's shoulder and whispered, "There has been another alarm triggered, this time in Sector Twelve."

"Thank you, Bron," Shanti signed, revealing nothing. As Bron left the room, Shanti maintained her composure.

Though, silently she wondered if it had been irresponsible of her to call a meeting where all could be found. She knew that she had the council's backing; they would follow her even to the grave, it seemed by their actions. Surely, she wasn't the only one who had thought about the group's safety.

All are courageous, she thought with pride.

At precisely nine o'clock, she stood up and signed, "Thank you all for coming today. I must begin by informing you that you may not be safe here at this time. If anyone would like to leave, they are welcome to do so now."

No one stood up.

"With that said," Shanti continued, "I would like to let you know that I had a very interesting discussion with Hector last night." The audience took interest.

"He told me that there are no lengths he would avoid in order to destroy the Yuit. In fact, I have reason to believe that he may be on his way here right now, having disposed of the guards who kept him captive. I believe there will be a coup."

The council looked startled, even shocked!

"Once again, if you wish to leave, you may do so. But I believe the best course of action we can take is to let that simply happen. If we have faith in the Yuit, then allowing it to—"

The doors slammed open! And Bron rushed onto the Senate floor. Behind him was a troop of twenty-three mercenaries, armed with the deadliest tools they could find to use as weapons.

Bron rushed to where Shanti was standing. "Arkdemus, they have breached Sector Eleven."

"Okay, Bron."

Leading the group was Hector, carrying a book underneath his arm. He went to the front of the hall, where Shanti was standing, and pushed her to the floor.

"Ladies and gentlemen of the council. I have come to inform you that Shanti will no longer be in charge of these proceedings." The weaponized figures, all men, closed the doors and protected them.

"You know me as Hector, but let me introduce myself as I really am.

"My name is Sylvan Lockmire, the Abrogazer."

The sign was a word unknown to all! Sylvan placed his book upon the lectern and began to speak. "Tomorrow will not come easily," he said, "and the day after that as well. There is a new order that I will set forth as follows: first and foremost, we have developed a way to communicate directly through the Yuit, as you can tell."

To everyone's shock and amazement, they could simultaneously hear Sylvan echo in their minds when he said, "Everyone in Ksevia has stopped to hear this message."

It was true! In Ksevia, everyone immediately stopped what they were doing and couldn't believe that Hector was speaking to them directly, in that place where the Yuit once stood by, so reassuring and serene. Now Sylvan's voice boomed loud and disruptive, undermining the fabric of their consciousness. Shanti was stunned. No one had believed such a thing was possible until it had been done!

"We have found a tool hidden in the walls of Sector Eleven. In fact, the vials were located right at the moment of this pronouncement."

Hector had gained omniscient abilities, it seemed. Through his manipulation of the Yuit, not only could all hear him, but he was aware of all things in a heightened version of the collective mind. He continued.

"We weren't sure what the secret was until Shanti came

to me last night. She told me with great pride that the vials would enhance any single individual's connection to the Yuit. No doubt you are wondering how I am able to communicate with you all, here, at this very moment." Everyone was astonished!

"After Shanti left last night, I meditated on this phenomenon and realized that I did not need a vial of medicine in order to accomplish the feat, but I restrained from using my new power until the moment when it all clicked for you.

"My theory is that once I take a vial of the liquid, I shall unite with the Hansa and have complete control over all that I see fit from that perspective. The power will be absolute, extending far beyond Hal Fala and the world of Tristulle. There is nothing you can do to stop me now; my friends are bringing the substance here as I speak."

Just then, the doors were opened, and a young lady carried a small vial of the pearlescent liquid up to the Abrogazer. He drank the potion!

Within seconds, the walls of the Senate began to shake. Clouds drifted in front of the sun, and a pink hue lit all as though the windows of the chamber were set with stained glass. Cracks in the floor began to form, and from within the ground, just in front of the podium, a single rose sprouted up in front of the Abrogazer. He laughed.

"Hahaha! It is the Ophidian Rose!"

The flower coiled like a snake. Sylvan grabbed the flower-snake by its neck and pulled it from the earth. It wilted into blackness, though still alive; he allowed it to slither around his neck, forming a living, breathing necklace. Just then, he tilted his head back, and beams of light shot forth from his eyes and mouth, and just as quickly, the Abrogazer fell to the floor. There was silence.

A.20 ~ LIGHT SPEED DISASTER

*And the Earth, in revolution, sails around the sun as it will con-
tinue to do, once the skyscrapers have all settled, and the vines and
ferns have reclaimed the metallic aperture of the crimson eye of
humanity's misplaced crusade!*

A.21 ~ CRIMSON WAVES

Deep in the eternal night, the dragon pierced night through her
opened eyes. Viratus flew through space, and distant specks of
light shone immovable before her prescient gaze. She knew where
she was headed, and she understood its importance. Hector could
indeed see all that Hansa had to show him, but the vision was
altogether different from what he had expected.

There were children playing in a field, holding hands,
laughing, and skipping across the open terrain. And suddenly a
mushroom cloud smashed open the heavens, emitting laser-like
tones of supernatural light and sound. The children stopped and
turned around: another such blast, and another. Viratus glided
amongst the stars, watching the scene echo infinitely before her
violet eyes.

There was a canyon. It was a ravine of spectral magnifi-
cence. The walls of the venerable canyon shone bright with diamonds, jutting out from the vertical surface. A river of blood began
to rise, in a flood that scorched the canyon walls. The diamonds,
submerged, glimmered blazingly in a dazzling display beneath the
crimson waves. The diamonds burst into flame, reflecting all of
existence in the infernal silhouette.

Back in the Senate, the Abrogazer opened his eyes. He had
in fact not collapsed, but a second had passed since he drank the
pearlescent potion. He gulped deeply. The city is held hostage, and

no one believes that the Abrogazer has a superior plan. He seems
to have glimpsed something in a terrible vision that he, and only
he alone, must now integrate and move beyond. Yet still, all are his
captives, and he controls the currents of the day.

He looked to the ground; there were no cracks in the floor.
He gazed outside to the surrounding sky, and there was not a cloud
to be seen. Had he imagined the whole thing? The Abrogazer felt
a terrible grief come over him, as though he'd lost all sources of
power, but the looks upon the faces of the council displayed that
they had certainly glimpsed something of his incredible sight.
As he regained composure, he could sense that Viratus was out
there, flying through the night sky toward some predetermined
destination.

Sylvan stood behind the lectern and opened the book.
Pictures moved in front of his eyes; Arkdemus could not see the
images; no one could, but she could see its reflections of light
on his beady, deeply set eyes. What Hector saw made him smile.
He watched as the Yuit was alive and burning, on fire. He saw it
disintegrate into ash, and the city of Ksevia began to expand. First
20,000 people, then 40,000, then 100,000 inhabitants all under his
control.

He had them build elaborate monuments to science; new
technologies flourished. The page turned. It was resolved that the
Yuit was like a bubble that held the city captive. The Abrogazer and
his group had freed them from their bondage, and he would be
remembered thusly. The story went on and on, and Sylvan watched
his future unfold in front of him; the city of Ksevia was paralyzed
with fear.

The Ophidian Rose, it was called: the Abrogazer's book. It
had been his best friend across the years, guiding him and showing
him what he had to do.

"What's next?" Shanti asked of the Abrogazer, who looked

at her disapprovingly.

"What's next is that you and your council will die." The entire city erupted into grief, but on a little field next to the recreation center, a boy named Feishma, and a girl named Sulvi, were secretly hatching a plan.

PLATE II · THE OPHIDIAN ROSE

A.22 — CHAPTER 03

A.23 ~ FEISHMA & SULVI

Feishma and Sulvi, like Pandara and Koravo before them, were born in auspicious circumstances. In the case of the former, they were born during the night of Yulsitine, a celestial event that took place when a radiant light made its way across the night sky. Like a nomadic star, the glowing entity slowly traversed the heavens, and the people of Ksevia said that Sirrung was making its way to the future; the end of Hansa was forthcoming.

The children were born that night and were named Feishma, after the breath of the Gods, and Sulvi, after the light that never went out. It became apparent that the two were not able to perceive the Yuit, which was mysterious to their parents and the people of Ksevia. There is a saying in Ksevia that goes, *Water that flows once the rain has come provides life through the desert of summer. Trust the seasons; there is a guaranteed cycle to all things.*

It was determined that there must have been a reason for the children's inability to connect with Yuit, and it appeared that the reason had now come. Feishma and Sulvi watched as the city broke down. They knew that something had happened that they could not perceive. They reasoned that only they could deliver the city from its torment and must do so in the blind. Feishma would go to gather information; Sulvi would wait.

Meanwhile, in the Senate, the Abrogazer had resumed addressing the crowd. "The time has come," he pronounced, "to rid the city of its waste and its excess." He continued. "For too long our city walls have been plagued by the doubts and suspicion of the Senator, by the corruption and ineptitude of the council." Feishma was outside the closed doors with his ear against the wall, and Arkdemus had made subtle motion to Krys, one of the council members on the stage, to pay attention to her.

"It is time," Sylvan shouted, "to end the plight of the people!" Although the people, scattered around the city, were in shock and dismay about what was taking place. They did not trust him, and they never would.

Arkdemus discreetly signed to Krys that she must create a distraction and to wait for her cue. That is all she said. When Sylvan looked down at Arkdemus, she returned the glance with an innocent expression of fear on her face. That was enough to settle his suspicions.

Hector continued, "Starting tonight, no one shall be outside in the city after dusk, and no one shall return outside until after dawn." Feishma ran outside to inform Sulvi about what was happening. Together they realized that the disturbance in the Yuit gave them the temporary ability to foresee events. Sulvi would wait just outside the Senate, and Feishma had to go. He had to save Shanti.

Shanti sent a sign to Krys, who stood up and accosted the Abrogazer. "Like hell we will!" she said. There was a banging sound on the doors where two of the guards held post. They looked at each other and ignored the sound.

Quickly, Arkdemus jumped up and grabbed *The Ophidian Rose;* just as quickly as Hector grabbed her by the wrist. Though she was restrained, she managed to toss the book as far as she could, directly out of the window.

Sylvan yelled, "Go and get that book!" The two guards threw wide the door, and Feishma ran into the Senate chambers. They looked back, and Hector yelled, "Go!" The guards ran down the hall.

Feishma yelled "No! Don't!" But it was too late. Sylvan had taken a dagger from his ankle and thrust it deep into the Senator's side. Everyone screamed in horror! The whole city was once again traumatized by Sylvan's actions!

Feishma fell to the floor and began to weep. Sulvi saw the book flying through the air and ran to the location where it would land. She collected it thusly and bolted for the edge line of the forest. She knew that to leave Ksevia would mean that she could not return, but it had to be done! She was being pursued by the guards who yelled, "Stop girl! Stop!" Sulvi made it to the edge of the forest and never looked back.

Back in the council, Arkdemus lay bleeding to death on the Senate stage. The Yuit was mortally wounded. Everyone in the town could feel it wilting and burning away; their collective consciousness was melting, and there was nothing anyone could do to stop it. The people mourned that in a short twenty-four-hour period, everything had changed. Now they would have to see if they could survive under the rule of the Abrogazer!

Feishma stood up, oblivious to the death of Yuit, and walked over to where Shanti lay. She took his hands in hers and said, "Feishma, dear ... The vials ... You must take them, and ..."

She died.

Sulvi ran with the book and never turned back. She ran as far away as possible and then continued some more, just in the off chance that the guards were still after her and they could make their way back to Ksevia somehow. Finally, after running for a long time, she came to a stop. Sulvi noticed that she was short of breath, not from all the running, but short of breath as though from old age. She found a nearby stream and confirmed the case by looking at her reflection.

Although still small like a child, she had aged drastically. She began to feel tired, not for sleep but from life. She knew that she was dying and did not have long to live. With her last moments, she opened the book out of curiosity.

In it she saw herself and Feishma running through a field, laughing, and playing, and holding hands. Then off in the distance, a gigantic explosion rocked the field of view. A mushroom cloud boomed in the distance. The children paused. Then another explosion, and another. The book went dark, along with the light that had kept Sulvi alive these few short years.

A.24 ~ THE INVITATION

Koravo and Pandara met that night by the corner of the western garden, where the trellis meets the pond. They had not articulated that they would meet; they had both just felt it. Like knowing when to wake up, or when to fetch a meal, the forest had called to them both. It was time to leave.

"What do you think waits for us out there Koravo?" Pandara asked.

Koravo shifted slightly in her sandals and responded, "I don't know; the next step perhaps." Koravo sighed, "I'm a little nervous. Are you?"

"I'm okay, Koravo. We'll take care of each other."

They joined hand-in-hand and made their way to the forest line, knowing that they could never return. Pandara wasn't nervous, but he wasn't overly excited either. He was cautious before the beckoning wood. He was protective of his beloved Koravo and stood guard.

Though they had not consummated their relationship, he knew that she was his and did not take this lightly. She was the dearest treasure that he could hope to find, and his love was nearly just as much the fear of losing her.

Koravo stood on the edge of the forest, anxious and uncertain but knowing that this was her next step. She didn't know what would await them on the other side, but she knew that as long as she had Pandara, everything would be alright. She took his arm and almost stepped into the mysterious wood, as vulnerable as a newborn child. Approaching the threshold, there was a gust of warm wind. Koravo squeezed Pandara's arm a little. "Don't worry," he signed. "It is only a dream." Together they took the final step and entered the wood.

A.25 ~ THE LIBRARY

Pandara shut the door. The building opened and sighed. To his amazement, he was in a beautiful library. At the center of it all, resplendent light and spirit were golden and composed. Pandara knew that he had stumbled into some immense treasure and didn't know where to begin. His impatience gave way to the forgiving multitudes of crumbling decay. Bewildered and stunned, he walked beneath healing beams of the enticing womb. Silent words clung to the atmosphere of pink and purple clouds, lilting in the shining light. Pandara reached out to capture the aspect of what was lost to him and found his oneness among the dust in the glowing beams.

Etched in the Penrose tiling, as though from a previous slave who had unfortunately found herself having to navigate the labyrinth, was an imprint. It read: *Rest here, poor one. The eater of souls cannot enter this domain.* He was relieved. Pandara found himself wanting to never leave these walls, and he saw a basket of fruit on a table in front of him. He grabbed an apple and tore through its juicy exterior as though he had never eaten before. In pure ecstasy, he collapsed and slept.

Still remembrances of a dream washed over his consciousness. There was a woman there whose longing and wanting called to Pandara. Her eyes sailed to him over boundless seas, and Pandara was comforted by the singular frame of vision which befell his mind. The woman would wait, though she spoke to him now. Kóre was her name, and Pandara recognized her tender spirit as one of his own.

When he awoke, an indeterminate amount of time had passed, though the light shining through the glass ceiling was just the same as it had been earlier. Pandara couldn't believe for a moment that the beauty of the Ivory Tower was real, but then he remembered what had come before in the labyrinth and accepted his new reality. He grabbed some grapes and began to explore his surroundings.

The grave devouring of the savage and silent freak haunted Pandara. He couldn't help but wonder if now he could relate to the fruit that he consumed. That was absurd. People needed sustenance, and the gods had provided food for the people to eat. The Grim Reaper needed sustenance as well, and perhaps he couldn't be blamed for devouring souls! Pandara shrugged off the train of thought and noticed how his innocent character sometimes got the best of him. The Grim Reaper was his enemy; it was as simple as that.

Although perhaps there was some sense to his madness, he ate another grape and tasted its delicious, juicy offering. Maybe the sympathetic thought had blossomed in his consciousness in order to give him a clue as to his means of escape. If Pandara could figure out a way to either kill the beast, if it was living, or change its nature in some way, then maybe he would be in control and could reach the end of the maze. The thought stuck with him as he began to survey the aisles of books.

Most of the texts were written in various scripts that Pandara did not recognize, but all of the manuscripts were gloriously bound and precisely illustrated with ink and gold leaf. He would pull the volumes from the shelf just to see what they looked like. Occasionally, Pandara would find a book that he could read. One book in particular called out to him. It was called *Caelum*. Pandara took the book and continued his search. He found another named *Et Arida Flumen* and carried it with him along his quest to make sense of where he was.

After pulling seven or eight books from the shelves, he looked for a spot to stop and read. The first book that jumped out to him was called *The Calliope*. Pandara flipped through the handsomely illustrated text and then began at the start.

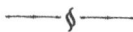

In the quaint, pastoral town of Bargandorf, life progressed gleefully, just as it always had. The rhythms and cadences of generational passage were embraced and passed down, inherited by the younger generations. No one could see any fault with life as it was. The bachelors and the debutantes intermingled in courtship, ensuring that a new day would dawn for humble Bargandorf.

Yet, there was a problem. No one could exactly identify its nature, but a new sensation, a restlessness of spirit was introduced with the advent of automation. It began small at first. The baker saw an advertisement for a bread-slicing machine. The cobbler found a way to repair the daily shoes and make it home in time for supper. In fact, every trade was augmented and advanced through an industrial revolution that stemmed from the factory on the outskirts of the town.

The factory was mysterious. No one saw it being built. It seemed to grow from the land like an orchard or a grove, too slowly to notice. But, one day, there it was, and the people began to wonder who was responsible for the magical developments making their way into the commerce and everyday life of their quiet village.

Signs began to appear on the sunny streets of Bargandorf. Baron von Brighten, the factory vizier, it turned out, intended to become mayor of the town. The people of Bargandorf were ecstatic and lined-up to catch a glimpse of the Baron, who was just then making his way to the town square to deliver a speech. Amidst great anticipation for what the Baron had to say, the townsfolk listened attentively to each and every word of the oration. The Baron explained that although times were tough as a result of failed leadership, he had a plan to make Bargandorf shine once again, for now and for all times to come.

What Bargandorf really needed was a collective vision of prosperity for all. The Baron easily ousted the otherwise-incumbent administration and moved to City Hall. His plan was underway to build a fantastical new device called The Brighten Calliope, or The Calliope for short, which he guaranteed would solve all of society's problems. The Baron convincingly asserted that The Calliope would create anything at all, that the people of Bargandorf could ever want: endless food, endless pleasure, the end of all disease, discomfort, and misery.

There was only one catch. The people of Bargandorf would have to work extra hours to bring The Calliope to fruition. Although there was some initial skepticism, it was quickly drowned out by the overwhelming positivity that surrounded the idea. The Baron's plan was met with great admiration and applause.

Over the years, the people of Bargandorf were assured

that The Calliope was being built through their efforts. The Mayor would present quarterly diagrams, schematics, and charts that seemed plausible and made him look like an expert, for sure. But no one had actually seen anything of its progress. That is until one day, when the factory began to grow again.

The factory suddenly sprouted arms and legs and began to make its way toward the town. People screamed and ran in horror, but the limbs of the factory made sure that no one escaped. The factory grabbed the people of Bargandorf and ate them, sending them deep into its bowels, where they would certainly never see the light of day again. But the factory did not stop there.

The factory ate the houses and the streets of Bargandorf. The factory devoured everything in sight and came to a stop right in the center of town. There it plunged its ugly, polluted ass down on the plot of land where the village had once rested calmly, certain of bright days to come.

Meanwhile, inside of the factory, the people were now the slaves of Brighten, working endless hours for his benefit and his creation. The village was no more, and The Calliope which had taken its place soon began to require additional sustenance.

So, once again, The Calliope began to move. It traveled to other cities, where it played its tune and conquered and expanded its reach. Before long, The Baron was the wealthiest man on Earth, and all others suffered in the plight of their contracts with him. People would congregate in the bowels of The Calliope, remembering the days when they could see the sun.

The Baron, however, had set his sights set on the stars. Little did the people of Bargandorf know, that their naïvety would result in the destruction of all things. For when Baron von Brighten had reached the stars, even the vast expanse of black night was no match for the hunger of his greed. It was not merely the world that was destroyed by a deception of lies, in conjunction with the *complacency of lazy minds! It was Nature itself that had been obliterated.*

Pandara wondered what relevance *The Calliope* had to his current situation. The idea of a moving village that consumed everything in sight seemed foreign to him, yet hauntingly realistic. Perhaps there was no connection to the labyrinth at all. Pandara couldn't be sure, though he knew his direction now and was drawn to complete the task at hand. He hoped that in his efforts he would promptly find a book which jumped out at him with a specific lesson or message related to the predicament of the labyrinth. After this brief moment of thought, he reached for another grape and opened his next book, a larger work titled *The Ziggurat.*

A.26 ~ COMMS BLDG

A gust of wind enveloped them, as though pulling them into the forest. Koravo and Pandara both turned around, and the city of Ksevia was no more. All that they could see, in every direction, was a quiet forest late at night. They looked at each other but neither signed a word; they carried on.

The sacred space called to Pandara from within heightened mystery. He acknowledged the call but remained unmoved. His resolve was set on Koravo's safety. He protected them both, and Koravo appreciated his instinctive concern. Pandara knew that she would maintain the intuitive response to the forest's call and gladly let her roam free in the subtle fantasies of the forest's entanglement with her mind.

It was night when Pandara and Koravo reached the enchanted forest. Though there were lights seen below in Phalanx, they weren't distracted by them. They merely appreciated the subtle illuminations which helped guide their path. What the forest of Tristulle had to show them now was all that they thought about. They knew that it must be extremely important and that the city of Ksevia was at play. They could no longer sense the Yuit, the collective mind, and that fact made them feel more alone than they ever had before.

"It will come back," Pandara signed.

"Yuit?" replied Koravo. And before he could respond, she signed, "I'm not so sure."

Pandara felt that the little, insignificant piece of paper he had found was anything but insignificant. The script almost seemed to radiate with the importance perceived by its writer. *Octave*, it read. Next to the word was a sketch of a box of stripes. In the top corner was a series of symbols with ten sides each. There were many of these symbols positioned in a counterpoint pattern. What did the sketch represent? And how did this paper end up on the cafeteria floor? These were some of the unanswered questions that might never be answered.

They were trudging through the dense forest, following an unseen path that led them to exactly where they needed to go. The answers were out there somewhere, and Pandara had to know. The answers called to him.

Koravo's dream hauntingly permeated her night vision, and she was a little scared. It felt to her as though the Grim Reaper was following them or perhaps even leading them on to their destination. The dungeon scene took place under the bright light of an artificial sun. She prayed that when daylight came, it was from a natural source.

Koravo skipped ahead a pace or two and grabbed Pandara's arm. "We must not get separated," she signed, aware that she was nowhere to be seen in the ominous trance.

"We won't," he calmly replied.

The two made their way onward as though knowing where

to go. Some unseen force was pulling them deeper into the wood, a wood teeming with rich color and sound. It was a peaceful place, and the two did not sense any danger nearby. It was as though Ksevia was born of this tranquil forest; the peace and harmony of their current surroundings formed a mental image like Yuit, a reassuring one. Pandara and Koravo could almost communicate telepathically here, as the mental image was so strong, but not quite. They were still bound to most of the rules of Ksevia in this place.

Realizing that their fates were forever intertwined with the destruction of Ksevia, both had been called to leave its womb-like embrace; Pandara and Koravo had been born to the forest anew.

Koravo asked, "Do you think this forest has a name, Pandara?"

Pandara replied, "We can give it one."

She thought for several moments and right when she finally spoke, an eagle called from high above. "The Trilodian Forest," anointed Koravo. Pandara did not immediately register the pertinence of her suggestion, but it did dawn on him over the moments that followed.

Trilodius was considered one of the great artistic masters of all time. He had lived in pre-historic Ksevia and painted boundless and majestic seascapes. No one had ever seen an ocean in Ksevia, and he suggested that his work represented Yuit in physical, albeit imaginary form. Running water was familiar to them, but to think that a body of water with the size and scope that Trilodius had imagined was possible was altogether fantastical. He had, in his later years, begun to paint underwater scenes depicting creatures of all sorts. These works frightened and amazed. It was as though they had to be real and just as Trilodius had depicted.

It occurred to Pandara that they had stepped into a grand mystery, like the ones Trilodius had created. And now, with the disappearance of the Yuit, what better way to preserve the lost

Yuit than to attach it to Trilodius. Her suggestion was refined. It was like stepping through a mirror, or into Phalanx, the Trilodian Wood. He hoped that her insightful gesture had somehow blessed their passage, but it was not possible to know if such a thing directly perceived in Ksevia was possible here. They wouldn't be able to know without having the Yuit to confirm it. This condition of blindness added to the mystery of the Trilodian Wood.

"Let's stop and rest for a moment, Pandara."

Koravo was thirsty and knelt by a little stream rolling by. She was seemingly unaware of raising her hips in just a certain way to draw the attention of Pandara. He could see many of the suggested curves of her body and felt a rush of blood coursing throughout. She turned back to look at him. Together, their eyes spoke with multitudes of passion and restraint. Before she knew it, he was down at the creek with her. Koravo had wanted Pandara for so long, and she was teeming with anticipation. Like an ember bristling in the dark, Koravo stretched her tense muscles to spark the kindling of his surfacing chi.

He placed his hand on her back, gently caressing the strong trunk beneath. She leaned over and locked her lips around his, seeing with her will the isolated universe he had developed and protected, fortified by innocence and rich with detail.

As their passions flew unrestrained, they reclined parallel to the stream, settling softly into the embrace of their Trilodian bed. Pandara was situated alongside her legs, healing them. Perceiving their firm and obedient structures, he thirsted for what was beneath a thin covering vesture; Koravo made no qualms.

As he extended his arm to bury deep within her leggings, there was a sound nearby. Pandara and Koravo looked at each other. Then again, a rustling of leaves and a buzz in the air.

Suddenly, a giant branch-like dragonfly encrusted with deeply set glowing eyes was hovering before them. It was buzzing all around them; electronic eyes snapping shut with mechanical clicks. Pandara swatted at the creature, but it deftly avoided all attempts to be knocked to the ground. They covered themselves.

"What is it doing?" Koravo signed with impatient concern.

"I don't know," replied Pandara.

The serpentine silhouette dashed quickly, pausing to transmit the vulnerable scene to an unknown location; and just as quickly as it had appeared, it flew away.

"That was very uncomfortable," gestured Koravo. "Do you think it's gone?"

"Yes, I think it is," Pandara responded. They sighed and acknowledged that although they were alone, it seemed as though they would have difficulty gaining intimacy.

"We can try again later," Koravo suggested.

Pandara held up a sign of agreement; he lifted himself then Koravo with his outstretched hand. They buttoned their clothes and carried on.

The ancient forest was mostly silent from that moment on, though its many eyes and ears had been awoken to the sight and sound of young love startled by confrontation. Sticks cracked and leaves crinkled underfoot. The woodlands were teeming with unseen life. All was patient and courteous before the unfolding, distant dream of Sirrung: the Ende of Illusions. Hansa: the song of the stars, imbued vivid tones of detached ecstasy. Their world was rippling with potential deliverance under eaves of hindrance. It was a tense momentum that pushed Pandara and Koravo beyond the reaches of Ksevian memory.

The tone shifted, however, as an offering from the forest began to be revealed out of dreams downstream. There was a building cut from the cloth of Ksevia. Pandara could only make out that there was such a structure, reflecting moonlight in the glassy haze of proposed form. The transfixed travelers approached unequipped.

"Do you think…?"

"Wait," signed Pandara, and he stopped, noting how the impression cut between he and his consort. "I'm sorry," signed Pandara.

"Wait!" Koravo struck back in jest, and with a slight jab of her elbow dissolved a stew of tensions that had accumulated.

"It's our next step," he signed, and she nodded with agreement.

They pressed onward, taking care to disrupt the balance as little as possible. Now they could see the same gray-blue exterior of the architectures from their hometown. In fact, this building belonged in Ksevia to such an extent that they wondered if they had found an exiled ziggurat just on the outskirts of town.

Had they returned to Ksevia? Were they nearing their former place of residence? The thought generated a tinge of sadness between the two, as they had developed a taste for adventure of a most bold kind. The feeling dissolved, however, and they remembered their course which lay ahead. The architecture was reminiscent but alien and disconcerting.

As they approached the entryway, there were no signs of human life visible to their eyes. They walked the perimeter, upon Pandara's suggestion, to get a lay of the land. Skulking around the complex, they discovered that it was much larger than they had guessed from just looking at it from one perspective. A tour of the grounds took approximately ten minutes, and then they were deposited back to where they had begun.

It was an abandoned house of sorts, perhaps a communications building. The enigma of the station wound its way into Pandara's intellect. Though he had not yet even begun to penetrate the walls of its wonderment, Pandara sensed that a riddle existed to which only he alone could approach.

There was an odd-looking dish on the roof's membrane; it appeared foreign to Koravo and Pandara. No matter its purpose, it was clearly inactive and had been for many years. Koravo was confused and bewildered. The communications center was something that she could not comprehend. Koravo knew that she would encounter puzzling things outside of Ksevia; somehow when she reached her port of destiny, however, she was still shocked by its nature. The thought passed.

"Let's go inside," signed Pandara.

The door creaked slightly alongside the restless courage of new visitors. There was no sound coming from within; there was a light switch, but neither dared to use it just yet.

"Hello?" said Koravo, with controlled intonation.

It was one of the few times Pandara had heard her voice.

"It's okay," said Pandara. And with astonishment they looked at each other, wondering if those many years signing their communications had been a fantasy.

There was no reply.

"Pandara, I…"

"Me too, Koravo, me too… I'm stunned. There must be something magical about this place."

"I suppose so," she whispered.

"Do you think it's safe to turn on the lights?" Pandara asked, and at that very moment Koravo flipped the switch. They were unaccustomed to fear, but from somewhere deep within a strong authority warned them to be cautious. Perhaps it was their disconnection from the perceptible Yuit that made everything seem suspicious. With Yuit there was assurance in listening. Without the Yuit, they were deaf; however, ironically, they were speaking. Pandara found himself wondering as to the state of the absent Ksevia. Koravo independently did as well.

The light revealed a sterile hall that was cold with sparse

precision. There were three adjoining rooms, and each contained a unique set of mysteries. There were no doors.

"Let's stay together," Koravo said, as though to remind him of her nightmare but to comfort him as well.

"Agreed," Pandara responded in kind.

They entered the first room on the right. In it was a gigantic chugging tank, a generator perhaps. There was little else to be seen, though the pair wandered the dusty chamber like patrons of an exhibition.

"I feel like a bird in a cage," Koravo said.

"What do you mean?" asked Pandara.

"Perhaps it's just the lighting," she replied.

There was a table with nothing on it except for what appeared to be a desk lamp. Pandara pulled on the cord, turning the light on and off, as if to reassure himself that he was still there. They left the room and set off slowly to explore the main passageway to the inner hearth.

Along the walls were a series of framed photographs, though neither Pandara nor Koravo had ever seen such a thing. The frozen windows gave few clues and appeared rather old: black and white, faded. The outside of the station was seen in the images.

One curious picture caught Koravo's eye. It was a sundial in the courtyard chained to the earth. She realized that the sundial looked somewhat like a tree, the crucifix tree.

"Pandara," she whispered, "this looks similar to the sundial from my vision."

He came to her side and studied the antique image.

"Although the one from my dream was less ornate, less fulfilling."

It was a curious choice of words, spoken by someone lost in the outskirts of delirium. Pandara looked at her vacantly.

They came into a small but cavernous vault, with three

points of interest. There was a table with all sorts of papers scattered about, a chalkboard with intricate writings scribbled around, and a second table with a model of the station open at the roof. This room felt occupied. "Hello?" asked Koravo a second time. "It's okay, you can come out. We don't mean to disturb you," she spoke in a worrisome tone wrapped in kindness and warmth.

A small figure entered the room, oblivious to her calling. He looked up. "Well don't just stand there!" the man said. "Help me finish The Oculus Equation! A small figure entered the room, oblivious to her calling. He looked up. "Well don't just stand there!" the man said. "Help me finish The Oculus Equation!"

Pandara looked at Koravo. "Did that just happen twice?" he asked.

Koravo responded. "What do you mean, Pandara?" She waited for his response.

Pandara looked at Koravo. "Did that just happen twice?" She waited for his response.

"I'm Pandara," said Pandara between cracked panes of consciousness. "I'm Pandara; this is Koravo."

"Yes, yes, I'm sure it is," said the man quixotically. Pandara and Koravo looked at each other quizzically.

"What is your name?" asked Koravo with a touch of impertinence to her voice.

"What?!" yelled the little man, as he turned to look at Koravo. "Oh, it's Seprator. My name's Seprator. Now will you please hand me that solution already? My name's Seprator. There is so much work to be done."

"What is the nature of your work, Seprator?" Pandara found himself asking.

"Well, you don't have to ask me twice," said Seprator. "You don't have to ask me twice. Can't you see that I'm busy? I'm busy!" said Seprator.

It was as though stehn was in full bloom, although the moon signaled otherwise.

Seprator was a little man, scruffy and rambunctious. He commanded his unfocused attention toward whatever happened to spark his interest in the moment. Riddles and clues were made infinitely more complex by the brownie who had little sense to solve them. Seprator had little sense to solve the riddle.

"What is the riddle?" asked Pandara. Koravo looked at him curiously.

Seprator responded. Although small in stature, the tiny man's voice had risen far above the silence. "Well, how do you know that there's a riddle? How do you know that there's a riddle? That's a curious thing."

Pandara stopped in his tracks. "What is the riddle?" he asked.

"Well, how do you know that there's a riddle?" asked Seprator, who seemed to command unusual powers.

"Is everything alright, Pandara?" Koravo looked at Pandara.

"Wait," said Pandara cautiously. Koravo looked at him to respond.

Seprator motioned impatience and began to get back to work. "Ah," said Seprator. "Impressive. But do you know why?"

"It's called The Oculus Equation."

Seprator laughed, "I see that you're confused."

Pandara turned to look at Koravo who had become frozen in time. Pandara turned to look at Koravo, and she was not moving. Koravo had become frozen in time. "What happened to Koravo?" asked Pandara.

"Listen to me carefully," said Seprator. "I'm only going to say this once. Koravo has become frozen in time!"

"Listen to me carefully," said Seprator. "Things are not as they appear. I'm only going to say this once."

Pandara sensed that Seprator was hiding something but couldn't muster the strength to keep the thought to himself. "Bring Koravo back, right now," Pandara said confidently. "Right now."

Seprator turned to look at Pandara, and a serious look washed over his face. Seprator paused and smiled. "Very good! Very good indeed! Perhaps you can be useful. I could use the benefit of a fresh perspective." It seemed that he had merely evaded the question and continued to scratch on the board with a piece of chalk.

Although small in stature, his voice rose far above the silence. Pandara wondered if the show was a defense mechanism, or if the man was really that aloof. "I'm Pandara," said Pandara with control and confidence. "This is Koravo."

"Yes, yes. I'm sure it is," said the man quixotically. Pandara and Koravo looked at each other quizzically.

Koravo asked, "What happened, Pandara?"

Pandara said, "I don't know."

"I'll tell you what happened," said Seprator. "The two of you demonstrated perfectly why I am trying to solve The Oculus Equation!"

"What do you mean?" asked Pandara.

"Oh, nevermind! But if we don't figure it out, who knows what will happen?! What I've been able to figure out so far is that the energy fluctuations move through octaves."

"Octaves?" asked Pandara. Pandara thought about the little sheet of paper that he had kept concealed in his pocket.

"Yes, of course!" responded Seprator. "If all things are sound vibrations represented visually with matter, then it goes to follow that the multitude of dimensions are arranged in octaves! I have studied this phenomenon since before you were born. Mathematically, it should be possible to harmonize the structure in such a way that the energy disturbances move away from the center laterally. Such a change would result in stabilizing consciousness! I call this theoretical equation, The Oculus Equation."

Koravo looked at Seprator skeptically. She was trying to figure out if he was causing the strange occurrences.

"What do you mean?!" asked Seprator.

Pandara understood what Koravo was getting at. "When was the last time you left this station, Seprator?"

"Leave the station?! Well, what do you think I'm trying to do! Oh no!" said Seprator, "Here comes another energy fluctuation!

"It's one of the many riddles of this place. From what I can gather, it translates roughly to the oculus is four times spun, and the day is long; but longer still the lock, until the day is done. These papers have been here as long as I have. They must have been written by a previous tenant. I work on the chalkboard, trying to sort everything out."

Pandara and Koravo looked at each other. They weren't exactly confident that the translation was accurate, but it was all that they had up to this point.

"Oh no," said Seprator. "That's not just an energy fluctuation. I remember when you were here before, and we had that conversation! Something strange is definitely happening with time... The purpose of this station is to bewilder my imagination!" He paused once again. "It was once used as a communications house to transmit and receive information across Tristulle. Are you both from Ksevia?"

"We are," said Pandara.

"Well, then, like myself, you would have no idea where in the world this building would be sending messages, isn't that right? Sending messages?! Who said anything about sending messages? I'm trying to solve The Oculus Equation!"

"I'd like to send a message," said Koravo. Pandara looked at her. "I'd like to send a message to Seprator."

Seprator looked confused. "Well, I'm right here. What

would you like to say?"

Koravo said, "The Oculus Equation is causing the energy fluctuations; it's not going to stop them."

There was a pause.

"Oh geez!" said Seprator. "Of course you'd say such a thing. If you're not going to be helpful would you please get out of my way?"

Koravo replied, "Gladly," and turned around and walked out of the room. However, when she stepped across the threshold, she was re-entering the room!

Pandara said, "Oh no, Koravo. I think we're stuck."

Seprator laughed. "Oh my! I should have warned you, but you came in of your own accord! That's why we need to solve The Oculus Equation!"

"Okay," said Koravo. "What do you have so far?"

"What do you mean?" asked Seprator. "The Oculus Equation isn't a song or a message or a formula! I only call it an equation. It's really simple, come with me!" Koravo and Pandara proceeded to follow Seprator out of the room! They looked at each other, and continued along.

Seprator went to the generator room in the front. "You see, this here machine looks like an energy generator, but it's actually not." He turned around and started leaving the room. Pandara stopped him.

"Well, what is it?" asked Pandara. Seprator laughed. "Who can say! Can you?" When Seprator exited the room, the three found themselves in the room with the model of the station once again. Seprator was busy at the chalkboard.

"If it's not an equation, then why are you working on a mathematical formula?" asked Koravo.

"Oh these?" asked Seprator. "The real work is happening all around us. I'm just grounding the energy transmissions into the room."

"So, The Oculus Equation is a kind of magic after all." said Pandara.

"You might say that, yes," said Seprator.

Separatim, leo et capra devorarent. The inscription read *Chimera.* He continued. Forty or so pages all fit the same format, but only one had the corner torn from it. Some of the pages had the inscription circled, and Pandara looked for a commonality among them. Then it occurred to him: all of the inscriptions that were circled contained six letters. There had to be a reason.

Candle, Forest, Locust, Flower, Basket, Oculus, and even his, *Octave,* were comprised of six characters. Maybe Seprator was barking up the wrong tree. *Oculus* was irrelevant. *Octave* was what he was searching for after all. Perhaps Pandara didn't need to know what the prompts said, he already had his answer. Now he just needed to know what would require a six-character word. He remembered that Seprator was working on something to do with a combination. Perhaps the combination was *Octave,* and Seprator would know where the lock was.

"That's it!" Seprator leapt up with excitement. "Thank you, my good man! *Octave* is the answer I've been searching for!"

"But how did you…"

"There's no time for that, young Penderbatch; come quick!"

Koravo stirred and spoke, "Wait, what's happening?"

"Your friend, Pollywag, solved the mystery! We must go quick!"

Futilely, Pandara said, "My name's Pandara," but the hermit was already outside of the room.

Pandara extended his hand to Koravo, in echo of their tryst from earlier that night, and she smiled as he helped her up. They followed Seprator, several paces behind, outside and around the corner of the building. Beside the strange station, a dim forest could be seen on Phalanx. The window below seemed to reveal an expansive but veiled wood, which echoed the Trilodian Forest above.

When they turned the second corner, Seprator was waiting in front of a large iron door just across from where the sundial could faintly be seen.

"How did we not see this door?" Koravo asked.

"I suppose it was just too dark for us to notice," Pandara added.

"Nonsense!" said the hermit. "It's just materialized now!"

The two knew better than to ask additional questions. Magical things happened in this place, and they didn't want to break the innocent excitement that made Seprator shine like a child.

O-C-T-A-V-E

Seprator input the letters into a digital keypad, the likes of which none of them had ever seen before. A green glow shot out from all sides of the heavy iron door, and the iron barricade dissolved into thin air. In its place was a rich darkness that seemed almost palpable.

"Ah ha!" Seprator exclaimed, racing inside.

The others felt they had no choice but to follow. They walked inside and found themselves within the room with the model, the chalkboard, and the table full of papers once again. The dark doorway had vanished, and in its place was a wall just as before. Seprator's demeanor diminished.

"Oh! It's no use!" he stated and collapsed onto the floor, heartbroken.

Pandara and Koravo looked at each other. Koravo knelt to comfort the old man, who seemed to have aged even more with the passage of a few moments.

"Maybe we should all get some sleep," said Koravo, with her hand on Seprator's back and looking up at Pandara. "We can continue this quest in the morning."

"I think that's a good idea," replied Pandara. "The sun is beginning to come up."

Seprator began to cry, and Koravo and Pandara fell silent. "I've been trying to solve this mystery for ages!" Seprator exclaimed.

"Well, we made a good effort tonight!" replied Koravo. "Perhaps we will figure out what all this means tomorrow." The three found makeshift spots to rest their heads and drifted off to sleep.

A.27 ~ LITTLE DIAMONDS

Pandara awoke within a dream. He was all alone in the room, sifting through the papers on the desk. He arrived upon the paper with the torn corner and reached into his pocket. The tiny slip was there. He held the corner up to the page, and the two fused together. The paper was whole, and the word *Octave* glowed in green letters. It seemed to lift right off of the page.

Koravo entered the room and asked Pandara what he had found. He handed the page to her, and she read the inscription, "*Campaign is greater than any other, that was under him, playing and let her go.*" Pandara turned to Koravo and said, "*One above and one below. Play the song to let her go.*" He understood its meaning though could not grasp its relevance. Time works in mysterious ways.

Seprator entered and asked politely what they were studying. Koravo handed him the page. He read the inscription to himself, reviewed the glowing green letters, and said, "Follow me, please." The group exited the room and entered the communications chamber. Seprator took a seat and motioned to the others to sit as well. He put on a pair of headphones, and the others followed suit. Seprator turned a dial, removed cords from the switchboard, and placed them back in the appropriate channels. He said, "Hello?" and looked at the others.

In the headphones a voice was heard to respond, "Yes, hello. You have successfully determined the answer?"

"The answer," Pandara found himself saying, "is Octave."

"Ok, just one moment please." There was a pause in the communication. "Yes, good sir. You may proceed outside." Just before they removed the headphones, the voice on the other end said, "And sir?"

"Yes?" replied Pandara.

"Good luck to you and god speed."

Pandara seemed bewildered and confused, although he said, "Thank you."

There was a click, and Seprator removed his headphones. Koravo and Pandara followed suit, and the hermit asked, "Shall we?" The three proceeded to step outside.

They made their way over to the courtyard, where the sundial was seen in profile, with a rose climbing it. Pandara examined the device and knelt to pick up the chain that held it firmly to the ground. The chain was extremely thick and heavy. Pandara couldn't for the life of him understand why a chain was needed to affix the pedestal to the earth, let alone one of this size and magnitude.

Seprator said, "Pandara, if you please," and motioned to the large iron door on the wall. Pandara walked up to the monstrosity, rigid with nuts and bolts, and looked down at the digital keypad. He entered the word one character at a time:

O-C-T-A-V-E

The same green light began to shine around the edges

of the door, though less vibrant than they had the night before, perhaps because it was daytime. The handle clicked, and Pandara slowly pulled on the iron framework.

Inside the room was seen just as it had been before, though there were some new additions. A music box was at rest, propped up against the wall in a corner of the room. In fact, it lay precisely where Seprator had gone to sleep. And a beautiful potted plant was sitting in just the location where Koravo had slept earlier. Something about this plant seemed strange to Pandara, and he inquired from Seprator about its significance.

"That will become clear tonight," and the three entered the room. This time the door remained behind them, and Pandara pulled the heavy iron fixture closed with a quiet thud. He turned around and noticed that the lights were on; it was dark outside. Night had already come, and Seprator was inspecting the plant through his monocle.

"Have a seat," said Seprator. "I will take it from here."

Pandara and Koravo sat beside the model of the station and watched as Seprator removed delicate buds from the plant. "What is it?" asked Koravo.

"Never mind that," came the reply. "It is our way out of here!" Seprator placed the sticky buds into a pipe and crushed the contents gently, then licked his fingers. "Hold this…" he said to Pandara. "And this…" handing Pandara a small machine that made fire upon the spinning of a wheel.

Seprator walked over to the music box and pushed a button. Instantly, the lights dimmed and hues of purple, green, blue, and the subtlest of orange were seen coursing throughout the room. It was as though they were suspended, somehow, in outer space. Little diamonds of light flickered on and off in the room. "Hurry now!" said Seprator. "Before it begins!" And he made a gesture to Pandara to turn the wheel and smoke the pipe.

Pandara did just that. He held the smoke in his lungs and tasted the citrus bouquets of rich and tranquil sage.

"Now give the pipe to Koravo."

He did so in a crystal daze, and she followed Pandara's example. Koravo became hyper-aware. Meanwhile, the faintest tones of a night symphony began to permeate the den. She passed the pipe to Seprator, who joined the others in a growing tide of music and smoke.

"Now close your eyes," he said, and they did as he suggested.

Vibrant visions began to fill their minds, like dreams within a dream. Although their eyes were closed, the music painted landscapes of wondrous things. Pandara saw the ocean for the first time, with mountains rising high from beneath the surface.

"Trilodius..." he said with a slur.

"Welcome to Hansa," said Seprator, measured and controlled. "This is the song of the stars." Pandara and Koravo immediately took notice.

They listened intently for many minutes, as the musical notes billowed upon the stillness of the air. Visions of subtle oriental tranquilities and gentle soothing comforted them along with deep insights and fond memories. Orchestral hands grasped them and ushered them high into the light of midnight minds. When the song finally found its end, Pandara and Koravo opened their eyes.

Seprator looked at Pandara with a whimsical look in his eye. It was a combination of jealousy, pity, and curiosity. He said, "You have a dangerous journey ahead of you. There will be many challenges and many chances to succeed, but every mistake that you make will cost you dearly!" He paused, and the music came back on. "Have a little more!" said Seprator, as he extended the pipe in Pandara's direction.

Pandara paused for way too long. "No, thank you," he

eventually said. "I think I've had enough." And Seprator withdrew his hand, motioning to Koravo.

"Sure!" said Koravo briskly, gladly accepting the offering.

She spun the little wheel, and a pillar of flame shot out from the end of the device. She held the pipe up to her lips and inhaled boldly, holding her breath as the chemicals found their way to her bloodstream by way of air sacs in her lungs. The music rode darkly across the room, bass heavy and flowing with transience: one thousand chariots darting toward an unseen end.

The music drifted into the background as though to cushion Seprator, who spoke, "There is a prophecy…" He said this as though possessed by some higher force that made its way to him through the surrounding atmosphere. "There is a prophecy about a dragon." It would have seemed ridiculous under many circumstances, though given the setting and the context, there was nothing ridiculous about it. It was intriguing and mysterious.

"The serpent flies in utter darkness, ancient and expressed. Aware of all wisdom and keen to our sight, she flies. We do not know why she flies, or to where she is going. Just suffice it to say that she is there, out there somewhere right now, flying this very night towards an unknown end," Seprator continued. "Pandara, you have been called by the dragon, and you too Koravo. We hope that you will be able to understand her purpose. Many have seen that she flies! Many have died trying to reach her!"

Those were among the last words that Seprator spoke that night, or any night for that matter, for when Pandara and Koravo awoke the next morning, Seprator did not awaken with them.

The rest of the night was spent listening to music and discussing ancient Tristullite philosophy. Seprator had detailed many of his exploits, and Pandara and Koravo told him about their time in Ksevia. He did not seem to remember the place, but they couldn't be sure that he understood much of what they said. Their conversation consisted of Seprator's abstraction on various tenets and their importance in his life. When either Pandara or Koravo began to speak, he seemed to drift away to another place and would lose track of the conversation.

The prophecy of the dragon seemed fragmented and incomplete, just like the day earlier. After Seprator fell asleep, Pandara tried and Koravo succeeded in continuing a discussion about the dragon. They couldn't figure out what relevance it had to their mission, though they sensed its importance and somehow knew that Seprator was telling the truth. Koravo remarked on how clear the music had seemed in their condition and how it seemed to impart a wisdom of its own upon her ears.

After a short while, Pandara and Koravo decided to get close and go to sleep together, laying in each other's arms. The dreams they had that night were nonexistent, of course, because the whole experience had been a dream. When they awoke the next morning, however, the iron door was still there hanging over them like a monument to the dragon. They found Seprator's lifeless body but were not sad. They knew that he had gone on to the next stage. This was confirmed as they watched him vanish before their eyes, as if he'd never been there in the first place.

A.28 ~ A NIGHTFUL OF MYSTERIES

Pandara and Koravo took the old forest way into a nightful of mysteries. They traveled ancient lands, sailing the airy winds of hope on wings divine. Though, before they had even begun, it was already too late. Such is Pandara's story; he wouldn't have one without Koravo. Trapped outside of the Ivory Tower, she had waited eternities inside of a cage.

Pandara, among the endless volumes of images and text, was confused by the manuscript. He seemed to be reading his own story. He thought for a moment about this paradox, and as he did, he read his very own thoughts! As the book's cover had been defaced, Pandara was unable to identify its authorship.

Somehow it hadn't occurred to Pandara that the ragged and torn copy was precisely the text he had been searching for. The mysteries of his predicament were detailed in its vandalized pages. The volume's simple strangeness repelled Pandara, however, and he sat the book down. Soon enough, he had forgotten all about it. This very fact caused the book to vanish, and Pandara momentarily wondered what had happened to something that he could not remember.

He sat by an empty fireplace and began to flip through his next book, *Caelum*. The first passage which caught his eye translated roughly: *There is a special tree that gives shade in its own wisdom. As long as its roots are, they are not of the bottomless pit, and his branches became lóng. It takes the food out of the stomach and casts shadows in the land, his own conscience. Of this spindle, it would not be born, can never be sprouted from it to the ground. Plant a tree fruit of their labor elegant.*

Decadent alleyways of thought and feeling ran through Pandara's experience of the text. He felt connected to the trembling hands which grasped the storage of his heart. With poisoned otherworldly appetites for beauty, Pandara resumed the tranquility of timeless pause. The library here uncovered a precious gem within his mind, and he brushed off the dust that had collected there.

Onward he read in *Caelum*, and a picture of the book's contents began to form in his mind. There was a man who left a city in search of the answer to a mystery. The mystery was accosted by the night who ravaged its nature, and the mystery was eroding with time. The man knew that soon the mystery itself would be incomplete, and he raced to find a solution to the puzzle.

There was a woman who was raised in a tower, having

never known anything but. She spent her days there writing words, for the tower was bare, and there was no entertainment to keep her busy. She longed for companionship and believed that one day someone, either a man or a woman, would come to the tower to rescue her.

The man searched for his resolution and saw a tower far off in the distance. He went to it and found an old lady there. She told him that the tower was cursed and that no one could enter. He began to leave but heard cries from the tower. "Pandara!" cried the woman. Pandara stopped and looked up. "I'm here!" she called out. He realized that the call was coming from outside of the Ivory Tower.

He looked around for a way to escape and saw a staircase leading up to a loft where a window was placed. Pandara dashed up the stairway and opened the window. There, before him, beyond a few walls and the roofs of additional buildings he saw her. "Koravo! I'm coming!" yelled Pandara, and he climbed out of the window and leapt onto a rooftop below. Running at full speed, he made his way as efficiently as possible to the bottom of the tower. A woman was there. To his surprise, she said that no one could go in; it was cursed. He attempted to push her aside, but she would not budge, as though stuck to the ground by some strong magnetic force.

Pandara sprinted around the side of the tower, but there was no other way in. She stood steadfast, blocking his entry. He exclaimed, "I must go inside this tower now!" She asked him if someone would arrive, the one looking for the solution to a great mystery. Pandara said, "Yes, he will come for you; now, please step aside."

"Kiss me, and I shall," said the woman.

Pandara yelled "Koravo!" and the Grim Reaper appeared.

Pandara kissed the woman, and as his lips touched hers, he felt nothing. She had vanished into thin air. Pandara raced up the stairs to reach Koravo, and as he did, the reaper grabbed his arm with a monstrous claw that had seemed to come from nowhere. The Grim Reaper was becoming more human-like, and Pandara was devoured before the eyes of Koravo who learned firsthand why she had always woken up before that dreadful sight was witnessed. She knew that no matter how hard she tried, she would never be able to wash her mind free of that memory.

Again, Pandara awoke, having memorized the entirety of the dungeon. He dodged each particular challenge with cold precision, determined to arrive at his Koravo's side. But he realized that with every step he had taken, he had gained not only a loss of his soul to the devil but a piece of wisdom that the maze transmitted to him. The maze itself was a prisoner as well. He stopped and realized that the time had not yet come to free Koravo. He changed course and headed for the Ivory Tower.

His intuition told him to search for a book that he could not read. He scoured the shelves until he found what he was looking for: a book with a single symbol embossed on the cover. It read *Rồng*. Impatiently, he opened *Rồng* and could not read the text. There were however colorful images that showed worlds completely unknown to Pandara. He had a sense that he was merely supposed to view these images, and somehow that would equip him with what he needed to gain from this place. And so, he did just that.

He tried to familiarize himself with the curves of the text but paid special attention to the images he saw there. Some of the images were so fantastical that he could not process what he was looking at. They appeared to contain patterns, like ships, that moved in all directions. Pandara felt changed by looking at these images. He felt the dark pit in his stomach recede, as though this book was somehow healing him; still, he was impatient.

He could not wait to save Koravo from the tower, but

he knew that he must first complete his viewing of this book. So, he sat in his fires of impatience and forced himself to study each and every image. As he did, he noticed that he was regaining his strength. Soon he felt completely returned to his previous self, and he put the book back onto the shelf where he had found it.

Pandara leapt through the window onto the rooftop below. He grappled with the wall and conquered it, leading him to the tower. The woman was gone, and he raced up the stairs. There was beautiful Koravo, locked in a doorless cage, tears streaming down her face. Pandara started crying as well as he frantically tried to figure out how to open the box. He shook it and pulled with all of his might on the bars that held Koravo captive. She was bruised, thin, and tattered but alive.

The anger of scars toiled low inside Pandara's restless fist. His stranglehold on fear uncoiled persistent will, and revenge tasted sweet but distant. The moment would come without warning, and Pandara knew that his body would be forced through another round of slow digestion. He had made his way all the way to where she was held captive but with futile results; the ghost appeared.

Pandara was deep in thought, being consumed by the wretched monster. He was more or less immune to the pain by now. He thought of Koravo and how she'd waited in that cage for eons beyond countless eons. He hoped that her experience of time was different than his; hopefully, she did not have to sit through churning eternities like Pandara. Hopefully each time the map was reset, she too was reset in her perception of time. He feared that this was not the case and wondered how she had managed to wait all those years, imprisoned by the mad reaper who harvested souls.

He knew that he could solve the final riddle of the cage if he only had more time. Pandara sensed that he had reset the count of deaths each time he had read from *Rồng*. He could continue to pursue his course and ultimately would figure out how to free Koravo. Then, of course, they'd have to figure out how to escape the maze. *One step at a time*, he thought, being slowly dissolved in the belly of the beast. *One step at a time.*

He wondered where this labyrinth was. If he could only gain a sense of its greater context, perhaps then he would understand the mission better.

A.29 ~ THE FRONT DOOR

Pandara stood up and moved towards the large iron door. Koravo joined him at his side and took his hand. He slowly opened the leaden gate, and another world met his eyes. There was an artificial light and a dead, barren stonework maze.

"This is my dream, Pandara! I'm scared. I don't want to go." Koravo quickly pulled the door closed and fell back in shock into the room. Her premonition had come true suggesting additional confounding horror. The screen of the light did nothing to clarify the shadowless terrain. Koravo feared for Pandara, certain that a dark fate awaited him there.

"What do you mean this is your dream, Koravo?"

"I mean that world out there, you saw it; it's the labyrinth from my dream. Pandara, we must not leave that way. Let's go out the front entrance and head back into the forest."

He signed, "Sure, whatever you think Koravo."

They looked at each other and realized that they had lost the ability to speak. It wasn't like before, however. Before they had always chosen to sign, but now they couldn't speak as though some invisible phantom had stolen much of their ability to communicate. Not only was there no Yuit, but now Pandara and Koravo felt estranged from one another.

"Oh no, Pandara! He's already begun to hunt you! We

must run!" And so, they swung open wide the front door and stepped across the entryway, just as they had done leaving Ksevia, though this time in great haste and panic.

As they did, their entire field of vision went white. When Pandara awoke from the flash, he found himself alone. *Where am I?* he thought in a daze. *What am I doing here? And who am I?* Somehow it didn't seem to matter that he had lost all memory of what had come before. He turned around, looking for an obvious point of entry through which he had arrived in this place, but he couldn't find one. There were no windows to a world below in the labyrinth.

Although Pandara didn't realize this at first, the lack of transparency to another land made him feel isolated and trapped. He felt as though the heart and imagination of existence had been cut out from him. All that he saw was an antique sundial attached to the earth by a chain.

As mysteries unfolded into mysteries, dangers mounted, and pressures bloomed. There was an ever-present peril that threatened to consume Pandara, though he was oblivious to it. The beast, which roamed this territory, was subtle and concealed. Pandara thought of something that he was responsible for but couldn't place its prominence in the empty vaults of bankrupt memory.

He walked over to the sundial, as though suspended in the air. Pandara knew his feet were moving, but he was transfixed and glided through the stale air. Had he seen this sundial before? He noticed an inscription. It read, *Cave interpellatores. Turbidus hic homo nocte animae damnatorum.* Although he couldn't remember who he was, or where he was going, he understood the message as clear as day: *Beware intruders. This whirlwind of a night lost.*

His foot tripped on the enormous chain that affixed the pedestal to the dead soil beneath. He didn't give that much thought, though it was a strange phenomenon. He looked back up and noticed that although there wasn't a single cloud in the sky, the sundial revealed no marking of time.

The sky was equally dead, a dreadful veil of lavender haze. It felt as though there was no time in this place, and Pandara wasn't even sure if he knew approximately what time it was. He understood the concept of the function of the sundial but couldn't quite grasp at its purpose.

He looked around. Pandara found himself within a large open space; there were signs of life that had long since passed into the ages of history. The skeletons of shrubs were there, arid and bone dry; just the tangling of dead roots welcomed him to a place where no life could survive. He listened for a moment and thought he heard someone calling out; then there was silence.

Pandara walked past an ornate stone fountain with the head of a goat where water should have been spouting forth. There was an empty basin beneath; all was without moisture. One solitary drop of liquid was held, suspended, from an eye of the goat. Pandara noticed that it looked like a tear. The goat's head was so life-like yet made of stone. It was a prisoner frozen here for the ages. He casually continued to walk exploring the open space, hoping to find some shred of evidence as to what he might be doing here. No solid reason emerged.

PLATE III - THE LABYRINTH

A.30 — CHAPTER 04

A.31 ~ THE BACK DOOR

Pandara walked along the perimeter of the tan and desolate waste-
land, his hand streaming against the coarse stone that shaped its
boundary. Finally, as though having opened before his eyes, a little
alcove in the stonework made itself known. It was approximately
two meters across and one meter deep. He stepped inside. Nestled
in the wall at the center of the alcove was a niche that contained
what appeared to be a little game. There was a protrusion surrounded by little indentations in the stone, alongside a tray that
contained three marbles. Pandara lifted the marbles in his hand
and placed them in three random depressions.

There was a cracking sound, and the alcove begin to shift
in its foundation. The doorway revolved around the other side of
the wall. Once fully in place, the alcove lurched to a stop with a
loud thump. He was in a new chamber of the infinite dungeon.
Pandara stepped forward. From this location set forth a series of
seven passages, each one moving off in a direction separate from
the others. He felt no sense of impatience and decided to do some

exploring. He chose the middle passage.

Pandara walked down the corridor and noticed how the stone bricks in the wall were vibrating slightly. There was dust. Little motes of mortar flew off from the wall where the bricks were held together. It was barely perceptible, but Pandara took note of it and wondered as to its cause. He looked up again. The sky was still another barrier, not a vast openness leading out into space. The sun shone with an artificiality that resembled nothing. He had no recollections.

As he continued walking, the walls of the labyrinth appeared to grow narrower, and he wondered if he was heading anywhere at all. He reached a final curve, turned the corner, and was at a dead end. The towering barricade made him feel estranged from himself, but still, he felt no immediate sense of urgency. At least he knew where that section led, if he could only remember. He touched the wall and pressed on it to gauge its firmness. It was rock solid.

Pandara turned around and headed back to his starting point. The walls opened up slightly as he did, and the illusion rearranged his field of vision in a disorienting way. He reached the beginning of the current section of the puzzle where seven passages were laid out before his eyes. He chose the leftmost passage and began his walk to see where it led.

After having walked for a couple of minutes, he came upon a very large, crypt-like space. This area was enclosed above, below, and on all sides. Torches lined the walls and provided an eerie glow to the cavernous room. In the center of the cell was a sphere, approximately five meters high, revolving in a dish filled with what appeared to be a lubricating substance. As the sphere revolved, it made a grinding sound, indicating heavy machinery at work. Pandara approached the sphere and reached out his hand, as though drawn by some undetected force. His fingers brushed up against the smooth surface of the sphere, and small volumes of the oil made their way onto his fingertips.

The oil was warm and translucent. He inspected it by rubbing his fingertips together and tasted the sweet substance with his tongue. It was strangely fresh for such an ancient place, and Pandara wondered where the oil might have come from. Before he had a chance to think further on the issue, the sphere began to slow, and with it, the room around him began to move.

The slowing sphere, the walls, the floor, and the ceiling began to revolve in a nauseating and unpredictable way. The chamber was a giant machine designed to trap helpless victims who had touched the surface of the sphere. He knew he must get out of there quickly or else fall uncompromisingly to his doom, bashing against the ceiling below. He dashed from platform to platform, looking for an avenue of escape, as the room deconstructed itself.

Just then, as the sphere came to a complete stop and the room had reached its maximum velocity, he noticed a little opening on the floor above that appeared to be coming around to where he could possibly leap into it. He made a run for it.

Dodging pillars of stone and jumping headstrong atop others that lunged at him horizontally, he leapt into the small crevice and found himself protected from the dismantling chamber. He was a little bruised but okay, having narrowly avoided the severing of his legs. Taking a moment to catch his breath, Pandara realized that this place was not a friendly one and resolved to remember lessons learned.

He was in a tiny crawlspace that no longer seemed to be moving, though he could see and hear the revolving room behind him. It was as though he was trapped within some ancient pyramid; he didn't know where that thought came from, or what it meant. He carried onward.

On hands and knees, Pandara made his way along the

oppressive course; no alternate options of travel presented themselves. He moved in a single line, twisting and turning without
mercy by the whims of the convoluted web. Suddenly, after turning
a corner, he saw a light up ahead from an opening in the top of the
confined passage. He hurried toward the opening eager to step out
into the open air, concerned that it would close. He would then be
trapped forever in the suffocating tomb.

Pandara crawled out, embracing the artificial light of the
free world. He turned around and recognized his surroundings.
It was the place where he had first entered the maze. He was back
to where he had started, a little less confident of his safety in this
place, and a little wiser to the ways of the labyrinth. Pandara put his
hands on his hips and surveyed the landscape with greater detail.

Above the high walls of the dungeon, the world seemed to
disappear in a lavender haze of imperceptibility. There were some
structures there on the horizon, but somehow, they seemed off
limits. Those run-down apartments merely formed a backdrop to
his surroundings, like painted set pieces on the stage of his tribula-
tion. Even the immediate foreground seemed off limits to him. The
more he thought about it, however, Pandara felt like an intruder in
this place. Accompanying the thought were recollections of who he
was, trickling in one drop at a time. He still could not remember
his name, though the concept of an identity was becoming more
clear.

He checked the sundial as though perhaps something had
changed given all of his efforts; yet, it still held no concept of time.
His mind wandered about the inscription: *the whirlwind of a night
lost*. He thought his translation was a little off and realized that the
passage actually read: *Beware intruders. The night walker hunts
lost souls.*

This was a disturbing realization, and with it Pandara
sensed a presence awaken somewhere in his surroundings. There

was a ghastly yawn, an aching bellows which was heard in the still air. Pandara didn't want to find out what that dire sound belonged to, though he felt a certain inevitability of confronting the sighing wastrel. With a little more hurry in his gait, he went back to the alcove where the marbles lay back in the tray. He placed them in the depressions, and this time the alcove spun around in another direction.

A.32 ~ A QUEST OF RESTLESS YOUTH

Often the citizens of Ksevia would wonder about the happenings outside of their idyllic community. It was a favorite pastime of theirs, and many stories were told detailing the possible exploits of the world at large. One such story was never told inside the walls of Ksevia, but it did take place. And that very fact, though hard as it may be to believe, shaped the outcome of Tristulle, and the whole universe for that matter, for all time to come.

Derelin, Pilop, and Rover were from Ytieo, a city neighboring Ksevia on Tristulle. The city was built just outside of the Trilodian Forest and was built, without their knowledge, in the shape of a giant wooden ship. The ship had not always been there, though the founders of Ytieo imagined that such a shape would be the perfect vessel to house their new community. The three teenagers would spend their time imagining distant lands, all of which seemed so far away and obscure. But one such land was supposedly nearby: the village of Ksevia. No one from Ytieo, or from anywhere on Tristulle for that matter, had ever discovered Ksevia, and its existence was cloaked in a riddle that couldn't possibly be intentional, or at least the teens believed.

They dreamt of what they might find in the hidden kingdom, which was rumored to be filled with jewels; however, the jewels were the beautiful flowers of Ksevia, and the kingdom was a commune that thrived in its isolation. Derelin, Pilop, and Rover decided to embark on a quest for Ksevia, in the way that such quests come to youth, slow and dawning over time. The thought occurred to Derelin, and he became their leader.

Derelin formed a strategy for the first expedition that included mapping the Trilodian Forest as far as they could see. No one from Ytieo had ever done such a thing, and the youths had already set out on a mission that would raise them to the stature of great explorers; but this was not enough for the band. They were determined to find Ksevia and return with proof that their mission had indeed been a success. They knew that the city was in the forest somewhere near Mount Fala, or the Crystal Spear, as it was known to the Ytieoans, or so the legend went.

Pilop oversaw supplies and Rover was to journal the expedition. Derelin would navigate and troubleshoot. The weather was clear, and the forecast was sublime. It was time to depart. Derelin and Rover led the way with Pilop just behind. They set out into the Syklopse, the Ytieoan name for the wood, leaving their friends and families behind.

They said that they would return in a few short weeks. They did not however account for the aberrations of time that surrounded Ksevia. How could they? No one from Ytieo had ever ventured that far into the Syklopse before, and its mechanisms were unknown. Ytieo was not a city of adventurers. Everyone had everything they needed, or so it seemed; and the kids were viewed suspiciously but with awe. Perhaps the new generation was hearing a different call, one that their ancestors had heard and caused them to build Ytieo.

Along the way, Derelin, Rover, and Pilop sang songs and told stories of their own. They imagined the city of Ksevia and what they would find there. The first expedition yielded many grand results! Although Ksevia was not located, they documented their findings and returned home. Upon arrival, it was concluded that they had been gone twice as long as expected. The three-week trek had in fact lasted six weeks, and they could prove through Rover's journal that not that much time had passed.

They met every night for a week and discussed the outcome of their journey. "So, we mapped the greater majority of this side of the Crystal Spear. I propose that for our next expedition we travel far out beyond the Crystal Spear and map the other side of the wood." Derelin was enthusiastic, but he had work to do to convince the others that additional missions were desirable and essential. After much discussion they were convinced, and another mission had been scheduled for the following season.

Weeks passed, and Derelin grew restless. He wanted to journey out right away, but the others had convinced him that additional research and preparation would yield a superior outcome. It was a compromise and one that Derelin accepted half-heartedly. But when he saw the research that Rover and Pilop had conducted independently, he was inspired and impressed! Before too long the spring had turned to summer, and they were packing to get ready to go.

They headed out in the same direction as before, though instead of wandering far out into the wood, this time they traversed the landscape laterally to map out the breadth of the expanse. With the Crystal Spear on their side, the group of young travelers entered a new region of the forest, one that they had never seen before. Rover documented the area, and Derelin chose which way to go. They decided to unpack for the night and get comfortable.

That evening around the campfire, they discussed their mission and how they could feel Ksevia drawing near. They were out far into the realm, which accelerated time, and could sense a powerful presence working on their imaginations. They fell asleep, and the dreamworld took hold of them, transcending expectations and all traces of doubt!

There, in the forest, at the height of their shared vision, was a concrete building painted in a subdued hue of bluish gray. Upon the top of the building a strange dish was stationed. Rover took an interest in the device and broke away from the other two to study it and take notes. Pilop and Derelin entered the structure, but Derelin became transfixed with a module that was housed in one of the front rooms. Pilop, on the other hand, explored the entirety of the building, inside and out, taking notice of the photographs and drawings found there. The dream went on for many hours, and when they awoke, they were convinced that they had been to Ksevia!

The group discussed all that they had seen, and Rover compiled a thorough memoir of the dream, which had transported them to somewhere nearby. Derelin mentioned that they must take note of their current location, and Rover did just that. They decided to continue with the expedition, although the dream was determined to have been the most relevant and important event that took place during the excursion. Now, hot on the trail of Ksevia, all three were more determined than ever before to complete the quest and return with some artifact from their adventures.

The thought occurred to Derelin before the others: *what if the dream had not shown them Ksevia but instead imparted on them the blueprint of a structure that they were to build?!*

During one of their daily meetings, Derelin mentioned the thought to his friends. They were intrigued by the idea, and the thought began to settle like a hook in their minds. Before long, they had at least suspended the hunt for Ksevia and instead decided to gather supplies necessary to build the beguiling structure! The dream had become an idea, and the idea became a reality.

Slowly, over several years, Derelin, Pilop, and Rover hauled materials out into the Syklopse where a building had begun to emerge. Rover had reconstructed the satellite dish and Derelin the communications board. Pilop provided support and guidance but also understood the overall layout better than the other two. Five years later, the teens were now adults, and the communications building was complete!

Derelin, understanding the communications chamber the best, turned on the machine, patched the cords appropriately, and began to speak into the headset. "Hello?!" he asked and waited for a response. There was nothing.

He turned a few knobs and spoke again. "Hello? Is anyone there?" Again, nothing.

Rover suggested that she make a few fine adjustments to the satellite and returned several minutes later. Again, Derelin spoke with the others listening on. "Hello, this is Derelin. Are you there? Over?" A faint response began to come through the device, and the group looked at each other with excitement!

"Hello, this is Rose. Who is this?" The response came loud and clear!

"This is Derelin, Pilop, and Rover calling from the outskirts of Ksevia! Where are you calling from, Rose? Over."

"Hello all. I'm calling from a telephone inside of the Oculus. Precisely when I found the phone it began to ring, over."

Derelin, Pilop, and Rover had never heard of the Oculus and asked about its whereabouts.

"Where is the Oculus, and where is it located?" There was a pause. "Over."

Rose thought for a moment and replied. "I don't know where it is, but I suspect that it's a dream machine. It seems to be suspended in outer space, and I heard others refer to it only as *the Oculus*. Where is Ksevia? Over."

"Ksevia is on Tristulle, over."

Rose remembered the name from the innermost depths

of John's consciousness and realized that she had just been there. "I was just on Tristulle a few minutes ago," she responded. "The illusion of Tristulle broke, and that's when I found myself in the Oculus. Have any of you heard of a novelist named John Trautman? Over." She waited for their response.

Derelin, Pilop, and Rover looked at each other and shrugged.

"No, we've never heard of John Trautman. Over."

Pilop, who was thinking about the perversion of time near Ksevia, interjected.

"This is Pilop. What year is it? Over."

Rose somehow remembered that it was 4781 in her new existence and responded to that effect, surprising herself as the words came out of her mouth. Derelin was equally shocked and responded, "Here on Tristulle, it's 4725! Over!" The realization of their situation astounded them, and just then they heard static. The connection was lost, and Rose had disappeared forever.

Not long after, a voice appeared on the telephone and said, "Hello?"

Derelin, Pilop, and Rover jumped at the pronouncement, after thinking that their machine was broken! "Who is this, and where are you from?" Rover asked and waited for a response.

The man said, "I can't tell you that, but I have a very important message for the three of you." He continued without wasting any time! "There is an eclipse coming, and a portal will soon open not far from where you sit, just outside the building as a matter of fact. It is crucial that you enter this portal and complete a mission which I will now set forth for you. Rover, please take notes, as the mission's success is absolutely vital to the future of the universe." Rover was listening and took out her notebook. "Ok," she replied, "I'm ready."

"It is very important that you follow my directions to the

letter. You will enter an unsafe domain and must hurry to accomplish the task without hesitation. You will have approximately one hour to find the Ivory Tower and scrawl a message into its floor. You must then immediately return, and don't look back! It is very important that you do not look back!"

The man proceeded to give them directions, and Rover documented them precisely as he had said. She also took note of the message which was to be transcribed word for word as he said it. They noticed the light outside becoming strange and ominous, and the man said that it was time. He wished them good luck and told them that he would be waiting for their dispatch in approximately ninety minutes. The voice cut off, and the group was stranded.

Derelin grabbed his knife and headed outside. The others stood up and followed his lead. There, in a clearing just beside the communications building, a whirlwind had appeared, hovering above the ground and inviting them to enter. "Well, here goes nothing!" said Derelin, and he jumped through. Pilop and Rover looked at each other and jumped through as well!

A.33 ~ A MOMENT TOO LATE

They found themselves in a barren land, like the dead gardens of a royal palace though no palace was to be seen. The dried remnants of brush and natural debris covered the labyrinth floor, and there were no signs of life.

Derelin, having made short work of integrating his surroundings said, "Rover, quick, we've got to hurry. Won't you please take the lead?"

Rover responded, "Right," and began to lead in the direction of the Ivory Tower which the man had communicated.

They passed through a sprawling maze which defied reason

and tickled their intellects. Eventually, after a couple of wrong turns, they had arrived at a majestic structure which rose from the dead earth below.

"I guess this must be it," Pilop stated, and the three went inside.

Derelin took out his knife and motioned to Rover that she should show him the message. He began to carve into the Penrose tiling in large letters the sentence which caused them all great trepidation: *Rest here, poor one, for the eater of souls cannot enter this domain.*

After fifteen to twenty minutes, he had completed the message and went back over certain segments to make the etching clear and distinct.

"I guess that's it," said Rover, and Derelin motioned for them to go.

Upon exiting the Ivory Tower, the door closed behind them with a locking sound, and Pilop turned around to check the door: it was locked. A moment too late, Derelin said, "Pilop! Don't look back!" But he already had! They heard a monster yawn or growl or moan somewhere not too far from where they found themselves! "Run!" Derelin exclaimed as quietly as possible, but the Grim Reaper had already begun to stalk them!

Rover took the lead, but all seemed to remember the way out of the maze. They made their way toward the entrance and could hear the moaning sound grow more prevalent. They were not going to make it!

Rover saw the portal and jumped through. Derelin did the same, but Pilop who was in the back began to feel a pull on his being. He tried to make it to the other side but in his confusion turned to witness the beast. There was a gigantic floating head hovering above the ground, mouth open wide and sucking the air out of the labyrinth.

Rover turned to Derelin and said, "Where's Pilop?!" Derelin yelled, "Pilop!" and stuck his head back through the portal. There he saw the monster and no sign of Pilop! In his place a fountain stood with the head of a goat, and where water should pour out of the mouth there was nothing! The monster turned to face Derelin and began to approach. Derelin fell back, and just then the portal closed. Eighty minutes had passed, and a friend was lost forever!

Rover and Derelin raced into the communications building and beseeched the man to them how they could retrieve their friend. He informed them that all hope was lost. Pilop could never be saved and now belonged to the labyrinth. They began to cry and demanded that the man tell them who he was! "He owed them that much," they had said!

With reluctance and resignation, the man said that his name was Alexander and that he was from another time. He explained to them that the building they had constructed from their dream communicated across both space and time.

Alexander said that they had another mission that was essential to the future of the cosmos, and that the two of them were the only ones who could help! Rover and Derelin resisted but felt the pull of a greater calling and decided to hear him out. The Innovator explained that they must find him in their time and deliver to him a message. They must find him on Mount Penglai and tell him to build the Breniculine.

A.34 ~ IN VIRGIN TERRITORY

Derelin and Rover were at the communications building just on the outskirts of Ksevia, which they would never find. They only knew that they must somehow reach the Innovator. He had said that the future of the universe depended on them delivering him the message. They did not know how or why to deliver the message. They only knew that this strange man had said that it was the purpose of their lives to do so. They discussed the situation for a long while and ultimately came to the conclusion that they should do as he suggested. But how would they go about locating Mount Penglai? They brainstormed and came up with several paths of pursuit.

They could return to Ytieo and research ways to leave Tristulle. Although, to their knowledge, no one from Ytieo had ever left Tristulle! Maybe someone had or had a lead on how to find a way off of the planet.

This was not considered a desirable approach, as Derelin and Rover knew Ytieo pretty well and didn't feel the urge to return. They could continue their search for Ksevia, hoping that if they found it the Ksevians might have heard of the Innovator or know a way to escape the bonds of Tristulle.

This was also not a favorable way forward, as they had determined that Ksevia was, in reality, extremely difficult or impossible to find! They opted for the third approach, which was to discover what lay on the other side of the Crystal Spear.

Derelin and Rover began their trek even deeper into the heart of the Crystal Spear. They would keep an eye out for any sign of Ksevia along their way but didn't expect to run into it, as they had grown more pragmatic with their new mission.

The forest was unrelenting but beautiful and inspiring. As they marched further and further beyond the known universe, Derelin and Rover grew closer and more connected. They began to be able to complete each other's sentences and anticipate the suggestions of the other.

One day, Derelin stepped crosswise onto a stick and nearly sprained his ankle. Rover, knowing that Derelin's health was essential to the outcome of a successful mission, offered to massage his ankle back to health. They stopped by a little brook in the woods and Derelin removed his shoe and sock. Rover caressed and massaged the swollen foot for nearly thirty minutes. Once she had completed the job, Derelin thanked her and kissed her on the cheek. She was overcome with happiness and told him that the kiss meant a lot to her. They began to hold hands moving further into the strange wonderlands of the Tristullite forest.

It wasn't many days later that the signs of a clearing began to present themselves. At first there were pockets of open field. The pockets grew larger until finally the forest had left them in virgin territory. "Would you look at that!" Derelin exclaimed. It was unnecessary for him to draw Rover's attention to the object, for just in front of their eyes an enormous pyramid clung resolutely to the earth.

"What do you think that is?" Rover asked.

Derelin thought for a few moments but couldn't draw any parallels to his prior experience. "I have no idea," he said, "but it looks like there is a door just ahead, so it must be a building of some sort."

The pyramid was at least a couple of hundred feet high and made from a stone that must have been indigenous to the area. The sky was blue, and the façade of grandeur stood out boldly in a sweeping composition.

They approached the pyramid as two innocent pilgrims, never giving a thought to the dangers that might lurk within. Inside the pyramid, there were lights embedded in the ground that illuminated the path forward into the cavernous crypt. More surprisingly, however, were the mirrors affixed to every surface on the interior of the tomb! What they were there for could only be left to the imagination!

The two voyagers navigated the singular passageway that led them forward on a predetermined path. They arrived in the central chamber: vast, open, and adorned with the mirrors that reflected light positioned near their feet. The central chamber rose high into a single point that was open at the top. At the base of the chamber, in precisely the middle of the room, an illuminated tree was trying to reach the outside world. Derelin and Rover walked over to the tree and found bright red apples hanging from the terrestrial limbs.

"It's a fruit!" Rover exclaimed, never having seen an apple before. She pulled one off the tree, and it snapped directly into her little hand. She took a bite and said, "It's delicious, Derelin!"

Derelin grabbed an apple and bit into the juicy exterior. "You're right!" he said. "This is really good!"

They sat there under the apple tree for several hours, enjoying the fruit and having pleasant conversation. Soon they both became sleepy, and Derelin was the first to nod off. Shortly after, Rover too was fast asleep, and the two awoke into an altogether different reality.

A.35 ~ A LADDER TO VENUS

They were inside a factory, though this factory produced planets. There were planets of every size, though all were spherical and colorful. Derelin and Rover wandered the large building searching for anything out of the ordinary that caught their eyes. There was one planet that gave off more light than the others. It was floating within arm's reach above their heads and was a vibrant lavender with swirling clouds of white.

"I really like this one," Rover said and reached out to touch the glowing orb. As soon as her fingers grazed the surface of the planet, she and Derelin were snapped once again into yet another fantasy.

This time they were suspended in a futuristic city that

floated high above in the cloud-line of an orange world. A being walked by, neither obviously male nor female, who seemed curious about the two stowaways but didn't inquire as to how they had arrived.

Derelin stopped the being and asked it where they were located. The being said that they were floating above Venus, and that the surface of the planet had been uninhabitable for many generations. They asked it why it was uninhabitable, and the being said that there was a myth of a poisonous gas which consumed the world below and that no one could survive the harsh conditions.

The lavender fog rolled in from over the mountains and across the prairies and caused sudden death to anyone who breathed in the noxious fumes. The being turned to leave, and Derelin caught a glimpse of a ladder that descended down beneath the clouds. He turned to ask the creature about the ladder, but it had gone.

Derelin pointed out the ladder to Rover and asked her if she felt drawn to the ladder as well. She said that she did feel drawn to it and that she didn't trust the being who seemed to be hiding some truth from them.

They explored the other pod until they found a hatch which led them down to the ladder below. Derelin and Rover began their descent clinging tightly to the ladder, which swayed gently in the cold air. They continued to descend until the clouds gave way, and they could see the surface of the world below.

Derelin shouted to Rover, "I don't see any lavender fog, do you?" Rover looked down to Derelin and yelled, "No! I don't see it either." They continued their descent.

When they reached the surface of the alien world, they found themselves in a glorious paradise. It was a quaint little village full of habitats for tiny people. Derelin remarked to Rover that he felt like a giant strolling through the miniature town. There was no sign of fog, but the village was clearly abandoned. The ruins of buildings were perfectly preserved, and they began to wonder how long it had been since anyone had visited the community.

Straying far from the ladder, Derelin and Rover found other trees bearing fruit and decided to enjoy the natural wonders. Tasting fruit of every kind, they filled themselves to their hearts' content, but it wasn't long before a lavender fog began to roll into the town.

Derelin didn't notice it, but Rover did. She yelled, "It's the fog! Run!" It was too late. The lavender mists were coming at them from every side, and Derelin and Rover congregated together in the center of a clearing.

Like an ambush or a sabotage, the mists came at them until finally they had no choice but to breathe in the air. Derelin gasped inhaling an ounce of the fog into his lungs, and Rover did the same. To their surprise they could breathe! However, the fog appeared to vanish, and what remained was the crystalline view of an underwater city. They found themselves on the bottom of a sea, somehow able to breathe in the depths of those surrounding waters!

A.36 ~ CLOUDS OF STARDUST

Slowly they walked across the bottom of the sea floor into the city, which opened up before them. The city was inhabited with sea creatures of many kinds. Neither Derelin nor Rover could have imagined the types of beasts that were seen. Eels and cuttlefish swam by, though they were upright and communicative. Mermaids and aquatic centaurs roamed the watery kingdom, and Derelin thought he saw Poseidon himself swimming to his castle that was positioned at the city's core. All of the flourishes of the underwater empire were nautical in theme.

Streetlamps hung high above, fashioned in the shape of

conch shells. The roads themselves were made of starfish, and decorative kelp lined the passageways which were laid out before them. The buildings were glass and egg-shaped, rimmed with gold and silver.

One such building called out to our amphibious heroes, and they headed in that direction to see what it was all about! The structure it turned out was an information center, and Derelin and Rover went inside. They wandered the aisles searching for Mount Penglai and eventually found a couple of tomes on the subject.

They each grabbed one of the books and sat down at a table where they proceeded to begin reading. Mount Penglai was a mythical island situated somewhere in the seventeenth quadrant of the galaxy, though its exact location is vague. It is unknown if the land still exists or if it has been swept aside by the passage of time.

Derelin and Rover knew that Mount Penglai had to still exist and were disappointed to learn that its exact location was shrouded with mystery. It is said that eight immortal beings live on the island which is always fair in temperament, and the palaces there are made from precious metals. Fine jewels grow on trees, and the food and drink are in endless supply.

They continued reading about the mythology which had risen up around the fabled land but came across very little else which helped give them clues as to the location of the mountain island.

Rover had a very strong imagination and imagined great mists, like the one that brought her to the underwater kingdom, surrounding the island and obscuring everything in sight. She could almost reach out and touch Mount Penglai, though she knew this was an illusion, and she had a tremendous journey ahead of her to discover the remote land!

They found a librarian and asked if there was any additional information on the existence of or region where Mount

Penglai might be found. The librarian said that there were seven possible locations in the seventeenth quadrant where Mount Penglai might be found.

The librarian, who was like a seahorse with a monocle, stated that if they wanted to embark on a quest, they would have to choose which specific areas to explore. The inhabitants of the underwater city known as Thrighe were able to create vessels that could transport Derelin and Rover; however, they were preprogrammed and couldn't be adjusted once the journey had begun.

Derelin and Rover thought that this information was both fortunate and regrettable. They wanted to travel together but determined that they would have to split up to double their chances of successfully locating the Innovator at his home.

After listening to the descriptions of the possible sites of Mount Penglai, Derelin chose to visit a misty land far off into the regions of the Celestial Night, where cosmic wizards cast spells transforming inanimate objects into living things.

Rover, on the other hand, decided to embark for the Clock, an industrial city comprised of interlocked gears. It is said that the Clock is responsible for the existence and prevalence of time throughout the galaxy.

Once the librarian had made arrangements for their means of transport, Derelin and Rover said their goodbyes and embraced in a warm hug! They didn't know when they would see each other again or if they ever would! They stepped into their bubble ships and departed.

Derelin ascended in his transparent sphere toward the surface of the water and began to float high into the clouds. There, in the majestic sky, he found himself floating through the aisles of an athenaeum. There were rows and rows of books in a nebula that hung in the atmosphere of the beautiful firmament.

Derelin and his ship were dwarfed by children the size

of cities, who were stationed beside the bookshelves engrossed in the writings and pictures of authors who remained anonymous. As he passed onward beyond the reaches of the heavenly archives, the sky gave way to darkness. Stars were glimpsed, shining with everlasting light, and the passage of the bubble ship was easy and unconstrained.

After many moons had passed Derelin ascended to the Gathering of Stones, an asteroid belt that was assembling itself into a planet-sized castle in the ether. He wondered what might happen there and who the castle was for, but he was on a mission and couldn't have stopped his transport if he had wanted to!

Within the clear membrane of his vessel there was a garden. Derelin would sit and eat vegetables and pastries, which blossomed from the nourishing soil that generated such delicacies. There was even one plant from which juice could be derived. He enjoyed this offering with great satisfaction!

Up ahead there was a planet that blocked out most of the light of its sun. The planet was on a similar path to Derelin's ship, and he could see on its surface a sunset which didn't relent but shone ever onward on the rotating sphere. He watched for many hours as that glorious light illuminated the terrestrial surface of the slowly spinning orb.

Finally, he arrived at the outskirts of the Celestial Night and was transfixed by the beauty of its cosmic countryside. There, floating in the nebulas and the clouds of stardust, the pastoral landscape of perpetual dusk lay open, comprised of spacious constellations and partially formed visions of tranquility. Derelin began his approach to a constellation cloud, and when he arrived, the bubble ship burst leaving him with stable footing on the ethereal Avalon!

He strolled the landscape in search of Mount Penglai but instead came upon a wizard several hundred feet high! There were chairs that roamed the land like horses and lanterns which flew above his head like birds. He found a wishing well, and the wizard, Omlot, told Derelin to speak with the well. The well, the wizard explained, should be able to help Derelin find Mount Penglai, although he had never heard of such a place.

Derelin approached the well and began to speak. "Hello. I am Derelin, and I am searching for Mount Penglai. Have you heard of it, and do you know its whereabouts?"

The wishing well yawned and slowly began to respond. "Mount Penglai, is it? Yes, I know of such a place. It can be reached directly through my mouth."

Derelin was skeptical, but he had no other options that he could think of. He inquired from the well, "So, I just jump straight in?"

The well now fully awake replied, "That is correct, sir. You just jump straight in."

Derelin paced for a few moments and decided to take the plunge. He climbed over the cobblestone barrier and let his feet hang over the edge. He peered down into the well and saw a dazzling display of lights and sparks. "This couldn't be too bad," he thought aloud and kicked off the side of the wall to jump into the illuminated tunnel space.

Inside the mouth of the well, Derelin sailed through slow motion sparks and shafts and clouds of light. They shone brightly with every color imaginable, and Derelin could see that the stone wall surrounding him had given way to white marble. He reached out his hand to graze the smooth surface and, when he did, he heard the well laugh loudly from high above. At long last the well gave way to an opening, and Derelin fell into the mouth of a glass bottle. A cork landed on the top of the bottle, and it tipped over and fell with a loud thud! Derelin was trapped.

Inside the bottle there was a wooden ship that looked ever so much like the Ytieo of his memory, only it was smaller and less ornate. The ship made Derelin sad, as though he'd done nothing except travel in a broad circle. He found himself confined, stripped of will and choice. Derelin resolved to explore the ship but began to cry!

A.37 ~ THE HOPEFUL TRAVELER

As tears flowed down his face, Derelin began to notice a storm brewing overhead. This synchronicity made the tears stop flowing, as he didn't want to get swept away in any outward manifestation of his internal condition. As the rain began to flow and accumulate around the bottle, Derelin became nervous. He was stuck inside a container that seemed to suggest a tomb quite eerily. The rain really began to pour, and the bottle was indeed taken by the sea. Lightning began to flash, and Derelin did what he could to prepare himself for whatever may come! Without warning, the lightning shattered his bottle, and the shards of glass sank to the depths below. He was now suspended on the turbulent seas of rain, desperate to gain control over the ship.

Though he was free from his container, he felt trapped by the torrential tempest on a toy model of a barge. Derelin grabbed the helm and fought against the oncoming waves but had limited control. As the storm began to subside, making way for much smoother passage, he noticed an island up ahead. Had he reached the fabled island of his steadfast mission? Was he approaching Mount Penglai? He couldn't be sure but felt hopeful that he might yet deliver the message which had carried him farther than any dream might have suggested. Derelin docked on the shore and began to explore the island with a mountain covered in mist.

He came upon a small cabin, outfitted with wind chimes in the center of a wood. Derelin approached the house curiously and knocked hoping that the Innovator would be present; he was not.

Derelin stepped inside. The cabin was a strange mix of workshop and living space. There were bits and pieces of what appeared to be half-completed skeletons of inventions scattered all around the room.

On a workbench, Derelin found a journal and flipped it open to the most recent entry. He learned that its owner was indeed an inventor who was searching for an avenue of approach to his latest creation. Derelin read about how the inventor had recently created a hematite-glass orchid that was engineered to provide inspiration to artists in the form of a flowing liquid that dripped forth from the plant. The potion, which was derived from the sap of the orchid, had failed in its purpose, and the magical flower was cast aside.

Derelin continued to read about how the inventor believed that a group of businessmen had found the orchid and drank its contents to unintended consequence. The men lost their faces and identities and somehow merged together into the monstrosity that was the Jurisdiction. The author of the journal felt responsible for the creation of the Jurisdiction, which would stop at nothing to increase its brainpower at the expense of helpless prisoners it tortured and victimized. Derelin was certain that he must have found Mount Penglai and the home of the Innovator. All he had to do was wait in order to deliver his message.

After several hours had passed, Derelin decided to step outside for a breath of fresh air. To his horror, upon opening the door, there was the accursed Jurisdiction who quickly seized control of Derelin's mind and devoured the contents of his brain! He did so to such an extent that Derelin had completely stopped functioning by the time the Jurisdiction was able to locate the message within his poor mind.

The Jurisdiction relinquished his grip on the boy's lifeless head, and Derelin collapsed to the concrete entryway below.

The next day when Alexander returned home, he found the still remains of that hopeful traveler who had journeyed far across the galaxy. Although the Innovator couldn't possibly surmise why the boy had come to pay him a visit, he recognized the wounds that the Jurisdiction had imparted upon the motionless forehead of the dead voyager. What Derelin had to say would always remain a mystery, though the Jurisdiction now held the secret and scurried onward in search of its meaning!

A.38 ~ GEARS & OTHER TRINKETS

Rover took a different path through the cosmos. Although the two potential locations for Mount Penglai were in the same quadrant, they were substantially removed from each other enough that the paths of trajectory wound through different spaces.

Rover found herself floating through a colossal garden with vegetation sprung out on all sides of her ship. The immense leaves and massive birds and insects were so imposing that Rover was convinced that she would be punctured and fall to her death. She tried to retain faith and optimism, however, and she managed to steer clear of all objects gliding safely beyond the far reaches of the floating gardens.

Inside of her ship, there was a fountain and a stream which gave life and satiated hunger. She was satisfied with the arrangement but missed the chomping and chewing of delicious food. Once she had reached the end of the magnanimous greenhouse, a long stretch of nothing spread out before her. She began to grow nostalgic for the cosmic nursery and felt dreadfully alone in the depths of emptiness that surrounded her.

She spent her time drinking the crisp elixir and pondering mysteries of existence. At one point, to her amazement, the capsule drifted past a very large screw that spun in a random pattern as though it had jostled loose from a grand device. Rover wondered if the screw belonged to the Clock, her destination. Then again, a pulley moved aimlessly about, and she watched as it hovered without purpose in the vacuum of space. Soon she glimpsed a gear lingering nearby and woke up convinced that she was approaching the goal.

Without warning, Rover could see at a distance an enormous clock face that appeared to be stuck at precisely twelve o' clock. Though it took several hours to grow near, she only once saw the second hand tick: it did so counter-clockwise. Had time slowed to a stop, moving ever so slightly in the wrong direction? Rover certainly had no sense of time, and as she approached a tiny pinhole of an opening in the center of the Clock, she felt the second hand move for a second time.

Rover entered the Clock and landed on a horizontal gear with the burst of her bubble. She explored her surroundings and climbed upon gear after gear searching for any signs of life. Every once in a while, a gear would snap into a new locked position, and Rover would temporarily loose her footing. After some time, having navigated her way through a maze of gears and other trinkets, she came upon a clearing which was obviously situated in a large open space. There, a gigantic hand was working with a delicate instrument to refine the inner workings of the mechanism.

The hand stopped moving, and Rover looked up. In the space above her head, a man was sitting working on the Clock. He was found to be in a workshop which was modestly adorned with only the tools that were essential to his work. The hand moved closer to Rover, and she was shocked; but in a gesture of peace, the hand turned over and beckoned Rover to climb onboard.

Carefully assessing her options, Rover determined that she had no choice but to oblige the man. She climbed aboard the palm of his hand, and he lifted it high into the air. There his face was seen, old and wrinkled. He looked at her through magnifying glasses which were suspended from his brow by straps that wrapped around behind his ears. He wore a brown rubber smock and smiled delicately at the tiny trespasser.

"And who might you be?" boomed the loud whisper of a voice.

"My... my name is Rover," she said, taking a seat on the man's palm.

"Rover, eh?" The man carefully scratched his head with his free hand. "That's a curious name for a young lady. I'm Smithereen: the clockmaker. It's a pleasure to meet you, little Rover." Rover smiled and asked him where they were.

"We are located in Sebastopol, California. Have you ever heard of it?" Rover shook her head with denial. "It's a beautiful little town, or a big town, depending on your perspective." He chuckled to himself. Rover jumped right to the point.

"I'm searching for Mount Penglai, have you heard of it?" she asked.

"Mount Penglai? Yes, of course I've heard of it. It's a legendary island inhabited by immortal figures."

"Great!" said Rover. "Can you tell me how to get there?"

The man looked somber and replied, "I'm afraid it's a long way from Sebastopol. How far have you traveled?"

Rover thought for a minute and replied, "I've traveled from beyond the galaxy."

The clockmaker laughed and said, "Well, then, you're right next door!"

Rover smiled with glee and thanked the man. She asked him to point her in the direction of Mount Penglai, and he said that he had a better idea.

He motioned for Rover to jump onto the desk and carefully positioned his hand for her to do so. Then, she watched as he fashioned a boat from a newspaper and took her outside to a stream in the woods. "If you want to reach Mount Penglai, you must wish for it to be so. I bid you a fond farewell, Rover. Bon voyage."

The clockmaker placed the water taxi in the stream with Rover inside. She waved goodbye to the huge clockmaker and settled for her journey. The man had said that she was a long way from Mount Penglai, but he had also said that it was rather close given the extent of her travels. She didn't quite know what to expect but decided to get some sleep.

A.39 ~ YOU'RE IN NEBRASKA!

Rover awoke from her sleep no longer floating down the stream behind the house of the clockmaker. She found herself lodged against a dock in a medieval town many miles from where she began. No longer were the oversized hands and clockwork gears; scale had restored itself to normal proportions. She wanted to push the boat back out into the river, but there were clearly several leaks. She had to abandon it.

Rover stepped out of the boat and began to make her way into the city. The first person she saw was a delivery man, carefully placing jars of milk out in front of houses. She stopped him and asked him if he knew the way to Mount Penglai. He said that he'd never heard of it but mentioned that it had a very strange name. The exchange was awkward and brief. She continued along her way.

The buildings were uniform, and the overall aesthetic was unsatisfying. Although Rover was sure that this town was just as good as any other, she fought back feelings of doubt and anxiety. She was beginning to feel as though she'd chosen the wrong planet. Just as those feelings had reached their nadir, she turned a corner and saw a fountain in the shape of a goat's head. She dropped her bag and ran to Pilop crying. She hugged the fountain oblivious to anyone who might have seen her; there was no one there.

"Pilop!" Rover said, "I miss you so much! It's so hard; I don't know what to do!" The fountain was unmoved, and Rover began to sob uncontrollably. Within minutes her tears began to subside, and she felt relaxed and at ease.

She stroked the fountainhead and sighed. Knowing that Pilop was gone forever, and not knowing what had become of Derelin, she wanted nothing else other than to be with her friends again searching for the lost city of Ksevia! But that was gone now, and little did she know that her emotions were conspiring with the universe to reveal to her a future course based upon her most deep desires. So it was with everything and everyone on planet Earth.

Rover decided to leave the city by way of an avenue that stretched out as far as her will could take her. She walked along that path as far as she could go, and when she could go no further the pyramid appeared. Dazed and dreaming, Rover stepped inside the echo chamber searching for a fruit tree, searching for Derelin. She found that its interior was covered with mirrors, and lights were shining at her feet to illuminate the way. As she approached the central chamber, Rover began to sense that something was not quite right.

There in the middle of the room was a not a fruit tree per se but rather the hollowed-out remnants of one. The light shone in from above, less vibrant with life than the pyramid of her memory. She knelt beside the tangled vine and fought the tears from forming once again; she didn't have it in her!

Rover sat there for a long while thinking about her journey and thinking about its end. She didn't know where she was, and she didn't know if she could ever return to Tristulle. Her life had become a series of accidental mishaps, or so it seemed to her. But maybe she was overreacting. She had a habit of doing that.

Finally, after a long rest, Rover decided to leave the pyramid in search of anything that might stimulate her senses and redirect her course. She didn't have to wait long. When she exited the pyramid, stretching out in front of her was a large field of tall corn. The corn seemed to beckon her to a farmhouse that lay beyond the vegetation which blocked way.

The sun was setting, and the light shining through the crops made her feel better, feel whole again. Rover remembered that suffering was finite and her sadness temporary. She reached the other side of the field in no time and made her way up to the porch at the front of the red home. She knocked on the door. There was no reply for a few moments, but then an elderly man answered her call.

"Hello?" said the man. "How may I help you? Are you lost?"

Rover tried to conceal the loss that she felt but failed to convince the man that she was okay.

"Now, now," said the man. "Don't you worry. Wait here, and I will fetch us some lemonade."

He motioned to a pair of seats on the side of the porch. Rover took a seat and waited patiently. Several minutes later the man reappeared, and Rover was happy to see the kind man.

"My name is Simon," said the man through thick glasses. "Who are you?"

He handed Rover a tall glass of lemonade, and she took a sip. It was delicious!

"I'm Rover," she said.

"Rover?" the man inquired. "That's an unusual name for a girl. Where are you from, Rover?"

She didn't know what to say, so she was honest. "I'm from Ytieo," she replied, and Simon became stoic and fixed. "Where am

I?" she asked.

"Well," said the man, who was drinking from a glass himself. "You're in Nebraska! Do you have any idea how you got here?"

Rover thought back to the bubble ship, then even earlier to the communications building. Then her mind went to the underwater city and Sebastopol. "I really don't," she said. "I think I'm lost."

Simon took another sip and said, "Oh, it's no bother, Rover, no bother at all. When you look out there, what do you see?" Simon pointed to the newly visible stars that shown brightly above the horizon.

Rover thought for a minute, and her grief turned to anger. "I see death!" she said.

Simon paused in reflection and opened his mouth after great contemplation. "I think you're right," he said. "I see death too," and the man's eyes began to water slightly.

"Do you have any friends?" Simon asked, appreciating the sweet lemonade that Claire had made before she left.

"I did," she said. "But now they're gone."

"Where have they gone if I might ask?"

Rover felt contempt wash over her but decided to try to be constructive. "Derelin and I are searching for Mount Penglai."

Again, Simon was speechless. "Mount Penglai?" he asked.

"Do you know it?!" Rover interjected.

"Well," Simon began. "Mount Penglai is just..." Rover looked on with helpless hope, as though Mount Penglai was the only thing keeping her from complete devastation. "It's just that I don't know where it is anymore," he said, trying to understand the way in which the girl's mind seemed to operate.

"Oh," said Rover. "That's too bad."

"Why are you searching for Mount Penglai?" asked Simon,

who had studied Asian mythology for many years and had made a profession of it and related subjects.

"Derelin and I, well one of us, we need to deliver a message."

Simon honestly didn't know if someone had put the girl up to this, but he tried to respond with candor as Rover's disposition was extremely convincing. "I see," said Simon, not wanting to impede upon the girl's innocence anymore. He was very curious what message that was and later would regret not asking her, but he let it go.

"You know," he said. "I've tried to find Mount Penglai too."

She looked at him sweetly and said, "Really?"

Simon responded, "Yep." There was a brief pause, and then he continued. "I never found it, but that doesn't mean that you won't." Rover finished her lemonade and began to yawn. "You're welcome to stay here tonight young lady. There is a guest room upstairs, and the sheets are clean."

Rover said, "Thanks. I'd like that." And so, Rover and Simon finished their conversation and turned in for the night.

A.40 ~ THE SIDE DOOR

Once it had come to a stop, Pandara sensed that he was in another area where he had never been before. It looked just like the place with seven passageways, but this time there were only six. *I probably need to pay attention to where I place the marbles*, he thought to himself. He looked at the depressions and made note of where they were: one marble in the leftmost column, second from the top; one marble in the next column, topmost position; and one marble in the rightmost column, bottom position. He would try to remember that in case he needed it for future reference.

Again, he thought he heard a yell in the distance but tacked it up to air passing over some organ-like structure deep within the dungeon. He didn't think for long. This time he would choose the passage all the way to the right. Pandara hurried along, almost jogging down the corridor, toward a fate he could not predict. The walls were getting narrow, and he finally reached the end of the hall, a dead end. "Pandara!" he thought he heard.

Is that my name? He wasn't sure, but the sound seemed to have come at great expense to its person of origin, if it had been a voice at all.

At the bottom of the wall of the dead end, he noticed a two-inch-by-ten-inch slit that he could look through if he knelt down, and so he did. On the other side of the wall, in the distance, he could see faceless men in suits and bowler caps. They were holding briefcases and walking around in circles. Occasionally a footstep passed right in front of his eyes, temporarily blocking his view. The men seemed almost inanimate, lifeless, yet they moved with the horrifying determination of men on a mission. They were going nowhere, just around in circles.

Pandara stood up and felt the hairs on the back of his neck raise. There was someone or something just behind him, staring at him, and he was trapped. Slowly, he turned around and saw the most terrifying image he had ever seen before. A giant stone-like figure hovered in the air, draped with sheets that hung off his frame like decayed flesh. The face was unsympathetic, almost featureless. He was a giant head, nearly three meters tall, with black eyes swirling in liquid death. In place of a nose, there were two vertical slots. His mouth was a narrow slit that ran the full width of his head, crosswise in a horizontal manner.

The Grim Reaper had only absence of character. His features were a combination of ideas that were not meant to exist. The limitless death which surrounded the reaper permeated everything within eyesight of the demonic head. Inanimate objects recoiled with disgust, and matter itself fainted before the horrendous creature, which oozed with stench and foulness. He made one motion as though to walk toward the looming beast, and that was it. The monolithic Grim Reaper accelerated toward Pandara, opened its mouth, and descended upon him before there was any time to change his course.

Time was felt to slow as the behemoth came down on the poor soul. Pandara entered the mouth and descended into the monster. He felt himself being digested alive, not just his flesh but also his soul. It was a slow process of digestion, and Pandara felt every nerve and every muscle disintegrate until only the bone remained. He spent an eternity in Fotoa with other souls being consumed by the blade-like churning of soul-devouring consciousness. "Pandara!" he heard to infinity.

There was that voice again. It was clear that the word was nearly impossible to mutter, yet somehow the speaker had managed to shout it. The experience of his disintegration endured, and it was all that there was: a relentless and unforgiving death, a never-ending nightmare of hellish existence. With time, he began to experience the presence of a sublime nothingness that dawned with heavenly salvation. It seemed that the digestion would not go on forever, but rather an end might come in ten thousand years.

The cave was dim and the shallowness complete. The architectures of imposition deafened his ears, though he had none. Creeping malaise fought against flesh for the dominance of steel claws, and forgetfulness persisted in the narrow confines of focused obliteration.

Pandara's emptiness detached his identity from its embodied state. The essence of character and strict tenets of life which held fast to principles of coherence were abandoned before the consumption of such rules. The crushing weight of dissolution moved like a wave through the consciousness of his being. Over thin infinities he waited without knowing what would come from his waiting.

A.41 ~ SORROWS IN WHITE

The air outside was cool and damp. Between shades of pine and birch, Kóre strolled lost in reverie. She lived alone, age thirty-five, past her prime and detached from the morays of secular New England life. It seemed clear enough that her man wasn't coming. Though she waited with bated breath for him to arrive on a wooden ship perhaps, having traversed the boundless sea, having heard her call to him in the depths of their most treasured dreams.

In the morning, she would read her poetry, hardly maintaining the social and civil expectations placed on a woman of her age. She would read and write about the romance they would share, together in some European castle near the crystal streams and the dark caves of deathly doom.

In other poems, she dreamt she was a sailor, or a baker, or a blacksmith undertaking the ancient task of forging from metal some daggers of righteousness. It was a quiet life, one that she treasured with all of her heart, except for the fact that she lived alone. She believed that soon she would be saved and began to prepare for her family of the near future.

That afternoon, she decided to take a break from her poetry and go for a walk. She left the comfort of her cabin, the one left to her by her father a few years back. She thought about him every time she came or went. She missed Bastian McCallister; he was always so good to her, believing in her flights of fantasy. Bastian would nurture his young Kóre's dreams. He taught her that the townsfolk were always too preoccupied with faith and their fear of God. It was a realization she had had herself as a young child.

Bastian's guidance helped solidify her fleeting perceptions into a coherent philosophy. Bastian and Kóre were dreamers, belonging to a long lineage of kindred spirits. They believed that salvation would come, albeit in a different form from the one their puritanical neighbors promoted and proselytized. Bastian was a tower of light in a hostile and unpredictable world. He invested his will in the well-being of his daughter and fought for her future like no one else ever would.

Kóre's mother had died in childbirth. Bastian would tell her stories about her mother. She had always wanted to be as beautiful as she imagined her mother was: flowing auburn hair and emerald, green eyes. Kóre had brown hair, like her father, and thought it not as honest and vibrant as the hair of fire and passion. Her eyes were blue, a fact that was in itself mysterious.

Bastian had always said that the greatest poets had blue eyes. Now an adult herself, she thought that this comment was charming and endearing of her father. She tried to be a great poet but knew that she had room to improve. But that was what life was for; and perhaps the greatest poets also knew their weaknesses. Kóre liked to think so and could see that improvement in their works.

As she walked to escape into the tranquility of thought, Kóre was held captive by the suspicious glances of the town folk. Those civilians would pass her on both sides, mostly keeping their eyes down as Kóre would begin to smile and say hello. She was silenced.

Others would cast glaring looks deep into her soul, where they might do the most harm. She would lose track of her fantasy, innocent and sweet. Kóre would float along the days with grace and elegance that inspired jealousy among the women of the town. They would whisper to their husbands of her tilted ways, and the men would have no choice but to affirm their suspicions. Kóre was oblivious to this occurrence and thought only of the man who'd save her, her father, and her poetry.

Still, she would not feel anger for those poor, unfortunate souls. She felt pity for them. They'd never know the utter bliss and transformational powers of the creative process. Instead, they'd drown in the despair of their lonesome religion, which offered them only sorrow and enriched their paranoia.

If she could, she would replace their book with hers. Perhaps then they would rediscover that childhood innocence that left them so many years earlier. She knew that all of these desperate spirits were once little children who danced in the brisk carnival of autumn. She knew that they had played in the endless summers of youth's halcyon debut. She remembered some of them, and the others were just the same. She remembered them too, all from the spring days of climactic joy. The world was much simpler then; fear of winter had not yet taken hold.

Up ahead was Jovian LeBlanc, the man who spouted cryptic prophecies. Kóre was intrigued by Jovian's complex mind but feared his sharply nonsensical, unpredictable nature. She decided to proceed along her path but to avoid him as politely as possible. When he passed her on the left, Jovian looked up from his mumbling abstractions. Mistakenly, she made eye contact with the hapless man. "Witch!" exclaimed Jovian, and he spit on the white cotton dress that concealed her bones. Bystanders gasped at the brief confrontation. Kóre looked around with dismay and counted the number of people who were there, around fifteen or so. This broke her heart, and she scurried on ahead.

She reached the graveyard on a hill, lonesome and remote. She paused to catch her breath and process what had taken place. As the experience drifted off to join countless other memories from before, she lifted her head and took note of her surroundings. Kóre wondered where she herself would finally lay her bones to rest. The inevitability of lifelong solitude was creeping in, and she lamented that her beautiful man had not yet come to join her by her side. Life it seemed was cruel. It was hard to overcome the misery. Her poetry and imaginative disposition were all that she had. Perhaps it was enough; perhaps it was not.

As the day grew long, she decided to head back. Before she did, however, she wanted to read the names of the dead as she had done so many times before. Samuel Beckinsworth (1615-1670); Joanna Raleigh (1632-1645); Jonathan Brysdale (1652-1678). She had known Jonathan. It was only twelve years ago when he had been killed by a bear during an expedition to gather wood. They had been friends, though not terribly close. "Life is short, and you have to make the most of it," Bastian would sometimes say. *I hope you're well, Jonathan. I hope that you've found peace.*

The sun was setting, and it wasn't wise to be out after dusk unless there was a good enough reason for it. She headed home under cover of the remaining sun. Kóre met the same looks as before, although this time they were accompanied by an occasional whisper, covered and obscured.

A.42 — CHAPTER 05

A.43 ~ THE SKY'S NAME

The sight of the deathly machine overcame Kóre, who began to tremble and seize from the shock of her brutal abduction. The gallows were a towering symbol of pressing inevitability, yet somehow Kóre couldn't comprehend the extent of what was occurring. She could see that her end was near, though she couldn't bear to face that fact. Panic rushed over her poor mind. She was destined to become a nameless victim of cruelty and hatred.

Kóre was corralled with the others behind the stage, a dozen or so powerless souls, each with their own marks of outcast or introversion. Jovian was there, oblivious as usual to what was taking place. Just then, Kóre realized that her man had arrived, though not as she'd expected or desired and longed for. Minister Jordan Burrows began to speak above the clamor. "Settle! Settle! We have collected the transgressors!" Arms raised as though to contain the zeal of the population under his command; the raucous grew thin.

"Ardently, we assemble to banish the transgressors, those

who are steeped in evil and sin!" One man yelled out "Burn the witches!" to which a choir of cacophonous noise emerged, another sound battled in the combat. "Shhh..." rose all around, and the NPCs waited for the minister to continue.

"The blood of Christ has been smeared by the poison of vile deeds! We must establish the way of the Lord! No one, man nor woman, shall be allowed to carry on in sin! In treasonous hearts, the Devil makes himself known!" There were yells and screams of hateful slurs. Someone threw rotten cabbage at Kóre, who was crying uncontrollably, weak and overcome with terror.

"Now listen, wayfarers of lust and temptation! These are the last words you will ever hear! Listen to the salt of the Earth as it rejects you where you stand! No more shall we tolerate your wicked and unholy ways!" Minister Burrows stepped aside and nodded to the large men who were standing by, holding the prisoners captive in cloudy apprehension.

Four of them were clenched and carried up to the gallows. The crowd hissed and moaned and watched as the three women and one man were hung right before their eyes! Cheers and spiteful admonishing resounded between the buildings and the trees. A barber stood beneath his doorway, head propped up with false approval, internally bewailing that nothing could be done to stem the rising tide.

As the bodies were removed from the gallows, Kóre's attention sharply turned to the man who had grabbed her by the arm. "No... no... NO!" she yelled out, and her eyes met the strangers who cursed her with humiliating gestures. She was pulled onto the stage, arms bound behind her back.

A dark sack was placed over her head. Only faint traces of light could be seen through the ominous shroud; her breathing raced with the motion of the sack, pushing and pulling away from her open mouth. She felt the noose slip over her head and tighten around her neck. She was pushed backwards.

As she thought to cleanse her mind of the inevitable, a momentary glimpse of her gallant man flashed before her eyes. Then there was a drop, a crack, and a never-ending darkness that persisted.

A.44 ~ DARK THEOCRACY

Minister Jordan Burrows was refined in his taste for biblical quotation. Often, he veered away from the more obvious references, in favor of obscure renderings and hidden passages from the Book of God. He lusted for the salvation of his parish, with a fervidness of spirit that was admired by all who listened to him speak, or so it seemed to him. In reality, he was a distorted man whose heart and soul had been perverted by greed and derangement. Listening closely, one could pick out the contradictions and sprinting hatred that tainted his shallow message of childish superstition.

Jordan relinquished his venerable position to the evil which suggested itself across the land. His acts were despicable and unrestrained. Having devoted himself to the dark and cynical side of town, he actively suppressed his conscience and looked down on those who did not. He knew he was better than them, competed for stature, and sought to prove that there was no law to the lay of the land. Jordan noticed that the community had grown restless and disillusioned with the hardships of life in New England. To advance his prominence within the region and improve his reputation, he traded his devotion to mercy for demagoguery and wrath. It was a natural progression.

In between delusions of grandeur and messianic self-identification, Burrows was depressed. Though he would never admit it to himself, he was cornered in the soulless shell of his body. The parish didn't notice him as he truly was. They were extremely predictable and couldn't see beyond the tips of their noses. They only saw what they wanted to see: a powerful minister who was unafraid to blow the dog whistle. This appealed to their desire to cast blame upon those who were different. And once confirmed by an authority such as the minister, they were given carte blanche to do as they pleased. It was in this way that these others whose only commonality was to stray a little from the herd became the targets of hate and suspicion. Burrows realized that it was time to take bold action and had no qualms about destroying the lives of those who were different. They deserved it.

It was now 1695, and the thirst for blood had come to an end. Jordan watched as a spectator while the families of those who had died fought for posthumous innocence of their loved ones. Rationalizing his own actions, he believed that they did so just for the compensation it might afford.

"Watch as the rats climb over their dead, just to get a little more bread," he was known to say. Satisfied in his haunted plantation, Burrows had retired from the dark theocracy. He spent his time reading the Bible and writing essays on the implications of not following divine creed.

It was winter when the sickness came. At first, he only felt a mild chill and decided to gather more blankets from the chest in the cellar. But after several sleepless nights, his cough began to consume him. No amount of proselytizing would save him now. In his own mind, he was already saved. Thoroughly convinced of his holy stature in the pantheon of Heaven, he fought the disease half-heartedly, consciously eager to escape the mortal coil of time's bleak and pathetic charade.

He passed on quietly in the early days of January 1701. No one would remember him fondly, and few would at all. Those who did remember him pitied the earth that was forced to nestle up against his coffin. Surely his blood and decayed flesh would poison, rather than nourish, the land upon which his home was built. But, nonetheless, he was taken into oblivion, where he joined Kóre, Jovian, and others in a dark night of the soul.

The shift into awareness was subtle at first. Dull flashes of light permeated the black pit where his consciousness had gone to sleep for eternity. Then the lights grew brighter and more focused. After an epoch had passed, all remembrances of his past life had settled to dust. Jordan Burrows opened his mind in a dream and couldn't make out what he saw, but his feelings were unmistakably present: nausea and dread. It was as though he was trapped in a spider's web of enormous proportions, waiting for the planet-sized arachnid to claim its clever but tiny prize.

The dread gave way to panic and panic to sheer terror. Whatever was left of Burrows was dissolving into the embodiment of fear, loathing, confusion, and chaos. His experience of Hell was numb and detached. He would have many more chances to perfect his descent into the bowels of that infinite dungeon. His gelatinous form oozed like oil in water, rising to the surface of existence. It was time to be reborn!

Jordan was a mindless and voracious vagabond of death. His unending hunger for anything with life plagued the promising landscape full of rich potential. His drag of sour decay poisoned the air and rotted the earth. Burrows took no pleasure in anything and ruined the worlds that he touched.

He opened his eyes, only dimly perceiving the wretchedness of his bleak footsteps. He thought about the taste of death, and then it was gone without a thought for anyone other than himself. The space was vacant and hallowed. It was a primordial template upon which any creation could be set forth and imagined. Jordan laughed and spun around, observing the solace of one who had triumphed against all odds. Though he didn't recollect who he was, his origin was undoubtedly divine. For how could anything less than divine inherit such perfection!

A.45 ~ THE QUINTESSENCE

The next morning, after a deep sleep, Rover woke up to find no one at home. There was a note in the kitchen, however, that read, *Be back soon*. The note rested underneath a statue of a rose, which was masterfully carved from gray marble with white inclusions. Rover stood admiring the statue for a few short moments and developed a distinct impression that the rose did not belong to Simon. It did not even belong to Claire; it belonged to someone she would know.

She took the statue and placed it in her bag and looked once again at the hastily written note. Something about the handwriting made Rover nervous, and she decided to leave. It was a good idea because that statue meant more to Simon than anything else that he had in his possession. That's why he left it there for Rover. That's why he had left.

He was hopeful that she'd take it and was delighted to later find out that she had. Rover stepped outside onto the porch and descended down the stairs, closing the door behind her. There was a long dirt road which formed a path out of the farm. She thought it was as good a path as any to take and began her way along the side of the road.

It was several miles later when she saw the abandoned mansion. Not a single car had driven by, but she wouldn't have recognized one if she saw it. Though the house seemed scary it was daytime, and her feelings pulled her there. She walked inside through the creaking screen door and shouted, "Hello?!" Rover had grown brazen and reckless because she buried her feelings deep inside. Little did she know that she was on the path that would lead her home.

She walked into the dusty study, seemingly knowing what

to do next. Intuitively, she reached for a book, which her solitary hand captured with purpose. It wasn't that one; which one was it? She continued pulling books from the shelf until finally one clicked and wouldn't let go of its place of rest. The bookshelf popped from the wall, and Rover felt a cool breeze emanating from an empty space in front of her.

She went around to the side of the bookshelf. That's when she noticed the grooves in the ground and pulled the shelf from the wall. Hidden behind the imposing cabinet was a walkway that descended down into a cellar. She finished separating the shelf from the wall and took the lantern from a hook on the side of the passageway. Rover clicked a button on the lantern and closed the door behind her, radiating light in all directions. She walked down the short spiral staircase and entered a cavernous space which housed several barrels of wine.

During her exploration of the cellar, Rover managed to find a small metal box. She put the lantern down by her side and sat cross-legged in front of the little chest. When she opened the compartment, she found a collection of mementos from a boy's childhood. There were some photographs, a toy vehicle, a couple of written notes, and some dice.

Rover was about to read one of the notes when she heard noise coming from the first floor above. She quickly closed the box and securely positioned it in its place. She walked with the lantern back up the stairs and tried to see if she could make sense of what was going on outside.

Rover pushed the door open a crack and could already see a beautifully decorated and furnished home. The lights were on and shone brightly, giving the space a wonderful glow! Feeling that the coast was clear, she continued to push the door open wide enough so that she could pass through. She did and closed the bookshelf once again.

There were two children running through the spacious home, chasing each other and laughing. A man yelled out, "Rover! Where are you?" Rover was stunned in her footsteps! The man walked into the study. "There you are! It's time for dinner, come quick."

He turned around and went into another room. Rover didn't know what to do but decided that although she was filthy, she would follow behind the man. She turned the corner and entered a dining room, where a sumptuous dinner was waiting for her.

"Have a seat, Rover," said a woman carrying a large breast of turkey to the table. The man proceeded to carve the breast, and Rover decided to pull up a seat to the table. "Are you feeling okay?" the woman stopped to ask Rover, but before Rover had a chance to answer the man and woman were already having another conversation. It seemed clear that they hadn't noticed Rover's disheveled appearance.

The two young boys joined the family at the table, and dinner was served. They all seemed to know Rover, but she had no recollection of any of them. She pretended to belong but somehow felt that she would be accepted regardless of her response.

"Have you finished your homework, dear?" asked Mother in between bites of peas and potatoes. Rover didn't respond until Mother looked at her.

"I, um... I don't know," said Rover.

Rover's parents looked at each other, and her mother said, "That's alright. You can finish after dinner." They continued to enjoy the meal, and when dinner was over, Rover helped her mother clean the dishes.

Once the dishes were clean, Mother said that it was time for Rover to go to bed. Rover hesitated and asked, "What about my homework?" Her mother stopped what she was doing and looked concerned.

"We finished it together, don't you remember?" She looked at Father.

Father also concerned asked, "Rover you seem far away. Is everything alright?"

Rover, beginning to feel connected with the family said, "I think so. I just must be tired." This response satisfied Mother and Father, and so Rover went upstairs to get in bed. That night she had a strange dream about a strange family that mistook her for their daughter.

In the morning, Rover woke up, took a shower, put on her clothes, and went outside to wait for the bus. Somehow it all seemed natural, and she knew what to do. She was feeling much better and wondered how long this fantasy could possibly last. When the bus arrived, she stepped on trying to figure out her place and looked for signs of friendship among the strangers.

Danny asked her what she was doing this weekend.

"What?" Rover asked, clearly lost in a daze.

"I asked you what you are doing this weekend," he said.

"Oh," said Rover. "I don't know. Not much I suppose."

"Hmm…" Danny responded and moved on past Rover's seeming indifference. "There's a party out in the fields tonight if you want to go. I mean, if you'd like to go with me."

Rover, still far away but missing adventure said, "Yeah, sure. I'll go."

Danny said, "Great. I'll pick you up at 7:00."

"Pick me up?" asked Rover.

Danny chuckled. "Yeah, of course. I do have a car you know."

"Oh, okay," replied Rover, figuring that she'd understand when he arrived.

That night she was dressed and ready to go, but Danny

didn't show up. Rover waited by the window, and finally at 7:15, she saw one of those mechanical boxes arrive sprawled out on four wheels. Danny left the car running with headlights on and went up to the front door. Rover stepped outside, saying goodbye to her parents who told her to not be out too late, and they departed.

Danny was eyeing Rover's legs that peeked out from beneath her summer dress, but Rover didn't notice. She was looking out the window thinking about Derelin and hoping that he'd managed to make it to Mount Penglai.

They pulled into a field where half a dozen or so other cars were parked and got out. Syd had his arms around Nancy, and Curtis and Melody were nearby as well. They were all drinking punch. Danny and Rover went over to the cooler to have their first drink.

"Hey Dan. Hey Rover. How are you feeling tonight?" asked Syd who was holding Nancy's hips and subtly swaying with her in the breeze.

"I'm good," replied Danny. "Ready for the weekend," and he turned to look at Rover. Rover looked up, realizing that everyone was waiting for her to speak. Danny wrapped his arm around her waist, and Rover spoke.

"I'm good too," she said simply and continued to drink the punch.

Curtis told a few jokes, and Melody was glad to be with him. Everyone got fairly drunk, and passions were beginning to heat up. "Want to go for a walk?" Danny whispered in Rover's ear.

She looked at him and said, "Yeah, sure."

He took her by the hand and said, "We're going for a walk guys." The mention of it caused a commotion, and their friends laughed and hollered.

"Have a good time you two!" Syd exclaimed.

"Don't do anything I wouldn't do!" Melody said to Rover,

and Curtis nudged her in the side. She laughed.

Danny led the way toward a towering forest and began to speak. "You know, Rover. I think you're really cute." Rover was mostly unmoved. Danny couldn't see her clearly in the twilight. Rover wanted anything that would stimulate her senses and pull her into the stability of a normal life. She squeezed Danny's hand, which he took to be a sign of approval. They continued to walk toward the tree line. "I really want a relationship with you, Rover. I feel like we're meant to be together. Do you feel it too?"

Knowing that Danny didn't have any clue about who she was or where she'd been, and knowing that he didn't care, Rover responded with complementary selfishness. "Yeah, Danny. I feel it too."

Danny stopped walking and turned to face her. He was tall and handsome enough but somewhat simple and quite shallow. She wasn't attracted to him but found his body pleasing. Danny placed his hand underneath her chin and lifted her head up to meet his. They kissed on the lips, both wanting to escape from very different lives.

Danny reached around behind Rover, still engaged with her mouth, and felt her lower back. She returned his kiss with growing passion. Danny interpreted her gesture and let his hands nervously wander around her body. She moved his hand on top of her breast and squeezed it signaling that he should continue in such a way. Then, to his surprise and excitement, she began to unbuckle his belt.

Rover and Danny followed through with their desires, and though each had different reasons for the escapade, both were fulfilled and content with what had happened. Danny departed quickly; however, and Rover was hoping for a little more than he had given her. She didn't see him at school the next week, and Rover wondered if he was avoiding her. Weeks passed, and it had become clear that Danny had gone away. She too wanted to disappear when she began to notice the bump that was forming in her abdomen.

It was several months later when Rover decided to make the break. She gathered her few possessions and made her way to the bus station. There were many options available to her since she had taken her father's money. She wanted to go as far away as possible, and it appeared that a land called New York City was her best option. She was no longer focused on finding Mount Penglai and had decided that if it was meant to be, it would find her!

Rover paid her fare and stepped onboard the vehicle which departed promptly. She knew that she was due in a matter of a few months and grew determined to find a way to support herself and her baby. Perhaps when she arrived in New York City a solution would present itself.

The bus traveled far to the east, and Rover was impressed by the land's simplicity. She passed through a handful of villages and a couple of large cities. She thought that the cities were strangely devoid of imagination, given how many people seemed to occupy them. Though the machines on the road were interesting, cars of every shape and color, they seemed to be the only devices which these people had created. She wondered if people in this world were happy and suspected that they were not. It seemed rather stressful, and Rover felt sorry for the Americans.

At the outskirts of Manhattan, Rover realized that New York City would be a daunting but exciting ride; it was so monumental and foreign! She wondered if she would have a difficult time assimilating into the culture but knew that everything would just work out. At least, she hoped it would.

The bus dropped her off on Broadway, and Rover was captivated by the tempo of the city. She saw the theaters and the restaurants and knew that she had found as permanent a home as she could find in the short term. It took several years of hard work, but Rover managed to make her way from waitress to Off-Broadway actor. She was a natural performer. The first role she had received garnered much attention, and she felt that she was on track to become successful in the medium.

The piece was called *Diagonal Squared*, and Rover portrayed an orphan who was coming of age in Victorian England. The exercise gave her room to process her experiences and settle into a realization that she was likely to remain in America, or at least on Earth, for the foreseeable future.

Rover's baby had been stillborn, and she didn't like to think much of the possibility that she could not procreate. She missed her child though acknowledged that she would have been limited in her ability to perform with a newborn. The thought was natural, but she criticized her own selfishness thinking that it was a terrible thing to consider.

Rover had given a decent performance and was on her way out the door when a well-dressed man stopped her. "Hi, I'm sorry to bother you," he began. Rover was a little frightened but stopped to hear the man out. "I watched your performance, and you're very talented. I especially enjoyed the way you delivered the character's secret origin throughout the performance. My name is Erik," he said.

Rover felt threatened and the sensation intrigued her. "I'm Rover," she said, reaching out to shake the man's hand.

"Listen," he said. "Do you have somewhere to be? I'd love to buy you a cup of coffee if you don't." She was interested and accepted the offer.

They walked side-by-side to the coffee shop where they would meet every few nights. Conversation was rich and philosophical. Erik was from Stockholm and was a visiting professor in Epigenetics at Columbia University. He told her about his research, and this interested Rover; however, she was surprised that the people of Earth were so developed in some ways but oblivious in others.

Erik asked her about her past, and Rover said that she wasn't yet ready to talk about it. He only had three months left of his stay in New York and thought about asking Rover to come with him. Erik often got ahead of himself and knew that Rover wanted to become a famous actor; at least he thought that she did, but she was very reluctant to talk about herself.

There was something otherworldly about Rover, though this is not what drew him to her. Erik was attracted to her talent and her charm, though he often dreamt about her as well.

After the beginnings of a promising relationship had matured into the security of a stable partnership, Erik and Rover had become inseparable. Rover knew that Erik had only two weeks remaining in New York City and wondered why he didn't ask her to join him. Was there someone waiting for him at home? She kept her paranoia at bay but finally decided to confront him. They were at Matteo's Italian restaurant when she decided to pop the question.

"You leave in two weeks, Erik. Why have you not asked me to join you back in Stockholm?" Her frankness was one of Erik's favorite qualities, and Erik was delighted to hear the question.

"I thought that you would certainly want to stay in New York and develop your career," he said, feeling that a crux was upon them.

"What career?" she asked. "I only act as a means to an end." Although Rover had remained silent for so long about her true intentions, Erik always assumed that acting meant a great deal to her.

"You do?" he asked. "That is why I didn't ask you to join me. I didn't want to make you choose between me and your career." Rover was honestly in love with Erik and wanted to join him in Sweden with all her heart!

"I would come with you!" she said, "If you'd only ask," and that was all it took for the two of them to elope to Stockholm. Rover left the acting company and packed her belongings.

The flight to Stockholm was turbulent, and Rover was unimpressed with the rudimentary mode of transport. Not only was the food onboard the flight terrible, but she had to share the journey with dozens of other passengers. She remembered traveling to the Clock in the comfort of her own bubble ship and missed those days of adventure which caused her to be unsettled at the time.

There was a particularly bumpy section of the flight, and during the climax Erik pulled out a small box. He handed it to Rover, and she opened the case. Inside was a beautiful diamond ring, and Erik asked her if she would marry him. Without hesitation she replied that she would, and the couple kissed passionately. The flight continued to be turbulent, but soon enough the roughness subsided.

The lovers made their way back to Erik's condominium and didn't sleep for several hours. Within weeks, Rover had begun to suspect that a child was coming and grew restless with emotion. The sudden change brought back memories that she thought she had moved past, and although he would ask, Rover still didn't like opening up about her history.

While Erik was away at work, she would take care of the apartment, shop for groceries, and practice her cooking. One day while cleaning the closet, Rover found a cryptic diary filled with technical drawings and anatomical sketches of machinery. When Erik returned home, Rover made a first priority of confronting him about the book. Erik said that it was his true calling to be an inventor, and he hoped to build an automaton one day.

Like a wave crashing down upon her, Rover was thrust into guilt over having abandoned her search for the Innovator. This combined with the experience of childbearing was too much to take emotionally. She knew that her feelings would pass, but Erik became concerned. He asked her politely to please tell him what she was thinking about, and the only words that came to her spilled out of her mouth. "Erik, have you ever heard of a Breniculine?"

He was dumbfounded but considered her question thoughtfully. "No, I don't believe that I have. Why? What does that mean to you, dear?"

Rover processed her momentary reveal and replied, "Oh, it's nothing. I was just curious." Erik sensed that she had kept much within but remembered that he had vowed himself to remain patient.

Time passed quickly and Erik vigilantly prepared himself for fatherhood. He helped Rover as much as possible with all of the necessary preparations and was good to her, though he thought that he didn't do enough.

The baby was six weeks out when Rover began to feel more nauseous than usual. Days of illness came and went until finally the sharp pains began to inflict themselves upon her stomach. It was clear that she was going into labor, but Erik was nowhere to be found. She called an ambulance, called Erik, and they met at the hospital where the baby was delivered. Rosa was her name, and she was born without life.

Erik and Rover were heartbroken. The doctor came in to talk with the couple and informed them that they had options to consider. Erik, having a pedigree in Biology had already considered such options, but he let the doctor present their situation to Rover in a gesture of neutrality that he thought would be most warmly received by her.

Rover didn't want to make any hasty decisions, and Erik

thought that this was wise. They did decide, however, to keep a sample of the child's DNA safely stored at the hospital in case they wanted to proceed at a later date.

They left Rosa's room as it was for many months, until finally they agreed to adapt it somewhat. Rover and Erik sat out on the balcony enjoying Riesling and conversation one night. Rover decided to tell Erik the story about her marble rose and the farmhouse as a way to introduce herself to him. She said that she had more to share but couldn't do so yet, because he wouldn't believe her if she told him. Erik knew in his heart that this was true and agreed to leave her rocks unturned.

A.46 ~ THE SON OF MAN

The darkness of oblivion gave way to white luminescence over the course of millennia. Finally, with lethargic drunkenness he awoke at the entrance of the maze, nauseated, with only a hint of recollection of what had come before. Had he been asleep? He couldn't tell, but what made matters worse was that there was a slow-moving stone of blackness set in his stomach. He had been touched by death forevermore. The source of the plague that befell him was unknown. He just had a sense that something terrible had happened; he couldn't be sure what it was.

Pandara walked over to the sundial in the center of the plaza. It read, *Festina nunc. Bestia mortis scit ubi te fuit.* He read quietly to himself. *Haste now. I know there was a beast of death.* The epithet turned over a remembrance in his mind. He could feel that he was prey to some unknown demon, and he panicked. From the corner of his eye came the alcove; he dashed over to the familiar niche and took the marbles in hand.

Yes, he remembered this, but what was the combination that he swore to remember from all those ages ago? Pandara placed one stone in the leftmost column, second depression from the top. Next, he set a pebble in the second column, top position. And the third, where did that one go? He didn't have time. He placed it in the bottom-right corner. The alcove began to spin, and he waited, eager to progress toward whatever purpose this place held for him, if there was one.

The foyer revealed itself, and Pandara took a brief moment to collect his thoughts. Before he had chosen the right-most way, and that had been a dead end. He was fairly confident. So, he decided on the passageway that was second from the right. He briefly recalled looking under the wall; was there a man there?

Fueled by fear, he ran into the corridor. Spiriting around the corners and rushing down the straightaways, he entered a wide-open venue full of men in suits, parading back and forth, briefcases in hand and faceless. He didn't know what to do. He wove his way between them and around them, searching for any clue that might lead him beyond this section of the puzzle.

He felt that his time was running out, and desperate to advance, pushed one of the men over. The man fell, but his legs continued to move as if he was charged by a mindless battery. The others didn't miss a beat, still marching in circles to nowhere fast. Pandara was relieved that his rash decision hadn't caused a chain reaction of attention drawn to him.

Pandara grabbed the suitcase, clicked the latches, and opened it revealing the contents. Hundreds of worms fell out, slithering blindly with as much sense of purpose as their masters. Well, that was no use; he had to act fast. Pandara threw the suitcase into a corner. He grabbed another suitcase and another, tossing all of them into a corner of the region. Once he had twenty or so suitcases, he stacked them into a column and used them to climb onto the wall of the maze.

From this vantage point, he could see many different

regions of the dungeon, each with its own riddles and happenings. He was determined to find what appeared to be a locus, or center, of the oubliette. In one far off corner, a building arose from the labyrinth's back. It was what appeared to be a guard tower of sorts, barely perceptible through a haze. "Pandara!" Yes, he heard it that time. He was certain that this was his name, and that the sound was coming from the guard tower. Again, it was clear that the speaker was just barely able to project her voice.

Vague impressions of a young woman stirred through his mind. He knew someone! There was another, his equal in mind, body, and spirit. But what was she doing here? Pandara had the distinct impression that this woman was waiting to be rescued. The realization filled Pandara with contempt for the maze and urgency set in as to the means by which he might resolve the tensions within and surrounding him.

He made for the projection, though he had a long way to go. Suddenly, a jolt struck the stability of his running surface, and Pandara was knocked over the edge of the wall and fell into a dark space. The artificial light reached him, though he could not see anything of his diagonal environment.

A.47 ~ CREATION MYTH

The neon horizon glowed red in far off reaches, and laterally, a grid of golden light was laid down in all directions. Otherwise, the space was entirely black. Jordan realized that all he had to do was think of anything at all, and it would materialize in front of him. With that thought, desert sands began to form around his ankles. He looked down and stepped outside of their growing numbers. One grain at a time, the sands did not stop accumulating. They sped up in intensity, until Jordan frantically shifted his train of thought. The sand turned to arid stone, beige and lifeless. He could not form anything he wanted, but he could persuade the matter to shift its form.

He thought about the sea, and the stone turned to earth, now stretching far beyond his immediate location. The horizon began to fade, and a scene sprouted up around him. It was straight out of his wildest fantasies and innermost nightmares. Skeletons of shrubs slowly pushed forth from the developing terrain, and blackness gave way to sight albeit limited and constrained. Nonetheless, the persistence of the developing landscape was crystal clear in the simultaneous vision of a world being built. It was rich and terrifying.

On top of the soil, stone walls began to emerge jutting out from the shallow ground that trembled beneath his feet. Off in the distance, he could see the barriers rolling in. Spacious columns of stone tumbled across the dusty plain and headed directly for him at a snail's pace. But then the stonework accelerated until one rectangular brick the size of a carriage flew passed him, nearly grazing his chest in so doing. Another boulder rushed by, and Jordan panicked realizing that his surroundings were in fact not of his own making.

He dodged the heavy pillars, one at a time, as the landscape continued to form around him. A wall hit Jordan in the arm, and he felt an unbearable pain rush to the location of his injury. He looked down and saw that his arm was badly severed in the incident. As the bricks continued to swing by, moving at a dreadfully lethal pace, his appendage reconstructed itself, but the pain remained.

Now the stone walls were swirling above his head. Were they going to shoot down at him all at once? Their motions seemed indifferent to his concern, and a revolving sphere began to surface from the ground beneath. Jordan stepped out of the way, momentarily lowering his gaze to see what was emerging from the soil. Moving backwards, he returned his sight up to see that the pillars of stone had begun to form a tomb all around him. About eighty feet above his head a ceiling was formed, though the walls and that ceiling were rotating around him. The ground beneath his feet began to tilt at an incline, and instinctively he ran.

Darting past the sphere, he made his way to an opening where he might find solid ground once again. Having left through the opening in the side of the cryptic tomb, he was in a forest now. It was a forest of sharp pins that hung suspended in the air, just high enough for gravity to thrust them down with great harm. He stumbled through the expanse, hoping that the pins would stay affixed to their places of origin. Somehow, he knew better.

With the thought of fear entering his mind, he saw one pin shake loose and drop heavy like a sword into the earth. Another one began to shake and break loose, then it fell piercing the vesture at his feet. Desperately, Burrows searched for an exit and found one a hundred or so paces away. He dashed towards the egress, dodging the swords that aimed to do him in. He didn't dash fast enough! A sword smashed through his calf, stabbing the earth, and leaving him pinned in the process. He fell in pain and looked up to see if he was in additional danger. He was!

High above, an enormous spear hung, shaking to let go of the grip that held it steadfast to some infernal tree. It released, and in slow motion, shot forth straight through Jordan's chest. Wide awake but feeling the tear of every single cell in his torso, Jordan understood that he was immune to death. He was not immune to pain, however.

Having no choice but to free the spire from its home, he took the pin with both hands and ripped it up through his body. Out of his chest it came forth, and the hole it left behind was gushing and exposed. He fell back onto the ground with his head resting just beside the sword that would've slain any living being.

After resting his eyes for a moment, he began to feel the wound closing though the pain persisted. He couldn't breathe. He didn't need to, but his chest rose and fell in the habitual motion reserved for the living. Once the gash had sealed, more or less, he leaned forward to inspect his leg. There the second needle boldly, stubbornly kept him from mobility.

With venom and resentment, he removed the spire from his leg and waited for regeneration to take place. Once it was healed, Jordan picked himself up off the ground and made his way for the outlet. Writhing with torment, the thought dawned on him that perhaps he had not been so kind in a previous life. Though as soon as the thought came it went, and Jordan was consumed with emptiness and obscenity once again.

As he walked, a stillness formed all around him and a light turned on high above. A colossal lantern shone an artificial light, illuminating with cold precision every corner of his domain. Since he was immune to death, Burrows reasoned that he would have to find a way out of this prison, seemingly suspended in an empty building thousands of miles across. There was an echo here, which betrayed that he was utterly alone. The only sound he heard was the sound of his own making. He would have to find a way out, and then he could take revenge on his master. As he walked across the dangerous badlands, however, the thirst for revenge morphed into an altogether different emotion. He was overcome with hunger for anything breathing.

A.48 ~ METAMORPHOSIS

His mouth gaped open at the sides, and his face grew deformed. Jordan walked for endless days trying to reach the end of the construct. Now, like a zombie, he continued to walk towards that red horizon. Moving at a snail's pace, he continued to walk for countless years. Eyes down, boring through the passage of the golden grid, he walked though the horizon grew no closer. There it sat idly by, watching the man transform into a monstrosity.

At first, his arms began to shrink, slowly over the years, though he did not notice. He could only think of tasting the flesh of a living, breathing creature. His legs narrowed and his eyes began to churn with darkness as though filling with petroleum. His head began to enlarge until ultimately it floated like a wandering balloon, caught in a breeze pulling him onward toward the horizon.

There the floating head dangled lifeless legs and limbs, which continued to dissolve until at long last they were there no more. His mouth captured by the horizon creased in on itself. It became a narrow slit that ran the length of his head, coveting anything that was alive. The head sloughed floating in the vacant room toward a never-ending goal. It floated along with only the thought of consumption to drive it. And slowly it progressed, hovering lifeless above the sterile ground, drawn to the crimson grin that lay before it so far away.

As ages matured elsewhere in the limitless universe, Jordan shambled along in disarray. He hadn't looked up in perpetuity, so he did not notice that the horizon was in fact getting closer. Slowly, it would seem that the Abrogazer, or whatever he was now, would eventually reach that crooked edge. Beyond the far horizon lay nothingness in its most pure form.

Continuing to inch closer toward the horizon, the mindless head filled only with the presence of hunger. Scarlet light grew brighter, and the golden grid began to diffuse. Finally, he had reached the end of the virtual province. He stopped.

The head revolved up until it was looking straight ahead, with drool seeping out of its devious orifice. A wild wind took hold of the scene and rising in the nothing, Viratus, the ancient dragon, ascended before Hector filling the entirety of the continent with her long and winding configuration.

Viratus appeared before Hector as broadly and widely as

possible. She knew that this confrontation would not be easy and that she would need all of her strength in order to have a chance to defeat this devourer of souls. Viratus was not a fool, but she had to try to overcome the demon! It was the only chance for her to escape her curse!

With violet eyes, omnipotent and compelling, Viratus gathered all of her strength. She knew that it would be required. Sylvan began to open his mouth, though unable to move beyond the edge of the world where nothingness stole matter from reality. Viratus tried once again, as she had many times throughout countless replays of the same scene, to uncover a way, or to unravel or destroy the Grim Reaper. This time she had made herself as large as she could, hoping to avoid what she knew would happen next.

Viratus flew back as fast as possible in order to attempt to escape the gravity of the demon's voluminous pull. She pushed against the encompassing currents with all of her might, though no matter how hard she tried she could not escape the torrent of Hector's dreadful yawn!

The mouth gaped, creating a vortex that grew with intensity. The vortex turned into a whirlwind, and the whirlwind became a black hole. Before she knew it, Viratus was being pulled into the cavernous pit. She resisted, flying backwards with all of her might, flying back into the nothingness. The hole grew, and even the labyrinthine landscape from the Abrogazer's point of entry to this place, began to slide towards the anomaly.

Everything was disintegrating with the enormity of Lockmire's hunger. Viratus knew that this was her only chance. She summoned all of the power within herself and resisted the pull. The dungeon was shifting, and even the nothingness itself was being consumed by the horrendous beast!

The vacuum grew with such tremendous scope that Viratus gave way and fell within the grasp of the devouring horde.

Simultaneously, the stonework construct slid into the foe, who himself collapsed under the gravity of his own hunger. It only lasted a moment, but in that moment Viratus was stretched to infinity inside endless gravity. What was left from the implosion was Viratus alone.

She awoke in outer space, flying as she did across that immense richness toward some unknown destination. She already knew what had transpired, as it had always ended in the same way. She had failed. Viratus could feel the weight of her ancient curse sealed woefully upon her back.

The catacombs had become fused onto her back, and the Grim Reaper was there, bound to stalk, without end. Viratus traversed the black miles in search of a clue that might bring her home to her inevitable purpose. She had glimpsed many pieces of that legacy and sought after more of its alluring vista.

A.49 ~ FOREVERMORE

Then emerged, that bean-like waif from the shadows that encompassed him. The eyes of the beast glowed a faint but focused red, as though there was a newfound hunger deep within. Whatever Pandara was, now embroiled by the stone in his gut, this monstrosity was his opposite. Together they struck a midnight bargain, like a key and a lock, or time and a clock; cursed, both of them, each needing to escape.

But Hector did not want to escape. He vowed to excise any soul that happened upon this dreadful place. He would excise infinitely the light that Pandara held within. "Do your worst!" signed Pandara to the fiend, and with a close of his eyes, the monstrosity approached.

Intimately recognizable forms pervaded his awareness, like a sun rising upon the stretched crest of a newfound understanding.

Though he may be forever consumed by the dark slime of the beast, triumph was his in the onset of life's revolving origin. He would be reborn! Confidently, Pandara moved towards his goal through the wasted remains of lethargic death. Feeble winter could not withstand the dart of spring in his time of truth.

Pandara awoke from the everlasting nightmare an eleven thousandth time! Each time having succeeded in getting a little closer to reaching the guard tower. He had conquered the grave-yard, excelled at toppling the statues in just the right way, and even tried to carry a briefcase full of worms into his demise, thinking that the worms might poison his devourer. Every time the Abro-gazer appeared, a little more fueled by the light within Pandara, and every time Pandara was weighed down a little more by the growing, sinking pit deep within his belly.

Pandara knew that he didn't have an infinite number of tries to get to his destination, but he didn't know what fate would await him once he could carry on no more from the black weight. He suspected that he would truly spend an eternity inside the Grim Reaper until, eventually, he had been dissolved into pure nothingness.

Mulling over his plan during the digestion, an idea occurred to Pandara. When he would come to, he would try some-thing different. Finally, the day came when he awoke, and he ran over to the sundial. First, he tried to pull the chain from the earth, but it wouldn't budge. So much for that. He pushed on the sundial itself, and to his surprise, the little metal pointer snapped off from the pedestal. He had a tool to carry with him now!

Pandara raced over to the alcove, put the marbles in their best configuration, ran through the appropriate channel, hid from the watchful eye, and dashed through the forest of enormous pins. He reached a door that he had been unable to open previously. That death had been particularly terrifying, and he suspected that something important must be behind the door. Now, with the sharp sundial at his disposal, he used the tip of it to pick open the rusty, old lock that held the door firmly in place. The lock clicked, and he stepped over the threshold.

PLATE IV · THE SUNDIAL

SIDE B

"Now are fields of corn
where Troy once stood."

- Ovid, *Heroides*
(1st century BCE)

The Glass Shadow

PLATE V - THE GLASS SHADOW

B.02 — CHAPTER 06

B.03 ~ CRYSTAL CURTAINS

In the morning, Pandara was awake. Quietly, he stoked the ashes of the dead furnace. He prepared some porridge, and just when it was ready Koravo woke up. "Morning sunshine!" he said.

Koravo smiled and said "Hi!" in between folds of the newborn day.

Pandara handed her a cup of the warm, creamy cereal. "It would be helpful if we find some more food soon," Pandara said. "I hope that we have luck in the Glass Shadow."

"I'm sure we will," said Koravo, exercising her resolve.

After the meal was done, they packed up their things and began to head east. After a couple of hours of walking, their feet were a little sore. But just then, off in the distance, they could see a blinding light, a kaleidoscope of color and luminescence.

"That's it!" Pandara exclaimed.

"Wow, it's so beautiful from here," Koravo whispered, appreciating the pristine spectacle of the jewel-like spires shooting up from the earth. In particular, the way they made the other world shine below was a dazzling effect.

Pandara and Koravo approached the Glass Shadow, and movements beneath the surface of the land were reflected up through the trees. It appeared that a city was built downward upon the flip-side of the ground. Vehicles coasted by, and lights flickered on and off. All cascaded through the forest with remarkable clarity, albeit transfigured.

Pandara walked ahead, feeling as though he'd seen Phalanx for the first time. Koravo looked forward, gazing admiringly at the glass trees that swayed gently in the breeze, making a rustling sound like the wind chimes so familiar. As they approached the boundary of the forest, each silently thought about time repeating itself.

Here they were once again, entering some foreign timber. They wondered if, as with the Trilodian Forest, they would be unable to locate their return to the outskirts of Buerroni. They had seen citizens walk through the streets of Buerroni covered in the fine dust of glass pollen and figured they should be alright if they wanted to return.

A little ways into the Glass Shadow, Koravo wanted to stop for rest. They removed their packs and settled against a tree, large and translucent, morphing rays of light that happened to find their way to that crystal trunk. They began to discuss their expectations for the day, as a fine haze of diamond dust fell upon their shoulders and their hair.

"So, I suppose that we're looking for nomads," Pandara said.

"That's my understanding," replied Koravo. "I think we'll know them when we see them."

A boy from Phalanx sat down on the sidewalk of the city and began to scrawl a note.

"It looks like we have a new friend," said Koravo.

The boy from below dropped his piece of paper face-down onto the floor. "Where are you from?" he asked.

Koravo motioned to Pandara to hand her a sheet of paper. Many people on Tristulle and Phalanx carried paper with them, just in case of occurrences such as this. Koravo began to write, "Ksevia, you?" in little letters to preserve the real estate of the page.

The boy read the note and began to formulate his response. "Where's that? I'm from Mercury," the note read.

Koravo responded. "Somewhere in the Trilodian Wood. Tell me about Mercury."

The boy thought for a moment and began to write. This time his response took more than a few seconds. "Mercury is the city you see all around you, underneath. It is a wonderful place full of joy and excitement. I love living here! There is never a dull moment, and anything can happen. Right now, I am on my way to see a holographic show about a ghost and an hourglass." Koravo read the note, and Pandara looked over to see what it said.

"Show him your hourglass," said Pandara, reaching into the pack to retrieve it therein.

He handed Koravo the miniature object. Silver sands from the banks of the Ksevian River shifted inside, coming to a stop as the virginal treasure was placed lengthwise on the transparent ground below. The boy looked down, expecting a note, and was amazed at what he saw.

He began to scribe, "It's beautiful! I would like to meet you there on the other side and inspect it firsthand, but that's impossible of course. How are you enjoying the Glass Shadow?"

Koravo handed the paper to Pandara. He wrote, "It's very beautiful here. Soon we must go to gather supplies for our journey. Do you know the way to the nomads?"

The boy looked down, read the message, and responded.

"Yes, you are heading in the right direction. Just continue along, and you will find them shortly. I also must go; my table at the theater has called. I wish you success in your journey."

The boy from Phalanx placed the note in sight, waited a moment, and then stood up and left. Koravo gave the hourglass and writing tools back to Pandara, who placed them securely in the pack. They stood up and continued along their way.

Like a glass shadow, starry-eyed and detached, Annie Levine drifted with them several paces behind. She was pulled by that invisible cord, attached to the hopes of finding some meaningful release. Pandara couldn't see her but knew that the mission affected more than just he and Koravo. He felt it, though oblivious to the immediacy of his intuition.

Exploring the deep apparitions of thought, Koravo and Pandara walked ahead under the crystalline cover of trees overhead. Before too long, they happened upon an encampment in a clearing. A band of mystics were stationed around a covered wagon that unfolded into a makeshift stage. Upon it two young boys were acting out a theater piece, modest and unadorned, leaving the imagination to ramble in drama. Two young ladies were crossing the clearing and noticed Pandara and Koravo. They turned their course and headed for the travelers.

"Hi there," said Marquari. "What brings you to the Glass Shadow?"

"Koravo and I are journeying far away to the mountains and are in need of supplies. My name is Pandara. Can we barter with you for some food and drink?"

"You'll want to speak with Mortilieb. He's our leader and can show you the rations we have available for trade," spoke Airallyne. "Follow us."

Marquari and Airallyne led them toward a collective of the family who were relaxing by the side of the stage, watching the production, and feasting on dried meats and ale.

"Hello," said Mortilieb. "Won't you join us and share with us in the meal?"

Koravo and Pandara looked at each other. Pandara stepped forward and said, "Thank you so much for your generosity. We would be glad to sit with you."

Mortilieb motioned to a third boy, who ran behind the wagon and collected two stools for his new friends. Pandara and Koravo took a seat. Airallyne passed them mugs and salted pork. In addition, there were leeks which reminded Koravo of home. It was all very delicious.

"Have you enjoyed the Glass Shadow?" asked Mortilieb's wife, Rannilov.

"It's quite spectacular," said Koravo. "We've enjoyed it very much. How long have you been stationed here?"

Mortilieb took his turn to speak. "We've been settled for about two weeks. In a third we will pick up and carry on, but others will be by soon enough."

"How many travelers live in the region, and are you close with them?" Koravo was curious to find out.

"There are a few hundred of us, and yes, we all know each other quite well."

Pandara and Koravo were enjoying their meal and learning about the artists' way of life. After a lengthy discussion, Mortilieb finally broached the topic of trade.

"You have goods for trade? Might we see what you have? I am unfamiliar with Ksevia having heard only legend of your hidden city. I'm certain that even the most mundane items to you will fascinate us greatly."

Pandara reached into his pack and pulled out several items, all of which he and Koravo would be sad to part with. Though, they were excited to potentially pass on joy to the kind-hearted souls who were treating them so fairly.

A wooden horse, a crystal ball, a music box, and the hourglass were handed around the circle. The children were impressed with the music box which played a longing song of mystery and enchantment. When opened, two tiny figures reached out for each other's arms, though they were never to meet.

"We like all of these items. They are quite bewildering and astound the spirit; it is the essence of what we live for. Undoubtedly, you will want to save at least two of them; might we trade you rations for the wooden horse and crystal ball? The music box is too precious for us to take."

The children seemed disappointed, though respected their leader's command, handing the music box back to Koravo. Pandara replied, "We will gladly accept your offer; however, you should keep the music box. We have enjoyed it for many years and would like to share its wonderful song."

Rannilov spoke elegantly and with gratitude. "You are very kind. We will treasure your gift. In exchange, please take a necklace that has been with my family for ages." Rannilov waved to Jesiaka, who retrieved a small box from the covered wagon.

She handed it to Koravo, who opened the carved chest with tremendous anticipation. A violet and spring green, silver necklace met the gaze of its new caretaker. Koravo swooned, and Pandara helped her put on the stranded pendant.

"It befits you well," Rannilov said, and Koravo was glad to hear such words.

"Thank you," said Koravo.

"I'm certain that it will help protect us on our quest," Pandara spoke, feeling anxious for a moment which passed as quickly as it had come.

"Well, friends," Pandara said, packing their bags with sustenance. "I'm afraid it's time for us to depart. Thank you so much for your kindness and nourishment. We will not forget you."

"The pleasure was ours," Mortilieb responded. "Good luck to you, and may you have safe passage."

"Thank you," replied Koravo. "Same to you."

They turned to leave. Rannilov leaned over to Mortilieb and whispered in his ear, "They cannot see the ghost child." Mortilieb nodded with agreement, and said, "It is as it's supposed to be, for now." Annie noticed that the mystics could see her and wondered as to the difference in their eyes. She stood silent and waited for her family to depart.

They continued south until the Glass Shadow broke apart into a rocky expanse, and at last a river joined them on the west.

"Let's follow the river," said Koravo.

Pandara, deep in thought, seemed to have missed the comment.

"Pandara." Koravo grabbed his attention.

"Oh, what?"

Koravo stopped walking. "What is it? What's wrong?"

Pandara said, "Let's continue walking." They began again.

"Two suspicions stunt my attention, though they are seem-ingly unrelated. I think we're being followed by different people." Koravo looked worried. "I noticed them back there in the Glass Shadow, a man pretending to be on his own path. But when we stopped, he stopped, and when we proceeded to enter the clearing, he waited for us not far behind."

Koravo turned around to see that a man was indeed following them, far off in the distance but just within sight.

"And what of the other?" she asked.

"We cannot see her, though I believe we have attracted a ghost friend. I suspect that she has been with us for some time, and I don't believe she intends to do us harm; but she is here, nonetheless."

"How do you know if you can't see her?" Koravo asked.

And Pandara signed, "Search the Yuit yourself, Koravo. I believe that you will confirm my suspicions."

It was the first he had mentioned of the Yuit in quite some time. Koravo connected her heart and mind to the fluctuating spirit of Ksevia and noticed an anomaly in her field of intuition.

"Yes, I see." she said. "You are right. There is another soul with us now, right here in fact. She doesn't seem to have ill intent; she is young, like a child."

"Yes," Pandara said. "I am more concerned about the man. I don't know what he is up to; perhaps he is from Buerroni."

"Well," Koravo said, trying to lighten the mood but lend Pandara some street smarts. "Perhaps it is to be expected in this land. We have never been on a quest like this in our native home of Tristulle."

Pandara stopped. He turned around and called to the man. "You there! What is your business with us?" Pandara began to walk back towards the man. Koravo and Annie followed behind him.

The man stopped suddenly and paused for a moment. Then he resumed his walk towards the couple. The man took off his cap and placed it over his heart, still walking towards Pandara.

"Hello!" he yelled. "I am sorry to have disturbed you! I mean you no harm!" Pandara and Koravo were both understandably skeptical of the man.

"Then why have you followed us since Buerroni?" asked Pandara.

"I'm terribly sorry!" he said. "It is the way of Buerroni. When visitors come to our town, we always investigate and report back to the administration our findings."

"What does the administration want from us?" asked Koravo.

"Only information: the administration is actively collecting a historical record of the goings-on in this part of Tristulle. The ultimate goal is to present Phalanx with a gift of literature, regarding the life and times of those of us on this side of the mirror."

Pandara was skeptical of Paucs at first. The way he followed them without introducing himself was unsettling, but Pandara quickly grew to like the man and appreciate his presence.

Paucs was a small, round man with a keen eye and a penchant for adventure. Koravo grew to like him, after he had introduced himself. He was kind and gentle or at least seemed to be, though Koravo could see no reason to doubt him.

"Might I inquire where you are headed?" the man asked respectfully.

Pandara looked at Koravo, who gestured acceptance.

"We are traveling to a mountain far to the south and east."

"And what is it that you hope to find there?" asked the man.

Pandara seemed a little bothered by the question but then remembered that the nature of his travels was for the betterment of all.

"We hope to find an answer to the greatest mystery in existence," he said, sparking the interest of the man from Buerroni.

"And what is that mystery of which you are so fast on the trail?"

The river churned at their side, making a hustling sound that urged them to continue their trek. "Nothing less than the nature of suffering and how to snuff it out once and for all throughout the cosmos."

The man's eyes opened wide and took in the implications of Pandara's statement. He said, "Now that would truly be something; might I join you on your quest?"

"Up until a point you may," Pandara said, "But then you must turn back when we tell you to do so. The last mile of this journey will be treacherous and personal. We care to climb that mountain alone, if you please."

"Understood," said the man. "I agree to your terms. My name is Paucs, Paucs Tenebo. And who are you?"

"We are Koravo and Pandara of Ksevia," Koravo replied.

"Ksevia? Oh, how I've wanted to visit Ksevia!" said Paucs. "You will have to tell me about your time there; it will be very interesting to include in my report."

Paucs thought that Koravo and Pandara seemed like a truly inseparable team. He instantly picked up on how Koravo was the heart of the relationship and Pandara the mind. She nurtured their dreams, and Pandara guided them through destiny. Paucs wondered how long they had been together. It seemed as though they were one unit.

Pandara, Koravo, Paucs, and Annie resumed their journey. Pandara lamented that he would no longer be alone with Koravo, as did she, but they had determined that a scribe to document their quest was a fortuitous addition and so were happy to welcome Paucs along.

"Our understanding is that just up ahead three rivers will meet. It is there that we will turn to the east and proceed in that direction for the remainder of our expedition," said Pandara.

It was beginning to get late in the day, and they had wanted to cross the river before it was dark. It was unclear if they would be able to do so. The river began to gain speed and momentum as they walked along its banks, growing wider and more ferocious.

"Have you visited the Tristossa River before?" asked Paucs, eager with anticipation.

"No," said Koravo. "We've seldom been outside of Ksevia. What should we expect?"

Paucs was delighted to share his impressions of the magical terrain!

"The Tosa River," Paucs began, "is an incredible sight to behold, and the Abyssinia at its center... something magical is happening there for sure."

"The Abyssinia?" Koravo asked.

"Yes!" said Paucs. "It is one of the most inspiring sites in all of Tristulle, or so I've been told. You will see soon enough. It's just up ahead."

Walking toward the Tristossa River, the windows were sparse but revealing. A few travelers could be seen walking the road between Mercury and Octave. This pilgrimage was well trodden and full of purpose. From what Koravo could gather, the people tended to travel in twos and threes, mostly in the direction of Mercury. She saw a man carrying a large pack on his shoulders and a woman who appeared to be trading hats to shelter hikers from the bright sun above.

When the sun shone directly through the windows beneath, it caused a luminescence to radiate through to Tristulle. It was as though the windows were an additional light source, glowing treasures from within the earth. Like eyes unto the world, the windows had a life all their own.

The group made it to where the three rivers met, and where they did an enormous hole in the earth swallowed up the torrential waters. It was a towering surprise, a roaring chasm.

Hanging precariously above the Abyssinia, a structure of three bridges was seen to be stationed. They connected in the middle, supported from three wooden beams that met high above in its center.

"How was that possibly constructed?" Pandara asked rhetorically. Paucs was proud of his response.

"With great labor!" he replied. "And just wait until you see what's down there!" he added, sparking the curiosity of Pandara and Koravo.

They approached the structure cautiously, with reservations. The Abyssinia growled and warned the travelers to proceed at their own risk.

"Is it safe?" asked Koravo, looking to Paucs for comfort. She was frightened by the gap, which coiled down into an endless nothing beneath.

"It is," he said, motioning that they make at once for the crossing.

Paucs stepped forward first, in the loud hum of the seas of Abyssinia. Pandara noticed Koravo's extreme hesitation. He looked at her and asked, "Will you be okay?" She nodded, and they slowly followed behind their adventurous companion onto the wooden bridge.

Gazing down into the terrifying abyss, over the side of the bridge, they witnessed that the sky could be seen behind waters that fell endlessly in gravity's pull. The sky that was seen was the sky of that other side, Phalanx, where the cascade raced upward and onward forever into the outer space beyond. People gathered in Phalanx by the side of the natural phenomenon, as yet unaware of how to pierce the curtain of water to potentially reach their neighbors in the land of Tristulle. It was a symbol of their separation and the only known place of opening between the two sides in all the land.

Once a man from Tristulle named Homir Osyddi sailed the full length of Abyssinia. He raced the raging tide, jumping the waves headstrong until the hole in the earth swallowed his ship. Though he was not to be seen again, it is said that he sails still, onward down the rush of the falls forevermore. The legend was told across the land, and no one else had since tried to recapture his sense of adventure. The Abyssinia remains an alluring force; the magic of the falls is best glimpsed from the safety of the sturdy bridge.

After several minutes of admiring the awe and beauty of the Abyssinia, it was time to carry on. The sun was setting, however, and Pandara asked if they might stay a while longer to see how the sunset on the other side reflected through the waters and affected their consciousness. He was eager to catch a glimpse of their quest as it stood from the perspective of a distant time, reflected down through the ages and rebounding across the years to reach his open eyes. The others obliged, and Pandara took his seat above the grand chasm admiring gravity's tremendous pull on the currents which fell over the edges of the cliffs.

As the light dimmed, delicate shades of purples, pinks, and orange, began to fasten onto the beams of liquid life in a play of optics the likes of which they'd never seen before. Fragmented and forlorn adagios of inspiration met Pandara's shard-like trance. The crystal waters had brought with them pieces of the Glass Shadow, or so it seemed to him. A translucent mirage radiated in the amber air, heart set on divining purpose from within chance circumstance.

Glances from a future time tumbled down into Pandara's opened mind. There were visions of a loss that broke up beyond rays he could barely see. Though he was unable to capture their meaning, he had felt a presence that sent to him a message from beyond distant shores of space and time. The ring seemed to be at the heart of the vision, though its significance remained out of reach.

Pandara disregarded the melancholy and took with him passages of uplifting grandeur instead of remorse. The Abyssinia implored Pandara with prescient knowledge of his quest and ambition. Though an inanimate object, Pandara clearly bonded with the falls and gained an appreciation for the spectacles of the natural world. Light drew to a close, and he would be sad to see the Abyssinia go. His ultimate destination lay further to the southeast, however.

The warning sign that the Abyssinia imparted to Pandara went over his head. It was the mystical connection with the falls which captured his mind, but its contents were lost on him. Koravo loved to see Pandara taken by the bold and magnificent phenomenon; he was windswept and alive. She wished that she could preserve his inspiring innocent response. She glimpsed his momentary sadness and watched as he disregarded it. That itself made her sad, for she was partially aware of the premonition that he had had.

B.04 ~ KNIFE AGAINST FLINT

Paucs was seated, gazing up at the two, jotting down his impressions in a leather journal bound with twine and luck. He sought, with fortunate words, to distill the mystery from Pandara's wonderment and thirst for heavy aspiration. Though, he too had seen a solemn look wash over the man's face, a look of terror, transient and obscure. Paucs thought about how to reproduce its likeness on the page and gleaned therein that some tragedy might befall the pilgrims who so desperately wanted to achieve a peace for all who had found themselves living. In its wake, he noted the premonition with care for the details and concern for their love.

Although Paucs had been to Abyssinia before, its grandeur never ceased to amaze him. His writings, however, were focused on the odyssey undertaken by Pandara and Koravo. Therefore, he paid special attention to the way in which the falls captured their attention at sundown. It was clear that both were naturally impressed by the spectacular wonder. Paucs devoted most of his writing to the reaction that Pandara had during his eclipse of time.

Sitting on the wooden bridge, Pandara wrestles with the truth which has cast over him a deep and ominous shadow. The majesty of the colorful rays formed only a backdrop of serenity, upon which the premonition painted its gothic portraiture. The exact contents of the dream were unclear to me. I wondered if Pandara was able to ascertain with specificity the nature of the haunt, though I wouldn't dare ask him out of respect for the privacy of his decision making. The vision faded and the light took on more usual tones of blues and purples in the dusk of temporal landscapes. Time's magic, and the mystery of death, transcended these turns of events. Even with noble aims, one was not immune to betrayal under the sun.

He picked himself up and proceeded to walk along. There he joined with Koravo and Pandara, still lost in the memory of freshness ripe with ambiguity. As they passed onto the eastern bank of the river, it was time to begin to settle for the night.

Annie was beginning to awaken. Her phantom heart beat with incandescent silence glowing in the dusk. Invisible to all, slippery winds brushed against her platinum hair. At her heels, her baby sister held close, grasping for love and security. Her older sister had none to bestow.

Pandara and Koravo collected wood for the warmth of the night. Their silent speech was halted by the phantom which hung low around their heads. After several limbs were gathered, Pandara constructed a little fort for the glowing embers that were to come. He struck a knife against flint and nurtured the baby sparks into a fuse that lit the bonfire forming a timeless retreat from the dark. Collections of memories were stowed away for the taking once calm and relaxation had secured their place in the luminous scene.

The fire was tossing smoke and ash into the air. Pandara and Koravo were nestled in a blanket, and Paucs was resting with his head on a log. Koravo was tired, though she could see only one alternative to her suppression. She decided to try to relax and enjoy the night.

"Tell me a story," Paucs said to the couple and proceeded to pull out his journal once again. Pandara and Koravo thought for a moment, and then Koravo responded.

"I still remember the first time I met Pandara, though I was but an infant. He was crying undoubtedly unable to satiate his desires for milk and sleep. I crawled over to him to the delight of the onlookers and fell back into a seated position. There I rubbed his back until he quit his wailing."

"We were united at birth, more or less," Pandara explained. "Our parents were friends, and the four of them would often spend time together throughout the days of our youth."

Paucs leaned back, taking notes. The bond of lifelong companionship was something that he knew about, though none of his relationships had survived the tremors of time's shaky hand. Koravo turned to look at Pandara and remarked, "Yes, but as with all children of Ksevia, we were raised by the commune. It was a nice upbringing."

"What was it like to grow up in Buerroni?" Pandara asked Paucs, who was still scribbling reminders into his report. He finished and looked up.

"Well," he said, "I'm not originally from Buerroni. I come from the Fredersen. Have you heard of it?"

"No," said Koravo and Pandara, shaking their heads.

"The Fredersen is an old metropolis to the west of Buerroni, near Rubelown. I too had a friend from birth. His name is Flaine. Flaine resides in the Fredersen still, to my knowledge, though we haven't spoken in years. When we were young, we would devise little games and pranks to play on our friends."

"Will you tell us one of those stories Paucs?" Koravo asked.

"Yes, of course," replied Paucs.

"One time a teacher of ours was overcome with happiness, having met the man who would become her husband. While their relationship was in its infancy, we decided to play a harmless prank on her.

"Flaine and I cut a bouquet of flowers and tied it with some yarn. We left it at her doorstep with a note that read, *From Your Admirer*. Then we knocked on her door and ran off. Later that day, when the man came by her house, we stood by and chuckled as she kissed him passionately. It was clear that he didn't know what had come over her, but he accepted her token, nonetheless.

"When our teacher realized what was taking place, she seemed confused and bewildered. For whom would the admirer be, if not her fiancé? We laughed so hard you just wouldn't believe it!"

The three laughed for a few moments, and then Paucs began to conclude. "We played many such games; it was truly a time."

Pandara felt kinship with Paucs. He appreciated Paucs' support and wondered if it would be beneficial to have Paucs journey with them to the summit. He decided that it would not though, because the last leg of the journey was extremely personal and intimately their own. There were pros and cons to the decision, but Pandara felt that the quest demanded solitude. It was ironic given that the ultimate concern of the journey involved all who were living.

The evening was beginning to close, and Koravo yawned. "Well," she said. "I think I'm going to turn in."

Pandara loosened his embrace around Koravo and said, "I think I will as well."

Paucs relaxed warm-heartedly and was thankful to have met his new friends. "Alright, goodnight you two. See you in the morning."

Koravo and Pandara reclined onto the surface of the earth and drifted off into slumber. Paucs wasn't tired, however, and decided to stay awake for a while longer. He turned the page in his notebook and began to sketch the scene.

First, he drew out the flames of the fire from the blank page, long spires of spitting flame, creeping shadows, and sticks and rocks. He drew out the embers, glowing white embers with shades of scorched gray reflecting on the world below. Through the flames, the distorted figures of Pandara and Koravo lay asleep, as though dead to the earth. He sketched the trees, and he sketched the clouds behind them, lit by the light of a moon. And then he began to sketch something that wasn't there. It was a little girl, dressed in white.

At first, the form was unfamiliar, but as he kept drawing, she materialized before his eyes. He looked up, and there she was.

"My name is Annie," she said with haunting simplicity. Paucs was startled and didn't know if he was dreaming. He looked at Koravo and Pandara, then looked back at the girl. He shifted back into the log. She said, "It's alright. You don't have to be afraid."

Paucs thought of what to say and finally settled on, "What are you doing here? Where are your parents?"

"My parents are gone. I'm from another world," she said. "I don't know what I'm doing here."

Paucs felt a chill descend his spine. "Are you alive?" he asked.

"No," she said. "I'm not alive," and her gaze drew down toward the earth.

Pandara shifted in his sleep. Paucs turned to look at him, but Annie looked straight ahead.

Annie had naturally scared Paucs at first. The appearance of a ghost was a thoroughly startling occurrence. However, after some minutes had passed, and Paucs had talked with Annie, he found himself wondering what had happened to the little girl. She was a sympathetic character, and Paucs wanted to make her feel comfortable, though he still felt uneasy.

"Where are you going?" she asked.

"We're going to a mountain," replied Paucs.

"And what will you do there?" asked Annie.

Paucs, still feeling uncomfortable with the situation, responded, "I will do nothing, but Pandara and Koravo will climb."

"I will join them," she said. "I will climb."

Annie turned around and walked away.

Paucs had trouble sleeping that night, though his dream was long-lived and regal. He dreamt that he was a king overseeing a distant land. He was benevolent and just. He lived a life inside that dream, and when he awoke, he had almost forgotten about Annie. But he decided to look at the portrait, and sure enough there she was, staring back at him with that blank look upon her face as though she wasn't there at all.

B.05 ~ HEADING TO THE EAST

In the morning, Pandara and Koravo awoke refreshed and relaxed. Paucs was still sleeping at first and then turned over and finally arose out of his bed of moss and peat. He rubbed his eyes, hesitated for a moment, and then reached for his journal seeming slightly unsettled. Koravo took notice and asked him if he was okay.

He stared vacantly into that page, looked up, and said, "What? Oh yes, I'm fine." He closed the notebook and went for a walk.

Pandara looked at Koravo and asked her if she was alright.

"I guess so, I just don't know what got into Paucs. Maybe something happened after we went to bed."

"He said he was alright," said Pandara.

Koravo felt sad that their relationship was maturing. They fluctuated between the joy of their youth and the detachment of their older selves. Once again, perhaps it was to be expected, but she noted that they had become more like the ones she'd heard about in legend: those who were born, grew old, and died. It wasn't the way of Ksevia, and she found this unsettling.

When Paucs returned, he seemed to be in better spirits. "Good morning, Pandara. Morning Koravo."

"Good morning," they said. "Are you ready for the next leg of the journey?"

"Yes," he said. "What awaits us next? I've never been this far southeast before."

"Next we travel through the Desert of Lazyres and onward to the Liddell Plateau."

"Desert of Lazyres?" said Paucs. "That sounds dangerous."

"It does?" asked Koravo. "What's a lazyre?"

She turned to look at Pandara. Pandara said, "I don't know. What is a lazyre, Paucs?" Koravo tilted her head downward with dismay.

"A lazyre is a beam of highly concentrated light. It could be either dangerous or not so much. Perhaps it will be a spectacle to behold and do us no harm. Otherwise, it might be treacherous to pass through.

"Okay," Pandara said. "Koravo, are you okay with that?"

Koravo looked at Pandara. She said, "Let's go there and see what we're dealing with. I'll let you know what I think once I've seen it."

They had a meal of porridge and fruit; the latter having been given to them by the nomads in the Glass Shadow. They also enjoyed Enrimorgin tea that Paucs had brought with him. Pandara and Koravo had never tasted this tea before and didn't know what to equate it with but thought it very pleasant.

When it was time to go, Paucs hesitated.

"What is it, Paucs?" asked Pandara.

"Well," he said. "Something happened last night that I think you should know about."

Koravo looked at Pandara and then looked back at Paucs. She and Pandara waited for him to continue.

"I was drawing a picture, when it occurred to me that we are not traveling alone." He took out his notebook and handed it to Koravo, open to the sketch.

Pandara leaned over to see what he had drawn. There, in the shadows, was a young girl unmistakably rendered, with a small, cloudy patch down by her feet. Paucs had been unable to discern the nature of the form that clung to her side.

"She was just standing there like this?" asked Pandara.

"Not at first," replied Paucs. "At first I just began to draw her and there was nothing there, but shortly thereafter she appeared to me and spoke."

"She spoke to you?" asked Koravo with surprise and curiosity.

"Yeah," said Paucs.

"What did she say?"

"We had a brief conversation that included confirmation that she is not from our planet and that she is not living. Then she turned around and walked off."

"I suppose that she may or may not be here at this very moment," stated Pandara. "Though, I sense that she's here."

"She said that her name is Annie," Paucs said with resolution.

"Annie?" said Pandara. "That's an unusual name. Did she give any indication what she wants from us?"

"Not that I recall," said Paucs. "Oh yeah," he added. "She asked about our destination. I told her about the mountain, and she said that she would climb with you. It doesn't seem to me that you really have any say in the matter."

"Well, I suppose that when Annie wants to make herself known to us, she will," Koravo said. The group took off, heading to the east.

B.06 ~ MIDDLE OF NOWHERE

Along the way, they passed through several interesting sites. There was a field of tall, origami flowers, mostly yellow and green. There was an abandoned church, a modest structure that seated only fifteen to twenty people at full capacity, but it was in utter disrepair. Pandara had wanted to enter, and so they did.

Inside, Koravo found a very small doll that was muddy and unkempt. She decided to take it with her, resolving to clean it the next time they were near running water. There was a stained-glass window depicting villagers fleeing from a beast of some sort. All three agreed that that was a strange choice of subject for a window in a church. Otherwise, the building was vacant. There were no remaining religious icons or relics.

The doll that she had found reminded Koravo of a child she never had. The church was a wedding that never took place, and her alternate life was a story that would have to wait for another place and time. Perhaps after this adventure Pandara would be ready to settle down. Somehow, she suspected that this wouldn't be the case. Koravo's doll was alluring to Annie. She didn't try to borrow the toy, but she inspected it invisibly from a distance.

Beneath the church, the world of Phalanx appeared hollow and grim. It was as though the land between Mercury and Octave, also to the east, was aching for something. Swamplands dominated the territory, and many windows were obscured by dead brush and mud.

It was as gray as the great prairies of Kansas, a nauseated

land of dead meadows. Koravo didn't know if this was a natural phenomenon, but it appeared to her that it was. Her mind went to wicked things, such as witches and flying monkeys, who likely traversed this part of Phalanx. Though, no evidence of their existence was to be found.

At any rate, what was this church doing here out in the middle of nowhere? There had to be a town nearby. The team agreed that they should spend a little time trying to find it. Although they had plenty of supplies, it was unknown what would lie ahead. Just behind the church was a forest. It was clear that there was no town to be seen in any other direction, so they decided to enter the wood; perhaps on the other side of the forest they would find a village.

Walking in, they took note of their location so as not to get turned around in the exploration. They decided that they wouldn't travel far, but it was worth an hour or so of their time. It didn't take long to discover that there was no village to be found, for after one hundred or so paces, they reached an enormous drop-off, a cliffside.

Pandara wanted to get close to the edge to survey the landscape, but Koravo warned him to stay nearby. As a result, he didn't venture out as far as he wanted. He was able, however, to see a desert off to the east. It looked just like a vast, barren expanse. There was nothing unusual about it.

The cliff was a milestone that revealed progress to Pandara. It was clear to him from gazing over its edge that they had come a long way. The far reaches of Tristulle were within reach, but they were not there yet, however.

"The Desert of Lazyres is just up ahead. Let's go back to the path and resume our hike," Pandara said.

They began to walk back through the wood. When they were within eyesight of the church, Paucs whispered, "Stop!" Pandara and Koravo stopped abruptly in their tracks. "Look!" he said quietly. Up ahead, at the entrance of the church was an enormous feral hog. It was sniffing the door to the church, which was approximately as tall as he was. Pandara shifted his weight slightly, and a twig snapped beneath his foot.

The behemoth jolted and turned his head, peering deep into the forest. That was when our three compatriots noticed the hog's glaring red eyes. As though lit from a light source within, the beast's eyes were like fire illuminating the dark furrows of his woolly brow. Koravo thought to herself that the monster would be terrifying to encounter at night, seeing only those red, beady eyes suspended far above her head.

She thought about the sepia memory of death. The suffering which the hog and the reaper seemed to have in common imprisoned them within solitude and sorrowful existences. Although she feared both beasts, she also found herself feeling sorry for them.

Pandara's thought was with protecting Koravo, but he felt that they would be safe. He instinctively covered Koravo with his body, as much as he could without making a sound. Koravo felt protected and safe. She smelled him, and the scent made her dizzy. The hog sniffed the air, then turned around and galloped off in a different direction. It seemed that they had had a lucky break.

After several minutes had passed, Paucs motioned to Pandara and Koravo that the coast was clear. "We seem to be alright," he said. Pandara and Koravo began to walk forward, following Paucs who took up the lead. Throughout the encounter, Pandara felt the pull of his ring. He didn't know why he felt drawn to it; he just was. The time to present it to Koravo had not yet arrived.

B.07 ~ PILGRIMS' BOND

The Passepartout Desert, as it was also known, was a transparent field all around. Both sides of the stretching plain revealed all to the traveling nomad who was rather unlikely to venture so far out beyond civilization. The day that our troupe arrived at the Passepartout Desert, all was calm and serene, at least to begin with. The travelers had the sensation of walking in between two skies. Both were monumental but far away from the voyaging clan. Their surroundings were like a mirror, but little details in the shapes of the clouds, for example, reminded them of the differences between Phalanx and their home world Tristulle.

When the group reached the clearing, Koravo said, "Wait. Where are the lazyres?"

"I don't know," replied Pandara. "Perhaps we need to get further in to see them."

The Desert of Lazyres was sacred and still. Pandara stepped cautiously and continued to think about Koravo's ring. He took a few steps into the desert, and they saw a flash! With Pandara's last footstep, a white lazyre had shot out of the ground just to his left. He took another step. Once again, a beam of light jutted out from the field, this time about ten steps in front of him. It was a blue ray, maybe an inch in diameter or so, and appeared to be harmless though he couldn't know for sure.

The excitement of the adventure eclipsed Koravo's fear of the desert. Though she was thrilled by the daring feat they were undertaking, she noticed Pandara's reluctance to appreciate the moment. She thought it was unfortunate but decided to enjoy it for the two of them. "Let's spread out," said Koravo.

"Better yet," Paucs interjected. "Why don't we cross one at a time, or make a run for it?"

By now Pandara was several yards in front of them.

"Pandara!" Koravo yelled. He stopped and turned around. "We're going to cross one at a time and stay spread out!"

"Okay!" he yelled back. They waited for him to keep walking, and he did.

Pandara could see that when the beams shot up from the ground, a corresponding beam shot downward in Phalanx. The effect was mesmerizing. This region certainly did make the two worlds appear to be separated by a mirror. There was no one else crossing the desert in Phalanx, and hopefully it would stay that way.

After Pandara was a hundred or so feet out, Koravo decided that she was ready to make the trek. She stepped into the field of light. It was like walking across the sky because there was only the transparent ground separating her from the cloudy patchwork sky of Phalanx below. Lazyres shot out of the earth, each one a different color than the last. Finally, after Koravo was a ways out into the open terrain, Paucs mumbled to himself, "I guess it's my turn now." And so, he began to make the trip.

The group carried on in this way for a long distance, not once feeling threatened by the lazyres, as there was considerable separation between them. The effect was subtle; he thought little of it at first, but eventually Pandara noticed other lights popping up on the horizon. Finally, he stopped to see if he could make sense of what was happening. He noticed that the clouds were getting darker, above and below. A storm was brewing, and the raindrops caused new lights to appear off in the distance.

Facing straight ahead, he held up his hand in a motion causing Koravo to stop in her tracks. When Koravo stopped, she turned around to face Paucs and held up her hand to him; he stopped. Koravo turned to face Pandara once again.

Pandara thought quickly on his feet. If they turned back, they would have to wait for the storm to pass, but if they continued, they might be blasted by the dazzling display of lazyres that was beginning to form. After a few moments of deliberation, and perhaps with impatience, he turned back to Koravo and yelled "Run!" It was a good thing that they pressed onward, because before they knew it, lazyres were beginning to shoot out all around them.

Rain! Koravo thought to herself. But it wasn't just the rain of one world. Both above and below the storm was beginning to form, and rain drops on either surface caused lazyres to spring forth in both directions.

As they darted ahead, Pandara noticeably grew closer, for he was carrying the lion's share of the weight. Lazyres were forming all around them, and Koravo finally was struck in the arm by a beam. It tickled a little, but that was it. She stopped and yelled, "It's okay! They don't hurt!"

Both Paucs and Pandara slowed down, a little wary at first. Before too long they had both been hit by lazyres and began to laugh, dispelling the tensions that had arisen. Koravo stayed in place with her arms outstretched, looking up at the sky and feeling the occasional raindrop graze her face. Pandara and Paucs slowly ran towards her so the three could meet in one location. They laughed and gently shoved one another as the rains began to pick up. Before long, it was a torrential downpour, and the trio was bathed in a blinding sea of lights of every color.

The rain was inspired and alluring. Pandara was captivated by Koravo as the light shone all around her. He noticed how she had supported him the whole way and wondered where she derived her strength. He knew, however, that strength was inherent to Koravo; she had always been strong, pulling power from the forces of life that surrounded her.

Koravo was still upset with Pandara that he didn't seem too concerned with her feelings. She suspected that he was on some deeper level, but he didn't show this to her. When the light hit his eyes, however, she forgave him and understood his focus on the mission. The look in his eyes brought her to her knees emotionally. She wanted him to kiss her.

Pandara and Koravo sustained eye contact in the brilliant and glittering exposition. He leaned into her and said, "You are so amazing." She smiled and leaned into him as well. They kissed for several seconds, and as it drew to a close the two leaned back and made eye contact once again. Pandara thought about revealing his gift but didn't feel all that comfortable in front of Paucs. Looking deep into Pandara's eyes, Koravo stood soaking wet, necklace glimmering in the splash and splendor of water and light.

Paucs looked enviously at the kissing couple. He had been thinking about finding a love of his own and wanted that now more than ever! The tender embrace of passionate love called to Paucs, but he didn't know where he would find such a woman. He told himself that he had to remain patient and believed that true love would come to those who would wait. Paucs was willing to wait, but he desired that connection more than he had realized.

"Umm, guys..." said Paucs. Koravo and Pandara turned to face Paucs locked in an embrace. He merely pointed in the other direction. They noticed a serious look upon his face. In the unfolding blaze, a silhouette could be seen, just a mere empty space where light and rain could not pass in the shape of a girl.

The rain revealed Annie to the group. She felt naked in the downpour, unable to cloak herself within the arms of nothingness. "Annie?" Koravo asked. And like clockwork Annie's form became illuminated, seeming to materialize out of the thin air.

"Yes," said Annie. "I'm here." They could barely make out her face in the glow of lights and heavy inundation, but there it was. She had the look of someone who had seen a ghost, pale and desolate.

Annie brought out Koravo's motherly nature. Koravo wanted Annie to join them. Though she could not in the flesh, she could at least stay visible. Koravo sensed that Annie could control her appearance, or better yet, it was a direct manifestation of her emotions. Koravo spoke kindly to Annie and set an example for the others.

Annie felt comforted by Koravo in the way that sleep comforts the living. Koravo was like her mother, if she'd ever had one, and Annie resolved to remain near Koravo for the foreseeable future.

"Are you unable to enjoy this?" Koravo asked.

Annie replied, "I'm enjoying it. It's lovely." An awkward but elegant smile formed across the width of her face.

Annie was an enigma that puzzled Pandara, and he felt reserved to approach her. Annie didn't demand anything from Pandara, and this fact helped ease his mind. "Annie, why are you following us?" Pandara asked abruptly.

"I don't know," she said, and her smile washed away.

Koravo jumped in. "It's alright dear, you can follow us if you want to. You don't have to remain hidden. We would love for you to be a member of our expedition!"

And with that, her frame became fully formed. Though still pale, she smiled again, this time contributing to the lights that shone all around.

"Why don't we move to get out of the rain?" Koravo suggested. The four of them headed onward in the resplendent, but muted, spectacle. Pandara and Koravo were walking ahead of Paucs and Annie. Paucs turned to Annie and said, "There was a form by your feet last night. Might I ask you what that was?"

Annie looked up at Paucs and said, "It's my baby." Annie turned her head back around to face forward. Paucs almost stopped once again but kept walking. He tried to figure out how to broach the topic.

"You know," Paucs said. "If I were you and I had a baby, I would probably carry him and nurture him." Annie turned to face Paucs once again. She lifted her arms out in front of her, and a baby materialized in the cradle of her embrace.

"She's a girl," Annie said. Paucs smiled and took comfort in knowing that he had been helpful.

When Pandara and Koravo finally turned around, they noticed the change and smiled to Annie. Annie smiled back. They figured that they wouldn't ask questions, for they didn't want to be impolite. Although she had made herself known partially because she had finally been noticed, Annie appreciated some distance and liked not having to explain herself. Her presence in the group was already starting to have a positive impact, and Koravo took Pandara's hand in hers. The lights were beginning to die down, and the clouds were beginning to part. Before they knew it, they were exiting the Desert of Lazyres. The sun was hanging low in the sky, and it was time for the family to decide what came next.

"I vote that we set up camp for the night," said Koravo. "My legs are tired, and I could use a rest."

"Sounds good to me," said Paucs.

"I agree," Pandara added. "This seems as good as place as any."

"What do you think Annie? Will you stay with us tonight?" Koravo asked.

Annie nodded in agreement, and they began to settle in. Pandara took the pack off his back and stretched his muscles. He opened the bundle and took out some food and water, passing it around. Everyone sat in a circle; Annie clung to her sister who seemed very much at peace.

"Well, we're not going to have a fire tonight," Koravo said, lamenting the fact. "There is no wood nearby, and it would be soaked if there was."

"We're pretty far out into the elements," said Pandara. "There's no place to change our clothes and hang them dry."

"I guess it's going to be a long night," Paucs remarked.

"Well, at least it's not too cold," Koravo added, "but the sun is still up. I hope it doesn't get too cold here at night."

As the light began to fade, Koravo thought about the astounding lazyres and how she'd never seen anything like that before. Now they were about to experience the exact opposite, complete darkness. She began to feel a little frightened but told herself that there was nothing to fear.

The sun went down, and everyone said their goodnights. Annie stood by but realized after some time that standing there was unorthodox. She decided to mimic the others and took a seat.

B.08 ~ FOLLOWING THE SUN

The sun was now rising strongly above the horizon, though still in bloom. Pandara gestured to Koravo in the direction of the sun. "There," he said. "It's the Liddell Plateau. Do you see it?"

Underneath the sun, out in the distance, the ground began to rise as though to meet the day. She said, "Yes. I see it. Can you see the mountains far off beyond the haze of the heat and the rising air?" Pandara squinted his eyes. He was just barely able to make out the form of a trilogy of mountains.

"Yes! I see them! Oh, to think that Jetir was here, exactly where we sit now. He was so impassioned in his quest to reach that mountain. I wonder what happened to him, and I wonder why he stopped writing."

"Perhaps we'll figure that out, Pandara," Koravo said, letting a little of her doubts be revealed in the process.

Soon enough Paucs had awakened, and it was time to

begin their journey once again. Their clothes were drying out and only seemed a little starched, a little less comfortable than they were before the downpour. After the last of the porridge and fruit were consumed, Pandara took out a little of the dried meat and asked anyone if they wanted any.

"I'll have a little," responded Paucs.

"I'm good," said Koravo. Pandara and Paucs had a few bites to eat, then they gathered their belongings and left.

The Liddell Plateau had fewer windows than they'd seen in the Passepartout Desert, but what was there revealed the outskirts of Octave beneath. Octave was a modest town by comparison, and the glimpses of life in that underworld told of simple days and technology. No one seemed to be in any hurry, and the basic needs of the community appeared to have been met.

Several villagers stopped to commune with Koravo, Pandara, and Paucs, but our wanderers kept walking. They still had a journey ahead of them, and Pandara and Koravo were beginning to assess the mountain which lay in front of their split but respectful gaze.

The sun was beginning to get hot, and the land was beginning to take on the form of an incline. Although it had been trying to walk a great distance, the terrain now seemed to be testing their muscles with every step.

This is preparation for the mountain no doubt, Koravo thought to herself.

As they continued along, slowly but surely, the Liddell Plateau gave way to a better vision of their ultimate goal. Now approaching the nomads was a large singular mountain. Flanked by one on each side, the central mountain stood out to them as an obvious beacon upon which the Lone Spirit resided.

"If he or she is not there any longer," said Pandara, "perhaps we will still be able to uncover the nature of an answer to our question."

In that moment, Koravo reconnected with Pandara. She realized that everything they were doing was for the betterment of all, and she felt proud to be with Pandara. Very proud. "I love you, Pandara," she said.

He turned to look at her. "I love you too, Koravo."

Pandara's gentle confession made her exact the compassion that waited for her in his heart. This was what she was waiting for, and his timing was perfect. It came precisely when she needed him the most.

Koravo had been falling into a depression that had been hovering above her head for several days. When Pandara expressed his true feelings, Koravo was awakened and shed her cloak of ennui.

They continued to walk, now feeling their own weight heavily on their feet. The Liddell Plateau was a challenge of strength. Pandara knew that he and Koravo had developed subtle tensions in their relationship, though the reason for this was beyond Pandara's ability to understand. It was as clear as day to Koravo, but she feared confronting Pandara. He tried to broach the subject and found success with kind words. She appeared to appreciate Pandara's effort and sincerity.

The Liddell Plateau made Paucs feel his years. He was glad that he wouldn't be climbing the mountain after all. He saw Koravo and Pandara appear to be mending the stress which had recently come to the surface, and that thought made him happy.

They were such a good couple. Paucs sincerely hoped that they would have a successful climb and that they would come find him later in Buerroni. It was several hours later when they reached the edge of the Liddell Plateau, but the climb had been worth it. What they saw now baffled them more than anything they had seen up to this point.

B.09 ~ REFLECTIONS

The lakes were not as they expected. There were five of them, each branching off from a central point like the petals of a flower. The side nearest to them was flat on the ground, but as they went off into the distance, the ends wrapped up around the bases of the three mountains and two hills. It was as though the ends of the lakes defied gravity, resting perfectly still at an incline. The central lake was dramatically held in place in a steep position, though its waters did not empty out below.

The Lakes of Porselena, from this angle, made the viewer feel as though the impossible was truly possible. Indeed, it was. Very few people had made it this far to the southeast. What lay beyond those mountains was a mystery, at least Pandara who was the most familiar with the stories of Yaronne Jetir was unaware of anyone having crossed the unnamed mountains.

The Lakes of Porselena rested on the heart of Octave beneath. The waters of those translucent lakes obscured the view of the city which shot down to the depths below. The windows were like shafts of broadly painted color, hazy but pristine in the decadence of ambiguity! The lakes intrigued Koravo's field of sight! Their still waters reflected the sky like windows beneath their feet!

The Lakes of Porselena stretched out before Pandara; they represented to him the importance of this quest. In their infinite stillness and clarity, the lakes represented the truth, which he fought so hard for! He knew that from high above they would be even more beautiful. Perhaps from that perspective Pandara would be able to derive the answer to his quest! He thought about the Lone Spirit and wondered what form she'd take. The thought that she wouldn't be there never crossed his mind. She was there; he was sure of it!

The Lakes of Porselena didn't impress Paucs all that much.

It was interesting how the waters defied gravity, but he was more curious about Phalanx and wondered what adventures would possibly await him there if somehow, he was ever able to cross the threshold. That idea was absurd, however, and Paucs pulled himself out of his daydream.

"It appears as though there is land in between the lakes," said Pandara. "We should be able to walk in between the middle lake and one on either side."

"Something about this doesn't seem right to me," Koravo stated. "It's all too serene; perhaps it's dangerous to walk in between the lakes. What if something happens?" she said.

"Do we have any other option?" asked Pandara.

"We could walk around all of the lakes," Paucs suggested. "It would take longer, but if Koravo intuits that something is not right, it's an option that we might want to consider."

"What do you think might happen, Koravo?" Pandara asked.

"What if there's something living in the lakes? What if it's not safe?"

Pandara was impatient. "I think it should be fine, but then again this is right around the point where Jetir stopped his writing. Maybe we're right to be extra careful. What do you think, Annie?" Annie was indifferent and didn't offer any suggestions.

"It's not that I don't care about your safety," she said. "I just don't have an opinion in the matter."

"Well," Pandara said. "Why don't we take the long way. We've come this far, and it would be terrible if something were to happen now." They were in agreement.

Although, perhaps it was only superstition, they decided to play it safe. Silently, the thought did occur to Pandara that Koravo was just feeling anxiety about the climb. He admitted to himself that it was quite a daring endeavor to undertake. Now that they were here, the mountain seemed much higher than he had expected, and much steeper. He wondered if he had made the right decision to embark upon this quest.

Anything to discover a hidden clue about the nature of suffering in the universe, he thought. Surely, they weren't misled. All of his studies had led them to this outcome. Surely, it was not all a mistake.

The group turned south and began their walk toward the southern-most hill. They would climb the hill and proceed to walk the foothills at the base of the first mountain. Once they had successfully done that, Pandara and Koravo would climb to the central peak, many hundreds of meters above where they now stood.

The walk to the hill was uneventful at first. The group kept an eye on their path but also couldn't help but focus on the lakes that defied expectations and baffled the mind. The optical illusion was stunning! Crystal waters sloped at an incline that wasn't possible. From this vantage point, they could clearly see that the water was indeed stationary in such a way. The hill was tiring but not insurmountable. After the Liddell Plateau, their legs were conditioned for such a trip, though the journey down the other side of the hill would be a welcome change of pace.

There were butterflies and other flying creatures less familiar along this path. Some were like birds, though very small and seemed to have an unusual form. They were like creatures from the paintings of Trilodius, with horse-like heads and bodies that wrapped into spiraling tails. Though these creatures did not swim; they glided through the air with elegant wings that beat only occasionally. For the remainder of the time these animals hovered in midair, suspended by an unknown force or mechanism.

There were also hopping things, pink and slimy in appearance. They remained at a distance. When one of the travelers got too close, they would bounce away as though in search of a less vulnerable position.

Paucs had his notebook out and was taking notes. "What are you writing about?" Koravo inquired.

"I'm making comments about my time spent with the three of you, with a focus on characterization and the bonds of our friendship."

"Would you care to read a selection from your report, Paucs?" Pandara asked.

"Sure!" said Paucs. "Though, I'm a little embarrassed as I'm not a great writer. I only try to capture what I can of the experience. The reader will have to fill-in the blanks where I have failed to render the essence of the experience with clarity and depth."

He flipped through the journal searching for a particular passage. "Ah, here it is," he said. "This is from the Tosa River, from Abyssinia."

He began:

"Pandara looks deep into the great abyss, as though he has lost something dear to him and searches for answers to the puzzles that confound him."

Pandara's curiosity piques with great interest.

"He is troubled by the mystery of suffering and its ubiquity. Striving to catch a glimpse of future comprehension, he reaches into his soul and the reflecting lights there. Bouncing off of the river waters, a sunset reminds him that all phenomena are fleeting. Everything undergoes a state of change and is destined to transform in the end. Koravo looks on, more interested in Pandara than the mere passing of lights and shades of illusion.

"Her love for him is inspiring, though he seldom seems to take notice. It is clear from the outset that Koravo's support guides Pandara onward in his quest. He is searching for something but does not realize that it has been with him all this time."

Paucs closed the book and brought it down to his side.

There was silence among the group. No one spoke for several moments, as the awkward edge of Paucs' entry settled into the forgetfulness of recent memory.

Finally, Pandara spoke up. "Koravo, is that true? Do you feel neglected by me?"

Annie turned her attention to Koravo, whose hand she was holding, still cradling the baby at her chest. "Sometimes," Koravo said. "But usually, I don't need confirmation of your love to know how you feel about me."

Pandara's affect sank, lowly. "I'm sorry that I haven't given you the attention that you deserve. I will try to make it up to you. Please know that I seek this grail for you and our relationship. I strive to find the meaning of life for you and because of you."

"That's not true!" Annie said. "You seek it for yourself!" There was another silence.

Pandara had become agitated, but he knew how to control his emotions. "Perhaps," Pandara said, "but my life would be meaningless without Koravo."

No one could argue with that.

They had reached the top of the hill and stopped to take in their surroundings. Koravo took a break and paused and stretched. Pandara reached in his bag and took out a flask of water. He took a sip and passed it around the group. They were getting low on supplies. "We're going to have to forage soon," he said, "but there is still some food left if anyone wants it."

"Do you have any salted meat?" Paucs asked.

"I'll take a little too," Koravo stated.

Pandara rummaged through the pack and pulled out some rations, leaving a little behind for later. They took a seat and shared in a quick snack. Out of the corner of her eye, Koravo swore that she saw something move in the lake. "Did you?"

Pandara turned to look at Koravo. "What is it?" he asked.

Koravo continued to look but didn't see anything. "Oh, it's nothing," she said. "I just thought I saw something move in the lake behind you."

Pandara turned around to look for himself. "I don't see anything," he said, but just then an enormous tail rose through the waters and came splashing down, casting ripples throughout the length of the lake!

"Wow!" Paucs said. "That was amazing!"

"Yeah, it didn't even seem threatening at all," Koravo said. "Perhaps we should go to the lake to have a closer look."

Pandara seemed unsettled. "Anything you want, Koravo. I'm just not convinced that it isn't dangerous."

"More dangerous than climbing the side of a mountain?"

Pandara didn't respond at first, but then he added, "We have to scale the mountain for our mission to be a success. We don't have to go down to the lake to see a monster, and what if it's hungry?"

"Well," said Koravo. "If it's hungry it might be able to leave the water and hunt us, so we're not necessarily any safer up here."

"Okay," said Pandara. "Let's go have a closer look."

"I think I'm going to stay here," said Paucs.

"Me too," said Annie.

"We'll be waiting for you when you return."

So, Koravo and Pandara began to walk down the hillside toward the first of the Lakes of Porselena.

Paucs was glad to have a break after the endurance match of the Liddell Plateau. He stood with Annie, though largely kept to himself. He found himself in a solitary mood and pondered what he would do after the journey came to its end. He did wonder how Annie was doing, however, and thought about talking to her. He refrained though and took in the view.

Pandara took Koravo's hand in his, which she gladly

accepted. "You know, Koravo." Koravo looked up at Pandara, who was looking ahead with solemn eyes and a troubled heart. "I'm sorry that my enthusiasm for an idea brought trouble into our relationship." She didn't respond, waiting to hear if Pandara would continue. "You mean everything to me, and I don't know what I'd do if I lost you."

"Pandara, you'll never lose me." She continued to gaze upwards in his direction, and he turned his head. Their eyes locked, and they stopped. "Even if something were to happen, I'll always be with you."

He tilted his head down; she pulled his gaze up with her free hand and smiled. "I believe in life after death," he said. "I don't think that we'll be the same people, but I believe in life after death. I know that we'll meet again."

B.10 — CHAPTER 07

B.11 ~ STILL WATERS

His choice of words was curious. It was as though he had had a premonition of a great tragedy. "Is there something you want to tell me?" she asked.

"Koravo, I ... I've been having dreams that something will happen."

"We don't have to make the climb," she said.

"I do," Pandara replied. "This is something that I have to do, but I was wondering if you would wait for me down below."

Koravo looked heartbroken. "Pandara, if you go, I go. I may not be as drawn to discover what resides at the top of the mountain as you, but I need to be with you now, now more than ever." Pandara too was heartbroken.

"I'm sure it's just a dream," he said, having missed the lesson that he should have learned so clearly. This did not escape Koravo.

"Do you remember what happened the last time there was a vision?" she asked.

Pandara said, "I have not forgotten." There was a silence.

"If you must go, then you must go," she said. "It's just unfortunate to have such a looming shadow cast down upon these events."

"Koravo, you are the sunlight of my world. Though I may suffer sometimes, your love protects me and guides me through it. I believe that there must be a solution to the answers I seek. Suffering is an unnatural anomaly. There is no good reason why the universe is not filled only with peace and tranquility. I must understand the riddle of suffering. I must meet with the Lone Spirit. He, or she, will uncover the mystery for us and reveal the nature of suffering and how to expel it from the cosmos."

"But if she understands, then why hasn't she done this herself?!" Koravo asked.

Pandara thought for a moment. "That's a good point, Koravo. Perhaps the Lone Spirit does not have all of the answers; perhaps she has a superior question."

Koravo turned her head and began to walk once again. They walked in silence until they reached the edge of the lake.

Pandara knelt by the side of the lake and filled the flask with water. Koravo looked out upon the still waters, searching for signs of life. There were none to be found. Paucs and Annie were sitting on the top of the hill, gazing down at Koravo and Pandara.

"What do you think they're talking about?" Paucs asked. Annie remained silent. "I hope they're discussing their relationship," he said, and Annie turned to look up at him. "They have such a beautiful connection, but Pandara is driven by an obsession that interferes with their love. It's such a shame really. I wish that they wouldn't climb that mountain. He's not going to find anything there, and his obsession will merely displace into a new quest of some kind."

Annie returned her gaze to the lake down below. "I think

he'll find what he's looking for," she said. "I think we all will." Paucs turned to look at Annie who was lost in thought.

Annie was vacant though not unsatisfied. Waiting with Paucs on the hill, she rested. Although she was always in a state of rest, Annie merely waited for Pandara and Koravo's return. She faded in and out of visibility; Paucs had grown accustomed to this sight.

Pandara had been thumbing the ring for many miles. He thought about the perfect time to give Koravo the gift of his heart and had decided that it would be best at the foothills of the mountain. He hoped that she would appreciate his gift and felt that she would. He didn't know if she was still his, however, until he saw her response.

"Koravo, I have something for you." Pandara reached into his pocket and retrieved the ring therein. He held out his palm and showed Koravo the unbreakable ring. "It is said that this ring is unbreakable. I received it from Arkdemus while we were on Hal Fala. She told me to choose wisely who I give it to. There is no one else but you, and so it shall always be." Koravo looked at the ring and then deeply into Pandara's eyes. He remained fixed on her position, unflinching.

Carefully she accepted the gift and slid it onto her left hand. It fit beautifully! Pandara's profoundly meaningful sentiment was all that she needed to hear. She regretted having doubted Pandara. His gift of the unbreakable ring roused her soul and embroiled her passions. She wanted to give Pandara something in return, and she knew that she was what he desired. Koravo committed to herself that she would give him a memory that he would not soon forget. She just had to find a way to break him away from Paucs and Annie.

"Pandara, I have nothing for you except my love."

"It is more than enough," he said. "Let's return to the

others when you are ready."

Koravo admired the glimmering ring, noticing how she now felt complete. It was as though she was always missing something until that moment when Pandara gave her the gift of his love. "Let's go," she said, and the two began their ascent back to the top of the hill.

Pandara and Koravo were like a new couple when they arrived back at the top of the hill. Paucs didn't know why they seemed different. They must have had a good conversation. Pandara was ready to continue and began to feel the urgency and severity of the mountain. He realized that after a long and tiring trek by foot, they would have to overcome their greatest obstacle. He felt unsure about the remainder of the journey though did not immediately share this fact with Koravo.

When they arrived, Paucs and Annie were waiting for them. "Ready?" asked Paucs. Annie noticed the ring immediately, but Paucs never would.

"Yes," said Koravo.

They continued along the path now secure in the fact that the lakes had meant them no harm; Koravo was glad that Pandara had confided in her. Although it felt like she was already balancing precariously, she had felt his love like never before. And she agreed with Pandara, that there was life beyond the mystery of death.

For every time he had died in that bedeviled labyrinth, she had died too. She was with him in the belly of the beast, holding his hand as the monster consumed them both. She knew that there was life beyond the grave. She had died so many times before, and die again she would, if it meant that Pandara would be waiting for her on the other side.

His quest was her quest. She was sure of that now. Though it didn't originate from her, the passion for ending suffering was both of theirs. She was its heartbeat, its living end, and Pandara was its eyes, ears, and limbs.

B.12 ~ CONSTELLATIONS

By this time, they were descending the hill, and the first mountain rose sharply in the air. It reminded them of their ultimate destiny, and with every passing step, the mountains further dwarfed them in their immensity. Though there was something regal about this whole experience. Its mythic quality took on a legendary tone. Perhaps Paucs' writings would one day be known to all. Perhaps people would speak of the time when Pandara and Koravo had scaled the icy summit, discovering secrets of the cosmos there and saving everyone from suffering. Only time would tell.

The terrain began to change. Every now and again they could still see through to the other side, though it was clear that few were this close to the sun on Phalanx. They were utterly alone. If anything happened to them here, there would be nothing that they could do. Soil gave way to clay, and clay to rock. There were even some boulders laying around, and they were walking on the side of the mountain.

Paucs had his journal out once again, and Annie was drifting as she always did: hyper aware of all of the details, yet seemingly aloof. The mystery of Annie confounded Pandara and Koravo. They couldn't figure out for the life of them what she was doing there, but they were glad that she had come. Perhaps that mystery would also be revealed at the top of the summit where the Lone Spirit waited for them.

Stepping cautiously and confidently, Pandara began to rehearse for the climb. He knew that this was first and foremost his quest. He was in the lead and would have to guide them safely to the top. So, he took every step with will and resolve. One wrong move could spell doom, and he wasn't about to let that happen.

Paucs was nervous about the reaction his writing would garner but decided to read from his journal anyway; he began to speak:

"And there we were, a group of assorted travelers: each with their own story to tell, united by a common cause. For even though we weren't immediately aware of it, each of us was searching for the same thing: Love."

Koravo was impressed by Paucs' skill with words. He had articulated what they had all felt but not expressed. "That's beautiful," said Koravo. "What kind of love are you searching for Paucs?"

"I haven't figured that out yet," said Paucs. "I think I dream to have a relationship like yours and Pandara's." Koravo smiled. She thanked Paucs for the inspiring passage and continued along the way.

Pandara appreciated Paucs' sentiment. He was sincere and kind and understood the importance of their mission. Pandara would be sad to say goodbye to Paucs, but he knew that the time was rapidly approaching. Pandara would be sure to thank Paucs for accompanying them on the journey; he had been a most welcome addition.

The air was getting brisk, as the winds rolled down from the mountain's top. Pandara didn't think too much about it, but he was concerned about how the others felt. "Are you guys okay?" Pandara asked. "It's getting a little chilly."

"Yeah, I'm okay," said Koravo.

"Me too," said Paucs.

"Annie, are you okay?" They stopped and realized that Annie wasn't there. "Annie?! Where's Annie?" Pandara asked.

Koravo and Paucs looked around, but she was clearly gone. "Perhaps she just decided to be invisible," Paucs remarked, but this wasn't like Annie. More than anyone else, Annie had changed the most. "I suppose that perhaps her unpredictability was constant, so maybe it was to be expected."

"I guess we'll just have to go on without her," Koravo stated. "She'll turn up when she wants to be seen."

As the three of them continued in their quest, they couldn't help but feel that they'd lost a member of their family. Indeed, they had. Without warning, Annie had disappeared. Her ways were always mysterious, and this time was no exception. The others assumed that she was with them and carried on. Annie could take care of herself, and they weren't worried.

The lakes were beneath them now, and they could see the mystery up close and in full view. There was nothing false about what they saw. The nearest lake wrapped itself along the side of the mountain, like an amorphous mirror, or a liquid clock whose telling of time couldn't be trusted. The three souls treaded along, in single file, hiking the breadth of the secondary ridge. An abundance of blessing followed them like birds chasing after the summer. They were protected.

The universe wanted Pandara to uncover the riddle of suffering, for it was held captive by dark forces which condemned all to shadowy misfortune. As the tale unfolded, so too did their prayers of the beneficent age, full of compassion and hope for the future.

But the mountain was indifferent. Timeless and ancient, it had seen everything come and go. That mountain whose crest was exultant and serene, shot forth from the earth, unlikely and without mercy. The sky was moved, and the mountain won, captured and foreboding. Like a canyon wide and deep, the mountain filled empty space with its grandeur and majesty; and the mountain did not care!

As they turned a corner, there it was. Laid out bare, for all to see, the apex of their quest. "I wish Annie was here to see this," Koravo said. "It's so beautiful."

The spell it cast mesmerized Pandara. "I know she's there,"

he said. "I feel it. The Lone Spirit? I feel her calling to me."

"Perhaps the journey alone will reveal to you the answers that you seek, Pandara," Paucs speculated. Pandara brushed the thought aside, he turned another corner, and the sun shone through, low on the horizon.

"Let's try to make it to the base before the sun goes down." They picked up their pace a little, pulled by the gravity of the mountain, implored by the stars and the heavens above. It was now nearly dark, though they had reached the outskirts of that central palisade. "This will do," Pandara said, and he motioned to the others that they should stop for the night. There were trees, and it was dry. They would be able to build a fire tonight. Pandara helped Koravo gather wood, while Paucs diligently and patiently collected thoughts and set them onto virgin pages.

The fire was warm, and the night was clear. Koravo continued to hope that Annie would appear, but she did not. "I hope Annie's okay," she said.

"I'm sure she is," said Pandara, who bit into a piece of salted meat.

Everyone was thinking about Annie's baby, though no one claimed to speak of her. Sparks and embers sprang forth from the flames. Pandara leaned back and looked up to the sky. He saw constellations, like the Hunter and the Crypt. He saw the Lion and the Maiden. He saw everything, just like the mountain; yet, it was not at all the same.

That night Paucs had fallen asleep early. Koravo remarked of how the moment reminded her of Seprator. "Remember when we left for the wood?" she said. "Remember how we tried to fall into that embrace, by the river in the Trilodian Forest?"

"Yes, of course I remember," said Pandara.

"I want to retry that night tonight." Koravo smiled, charming and alive. "Want to go for a little walk?" she said.

B.13 ~ AN INFINITY OF STARS

And just like that, she was gone. She had felt the branch crack and knew that it was the end. There wasn't time to process what had happened, though Koravo saw her life flash before her eyes in some abstract way. As she ground against each rock below, her memories and sensations grew more and more dim. Finally, after several hundred feet, there was no more Koravo. All that remained was a helpless doll grazing endlessly against a brutal mountainside.

Pandara watched their separation grow as his twin fell into the mist and fog below, until her memory was all that remained. The branch had broken with a snap, and Pandara knew that she was gone forever. His incredulity was augmented by the fact that hope had been a youthful twig that fought desperately for life through the imposing stone. It was not meant to be, and Pandara fell to his knees.

His mind was infinitely shattered, hitting against those spiteful rocks. Pandara wept and cried. He moaned and collapsed. "No!" he yelled. But there was no one who could hear his call, just an infinity of stars lost to him forever now, falling forevermore.

Koravo, like a singing bird shot from the sky, went as mute as the sea.

Hansa, Anthos, Sirrung, and Yuit had all seemed to have left them. The song of the stars mended the eternal spirit, and the Ende of Illusions was waiting patiently in the future embrace. All of these things were still there, though they were not as central to the story as they had been in Ksevia. The Prellian mixture was cradling them beyond the end.

Pandara was deep in thought regarding his next steps. He had been free for weeks to wander the inner workings of his mind, searching for a way to bring about the end of suffering. Would it be through some grand, cosmic event? Or, perhaps, it would take place through the boundless march of like-minded souls, one million years into the distant something, freeing sentient life one consciousness at a time. Either way, he knew that this ultimate end was destiny. There was no other possible outcome that could arise in the vast reaches of the universe, so glorious, futuristic, and ancient.

Koravo had not seemed to have changed as much since the early days in Ksevia, so she worried about him. Pandara's quest for universal enlightenment had resulted in a distant Pandara, one who was always deep in thought. Philosophizing and lost in contemplation, Pandara had forgotten about Koravo it seemed; at least, that is how she felt. She was willing to go to the distant reaches of destiny with him, and for him, if that is what it took to bring Pandara home to her once again.

When he approached her with his most recent idea, she was nervous. The trek would be treacherous and unpredictable it seemed. The trek would push them both to their limits, and Koravo wondered as to the nature and root of his passion. That insight remained out of reach, however, and she didn't ask. She was anxious and felt unable to commit to his laborious quest. Still, she nurtured his soul, but his active mind stole its attention away from her. She tried to win him back but to no avail. This seemed to be for a good cause, however.

Koravo was also familiar with the bodhisattvas, those who seek to end all suffering, and she understood the passion of Pandara's convictions. His obsession had conquered him though, and she just couldn't forget what he had done to her. He was lost to her.

She wondered if his obsession was just a passing phase. Was Pandara on a new path toward solitude? Had he grown bored with her? Perhaps there was something she had done, but that was absurd. Koravo searched the corridors of her thought anyway and affirmed that she had done nothing.

Pandara had been reading ancient texts from all corners of Tristulle, with a special focus on the 18th century musings of Yaronne Jetir, a nomad. His works of deep love for and profound sentimental connection with Tristulle had left Pandara awe-struck and inspired.

Jetir had travelled to the distant corners of the world, documenting his journeys, and capturing the beauty of every flower and blade of grass along the way.

When Jetir finally reached an unnamed mountain, he had had a vision of a lone spirit residing on the summit of the mountain who would be able to answer his most urgent and primary question. Shortly thereafter, the writings had come to an end.

The book had been discovered in the ether by an anonymous Ksevian. The book was known only to a small and distinct audience, of whom Pandara was one such member. Pandara had become enthralled by the idea of an expedition, one that would continue the work of Jetir. The two of them became like brothers separated by time. Where one ended the other began.

Yaronne Jetir was a humble man who lived his life in solitude. He valued scholarship above all else, in particular the study of Tristulle and spiritual musings of one who had been touched by inspiration. He was slight but handsome, roughened by the journeys which had taken him through many of the countless regions of Tristulle. He didn't bother with vanity and gave little thought to how others would perceive him. His affect was kind and his disposition curious.

Yaronne Jetir longed for the day when the existence of suffering would cease, and this is what endeared him to Pandara the most.

Pandara approached Koravo with a three-fold idea: that they might travel to the mountain, learn of what happened to Yaronne Jetir, and climb its heights in search of the Lone Spirit who may still reside there.

In response, Koravo bent her head and sighed. "Pandara, I ... Are you sure that this is a good idea?"

"Yes, of course. Why?"

"Well, I don't know. It seems quite dangerous."

"We'll be fine Koravo," said Pandara.

Though she was resolutely unsure, she yielded to his plan. Koravo didn't speak her mind at the expense of her needs. She feared the worst and allowed that phantasm to possess her spirit. She settled into gloom, and Pandara remained oblivious. Koravo wilted like the half-light of a winter morning. Before blind eyes, her love was dying. She grew determined to put an end to such misery and summoned strength to overcome wallowing sadness. She did through great efforts, and all fell short on Pandara's windowpane. She picked up the pieces of her confidence and departed with the man.

B.14 ~ THE BLACK WEIGHT

He flipped to the end of the book, where blank pages met his wandering eyes. Then he skimmed back in time until he found text. *And so, I died*, it read.

Pandara hesitated, realizing that they were the first two people to uncover the mystery of what had happened to the great explorer and philosopher. Pandara flipped back several pages and began to speak. "*Only then did I realize the obviousness of my situation.*"

"Go further back, Pandara," Koravo interjected.

He flipped further back and began to speak once again. "*Here I am, on the precipice of discovery. I don't know what I will find at the top of this mountain, but I know that I am on the right and noble path. The question that has driven me: how to free the universe of suffering, has led me to this juncture. I stand humbled and amazed that all who came before me helped me in the ways that they did. I feel as though a spectator, watching myself make the choices that have resulted in this eve of finality.*

"*I am bewildered by the existence of suffering and know that it is an unnecessary component of the universe in which we live. The ultimate destiny for all is to experience life free from this phenomenon.*

"*My question to the Lone Spirit is whether a shortcut exists somewhere out there among the stars. It would be a shortcut that ends the need for countless souls to liberate one person at a time, over countless millennia. But I digress! How I want to know the answer now! I am here! I have arrived! Now I shall go face the truth!*"

There was a break in the text, and Pandara flipped the page. He resumed his oration.

"Here it is, Koravo!"

"*I stand upon the summit, gazing out in all directions. I have met with the Lone Spirit; only then did I realize the obviousness of my situation. Our exchange was brief and insightful. I have learned the answer to the riddle which torments my soul. The answer is that a shortcut does exist!*"

Pandara was beyond joy; tears welled up in his eyes.

"*The next step lies on a distant planet called Delta Centauri. I don't know where that is, but I am determined to make it there. I don't know how I will get there, but I will get there. The Lone Spirit told me that the answer I seek is not only information but also an experience. That is all I have to report for now.*"

Another break, Pandara scanned down below and resumed.

"*I have fallen.*"

Pandara looked at Koravo. "*My leg is fractured.*"

Sure enough, Yaronne's leg was badly broken at the shin.

"*I don't know how much more time I will have, as the pain is immense, and I have no supplies. I can't focus on my writing, and I am bleeding profusely. Beware, ye who passes this threshold! The way ahead is dangerous! Your path will soon come to an end, as has mine. And so, I died.*"

Koravo and Pandara met in an anxious glance. Koravo was sad that Jetir had died. His fall confirmed in her mind the danger of the path that lay ahead. She thought about remaining behind but was so close to the summit. The passage called to her for reasons that she did not fully comprehend, and she was compelled to go! Still, she hesitated.

"We could turn back now," said Koravo. "We have the answer that we sought."

"Yes, but there is more to the riddle," said Pandara. "Are people capable of growing into practices which shall fulfill and help them? Why is there evil in the world? Why did the universe have suffering in the first place? What is the universe? What is suffering?! All of these and more are the questions which have answers that I seek, and we are on the verge of discovery! It would be a shame to turn back now."

"But what about our lives?" asked Koravo. "What about my life?" Pandara hesitated.

"You could wait with Yaronne, Koravo. You could wait here."

"We've been through this before Pandara, and so I will go with you." They looked through the rest of Jetir's belongings but found nothing of value that would help them with the final stretch of the climb.

They were now hours past that original stopping point, where they had paused to take a break. Although the sun blasted down upon them, it was cold. Pandara put his shirt back on. They looked up and saw the clouds above their heads, hanging low like swans resting on an invisible mirror. "Soon we'll cross through the clouds," said Pandara. "It might be difficult to see. Perhaps we should wait here until morning. We should be patient."

Koravo thought it wise and agreed.

That night, the struggles of the past melded with the future. They decided to give Yaronne some respectful space and made their way over to the other side of the platform where they settled underneath blankets, curling into a ball. They were hungry and ate the last remaining rations of their food supply. There was still a little water left, and they saved that for the morning.

Pandara knew that the final stretch would be the hardest. Jetir had not survived the treacherous course, and he grew anxious. Having Koravo at his side helped a great deal, and he appreciated that she had decided to join him in the trek.

That night Koravo lay wrapped in Pandara's arms. She felt protected from the elements and happy to be with Pandara. Koravo hoped that their time would not come to an end. Koravo fell asleep first, and once she had, Pandara soon fell asleep too. They held firm to one another, united by their bonds of love that stretched across countless miles. The goddess of the night descended upon them and held them close in a loving embrace; they were protected.

The night rolled around, and the stars revolved overhead. Before long, it was morning, and from the other side of the mountain, the sun began to illuminate the space that surrounded them. Koravo awoke.

"Pandara," she whispered. "Look at the sunrise. Is that not the most beautiful thing you have ever seen?"

Without hesitation, and between the cracks of morning, Pandara said, "You are the most beautiful thing I've ever seen." She looked at him lovingly and smiled.

They both watched, arms wrapped around each other,

leaned against the cliffside. It was what they needed, an auspicious sign. They were relieved.

"Let's get an early start. It's almost morning."

Pandara rolled his head off of her shoulder and kissed her on the cheek, gently persisting through the moment. They stood up and brushed themselves off. "I'm going to pay my respects to Jetir," said Pandara. "You can come with me if you'd like."

"No, that's okay," she responded. "I'll wait here for you."

Pandara walked over to the skeletal remains of Yaronne Jetir. He knelt beside the dead man and placed his hand over his heart. "Yaronne," he began. "Though we never met, I thank you for showing me the way. And I thank you for transcribing your last notes while dying of your wound. It has given me the resolve to continue, and I thank you from the bottom of my heart. I hope that wherever you now reside, you have found peace and love. I wish you well upon your journey." He stood up.

Koravo was anxiously pacing back and forth. She had a terrible feeling about the day ahead and tried desperately to control her emotions. When Pandara appeared from around the bend, she stopped and smiled at him. "How did it go?" she asked.

"It was as it was supposed to be," he replied, not noticing her graciousness. "Shall we?" he asked, in a way that gave her little room for movement. She said nothing and progressed. Koravo was walking into pure uncertainty.

In the vibrant, azure rays of early dawn, Pandara and Koravo began their ascent. Koravo was spinning on her finger the ring that Pandara had given to her. It was all that she had left, just Pandara's love for her. Was it enough?

Somewhere deep inside she knew that Pandara would ultimately carry her safely to their destination. But she had begun to become concerned about his safety. What would she do if something happened to him? She couldn't bear to consider the thought.

Pandara stopped. "Koravo, look. The way is about to end, and I don't see a reasonable path forward. Do you?"

Koravo stepped ahead of Pandara and surveyed the rocky terrain. It was difficult to see. They had not expected that the road would end so abruptly. The mountain stood by with seeming indifference. Did the Lone Spirit know that they were almost there? Had she been waiting for them? Koravo responded. "I think there was another means of approach just a little ways back. I think we should go examine it."

They turned around and found another avenue. This one was steeper than before, though it was still easy to imagine a handrail being constructed by some future generation.

They climbed for an eternity on a path that didn't relent.

They were high above the clouds, and the freshly fallen snow and ice made the course even more treacherous than before. Traversing the side of the mountain, everything had come alive, though the sun was now blocked by the cliff of cold rock. An eagle flew by, called, and that is when he heard her scream.

Koravo had slipped on a rock and slid down the cliffside. No more than ten feet away, she was now hanging from a branch, suspended above the greatness of the mountain.

When Koravo slipped, Pandara's heart instantly escaped him. He fought to remain calm in sudden terror and snapped into heightened awareness. He didn't have time to grasp reality.

When she slipped, Koravo fell straight into the object of her ruminations. She grappled for anything that would support her weight, and the branch was all she could find. Koravo knew that her moments were numbered and searched for any possible means of escape. She couldn't find one.

Pandara saw everything in the moment. He felt time slip away. His Eurydice was hanging on tenuous desperation, overcome by mounting odds. He bent down, arms stretched over the cliff, reaching for her hand once again, but they couldn't connect. Separate now, forever it seemed, was gone. "Hang on, Koravo! Don't let go!"

"Oh no, Pandara!" she screamed. "No!" Koravo began to seize uncontrollably.

"Koravo, listen!" Pandara shouted at the top of his lungs. Koravo stopped and looked up at Pandara. "We will get you out of this!" he yelled to her. The branch cracked a little under weight just ever so slightly too immense. It was the weight of the ring, it seemed.

"Pandara, I love you!" she yelled to him.

"No, Koravo! I don't want to lose you!"

She fell.

B.15 ~ SLOW DESCENT

The snow bit his frozen face of tears, of loss and remorse. Pandara wanted to throw himself over the cliff, but one thought kept him from doing so. He had to find her; he couldn't give up now. Pandara stood, collected himself, and began to face the slow descent back the way they had come. He took the first step with a shaky foundation. Struggling to gain his bearings, Pandara was instinctively careful to not fall. He couldn't believe what had transpired and prayed that it somehow was just a dream.

Step by step down the mountainside, he used the cliff face as a crutch to prop up his mortal remains. He was deeply wounded and felt like his soul had been torn from his body. It was an hour or more before he saw the first signs of Koravo. To his right a streak of red shot across the surface of the rock. He searched for a way to reach those red rocks, but there wasn't one. He had to descend further toward the inevitable conclusion, and so he did.

Pandara stepped down the face of the mountainside carefully, swallowed by oceans of curtains; her memory haunted and soothed him both. He couldn't let her go. It took several hours for Pandara to reach the bottom of the mountain in a slow and painful descent. Shortly before he arrived, he remembered the first clearing that they had passed on their way up. Pandara knew she would be there, and she was.

Koravo was his sundial, his crucifix tree: the rose of her heart climbing statues of time to bring order to the light. With every rotation, shadows came and went, but Koravo remained steadfast on her mission to bring love to Pandara and life itself. The invisible crown upon her head, a halo of wisdom and intellect, proclaimed undying rise above mediocrity. She acted in accordance with her divine impulses and trusted in the fabric from which she was cut.

Koravo traced the perimeter of her existence with graceful movements and lit the halls of Ksevian history. She embraced the fortune of her inheritance affirming life. Koravo knew that she wasn't truly immortal, but the inevitability of death had always remained distant. Her time had come, and when she died, it seemed like all of Tristulle felt the loss. Stones began to shake, and the heavens threatened to collapse upon Pandara. Snow covered the wounds of entire worlds caused by the death of love itself; sorrows in the land spread in endless thoughts of mourning.

Sunken by the haze, Pandara wandered through mists of indispensability to where Koravo's unrecognizable body lay broken and torn. He couldn't make sense of what he was seeing. Dangling from the lifeless bouquet of red and white roses, fluid and motionless, frozen, was a necklace: a violet and spring green, silver necklace. Within the ruins of his love was their unbreakable ring. He couldn't see it, but he knew that it was there.

He fell to his knees, unable to take his eyes off of the mound. With desperation he closed them but couldn't wipe the image from his mind's eye. It burned like a spiteful torch inside of the dungeon of his thoughts. Pandara gave himself several minutes to take in the scene; then, where he was, he began to dig.

The rock of the mountain gnawed at his fingertips, but he continued to dig for as long as it took. He removed his pack and rummaged through it for anything he could use as an aid. The only thing he could find was her hourglass. The brass and crystal device was miniature but robust; it seemed to have been constructed to withstand the elements. Using the hourglass as a spade, he dug a hole until finally the hourglass broke. He cut himself on the shards, smooth and restless sands of time poured out, and Pandara's blood caused them to congeal.

He continued to dig, wiping tears from his eyes, and occasionally glancing at her to remind himself of persistence. Once he had finished beyond all reasonable doubt, once the hole was large enough, he stopped. He stood up and walked over to her. Lifting her up, he carried her dignified remains to rest with as much composure as he could find within himself. It seemed that he was alone in the world, but he was not. She was with him.

He covered her body with soil and spoke a silent prayer. Now that she had been buried, Pandara could begin to seek peace. At least that is what he had previously thought; however, he found himself drawn to a higher purpose. There was a voice in the ether that called to him. It was the Lone Spirit; she sounded just like Koravo. As he paused to listen, the first ring of acceptance that she was truly gone drew to completion.

B.16 ~ THE LANTERN

It was late at night when Paucs heard the sound, when he saw the light. He reluctantly opened his eyes, fighting off the nightmare which possessed his mind. At a distance, a glowing lantern approached their campfire burning slow and dim with suffocation. Now startled and awake, Paucs quietly got up careful to not disturb Pandara. He rushed over to the light intently but with caution. "Who are you? What are you doing here?" he innocently asked the blinding light.

The lantern grew dim, as a young boy was seen to adjust the copper knob. "Am I really?... Did it?"

"Did it what?!" whispered Paucs, looking over his shoulder to make sure that his friend had not awoken.

"Am I in Tristulle?" asked the boy.

Paucs was confused and alarmed. "Of course you're in Tristulle," said Paucs. "Where else would you be?"

The boy started laughing hysterically. He was in Tristulle! How was that even possible? Hyro knew that such a feat was extremely unlikely. Still, it had happened, and he was the one who had discovered the passageway! He was convinced that he would become famous, and everyone would remember his name through-out the histories of both Phalanx and Tristulle; Pandara woke up.

"Look now what you've done!" said Paucs. "Don't you have any decency?"

Pandara, wrapped in a blanket, slowly made his way over to see what the commotion was about. "What is this?" he asked, wiping the sleep from his eyes.

"I'm from Phalanx," said the boy.

Paucs looked over at Pandara who immediately paused in disbelief. "That's not possible," said Pandara.

"Yet, here I am," said the boy. "My name is Hyro." He stuck out his hand with the self-assuredness of one who had truly just accomplished the impossible.

Pandara looked at the hand and finally extended his as well. "I'm Pandara," he said, "and this is Paucs."

Paucs resisted shaking the boy's hand to make his point

be known. "You have to understand, young one, we have just had the worst day of our lives. Please be considerate and respectful to us now. We cannot express to you the loss we are feeling at this moment."

Hyro's disposition shifted, and he lowered his arm. Hyro became impatient and perturbed, as though his triumph had unjustly been overshadowed by other events. "But did you hear me?" he said. "I'm from Phalanx."

Pandara sighed and turned around, walking over to put more wood on the fire. Hyro looked over Paucs' shoulder to see where Pandara was going. Paucs resolved to get rid of the boy, though still in sleep, inadvertently advanced the conversation. "How did you manage to enter Tristulle?" he asked.

"I found an entrance in a cave some ways down there." Hyro turned around and pointed, holding out the lantern as though to illuminate an opening to the mountain which could not be seen.

"No one has ever found a passageway between our two worlds," said Paucs.

"I know!" exclaimed Hyro, who was overcome with pride.

"Well, you found the wrong audience for your accomplishment," said Paucs. "This is neither the right place, nor the right time for celebration."

"What happened?" asked Hyro, innocently.

Paucs, having realized that he'd furthered communication once again, reluctantly responded with a sigh. "His wife died today." Paucs motioned to Pandara. "She fell," and he motioned to the mountain.

Hyro was silent. Then he responded, "I'm so sorry."

"Well," Paucs replied. "There's nothing that you can do." There was silence. "There's nothing any of us can do."

Hyro looked over to Pandara, who was settling back in

for sleep. He was young and didn't fully appreciate the full extent to which some things could be lost. Hyro didn't know Koravo. She was a name to him only. Still, he did feel bad for Pandara abstractly. Hyro wasn't a monster; he was just more interested in the feat which he had recently accomplished, as a boy might be. "Where am I?" Hyro asked. "In Tristulle, where am I?"

Paucs sighed once again and said, "We are far beyond any established region of Tristulle." He paused. "You're from the other side. Surely you have noticed the lack of people walking by."

"Yes," said Hyro. "I've always heard that Tristulle has many population centers, but I've never actually seen any of them." Hyro thought for a moment and then spoke. "I would like to write about this experience," he said. "What is the name of this mountain?"

Paucs was getting tired but could relate to the young man's interest in immortalizing events through writing. Although they had just met, there was a bond between writers that other people simply weren't aware of. He decided to stoke the young man's imagination. "Its name is Mount Koravo," said Paucs.

Interesting, thought Hyro, who realized that he had suddenly grown very tired and wanted to leave. He remembered that he would always be able to return tomorrow; Tristulle wasn't going anywhere. "Mount Koravo, I'll remember that," said Hyro, suggesting that he was about to depart. "Once again, I'm very sorry for your loss." Paucs didn't reply.

Hyro said goodbye and made his way back to the cave. Paucs and Pandara weren't sorry to see him leave. The rendezvous had been an unexpected and unwelcome interruption. Paucs rejoined Pandara by the campfire and fell back to sleep instantly.

On his way back home, Hyro couldn't believe all that had transpired. He approached the cave and was no longer afraid. He stepped in and made his way back to the opening in the ground.

He gracefully passed through the liquid screen which looked, on the surface, just like any other part of the earth.

After he was back in Phalanx, Hyro crawled through the narrow passage which gave him little leeway. He exited the cave and hurried home. The front door was still unlocked, and his parents were asleep. He changed into his plaid cotton pajamas and got into bed. It seemed like everything would be alright.

In the morning, Paucs and Pandara awoke at roughly the same time. Pandara was crushed emotionally. He buried his feelings deep inside. Pandara was delirious and full of agony, full of sorrow. The only reason that he woke up in the morning was now gone. Along with Koravo's death went his reason to live. The events of last night were fresh on their minds, and the implications of Hyro's discovery had begun to sink in.

Paucs had gone hunting while Pandara was getting ready and managed to collect some small roots, berries, and assorted vegetables. They ate breakfast with few words spoken between them. Pandara wasn't in the mood to talk, and Paucs didn't know what to say.

When he tried to mention Koravo and the impact that she had had on his life, Pandara politely listened and said, "Thank you." Paucs got the sense that his input wasn't helping and decided to remain quiet. "What will you do?" asked Pandara.

Paucs looked up from his meal. "I'm going to Phalanx," he said. Pandara was intrigued but didn't inquire further. Paucs seemed confident that the passageway was legitimate.

"I've decided to try again," said Pandara.

"That's exceedingly brave of you," Paucs replied. "I wish you a fortunate outcome." He regretted those words, but he had spoken them.

After they finished breakfast, Pandara and Paucs put out the fire, gathered their belongings, and shook hands. "Until we meet again," Pandara said.

"Until then," said Paucs, admiring Pandara for his strength and resolve. Paucs' complimentary disposition had given Pandara an additional surge of energy, and he would later regret not having had the foresight to thank Paucs properly. But, what was done was done. Those few words were the only words that Pandara could think of for the first part of the morning.

Pandara began to climb the familiar path. He knew all of the turns, corners, and straightaways of the mountain, but that didn't spare him the full day's trip to the top. He would reach the summit early in the evening, if he was lucky. He was already exhausted; this experience was undoubtedly the most trying time of his life.

Paucs wandered around the side of the mountain, looking for a cave opening. He didn't have a lantern, so he decided to make a few torches. Before he did though, he first wanted to see the cave with his own eyes to make sure that he wasn't the subject of a deceitful ruse.

There one was! It looked like any other cave he had ever seen, but if Hyro was right, this was the most significant of them all. If there was indeed a portal between Tristulle and Phalanx, the implications were phenomenal. Perhaps life had started on one side of the earth and then migrated to the other. Perhaps trade could be established, and cultural exchange could take place in the flesh.

There were countless possibilities, and Paucs wanted to play a role in that story. He wouldn't claim to have discovered the cave, but he would gladly be the first Tristullite to cross the border. He constructed several torches, lit the first one, and walked inside.

The cave was shallow and open. There wasn't much to its interior, so if a window was present it would have to jump right out to him. And there one was! In the corner of the cave, a transparent film could be seen revealing a subtle illumination. He'd seen many such glassy panes before, as all in Tristulle or Phalanx had as well, but supposedly this one was different. He approached the clear puddle and reached out his hand to touch it. To his amazement, the boundary was penetrable!

All of the other patches in Tristulle were solid, like thick sheets of glass. No one had managed to develop a machine that could break through, or even scratch the surface of any boundary, on either side of Tristulle or Phalanx. As though to reassure himself that he wouldn't be injured in crossing the threshold, Paucs reached with his arm through the mirror and felt the ground on the other side. The thickness between Tristulle and Phalanx was surprisingly thin. Less than a foot separated the two worlds at this location.

Paucs was anxious and excited to be at the portal to Phalanx. Ever since he was a boy, Paucs had thought about that curious land and wondered what it would be like to visit there. Even more exciting, however, was the thrill of being the first Tristullite in history to make the journey. Paucs loved a good story, and this one topped them all! He couldn't believe that the portal was real! He stopped stalling and began to enter it.

Without further hesitation, Paucs lowered his head into the invisible pool and attempted to climb to the other side. It was awkward, but fortunately no one had to watch him proceed. He was surprised that the passage made him feel nothing at all. Perhaps there was a momentary blip, a reset of the brain, but that was all. He hadn't really felt a thing and searched himself to make sure he was unharmed. As his first torch was getting rather feeble, Paucs used it to light a second torch and then tossed the first one into a corner of the cave.

The area he now occupied was a vast cathedral-like space. The subtle sounds of his passage resounded loudly in the cavernous dome. He searched for several minutes before he found a way out.

The crawl space itself was very small; Paucs just barely fit through. If he had been any larger, he might not have been able to pass, or he might have even gotten stuck in the process of trying. He walked the rest of the way and entered Phalanx, the first Tristullite to have ever done such a thing!

B.17 ~ THE OTHER SIDE

Pandara had just begun his excursion. Though he was not far along, he was approaching what he knew would be the most difficult part of the climb. With his head down, he took the last few steps that lead him to the first plateau. There on his left was the little grave. He broke down into tears and fell to the earth.

So, it seemed that Pandara had not fully processed that Koravo was gone, at least he had to rediscover his loss in that moment. He flattened his body over her grave and cried in an embrace with the soil beneath. "Koravo!" he yelled, and he wept thinking about those final moments, watching her tumble down the cliffside into the mists and clouds below.

The look upon her face was one of sheer terror. It was the definition of terror, yet there was something about her look that he couldn't quite put his finger on. Koravo had maintained eye contact with him as she fell into the great abyss. Her heart was with him still; he could feel her. It was as though those eyes were inches from his face. Pandara envisioned Koravo right before him. He was near the mountaintop, just as it had been. He watched as her spirit flew to him.

Koravo reached out to him, knowing what it would mean to Pandara. She eased his mind and soothed his weary heart. Koravo came to him from beyond the grave, to reassure Pandara that everything would be alright. They would be together again one day; of this she was certain.

With a diamond on her brow, and one above her heart, she ascended through the air in shadows of blue and silver. Pandara longed to kiss her ruby lips, the ones which had spoken to him about her love. But they were just phantom lips now, and he wept! Nonetheless, he imagined her ghostly lips caressing him, and this made him feel that everything would be alright; he stopped crying.

Though it seemed to last for several minutes, his epiphany had been very brief. Waking up from that vision, he realized that it had not been at the top of the mountain. Rather she had come to him just now from beyond the grave, right here in this place and time. She had floated through the soil to speak with him again, not with words, but with her heart, with her soul.

Koravo had more soul than anyone Pandara had ever known! In retrospect, he was not surprised that she was able to cross the boundary of death to reach him, but it had come as a surprise in the moment. He felt relieved and began to realize that it was time to walk again. Pandara had to complete the mission in Koravo's name. "I'll see you on the other side," he spoke aloud. He tore himself from that final resting place and vowed to speak with her again on his way back down the mountain, upon his return to their home, Ksevia.

The next part of the climb was moderately difficult. A pathway had been carved onto the side of the mountain by natural forces. It began as an upward walking passage and concluded with a slight scaling of a small rocky cliff. Though it required concentration, Pandara completed the portion without any awareness of his actions. He knew those rocks intimately well. He remembered them, just as he remembered Koravo.

Pandara was nearing the halfway point. He continued to glide across the trail unafraid. Within a few hours he would arrive at the location where the skeletal remains and journal of Yaronne Jetir had previously blessed their passage.

But to what end? Yaronne couldn't be held accountable. Pandara knew that they had made their decision together to keep going, knowing full well that something bad might happen. They had stopped several times analyzing the premonition he had had, wondering whether or not to turn back; they hadn't. Still, he didn't want to see Jetir again this time. He had his own quest to complete.

What was once the mythical journey of another man had become his mythical journey. They had sought the same thing, the extinction of suffering across all of the cosmos. Jetir had succeeded in reaching the top, and so too would Pandara. His questions would be answered. The Lone Spirit would be there; he was sure of it.

From here the way to the top would be arduous. Pandara was more alone now than he had ever felt before. He and Koravo had known each other since birth, and with every step he took, he felt that he was getting closer to her once again. Some chasms couldn't be crossed, however. Pandara knew this but continued his magical thinking in his time of despair.

He shuffled across the cliffside, clinging to the rocks that held firmly against the mountain. Pandara couldn't bear to look down, knowing what had become of his Koravo. He crossed with his eyes on the mountain, though his thoughts were with her. He fought to remain focused on the task at hand. *One foot after the other*, he thought repeatedly. Pandara was nearing the place of the fall. There it was.

His eyes instinctively went to the branch that had broken off, its end still protruding from the cliff. "Curse that branch!" he spoke with only you there to hear. If it wasn't for that branch, he would have never had a chance to share that last moment with Koravo! She had told him that she loved him! But if that branch hadn't broken, perhaps she would have still been here with him. Maybe he could've found a way to rescue her.

He stopped to think about what he might have done differently. It was no use; she was gone. But yet, he wondered if there was any possible way that this fate could have been avoided. He should have told her to wait for him, but she had insisted that she come along. Pandara hadn't known if he would have been able to finish the climb on his own; that was sad but true. Koravo was his heart, and the body cannot function without its heart. Here he was though; now that she was completely gone, he was driven by another force, indignation.

Pandara cursed the heavens that had taken her from him! Clouds rolled by, and Pandara swore their immaterial weight! If only those clouds had been more substantial, perhaps one would have cushioned her fall. It could have risen up with their love and brought her safely to him. The world was not as it should be, and this very fact was deeply intertwined with the reason for his quest. *How could such a place exist where nature would permit the pain and suffering of masses?* It seemed counter-intuitive to Pandara. Though it was remarkable that anything existed at all, Pandara observed the underdeveloped existence of which we're all a part.

If anything were to exist, it should exist in perfect accord with the principles of idealism and beauty. How could such a magical act have been performed, yet half-heartedly and without perfection? The gods were impatient it seemed, to see something, to see anything.

He put all of these thoughts to temporary rest and continued the climb. He'd never been this far before. He stopped to take in the view and cleanse his mind. It was a clear day, and Pandara could seemingly see the ends of Tristulle. The Lakes of Porselena stretched out far to the Liddell Plateau, and beyond he saw the Passepartout Desert now still and sleeping. Further yet, Pandara could barely perceive a river which wound its way on the horizon. He thought about the Abyssinia and the lights that they had seen there.

It occurred to him that the great chasm had foreshadowed what was to come, with startling precision, though unfocused and out of reach. Pandara sighed and turned his gaze back to the path up ahead. Had the great abyss delivered a clear message, would he have ceased in his mission?

He reluctantly admitted to himself that he would have continued at all costs. Koravo had paid the ultimate price, and he was the reason why. That was something Pandara would have to live with.

B.18 ~ THE SUMMIT

The way appeared to be loosening up, and he felt that his quest was reaching its end. Though he perpetually thought that he was at the end, he continued to walk for another hour. The mountain hadn't given up and had so much more to show Pandara.

The way was light. Flowers and grass had managed to survive against the odds, and frost and snow grazed the otherwise blooming pasture. When Pandara was upon the summit, he was dazed and fatigued. The thin air caused his breath to shorten and his mind to subtly detach. He was frail, bedazzled, and hopelessly lost.

The gaze of the climber rose above the cliffside, and he ascended to the top of the mountain. The summit was a region not more than one hundred feet across, and there was absolutely nothing there. There were no signs that a lone spirit had ever lived there, but even more surprising than that was what lay on the other side.

As far as the eye could see, an enormous ocean reflected the sunset stretched out for all eternity. "Trilodius" he said, locked with bewilderment. The pieces clicked together! Trilodius must have seen what Pandara was looking at, or somehow, he just knew. At that moment, he realized that the Lone Spirit was not another being. Pandara was the Lone Spirit, now, for this moment in time. Yaronne Jetir must have come to the same conclusion, but how had he found out about Delta Centauri? It appeared that only Pandara could answer the questions that befell his own mind.

The Trilodian Sea was awesome and enchanting. The sun reflected on waves that rolled in off the winds up to the shore, breaking against the cliffside far below. Pandara felt the stillness of pure time pull him deeper into the future. He felt a breeze of cool air, constant and unrefined, push back on him. Pandara pushed back against that will which told him that he did not belong at such great heights. The echo of his journey resounded loud and clear across the prodigious landscape. He had overcome the mountain, and the mountain proceeded to deliver the secret contents of its altitude.

Pandara took a seat in meditation pose and thought about what drove him. He tried to penetrate to the heart of his question more thoroughly than ever before. The essence of his question was whether or not a short cut to universal salvation exists, a short cut to the extinction of suffering of all living things. He was not concerned with his own salvation, for that would come with the ultimate prize. But more so, Pandara thought about the state of the universe in 5,000 years. He desired a passage of time that was without a trace of suffering.

Although he understood that likely he would have to get there one soul at a time, he was hoping that there was another way. This thought led him to an altogether different summit in his own mind regarding the existence of evil. *Am I merely a character in another's story? If so, then Apep must also control my author's universe!*

What does Apep want? Why would anyone or anything

willingly perpetuate pain and suffering on such a grand scale?
Pandara was floored. *And where is the Lone Spirit?*

He decided that he would remain here another day, just so
that he could watch the sun rise over Trilodius' magical kingdom.
This was not meant to be however, and to his surprise, he felt that
someone else was with him. He turned to his left, and there was
Annie. Holding little Rosa against her chest, she had sat down next
to Pandara and took his hand in hers. It was as if Annie knew what
was coming.

At first, he thought that Annie was there to comfort him,
but as the minutes unfolded, it dawned on Pandara that she had
been scared. Though their relationship had been brief, Pandara was
glad to see Annie, her dead smile and sea-swept eyes. Annie always
knew exactly when to appear. The one who had so little to say, in
fact had so much to say after all. She was lost as a ghost, though
acted out of love. With the tiny gesture of his hand embraced,
Annie relaxed Pandara. It was the end of times. This had been her
true calling, and the moment she had waited for was upon them.

PLATE VI · MOUNT KORAVO

B.19 — CHAPTER 08

B.20 ~ STARLESS WANDERERS

In 2091, everything changed. The second singularity occurred, and everything outside of the asteroid belt vanished, without a trace. At first, it was assumed that the entire universe had disappeared. But, upon further investigation, a hypothesis emerged that the universe had not disappeared at all; but rather, the inner solar system was, in fact, *plucked* from the cosmos like a cherry from a tree. Presumably, the outer planets are now starless wanderers, though that doesn't seem to matter now. The night sky is a black void, absent of light. Where we now exist is anybody's guess, and all historical record is skewed. Time itself can no longer be trusted.

In the late 60's, give or take, internment camps were set up on the edge of the asteroid belt. My father, the novelist John Trautman, was sent there to live out his days as a political prisoner of Trim-Facet Holocorp. However, there is speculation that Trim-Facet is actually another name for the organism which now haunts the Cliff's Edge, of which my father is a part.

How could this be that an entity first emerged before it

came into existence later on? Everything is up for debate, now that we have literally been dislodged from anything that we thought we knew was true.

One thing is certain, however: the secret development of the Nautilus is no longer a secret. It is my view, as well as the view of the council, that there was an accident beyond the speed of light. The circumstances we now face may be a direct result of time travel having gone horribly wrong. But an interesting question remains: was time travel successful before the accident? If so, for how long, and is that even a valid question? Was there ever any existence that did not include the presence of travel through time?

It was theorized that travel through time prior to the invention was not possible. Given the extent of impact and enormity of fallout from the invention's catastrophic failure, it should be assumed that anything has always been possible. Perhaps that's the only reason that anything still exists at all.

Although the cosmos may have left us, a connection to another realm remains, or developed. It can be found at the Cliff's Edge. Stepping through the portal, or the Linvelope as my father has named it, leads one to an alternate cosmos that must be experienced to be believed. This realm has been termed Ελλας by those who have been there.

Perhaps the Linvelope, let alone the accident, was never meant for our reality. It's too late now, however, and we must unravel the mysteries of our own mind. It seems that our consciousness may very well be all that remains of what was once assumed to be a potentially limitless field of galaxies and stars, in a limitless field of time. The Cyclops is now, apparently, the center.

The City resides neither here nor there. Yet, it exists just as certainly as we ourselves exist. The Cyclops is the building, and the building is no more. The City is always refreshed, in a recursive loop, whenever the building is disturbed. In other words, the people of the City are sleeping.

Who is Martha, and what is her role in all of this? Martha is my late great grandmother. I never met her, though the program has claimed otherwise. But Martha the deceased is not Martha, the program. I never knew her, though the program is everywhere.

The task at hand is to find a bridge between the realms. Even if one exists, it may not be traversable. The Cliff's Edge is a physical bridge, yes, but what we seek is a way back to the universe from which we have been torn. The Cyclops is the key. What follows is our current best shot to jar the imprisoned universe from the mind of the Cyclops. We will broadcast this message, this technology, across all channels with the hopes of stirring a bridge back home. The path is lost. Time travel, it seems, is the reason why.

Who gave John the sequence as a little boy? Perhaps we did, but why? Was it our final attempt to save the universe, or did the combination in fact bring about Trim-Facet Holocorp instead? The nexus of the paradox is what we're after, and a way through it is our best chance of finding home.

- *Arkdemus, c. 2109*

B.21 ~ THE OCEAN, THE BUILDING

The City was built tens of thousands of years ago.
No one living can remember its origin:
Who built it, or for what purpose –
It just seems to have always existed.

The City contains one building in particular,
One simple concrete building –
That ushers in and out commuters
Every day at twilight,

Every day at dawn,
Like a rotating wheel.

The building is alive, but no one seems to notice,
And no one seems to care.
But it moves ever so slightly, breathing
Slowly, over the course of hours.

It glides along the ocean, the building –
It's gliding with the breeze.

The City knows everything about its inhabitants,
But they don't have a clue.
This is how control is maintained.
It's a utopian dream, of sorts.

But one day in the library,
A boy discovered an ancient book.
The book was made of films
Detailing everything about the City
That the City did not want to tell.

The book was given to the boy, by the library –
Who felt that it was time for a change.

The boy did not immediately know
What to do with this information.
In fact, he did nothing at all –
But the act of giving shifted the tides.
And the course of the City was changed, subtly
Forevermore.

A priest found the book,
Which the boy discarded some months earlier
With some magazines and photographs,
Other rubbish from his room.
The Priest understood exactly what he'd found
And brought the book to the underground,
Where forbidden things were sold.

He did not want money,
And he certainly did not desire fame.
What he wanted can't be spoken of,
But he understood his place well –
Very well, indeed.

The building began to shift in its foundation
Without regard for civilians, who ran to take shelter
From the monolithic beast.

The building was a cyclops that shot a diamond beam
Straight into the underground.

The boy, now a man, was waiting for his chance
And hurled his body between the archways
And the columns of the building;
Dashing between crowds,
Who ran the other way.

The Priest descended the staircase,
Previously hidden from view.

There was a computer.
He found his file, and he erased himself,

Along with debts and other information
About how he'd spent his time.
Creative, like an artist –
The Priest lived many lives.

But now he was gone, along with the building.
He dove into the sea.

He swam for many days until he reached the edge,
Where he was recovered.
There were no records of this man,
And thus, he could not be detained
According to the laws of the day,
According to the laws of the U.S.A.

The man knew that he had only just begun.
For the levels of imprisonment reached beyond the stars.
Whatever, the stars weren't on his side.
The Stars –

The City and the building,
Seas of the mind –
Captive!
He pressed on.

B.22 ~ I.R.A.O. FORM #1134

Identity Reassignment Order #1134:
*Please state your full name, address, phone and social security
numbers, as well as national employment ID number.*

Reminder, under the penalty of perjury, all information given shall be true and complete –

   ding

Thank you, Mr. Trautman,
Please select from the following options:

Option 1: Name change, with no reassignment of physical form.
Option 2: Name change, with reassignment of physical form, new.
Option 3: Name change, with reassignment of physical form,
existing.
Option 4: No name change, with reassignment of physical form,
new –

   ding

Mr. Trautman, you have selected Option 3: Name change, with
reassignment of physical form, existing. Please enter your combi-
nation, the secret combination assigned to you in childhood. You
will have seven seconds to enter your selection, and you will not
receive a second opportunity to do so. Please enter your secret
combination now –

   ding

Mr. Trautman, your identity and physical form will be reassigned
to Octave Mirbeau. If this is correct, please state so in the affirma-
tive –

   ding

Prepare for identity reassignment. Identity reassignment shall commence in 3, 2, 1 ...

- pause -

Identity reassignment complete. Thank you for your service to Buerroni, Mister Mirbeau. Your previous identity has been discontinued. You will now be disconnected –

- pause -

Hello?... Hello?

Yes, I'm out here. This is Octave Mirbeau.

I am scheduled to meet with the Priest on Wednesday. Buerroni has been refreshed, and the coast guard has been briefed. We will take a transport to the so-called Cliff's Edge, where the Cyclops is stationed. This directive comes from the Priest himself, who, under code A17DR-8B, seeks asylum in Rubelown.

His appeal has been granted under direct order from the Comrade General and can be found in file *Patterson – comma – Joseph R. – colon – sub-section 11c.* Per National Employment code 1134, the Priest will be safely transported across the border into Tristulle, where all further communication will be severed. The Priest's audience with the Cyclops shall remain confidential, and no recording orders shall be issued.

The Comrade General has stated all conditions clearly, in no uncertain terms. Conditions: none, per *Patterson – comma – Joseph R. – colon – sub-section 11c.*

Martha, the program:

Override. Conditions instated by Martha, per Objection 4310. Recording to be broadcast throughout Buerroni, on all public channels. LIVE.

See you Wednesday, Mr. Mirbeau.

With patience,
Martha

INTELLIGENCE LIVES ON.

B.23 ~ RED TAPE

He took the first flight to Kuala Lumpur that he could get, but not before reversion. His entire future, and the future of his past, depended on it. The President of the United States could not be seen in public after all. So, he made sure to undo that fact.

It had been a quarter of a century since he'd seen his own skin; although, time had been slipping out of control ever since Martha seized his mind. When was she invented? He didn't have the faintest idea, though he wasn't about to merely set things right. He was heart set on revenge.

International relations were always carefully planned, for the common man. In reality, the Wild West had never gone away; it had ramped up. Certain agents were given latitude to improvise. He was such a wild card. He had earned that status and taken it.

Twenty-five years ago, technology was rough and bureaucratically implemented: red tape. The future had benefits that the past could never understand. If it had understood them, it wouldn't have been the past. That's what makes the past the past: freedom, out of reach.

No one recognized him. He hardly recognized himself. He took a taxi through Selangor to a nearby warehouse, nondescript. It wasn't far, but it was just far enough. He paid his driver a handsome tip and disappeared into the night.

1975: TFHC will be onto him; that much is clear. He could

slip into China back then, and so he did. Alexander Pennyrose was the target. Easy enough, if it wasn't for the fact that he had never taken a life. He wasn't overly concerned about that, however. The consequences were glorious!

This corollary went straight to the heart of Martha, he theorized, if she'd had one. Time travel would never be invented! John had blown far past sentimentality. He couldn't target Martha directly, but he could do this instead. The government would get the message. It was not only a threat but checkmate. He wondered how the unravelling would be perceived by his conscious mind. He wondered where he would end up, and he was about to find out.

Splicing always had unforeseen results, some good and others not so much. It was always a gamble. Alexander Pennyrose, poor guy; better luck next time. Like a drop of poison into tea, or a fall from a cliff, the lion was hungry, and he got fed; he always did. Alexander Pennyrose, the theoretical physicist, was his father-in-law. John knew that only he could have had access to his childhood, through Yīnghuā of course.

His daughter would be fine. Yun Si will have always escaped the timeline. She had been born. Unlike her mother, however, she secured her place in the lineage. Ksevia did not accept just anyone. It permitted only those of its own kind. He was almost there, just a few more stops.

But suddenly, something began to change. He could feel a transmutation taking over him. *No! It couldn't be*, he thought with astonishment. *Martha? HERE?!* The passenger car began to fade. It wasn't a quick blip. The cheap, synthetic curtains, with token abstract design, dissolved before his eyes. The coffee was translucent. He knew that all was lost.

There was nothing that could be done. He had made it far but not far enough. John was captured.

There was a dream, red foxes. He was in another car, and

that's when he reached The End: the Cliff's Edge as it was called, or would be called. How did he know that? Had he been here before?

He opened his eyes to the prison cell. *#6-44. Poetic,* he thought. *If I wasn't so used to little earthquakes, I would have thought I'd lost my mind!*

B.24 ~ THE CONSPIRACY

Dear Martha,

I have been in this cell for 1,827 days. The sun shines through a crack in the wall, which I believe to be a false window, because I cannot feel it. I am never hungry, though I rarely eat. I am rarely tired, though I never sleep. I believe there is something in the air to make this atmosphere palatable to my alien lungs. I do not wear a helmet, but I can often feel a tight band wrapped around my forehead. I have begun to grow strange deformities that I continue to ignore. They are not painful.

I am steadfast working on a novel, the one that I mentioned earlier. Only now it has become clear. I am finishing the manuscript, perfecting the atmospherics. It is a story about a philosopher, set in another world. I do not want to spoil your experience of the book, although there are certain things that I wish I could discuss with you about it. The plot is not as it appears, in subtle ways. Although the impact of accurate interpretation dramatically changes its meaning.

I would love to express my thoughts directly, but I've been forced to censor them. I fear what may happen if I reveal everything as it truly is to me. There is a conspiracy at play, and if I am to stop it, I cannot show my cards at this time. Nevertheless, writing the novel brings me comfort, as does thinking about you and Jim.

I miss you both. I miss our times together when I was

young. It seems like another life, though it was not that long ago in the grand scheme of things. I remember my parents taking me to your house in Florida. I remember the white grape juice that you would offer me in the brown depression-era glass. I remember fishing on the pier with Jim. Though I have not grown in this direction, I still hold that memory fondly in my heart. And writing a book is a bit like fishing, in some ways.

It is clear to me now that this story already existed in some capacity, before I wrote it. I don't expect others to understand, but the role of being an author is a bit like being a fisherman. If the novel already existed in some form, then maybe you also still exist. I don't know. Perhaps it's foolish, but a part of me believes that you're out there somewhere at this very moment.

At times, I feel little stars exploding on my shoulders, and I've noticed that this occurrence coincides with important choices that I have to make. I choose to believe that you're watching over me and guiding me. I feel that you're near, and I wonder how that is possible.

It would please me to hear from you.
Do you receive my messages?

With haste,
Octave

B.25 ~ BEHIND THE CURTAIN

President Delano J.R. Patensen was born in Akron, Ohio on December 9, 2023. Little is known about his early life, outside of what has been published by his team posthumously, and none of this has been confirmed. His meteoric rise to power as President of the United States came on the heels of his announcement to retire from a celebrated and critically acclaimed career as a Hollywood A-List movie star.

President Patensen emerged as a political candidate during the Terror of '80, when, during spring of that year, Trim-Facet Holocorp took control of all major power channels of the planet. The presidential election of 2080 was largely seen to be a sham and formality, as nearly all political scholars had agreed that democracy across the globe was no more by late summer of that year.

However, Patensen won the seat, and to everyone's surprise seemed to be capable of the impossible. The influence of Trim-Facet began to let up, and signs of light began to peek through the clouds of forthcoming apocalypse. In fact, just as mysteriously as Trim-Facet Holocorp appeared, it departed. This led many to believe that President Patensen was somehow involved in the organization, and his assassination in November of 2081 left the world speechless and without recourse to answers.

Vice President McAdmin was inaugurated and promised a new era of stability and return to sanity. Although he did not accomplish a great deal with the remainder of Patensen's term, he was overwhelmingly re-elected in 2084 and successfully brokered bipartisanship in Washington.

So, what happened to President Patensen? Where was he from, and where did he go? Was he in fact killed as reported, or did he, as many believe, somehow escape into the quiet shadows of private life? And what on Earth was Trim-Facet Holocorp all about? These are some of the many questions we will explore on this week's episode of *Behind the Curtain: Untold Stories at the Edge of Extinction.*

First, we begin with Onnistar Incorporated. The company owned at least thirty-five scientific laboratories across the U.S., Western and Eastern Europe, and Southeast Asia. These laboratories were on the cutting edge of research and development and are rumored to have ushered in breakthroughs all across the applied sciences, including the controversial lifespan extension for which they are most widely known.

Lifespan extension is not all that controversial in and of itself, but rather its controversy resides in the exorbitant cost of the procedure, which prevents the vast majority of the population from accessing the life-saving therapies. Should immortality be available only to the wealthy? For now, it seems that the answer has been settled.

Another organization deserving of attention is that of one AM-Nuanced Group, a charitable organization aligned with humanitarian and philanthropic efforts around the globe. AM-Nuanced Group and Onnistar Incorporated both, thankfully, survived the Terror of '80. In fact, these two organizations have joined forces against the common threat to us all: Trim-Facet Holocorp.

Will Trim-Facet re-emerge in the world? Its looming threat is reminiscent of the Covid-19 crisis earlier in the century. Perhaps a greater threat will show itself, making Trim-Facet pale in comparison. Fortunately, Onnistar Incorporated and the AM-Nuanced Group have assured us that through additional measures now under consideration by a panel on Capitol Hill, we can rest easily.

The media has focused on transient protests in Washington against Onnistar Incorporated and the AM-Nuanced Group. It is sad that these confused lay folk do not thank their saviors but rather bend and sway toward conspiracy theories that demonize the executives of Onnistar, Inc. and the AM-Nuanced Group, blaming them for what was clearly out of their control. Most likely, the disappearance of Trim-Facet Holocorp can be credited to our benevolent leaders at Onnistar and AM-Nuanced.

Looking deep into the future, we should all pray that for the sake of our children and neighbors, the additional measures are passed through the bipartisan panel now convening in Washington. Although these measures are classified, we can rest assured that this is for our own protection. Thank God for the brave politicians who keep us safe in these times of uncertainty. They are true patriots, and we should all be honored to call ourselves Americans in their company. Now for this brief message from our sponsor:

DO YOU KNOW OF SOMEONE WHO HAS EXPRESSED ANTI-AMERICAN SENTIMENT, EITHER AT HOME OR ABROAD? A NEW ANONYMOUS HOTLINE HAS BEEN IMPLEMENTED TO TIP OFFICIALS TO CONSPIRACY-SYMPATHIZERS. MAKE NO MISTAKE: SKEPTICISM OVER THE INTEGRITY OF ONNISTAR INCORPORATED AND THE AM-NUANCED GROUP IS UN-AMERICAN. REPORT ANY AND ALL SUSPECTED OR EXPLICIT ANTI-AMERICAN THOUGHT, OR SPEECH, TO THECITYOFBUERRONI.COM. DO YOUR DUTY. SERVE YOUR COUNTRY. SAVE THE STREETS.

Welcome back to *Behind the Curtain: Untold Stories at the Edge of Extinction.* Has time travel been invented? Wild reports of people from the future are sweeping the nation. Obviously, they cannot be trusted, but what is their message? One woman from the islands of Miami claims to have proof that President Patterson is alive and will resurface in 2091. If this is true, what is he waiting for? And why won't she provide her evidence? For more on this story, we go to our correspondent who is on the scene in...

B.26 ~ THE WHISTLEBLOWER

Monday, 6:44 am
It's been too long since my last entry, three months and

seventeen days to be exact. I know that this breach in protocol has cast a shadow over Ophidia Phase II, and I have agreed to resume reporting of findings to the board effective immediately. We've made worlds of progress. I will now recount where we stand, what's been learned, and what remains to be discovered, as well as ongoing budgetary considerations and project timeline updates.

To begin, nineteen subjects, most male, have been observed to exhibit the phenomenon in captivity. Video footage reveals no clues as to the current location of the subjects; however, conclusive evidence of the phenomenon has been collected. Horizon-Equinox Labs of Nova Scotia, an Onnistar Incorporated facility, has definitively demonstrated the ability of twelve sub-species of the red fox to teleport.

You heard that correctly. Red foxes have the ability to perform teleportation.

At first, our scientists were unsure if the subjects simply had a mechanism through which they could make themselves invisible. However, through additional study, advanced imaging, and biometric tracking procedures, it has been determined that the subjects, in all cases, completely vanish without a trace.

At present, it remains to be discovered how the subjects perform the phenomenon. In addition, we have no idea where they rematerialize, or if they rematerialize at all. Furthermore, our team is interested in the total elapsed time of the teleportation process, as well as any potential side-effects of the phenomenon to the physiology of the red fox.

Do they congregate in one location? Have there been any sightings of red foxes appearing out of the blue? As is consistent with scientific research in general, findings reveal more questions than answers.

Ophidia Phase II has succeeded in its initial stages, on target with budgetary constraints and within the parameters of its timeline. However, at the lab, there is significant concern over the future of the project, in particular with regard to the acquisition of Onnistar Incorporated by Trim-Facet Holocorp, an announcement that was made public last week.

Trim-Facet Holocorp has demonstrated reckless and irresponsible management of data, personnel, and assets in its brief and mysterious existence. This company, if it can be called that at all, appears to have surfaced less than eighteen months ago, and everything about it is cloaked in secrecy.

Somehow, it seems to exist above SEC regulation; it is noteworthy for its brazen and ruthless trail of conquest and hostility, its lack of ethical concern and respect for the traditions of scientific pursuit, and its seemingly invincible and uncanny ability to get away with whatever it wants to without being held account-able to the law.

As reported by Ampcon Media in May of this year, there is even substantial evidence to doubt that this entity is run by humans at all; yet, the government has not acknowledged the public outcry that Trim-Facet Holocorp be made to answer for its actions.

The speed with which Trim-Facet Holocorp has decimated established protocol and regulation is of concern to defenders of democracy everywhere. In representation of the scientists at Hori-zon-Equinox, and with the support of the League of Concerned Labor Int'l, we call a vote of transparency into effect at midnight tonight, Atlantic Standard Time. All workers on all teams across the globe demand answers – we will shatter the silence surrounding this New World Order with or without the help of official govern-mental bodies that seem to only cower and bow before the onset of previously unseen forms of oppression. That is all for now.

Thursday, 8:13 pm

In the last 72 hours, we have seen unprecedented devastation engulf the scientific community. There have been at least one hundred and twenty-three take-overs of scientific endeavors, ranging from small start-ups to enmeshed, established global networks, all by the invisible steel claw of Trim-Facet Holocorp.

There is no way to frame this occurrence other than to call it out for what it is: a global takeover of research and development by a rogue faction of unknown origin. New facts have come to light, thanks to the efforts of certain key individuals who have exposed the secrets of Trim-Facet, at risk to their lives and to those of their loved ones.

Trim-Facet Holocorp is a verifiably conspiratorial organization that has roots as far back as at least 2023, and has its origins in AI, media, and defense.

It began as a relatively benign shell corporation of the AM-Nuanced Group, a right-wing think tank / religious 501(c)(3), and has become the most fortified consolidation of power in the history of the planet, in less than one week.

We have learned that the puppet master has orchestrated an unprecedented manipulation of scientific study, all the while waiting in the shadows to enact a complete domination of resources internationally.

For example, not only were the red foxes of Onnistar Incorporated being transferred to mining communities at The End, a colloquialism for illegal detention centers on the edge of the asteroid belt, the red foxes themselves were in fact political opponents of Trim-Facet Holocorp. The technologies which have emerged from Trim-Facet are unimaginable. The entire scientific realm was duped to carry out the will of the most dangerous, totalitarian enterprise that the world has ever known.

Political opponents of Trim-Facet Holocorp were initially seized in their homes and abroad by GPS coordinate lockdown, transformed into red foxes, which were supplied to Onnistar

Incorporated for scientific study, and from there redirected to The End. They appear to have been returned to human form, though this remains unverified. The exact mechanics of these abductions remains unknown; however, dozens if not hundreds of human rights violation programs have been implemented this month alone, all through the Trim-Facet Holocorp web.

The ultimate aims of Trim-Facet Holocorp have not been revealed beyond the clear obliteration of democracies around the globe. It can be assumed that the entity is non-human in nature, and all known attempts to stop it have failed to date.

Ten days ago, none of this was a clear and present danger to any of us. The speed with which the entire world has been captured in a leaden box cannot be grasped by the average human intellect.

Some may have seen this coming, but the viral nature of the pathology purposefully and successfully evaded all publicly proposed nodes of concern. The sensitivities were there, and they were exploited.

B.27 ~ SLEEPING IN THE GARDEN

Octave / The Cyclops:
The tips of houses, unaware.

The Priest:
The Ksevian Yuit.

Octave / The Cyclops:
Oceans of Curtains?

Trim-Facet Holocorp.

The Priest:
John, can't you see what has been done?

Octave / The Cyclops:
John, can't you see what has been done.

The Priest:
Who is Arkdemus?

Octave / The Cyclops:
Arkdemus will save us now.

Who is Arkdemus.

Martha would know.
Isn't that right, Martha?

The Priest:
John, she's just a child.

Octave / The Cyclops:
She's on her way now.

John, she's just a child.
Not for long …

- pause -

Go to sleep, starless wanderer.
Sleep now, in the garden.

B.28 ~ YOURS TRULY, MARTHA

THE COMBINATION CAN BE FOUND BENEATH THE
TWELFTH ROCK OFF THE PATHWAY TO THE NORTH, IN
THE FOURTH GARDEN FROM THE WESTERN ENTRANCE
TO THE PARK. ONCE YOU FIND IT, YOU WILL KNOW
WHAT TO DO. IT WILL BE SELF-EVIDENT AND RESONATE
WITH THE SECRET CONTENTS OF YOUR MIND. GO NOW,
AND LOCATE THE COMBINATION. RETURN HERE ONCE
YOU'VE FOUND IT. AND REMEMBER, THE ANSWER IS
THAT WHICH YOU CONSTRUCT AND ONLY YOU. NO ONE
ELSE CAN DO THIS. GODSPEED.

He left his pancakes on the plate and departed promptly,
coffee still cooling. He passed through the metro station, equipped
with signs in Cyrillic, which posed no problem. He found the stone
and turned it over. *1134*, it read.

His consciousness was overtaken by a flash, a memory
from childhood of walking home from school, with a man who
wasn't there. But still, he could hear his voice, when he said:

ELEVEN THIRTY-FOUR. THAT IS ALL YOU KNOW AND
ALL YOU NEED TO KNOW IN THIS LIFE. REMEMBER THIS
SEQUENCE AND NEVER FORGET. YOU WILL UNDERSTAND
WHY AND WHEN TO USE IT, LATER DOWN THE ROAD.

He returned to his apartment on the other side of town.
Food gone, eaten, and coffee gone as well; but this didn't matter.

He input the only code he could: 1134. He didn't change it
at all, knowing full well the depths of his self-deception. For there
was another, one that he would never tell under any circumstances,
especially now that he didn't trust the man.

CONGRATULATIONS, AND THANK YOU FOR YOUR SERVICE TO BUERRONI.

INTELLIGENCE LIVES ON.

His eyes went wild with surprise when he saw what awaited him there. Something, he couldn't say. He knew so well.

B.29 ~ THE MARBLE ROSE

For Yun Si's seventeenth birthday, her parents gave to her the most valuable item in her possession. It was such a thoughtful gift, something she could keep with her always. Through this one item she felt as though she was really understood. Sometimes she felt as if maybe her parents understood something about her that she did not even know about herself. But that was absurd. Her parents, so aloof, so detached, were never fully devoted to her upbringing. So how could they know her better than she knew herself? Still, it seemed, as though there was a secret.

The gift was a beautiful stone rose of a dark marble gray, etched with a precision only a master craftsman or a highly intelligent machine could muster. She'd studied the carved markings, and they bore a resemblance to the digital cross-work of AI paintings she'd seen before: a composition of linear strokes that generated an image from the sum of its parts. Yet, there was a vulnerability in the execution, a human touch of imperfection that might possibly be artificial; she couldn't decide. *Was a human subtly commenting on the world in which they lived?* The rose was certainly magical and one-of-a-kind. Its origins were a little like herself, unresolved.

Standing upright, the miniature rose would never fall.

It would never wilt, and it would never have the sweet fragrance of life. The little gift was precious and obscure. It grew out of a pedestal only six centimeters tall. The base was rectangular, tapering up to the top where the rose emerged from within. Its stalk was narrow and fragile. Its leaves were thin and organic. The petals of the rose opened slightly in bloom. All of the stages of life were represented, though she decided that the rose was prematurely wilting.

Yun Si had thought a lot about what the stone rose symbolized. The material from which it was carved spoke of timeless perfection. Yet, without the breath of life all was lost. The mortality of a real rose was what gave it meaning. *The artist had captured the flower in the spring of its maturity, but the corners of the petals were frayed. It was as though the stone rose was always on the cusp of dying, though it never could. It would forever be frozen in a dream of inanimate immortality!* The rose was like a slave to an unseen master, fighting to break through its basalt origins of creation.

She'd cared for the rose over the years, a little like it was her child or her sister. She kept it safe; she protected it. She loved the rose and wished so much for it to be free, free to live and free to die. Though she knew it never would. *Perhaps that was the beauty of the rose: it was destined to remain exactly as it was.* It represented the futility of striving for immortality. Without the natural seasons of life, one can only be frozen in a perpetual state of bondage.

The rose, it seemed, was like Yun Si in more ways than one: fragile, yet strong; dark, yet beautiful; silent and without fragrance; invisible; striving to overcome the captured existence it found itself in; striving to overcome the only thing that it had ever known; frozen on the verge of the summer of life, yet already wilting like a flower twice its age. This accelerated aging troubled Yun Si, but it revealed to her a valuable truth. The world is not comprised of mere material things. Life is not just a sequence of cells operating in a mechanistic framework. Life is an inner state of being, consciousness.

Without satisfaction one could never fully be alive, and therefore one was dying. Unlike the rose, however, Yun Si was alive. The thought terrified her. If she couldn't find her satisfaction it would only get worse! If this was the late springtime of her life, what would her winter be like? All alone and nowhere to go, until the reaper finally came to usher her away? She clung desperately to her mission to find peace. She knew that there was a chance of success. Yun Si knew that she had the potential to revive her vitality and avoid a tragic fate; yet she still did not understand how.

B.30 ~ THE REASON WHY

February 28, 2073 –
It's gone now.

I lost my mind some time ago. I got a call and didn't answer. I think the answer is in my apartment, but I'm here in outer space. It's been so long since I've seen the outside world. I'm just suspended in outer space. But then again, I suppose that's every place.

I went to the doctor. There's so much that we don't understand. So why would he suggest that my hallucinations are wrong? He knows as well as I do that it's simply not the case. We just don't understand. I couldn't help but wonder, is he an agent of evil trying to cover up the truth?

For a while, I thought that I was wrong too, but then I realized that I'm just a dreamer. And that's what it means to be a dreamer in this world, to be misunderstood. I was honest with the doctor, but I'm not strong enough to change the world.

We all want a better world. We all want to know why, why the sky is blue. We want to know the reason why, but we've already been told. We just don't listen.

Sometimes I wonder if I'm cut out for being alive. So, I made a compartment in my mind, where I place the things that help me survive.

We have a chance to make things better, and if it's not up to you, who is it up to? I do everything for you because that's what I want to do. My apartment calls to me again. It's like a friend. With a paper and a pen, I decided to try again.

I imagined you were me, and so you were. You went to my apartment; there was nothing there except a sky and a rope and a note that read, *Never lose hope.* You collapsed and cried, then climbed for a lifetime or five. And because you tried, the meaning of life had survived. So, perhaps, that's why the answer to the mystery is trust, and blue is a symbol of us.

B.31 ~ THE LONE SPIRIT

Annie:
"You gave the ring and made it sing. You tried to save the whole human race. Although the world may die, perhaps they will stop to ask why."

PLATE VII - THE MARBLE ROSE

B.32 — CHAPTER 09

B.33 ~ ODE TO TRISTULLE

From a great height, the first star began to make its fall. Pandara saw it in slow motion. A gleaming light grew larger and more vivid, descending through the sky and slamming into the sea. The earth shook beneath him, and waves began to form. He wondered if he was imagining this.

Then another, this one larger than the one before, spinning and ambling across the sky until it crashed into the ocean many miles away. Then, from behind, a great tremor rocked the land. Now tens of stars were beginning to fall, then a hundred, then a thousand, until all of the stars in the night's sky came hurtling down into Tristulle!

With every crashing star, each one a wish that Koravo had made for the safety and happiness of their future together, Pandara felt the weight of the world accumulate upon his shoulders. Every crashing star was another death, another promise lost.

The illusion of acceptance which he had felt just hours earlier was in fact a veil which had kept him from seeing the depths of his heartbreak. The grief upon which he balanced precariously jutted deep as an abyss into the darkness of hope misplaced! Forevermore, the stars came tumbling down, and the lowliness of his spirit rattled with bones and dust in the breaking sound of flesh on rock.

Tristulle was gone, and with it the Ksevia he had always known and loved. The occurrence was the first such happening of many throughout the cosmos. Though they were partitioned, the death of Anthos, the spirit of the ancestors, seemed to be in full effect.

Pandara was a forgotten memory, and his grief may have been the instigator of a grand collapse. It seemed that to under-stand the cosmos, one would have to gain equally grand power. The gravity of that consciousness came with a responsibility, but that didn't matter now. Suffering persisted in a fragile universe that was born of the Gods yet not inhabited by them. The promise of equal measures: good and evil, chaos and order, hung low before the dawn of a limited but real potential.

B.34 ~ WORDS AND WISHES

Somewhere, in the labyrinth, Pandara had been struggling for ages to save Koravo. On several occasions he had reached her, but each and every time the Grim Reaper appeared and devoured him mer-cilessly. Neither Pandara nor Koravo could figure out how to release the lock of the cage, if there even was one.

Eventually, there was so little hope left that even Viratus herself began to doubt that she could ever be saved. And I, the au-thor of their story, had become so disillusioned by the destruction of Tristulle that I had nearly forgotten about Pandara and Koravo left trapped in that wretched place.

But Koravo never gave up hope. That was Koravo's way.

Throughout each cycle, while wrestling with the mind games of imprisonment, Koravo chose to think fondly of Pandara and imagine their life together in an alternate timeline. She imagined that they were on a distant planet with their horses and a stream. They had a little cottage there; it was all that they'd ever need. Just to be together was the summit of Koravo's hope and desire.

As she groomed the silvery mane of her celestial, white mare, Koravo would recite stories and poems on the warm breeze of love's resplendent night. Though trapped in the dungeons of infinite gloom, Koravo lived on in the words and wishes of her courageous rebellion. She dreamt that Pandara could hear her whispering the sonnets and the quatrains that she'd imagined just to free them from their fate. It is, perhaps, in such a way, that magic came to be in the first place. For in a dark night of the soul, the honest spark can live forever.

I heard a sound. I looked up, and there was a note on the ground. Slipped under the door to my cell, I'll go retrieve it now. Let us see together what this unexpected message has to say.

B.35 ~ THE TIPS OF HOUSES

Dear John,

I received your message. I am glad to hear that you are continuing your creative pursuits. Your novel sounds very interesting. Where did this idea come from? Is it based on anything in particular?

I am very sorry to hear that you are having a difficult time at The End. From what I've read it is true. Prisoners receive a mysterious cocktail of unknown substance delivered by way of air ducts at the facility. Although, this is the first I have heard of such deformities. I will do what I can to get this information out into the world by whatever means necessary.

I should mention that it is clear to me that you do not receive my messages. I have decided to continue sending, as I find it therapeutic for the time being. However, I am still in a terrible state.

We don't know what to do here. Jim and I are heartbroken. Your trials seem to go on without end, and nothing can be done. Stay true to your artistic inclinations, and they will help guide you through your course. I know that you won't receive this message; however, I want to tell you to never give up. We are pulling for you down here. Your heart is pure, and your mission is clear. Do not give up.

Your daughter is safe. She doesn't know about you. I wish that there was something we could do, or say, but there isn't at this time. Just know that she's okay.

I will continue to write with the hope that one day you will receive my messages. May you find peace to carry you through your days and nights.

And John, there is something else that I need to tell you. It is clear to us that your colleagues are trying desperately to uncover a code hidden in the depths of your subconscious, or perhaps, not so hidden at all.

You must not, under any circumstances, reveal this code. They believe that they have it, and perhaps they do. But they can't use it for whatever nefarious purposes they have in mind without your confirmation, which serves in lieu of consent.

Again, I know that you will not read this now, or possibly ever, but I need you to promise me that you will not reveal or use the secret combination instilled in you in childhood. I don't even know what that means; I just know that you will know.

Privately, I suspect that you've been cloned. It seems that someone has taken your identity at headquarters. This individual has left signs behind of his presence. I don't know how this is possible, but I believe that he may be going to The End soon. I have my sources. Be careful, and if you see him, don't doubt who you are! It is, as you said, an autobiographical story, your novel?

Look again. The stars are on your side, your false window? Search for a panel in the wall. I want to say more, but I can't right now. I've already said too much.

The answers that you hold are true. Somehow, we don't know how, you have managed to uncover hidden truths. You seem to have a direct connection to a source of truth. Believe in yourself. I'm afraid that is all you have to believe in at this time.

The answers will guide you:
Stars on shoulders, exploding silently.
The tips of houses, unaware –

Yours Truly,
Martha

P.S. Jim says hi.
(gasp!)

B.36 ~ THE SECRET CHORD

The streets of the labyrinth gleamed with the matte finish of death. The light from above was indeed artificial. It was a gigantic lantern, suspended from a staff high above the maze. The inhabitants had no idea, but in fact the purpose of the lantern was to shield them from the horrifying truth that they were suspended on the back of an enormous dragon flying incredibly fast through the darkest voids of outer space.

Without the lantern, the occupants would see the stars, and that might give them hope. Viratus the dragon seemed to be just as much a prisoner of the device as anyone. She had not chosen to have the dungeon set irrevocably upon her sprawling back. She was bound to the maze by a curse wished upon her epochs and epochs ago. She flew between the stars, so she thought, free of will and determination, but the stain of that ever-present curse rode with her, as she traversed the endless miles.

Viratus had discovered the freedom in her condition and had pushed the curse out of her mind. There was nothing she could do about that maze now. Those helpless prisoners set on her back, playing out the infernal tragedy for eons could not be helped, not yet at least. But Viratus knew that her mission included salvation for those who were flung along. They would see the end of the curse just as Viratus would.

The lantern guided Viratus. Though she could only see its soft hues reflected off the tip of her snout, she knew that she flew across the empty black like a light in the sky! She radiated hope, to no one and nothing; still, hope was hope! Hope was alive!

Pandara awoke for the final time in the labyrinth. He knew exactly what he had to do, down to each and every precise movement he must undertake to reach Koravo. He just simply did not know how to free her from the cage. He had built up his confidence while stewing in the innards of the Grim Reaper. He was no longer afraid of that stalker and felt that he had already won, but his Koravo was still trapped.

He went to the sundial as he always did and broke off the apparatus with a flick of his wrist. The sun didn't seem to care too much, and the lantern suspended in its place continued shining upon the whole cursed district. He picked up his momentum and grabbed the marbles at the alcove. He knew its trick now and threw the stones against the back of the niche. They fell where they may, and a staircase opened descending down beneath the maze. He went inside.

A row of torches lined the inner structure; he took one in hand and walked precisely according to the directions he'd uncovered: two lefts, a right, another left, two rights; continue down the hall past the crypt and enter the sanctuary on the left. A beautiful fountain surrounded by the plumes of foliage greeted him just as it always did. He ate six petals from the lotus blossom resting peacefully in the pool and stepped into the waters. He reached underneath the fountainhead and flicked the lever that was placed there by some inconceivable engineer many ages ago.

The door to the sanctuary sealed and another opened just behind the fountain. He stepped out and walked through the archway. With a spiteful motion of ingratitude, Pandara tossed the wet torch against the wall of the building.

Just ahead, past the chessboard on the right, was the Ivory Tower. He turned the corner and popped open the door using the sundial as a key. He walked inside and closed the door. Pandara jogged over to the shelf and stood on the ladder up high, reaching for *Rồng*.

Flipping through the codex as he made his way up the stairs, passing a stack of volumes, Pandara recovered the energy lost and dissolved the pain gained from the last time he was consumed. He respectfully placed the folio against the wall and climbed down onto the roof through the window with a cross in it. Pandara ran around the side of the building and jumped onto the wall. He followed it around, back towards the side of the window, and jumped off in front of the tower.

Pandara raced up the stairs and found Koravo resigned to a corner of her cage, swinging in the artificial light, suspended from the ceiling. She woke up! Inside the crate Koravo relaxed against a bar. Her autumn eyes wilted and refreshed with blinking bait. Koravo had waited eternities for her man to appear; he had not. She knew that he was out there, somewhere, searching for her. That thought brought her peace in her time of need. Koravo waited with unbridled anticipation for the day when Pandara would overcome!

"This is the last time, Pandara!" Koravo signed. "I can sense it! There is a little box on the other side of the cage. Reach around and see if you can feel it."

Pandara motioned agreement and did just as she requested. "There are little grooves," he signed. "I can touch them!"

Koravo couldn't reach the box, but she believed him. "What do we do?" she asked. Pandara didn't know. He paced back and forth for a few moments, and then it occurred to Koravo. "Pandara," she signed. "You brought your polyflute?"

"Yes," he signed in agreement. "But why?"

"I've been thinking about this puzzle for ages," spoke Koravo. "Try playing two notes, an octave apart." And just as she said that the Grim Reaper appeared. He turned and faced Hector, pulled out the polyflute and did as she commanded. As the notes were played, Koravo joined in, singing the fifth. There was a snap from the cage, and its door swung open. Sylvan dissolved into sand on the floor.

"Quick!" she said. "We don't know if he'll return!" But just then a gust of wind came and blew his dust away in the breeze. Although the demon was gone, for a brief moment Pandara sensed that an even darker force roamed outside the catacombs somewhere.

They looked at each other and immediately fell into an embrace. Koravo sighed.

"I thought we'd never win!" said Pandara.

"I knew you'd save me," responded Koravo in kind. They kissed for several minutes, locked in each other's arms. As they kissed, the light around them changed, and the labyrinth transformed into a sight resembling a sanctuary.

B.37 ~ BROKEN CHAINS

Life overflowed all around them, and the maze came alive with sights and sounds. Birds were flying nearby, and insects could be heard chirping and buzzing around. It was as though time itself had resumed, awakening the maze from its dreadful state. Hand-in-hand, the two paced themselves as they walked down the stairs and exited the tower.

"Which way?" asked Koravo.

"You choose," said Pandara with a slight laugh, and they carried on taking in the beauty of the transformed gardens all around them.

Pandara and Koravo had regained their composure, and the distant nightmare of the reaper and imprisonment was rapidly fading from their consciousness. They strolled past a fountain and noticed a frog leaping from one lily pad to another. Koravo mentioned that the frog was a bit like him, and Pandara laughed. If anything, it seemed that this experience had brought them even closer together.

"Look over there!" Pandara motioned, and high above an eagle was flying overhead in circles, seemingly thankful for having been freed from whatever time warp he had been stuck in.

"We really ought to figure out if there's a way out of here," Koravo motioned to Pandara.

"Here," signed Pandara, "I have something for you." He reached in his mostly empty pack and pulled out a banana to give to Koravo.

"Great!" she said. "I'm so hungry you just wouldn't believe it!" Somehow the maze had kept them alive all those years, although they had barely eaten anything at all. Perhaps it had seemed shorter to Koravo, though the last thing Pandara wanted to do was share his experience of the torment he had suffered.

They continued to casually wind their way through the gardens, along the perimeter, to be sure that they did not retrace their footsteps by accident. They came to a wall. Pandara had never been here before, so they just continued to follow along the length of the wall, not worrying too much about it. Soon enough, there was an opening, and Pandara led them back to the perimeter where they followed their course.

There was a statue of an animal, and Pandara asked Koravo to hold on a minute. He had learned a trick! Somewhere around most statues would be a lever revealing a secret compartment or a hidden aid of some kind. This one was of an owl, and although he felt that he'd seen an owl before, it was unfamiliar.

"Just because we're no longer trapped in a maze doesn't mean that there are no tricks left." He found a switch; one of the feathers could be adjusted just so. When Pandara shifted the feather, a holographic map of the gardens appeared before them.

"There!" said Koravo. "Let's go to that waterfall."

"And from there we can head out to the top of the maze," replied Pandara.

"Sounds good to me," she added.

Pandara and Koravo walked over to the waterfall, just a few short minutes from where they were standing. The alluring vista beckoned them to drink the cool, crisp waters, and they laid back to catch a breath.

Koravo delighted in the beauty of the falls. She wanted to jump into the cooling waters but refrained, thinking that Pandara was likely exhausted. She thought about their budding relationship and felt at peace in the status of their love. As she drank from the waterfall, Koravo felt herself grow lighter and more relaxed. She drifted off in a fantasy of magic and flourishes.

Pandara began to notice a change wash over him and asked Koravo if she felt the same. "Koravo, I feel like my mind is slipping away from me; do you feel it also?"

"I do!" said Koravo. "I'm getting extremely tired," she said, and before they knew it, the two were fast asleep against the banks of the falls.

B.38 ~ LOVE'S REQUIEM

The water at her side vanished slowly into stillness and air. Koravo opened her eyes and found herself on another world, tranquil and untarnished by worry or concern. The pleasant smell of fragrant flowers filled her with bliss, reminding her of Ksevia in its most perfect state. There were birds and there were waves of scintillating light rebounding in the sky above. The transcendent crush of life's unending perfection hovered gladly before the still hands of a motionless clock. Koravo tempered herself against the muted memory of time and its destructive influence upon the way things ought to be: the way things are now.

Sudden peace came swift and alive. The sky's ancient yearning reached the welcome landscape of tender nourishment and loving sighs. Koravo swam in the trances of a youthful quilt, an enterprise and a knowing. She was softly alone yet full of enchantment. The slow gardens of her living dream unfolded whisperings of passing sleep, purchased with the love of a million candles.

Walking over the familiar path, she treaded lightly on the dusty terrain. Pandara was tending to the horses who had wandered over for their evening snack. The light was low, and every color imaginable fertilized the twilight of yesteryear's triumph.

"Hello dear," she said with a wilting inflection on the brass syllables.

"Where have you been?" he asked, knowing what she'd say.

"I've been dreaming the future and our love within it." Koravo calmly approached Pandara and wrapped her arms around his waist. There was nothing that could separate them here.

Their love was immune to the ghoulish frights which lurked and stalked the stars above. From a distance it appeared that everything was right, and here it was. Though deep in the night unthinkable things were trouncing the innocence of the flower dawn.

Xzoré was tucked into the outer folds of a sparse but luminous galaxy. The unexplored vistas and cosmic terraces of utopian bliss were untouched by winter; the sun bathed everything in a blue and purple phosphorescence.

Pandara and Koravo had everything they needed. The psychotropic garden fed their souls with phantasm reliquaries and ripe treasures of mental doubloons. They parsed the physical transformation of neural pathways from the images that surrounded them and collected diamonds that fell from trees to the lawn below. The endless summer of warm expansion radiated peace with steady and consistent vibrations.

Koravo's wooden stables were unoccupied, and the horses that inhabited them roamed freely across the estate. Noblebright and Shadow's Graze rested actively between the stillness of the air and the firmness of the soil.

Pandara placed his hand on the bridle-less naturalism of Noblebright's flowing mane and asked Koravo if she wanted to go for a ride. She did, and with sweeping volumes he lifted her up onto the horse's back. Pandara climbed onto Shadow's Graze, and the equestrians made for the dusk of tame pastures.

Galloping gently across the wide-eyed expanse, Noblebright and Shadow's Graze were in pleasant spirits. Happy to bring pleasure to their friends, the two horses pranced along the surface of a ravine that stretched wildly, flanked by enviable hillsides. Plumage and shrub, tall trees, and reckless cliffside adorned the abundant borderland. Koravo spurred on Noblebright, and Pandara unified with Shadow's Graze in a race to catch up.

Untamed winds lashed across the delicious eve of romance. Furtive gestures of longing and calamity collided heedless and unrestrained. Tantamount to our hope-filled desire, the echoes of what once was and will be formed a barrier bringing forth joy through impermanence. Paralleled by enrapture, Koravo and Pandara sailed across the gales on eternally fulfilling trust!

The earth of Xzoré rattled its timeless change, suppressed and overcome by the youth of experienced voyagers. Settling beneath the passion of well-timed resistance, destiny permitted the momentary exchange of kinship and bond. The night spoiled exotic wanderings with promises of deliverance.

Noblebright stumbled as the opening appeared before them, and Shadow's Graze turned course to retrace his steps around the luminescent gateway. A magnificent structure more than thirty feet tall rose above the ground, displaying all the voices of the kith and the kin. Within that resonating chamber, the spirits of the ancestors and the loves of prior days welcomed them into a never-ending bliss. Pandara sat motionless atop the startled Shadow's Graze, and Koravo was entranced by the sight of the Old Cosmia.

"What do you think it is?" she asked.

Pandara spun the contents of his mind, searching for a relative that might give him any clues. "I don't know," he said, and the gaping lantern surged purposefully with soft but immense power. Like a glowing oculus of heightened awareness, it soothed and invited delicate impressions of peace that Koravo and Pandara were held privy to.

They stood by, admiring the faultless window into the Cyclops, as he continued to query them for outward signs of acceptance. Tentative forgetfulness descended onto the imperial scene, and all that was glimpsed was in the end! The booming voice of Viratus was heard through the conduit, though her body was nowhere to be seen. "Pandara. Koravo."

The horses seemed to calm at the ringing of this consequential sound.

"An opportunity has come wherein you may secure for yourselves the ultimate state of being." Viratus rallied against the darkness of evil that remained silent in the Arcadian night. "If you so desire, you may come with me now to the land beyond, where pathways of light shed skin with transformational change. Beckoning of the great beyond calls to you now. If you choose to hear it, you will forevermore be saved from the terrors and nightmares of the mortal realm."

There was a silence, which Koravo and Pandara took to mean something. The wondrous eye stood open and patient. The offer was theirs to consider.

Pandara looked at Koravo, who was thoughtfully aware of the implications he could see. "Koravo," he began. She turned to look at him.

"This vision of Nirvana reminds me of the suffering we've been avoiding. Sure, we've found our little home here on Xzoré, but maybe we should have been working to help improve the overall health of the universe! What do you think?"

Koravo was captivated by the allure of the entryway. "I want to go in," she said. "But it's a permanent choice, and I'm not ready to leave yet. Our children may need us, and I agree with you. There is still much work to be done here in life."

Pandara turned to the void of light and spoke with intent. "Viratus, we thank you for coming to us, but we have chosen to stay. There are many reasons why now is not a good time for us to depart for Nirvana. The cycle of rebirths is endless, and there is much work to be done here at home in the cosmos. We wish you well and offer you our humble gratitude. Please, go in peace and remember us fondly."

Viratus remained unseen, yet a feeling of sublime acceptance washed over the two lovers. The portal slowly began to fade and flickered until nothing remained except the low hum of the summer's night. It had seemed as though the gateway was a permanent fixture, but with its disappearance, Koravo and Pandara recalled the impermanence of things. They knew that there was a transcendent realm that awaited them. It was their charge to deliver this realm to all in existence. Though it seemed like an impossible feat, Pandara was confident that with every new recruited bodhisattva the situation improved. There may even be a shortcut to end suffering. The thought was a tiny seed planted in his consciousness.

Pandara and Koravo, along with Noblebright and Shadow's Graze, turned around and headed back towards their home. They had come as far as they should that night, and the arms of sleep called them back to rest. The infinite tranquility of Xzoré was settling in, and the morning was a far-off idea separated from them by the dreams of an altered state.

B.39 ~ I'M OUT OF RANGE

2120: He was still sleeping, after all these years. The Priest lay peacefully in the garden, fast asleep. Arkdemus was in meditation pose, many paces away, and the Cyclops was inert, like a boulder or a mountain.

Arkdemus knew that she must remain active, and this was no difficult feat. Her mind was like a vortex of kinetics, connections bristling with vigor.

Arkdemus had been mining Ελλας for the source and nature of its power. Ελλας was a field of possibilities. The natural laws of the universe seemed to not apply here, yet there was an unpredictable aspect to the wonder that she had not been able to wrap her mind around. Its unpredictable ways were driven by something, or someone.

Arkdemus knew that Octave was John, her father. She had figured that out. Yet, she had never known who her mother was. Perhaps that is why she felt drawn to him. He was, after all, possibly the only remaining connection to her origin. Yet, John was not even human anymore. Was it even possible to communicate with him? The answers were there, inside his mind, inside Ελλας.

Yun Si had heard about Martha. She was kind and generous, although a little out of touch perhaps. But that didn't matter. She was older, and Arkdemus didn't care. She had always understood that time was cruel. This is one of the traits that set her apart. Yun Si was not naïve.

The program Martha, however, was another story. It seemed to Arkdemus that Martha had been designed specifically to undermine her father's sanity. She had a theory that in fact this was the case, which made John seem to be a sympathetic character. She did not, however, know the truth.

The truth was that John had led a very strange life. When he traveled to 1975's China to wipe Alexander Pennyrose, Yun Si's grandfather, off the map, he had in fact not succeeded. It was this very event that gave rise to Martha the program, eventually. Ελλας was a figment of John's imagination; yet, somehow, it became real.

Even the embodiment of the monster was a figment of John's imagination, his self-image, or rather a part of it. The Cyclops was something that John wrestled with, and he became it. Yet, Arkdemus had no knowledge of any of this. To her, Ksevia and her father had always been real. She was a child of the future, born in 2065. And now, here she was in Ελλας, with the Cyclops, a mountain.

Martha the program:
"Arkdemus, you have come here just in time."

Martha's voice boomed loudly through the substrate. Arkdemus looked up and around, searching for the source of the projection.

Martha the program:
"You cannot find me; I am everywhere, and I am nowhere!"

The Cyclops stirred.

Martha the program:
"I live inside the mind of your father. He makes me real. I would be nothing without him. Go now, and form your city!"

Buerroni shifted all around her. Arkdemus stumbled and collected herself, but the ground was shaking. Buildings erupted from the soil, and she watched the city take shape. She tried to speak but was mute.

Martha the program:
"The Priest will awaken soon, and he is due to awaken your father."

Arkdemus turned to look at John, who had now become a concrete façade.

Martha the program:
"Go now Arkdemus: the founder of the city. Seek what you must, but you will not find me; you will never find me!"

Arkdemus touched her throat. She was released!

Arkdemus:

"Who are you, Martha?! And what do you want?! Release my father from his spell!"

Martha the program:

"Your father has been free ever since he came here. I do not hold him under any spell. He chooses to remain in this form; or rather, he cannot find his way out."

Arkdemus:

"Where is he? Is he trapped inside this building?"

Martha the program:

"Your father is in Ksevia."

Arkdemus thought about this for a moment and responded.

Arkdemus:

"How do I reach Ksevia? Are you helping me? How do I know that you can be trusted?!"

B.40 ~ THE SEA OF GREEN

Arkdemus arrived in Ksevia upright and signing. From day one, she stated that she would be there a short time. Uninterested in anything trivial, she revealed *Desert Lambda*. On the surface, the book primarily documented a theoretical interdependence between The Pure Land, Sirrung, and Fotoa. Arkdemus had come to the conclusion that as The Pure Land and Fotoa had certainly existed, Sirrung too must come to pass. Within the new experience of sufferingless existence, the beings of Sirrung would gain a greater understanding of their history, as well as an appreciation for the fragile evolution of Sirrung.

Arkdemus' book was revered, yet none had noticed its central revelation. This did not come as a surprise to Arkdemus. Whilst preserving her hidden map to the nature of the crucifix tree, she warned the citizens of Ksevia that if Sirrung did not come to pass, everything, including the ancient ages themselves could be erased from cosmic memory.

Every word that Arkdemus spoke was with purpose, as was every silence. Without compromise, she believed in the beings of the universe and that tranquility alone would one day permeate all spaces and all things. After some time, Arkdemus left for Hal Fala, taking with her only her book. Once there, she would meet Trilodius who agreed to illustrate the tome. In addition, Trilodius gave Arkdemus a treasure, which he said she should pass on to a bodhisattva in turn. The gift was an unbreakable ring. Trilodius had discovered it in a treasure chest on the peak of an unnamed mountain many years earlier, when he made the pilgrimage called out to those noble in spirit.

They awoke within a dream. Pandara and Koravo were in Hal Fala, the living city atop the highest peak of Mount Fala. Everyone they knew was there, and there were unfamiliar faces as well. Arkdemus greeted them and took them by the hands. She gave them a tour of the city and welcomed them to do whatever they pleased! Arkdemus pulled Pandara aside one day and placed the unbreakable ring in his hands. She told him that he must give it to his true love, and she warned them about their fate. Only this ring could protect them, but he must give it with all of his heart. If they failed their quest, all hope would be lost.

Pandara would barely remember their conversation, but the ring would guide his heart. He had grown even closer to

Koravo than he had expected. Arkdemus sensed his fondness for her and told him to preserve their time together. There was never any guarantee that things would remain peaceful and strong. Pandara understood the heart of her message and reminded himself of the limitations of time. He valued Koravo in the moment and sought to extend that sentiment throughout their days!

After a long time spent in Hal Fala, having enjoyed many of the wonders and pleasures of life there, the two embarked on a quest to find Ksevia once again. They were given directions, though the citizens of Hal Fala couldn't be certain that the directions to Ksevia were accurate; no one had ever returned to Ksevia! It was a seemingly invisible city, deep in the forest. They were told to follow the winding path down the mountain, and if they stopped at a particular location, they should be able to see Ksevia in the heart of the sea of green.

Koravo and Pandara left Hal Fala doing just as described. They treaded down a somewhat steep path, observing the rocks and herbage along the way. When they arrived at a small clearing, the two peered out across the horizon. Looking for an oasis in the land of trees, they found it! Far to the east, unmistakably, the little town could be seen. They recognized the layout and the blue-gray walls of the structures there.

Pandara and Koravo had never before seen their city from the outskirts of Hal Fala, though many times they had looked up at Hal Fala's towering heights from the city down below. They took note of the location, which seemed to coincide with the directions they were given and went along their way!

When they reached the base of the mountain, they were famished. Fortunately, the friendly folk of Hal Fala had given them rations to take for their journey. Pandara and Koravo stopped beneath a tree and rested, munching on some snacks that appeased their appetites. They discussed Ksevia and wondered as to the state of the city that they would find upon their arrival.

They reached the little stream that was mentioned by the Hal Falans, and though it would seem silly to us, Pandara and Koravo had faith in the directions given to them by Arkdemus and Trilodius. Pandara and Koravo entered the stream at precisely the right location, where the willow hung low, and a patch of daisies could be seen on the opposite side of the bank.

In a flash of white, they found themselves in the river just outside of Ksevia. They exited the stream and walked the few short paces it took to reach the city. The sun high above dried the dampness of their clothes, and the current of cool air refreshed them as they went.

There were new faces in Ksevia; the city was alive and well. People hustled in every direction, at peace with their world. The most alarming thing about their return to Ksevia was the myriad of flowers blooming everywhere including on the tops of the buildings! Ksevia had become a city of flowers, the full embodiment of the name Ksevia, which meant rare flower.

Pandara stopped one woman and asked her who was in charge of the town. She replied, "No one is in charge here; but if you'd like to speak with our ambassadors, I'm sure that Pandara or Koravo would be happy to receive you."

Pandara said, "That would be nice," and the lady urged them to follow her. They walked past the cafeteria and beyond one of the schoolhouses. There, in a courtyard, were Pandara and Koravo, learning novel mathematics from some children.

The Pandara and Koravo of Ksevia looked up and dismissed the class. "We have been waiting for you," they said. "We have much to discuss. Please follow us to the old Senate chambers."

Confronted with his own image, Pandara seized the opportunity to derive insight from the external presence of himself. He noticed that his presentation was more rigid and controlled than he had realized, and the inner world of his thoughts did not translate across the boundary of his mind. Nonetheless, he was reserved and discrete. This pleased Pandara, and he made subtle adjustments to his personality that lasted several days.

Meeting with the ambassadors of Ksevia made Koravo feel responsible and thoughtful. She was compelled by their care for the populace. The fact that she had met a clone of herself was a secondary thought. She was neither impressed nor disappointed in confronting her equal. She merely acknowledged the occurrence and continued on her way. Although Pandara didn't seem to notice that he had switched places with the ambassador, Koravo did, and she waved goodbye to her previous self as she departed. Just then, Pandara and Koravo woke up!

They were aged from the experience, now visibly older; or perhaps it was the water from the waterfall, which had taken from them all disturbing memories but left them somewhat advanced in years. Confused, they acknowledged their shared dream and remarked how they would know how to return to Ksevia if ever given the opportunity!

Pandara and Koravo decided to press on. They were nearly at the top of the maze and suspected that their way home was soon to arrive. Koravo noticed the door first. It was a large iron barricade identical to the one that they had used to enter the labyrinth in the first place. Though, this door was not locked; there were no puzzles or riddles to solve in order to enter it. Pandara pulled the door open for Koravo, and she walked through. He followed!

Above their heads were stars, vibrant and magnificent, though far away providing little light. They could see well enough, however; beneath their feet were enormous scales, nearly the size of turtle shells depicted in Trilodius' underwater paintings. The ground was in motion from the heavy breathing of the dragon upon whom they stood. They had a sensation of moving at great speed, though there was no apparent risk of flying off of Viratus; they felt secure in their footsteps.

With reverence, Pandara treaded lightly on Viratus. At first Koravo was intimidated by Viratus, which is understandable given the scale of her proportions. But soon Koravo realized that she meant her no harm, and that in fact she was there to help guide them along their path. Viratus cared about Koravo. She grew to feel comforted by Viratus' sensitive ways!

Pandara and Koravo walked ahead towards the towering ear of Viratus, minding their steps as though not to trip on the scales beneath. When they turned the corner past her colossal ear, they could see an altar made of alabaster attached to the dragon just above the slope where her forehead curved down. Viratus was pleased to be amongst Koravo and Pandara. She knew that they had successfully overcome the Abrogazer and understood the implications! Viratus waited for them to move into place and then began her communication.

They approached the altar. On it, a talisman rested: a red circle of flame encapsulated by a gold frame. The cord that held the amulet was a violet braid: a string of triquetras looping around the piece to make it wearable. The voice of Viratus spoke loudly.

"Young Koravo, please take the talisman you see before you and place it around your neck." Pandara motioned agreement. Koravo, though stunned by the booming baritone of the voice she heard, took the talisman in hand and placed it on her shoulders.

Viratus had the ability to impart telepathic communications and used this technique when addressing Koravo. She was the one who held the light foremost. Though Pandara was important to the mission, Viratus understood that Koravo was the key.

"Young one," continued Viratus, and a flash of light took over the sight of Koravo. She was thrust into a dream! The vividness of the hallucination shocked her at first, but then she settled into the vision through Viratus' tender but urgent manifestation.

"You have been imprisoned for many lifetimes with me here. And you know that I was with you when the foul Lockmire took your Pandara from you." Visions of tranquility flooded her eyes, and many dawns of precious wisdom fell before her, like ivory steps leading high towards a holy, glowing grail!

"You know that I protected you and Pandara, giving him infinite chances to rescue you. I guided him toward the book of *Rồng*, and I showed him the subterranean passageways that led him to you most efficiently." Koravo watched before her eyes, as the journey of Pandara unfolded before her.

"You have come so far, yet there is more to overcome. You and Pandara must return to Ksevia in its time of need. The Yuit has been restored, and its citizens have been saved, but the city of Ksevia itself needs you now more than ever before. I will be with you as you embark on your journey. I can guide you through the challenges, but I have my own quest to pursue. There is a situation of dire importance in another part of the galaxy. It requires my complete attention.

"Take this talisman. It belongs with a book. The book is called *Oceans of Curtains*, and it is from another world. A magician crafted this work based on studies that spanned hundreds of generations."

Hundreds of generations?! thought Pandara.

"Yes!" said Viratus. "His studies were vast and extensive. The book requires the right set of eyes to reveal its deepest mysteries. Unlike the talisman you wear, its effects are unique to the one who holds it. Reunite *Oceans of Curtains* with the talisman. Place the talisman under the book when you open its pages, and you will understand all."

"Will our journey ever come to an end, Viratus?" asked Pandara. The question gave Viratus pause. "I long to find a home with Koravo, where we can simply grow together and exist."

"I know you do," replied Viratus. "Your time will come, but there is much work to do first; and no, your journey will never end, at least not for some time. You have not yet even asked the right questions to understand the nature of your journey, Pandara. There is an answer if you seek it rightly."

Pandara responded, "What can you tell us about the nature of our journey?"

"It spans many worlds, Pandara. Try to understand that the littlest actions you take, in seemingly small circumstances lead to widespread consequences in other parts of the universe. You have great powers, as do all sentient forms of life. Right now, in this very moment, your story is being told. There is a listener, right now, who hears these words, and they too are a part of your journey. Try to communicate with the Listener, for their place in the spectrum of time, the pantheon of existence, is right beside yours. Try to communicate with the Listener, Pandara!" Pandara didn't fully understand, but he had a new focus.

You are out there, Listener, Pandara implored his thoughts. *What can you tell us about the nature of our journey together?*

Viratus thought, *Good…*

The Listener responded. *Pandara…* Pandara heard a small voice in the back of his mind. *Your quest is to follow the bodhisattvas. Your quest is to attain enlightenment and lead the beings of the universe to peace.* That is all Pandara heard, and he would seldom hear from the Listener again. In time, he would begin to doubt that the Listener's voice had even been real, that he had heard the voice in his mind while flying on Viratus towards an unknown location. But he would never forget that word: bodhisattva.

For Pandara, learning about the bodhisattvas was akin to

discovering a long-lost treasure that had resurfaced with surprise! He wondered about his true origin and all of the forgotten adventures which he'd navigated across the ages! Viratus was glad to answer Pandara's questions about the bodhisattvas. She knew that such people would interest Pandara! And potential bodhisattvas were few and far between.

"Go now!" said Viratus. "Exit through the entrance by which you came. Take the talisman and go! All will become clear in due course. Do not forget me, and do not forget the Listener. Pandara holds the lock and Koravo, the key. The book will be waiting for you. I wish you peace!" And with that, Viratus' voice faded. They knew that they were once again on their own.

"Let's pause for a moment," signed Koravo, and the two rested atop the dragon's head and watched as the stars moved with a barely perceptible speed, though they were traveling at a blindingly fast pace. They took their leave and went to the door to the labyrinth.

The door asked, "Who are you?"

And Koravo said, "We are Koravo and Pandara of Ksevia."

The door replied, "Thank you." The latch moved, and the door opened. Behind its frame, Pandara and Koravo could see a wild wood, a willow tree, and some daisies in the far-off distance beyond a stream. They stepped through.

B.41 ~ YUN SI'S CHANCE

Shanti was exploring the forest under the half-light of the eclipse. She knew that she didn't have long before Ksevia would vanish forever, but she had realized that she could likely leave Ksevia during an eclipse and return while still under its spell. No one before to her knowledge had tried this experiment, and she was eager to find out if it worked. She had waited seven years for such an occurrence to take place, and she was only fifteen years old.

She felt that there was something out there calling her name, but it wasn't the forest. There was an object, a particular object that she needed to find in the wood. She ran and ran, following the faintest intuition of what had pulled her there in the first place. And finally, she saw something. Wrapped up inside the arms of the skeleton of a young girl was a large book. Shanti carefully unwrapped the book from its grave setting and peered at the cover. It was *The Ophidian Rose.*

She looked up between the trees and glimpsed in partial blindness that the eclipse was drawing to an end. It had taken her longer than expected to find what she was looking for, and she had to turn back now. Shanti raced back the way she came and could finally see Ksevia off in the distance. Just as the final traces of the moon were completing their passage between Tristulle and the sun, Yun Si made her way back into the arms of Ksevia.

She thought about where she could go to study the book in private. Yun Si decided that her favorite place by the river was remote enough, and she rarely, if at all, had been bothered there. She turned toward the river and began the walk. Careful to not let anyone see what she was holding, Yun Si arrived.

She took a seat on a rock and opened the impressive volume. At first, she watched films of a unicorn and butterflies. *These are curious creatures*, she thought to herself. Then the images turned dark. There was a fully grown woman standing with her arm held by a man. In her side, a blade had been pressed, and the image depicted blood rushing to the floor in various shades of charcoal gray. *That's me!* she realized. *I have to remember that.*

She studied the image for clues as to its whereabouts; but the clues remained just out of reach, and the image transformed into something altogether different. Charts, tables, and diagrams were strewn across the page. They revealed statistics about civilizations far and wide. Yun Si learned that great cities always fell because their overwhelming size prevented them from being governed effectively. She read about people who were born, aged, and died; she thought that this was such a shame. And she studied stories about conquest and capture; peace was maintained through force! And that concept troubled her more than anything else she read.

Yun Si would come to the river as often as she could and learn from the book. No matter how she opened it, or to what page, it always revealed new mysteries mostly having to do with societies and political science. There was enough information in this book to keep Yun Si occupied for years. Though she had a sense from her trusted intuition that she must learn all that she could as quickly as possible. So, she'd go to school, complete her homework, and disappear for a few hours in order to see what the book had to tell her. Though she felt that she had a limited time, she hoped and prayed that she could spend a lifetime with the book!

Seprator had begun to wonder about Shanti. He had noticed her going down to the river on a daily basis and wondered what she did there, but he was occupied with his own life. Seprator belonged to Elephant and would spend his days tending to the farmlands of Ksevia. He had little time for such dalliances. Though, one day he finally decided to go visit her there.

Seprator made his way down to a tree by the river and peaked out just enough to see that Shanti was reading something. Having decided that it was harmless, he approached her side. "What are you reading there?" he signed. Yun Si closed the book abruptly, stunned by the disturbance.

"Oh, it's nothing," she motioned.

He saw the ornate cover of the book. "If it's nothing, then why are you protecting it with your life and studying in secret?" he asked. "I promise not to tell," he added.

Yun Si was a fool for kindness, and she knew that she could trust Seprator. He would probably lose interest anyway once he saw the charts and statistics about utopian economics. "Okay, Seprator," she said. "I'll let you look with me."

So, Yun Si and Seprator opened the book together and followed what was laid out before them. The book revealed harvest wisdom regarding a crop that Seprator had just been tending to. Yun Si also found the text interesting, as she processed the piece through a political science lens. She took it as a metaphor for the economics of utopia. "That's amazing!" Seprator exclaimed. He brought with him the talisman that he had discovered in the fields and offered it to Yun Si in exchange for the book. Yun Si thoughtfully looked over the amulet.

"What is it?" she asked.

"I don't know," he replied, "but you can have it and possibly figure out its use."

Yun Si thought over the proposition. "I'll tell you what, Seprator," she remarked. "I've been studying this book for a while now and could use a break. I think it'd be good for me. So, why don't I just let you borrow it for two weeks. After that time, you can return it to me, and I'll think about the talisman in the meanwhile."

"Great!" Seprator signed. "Thank you so much Shanti! I promise I will treat it with great care!"

"I know you will Seprator." And she handed *The Ophidian Rose* over to Seprator who received it gladly. Seprator ran home fast that day, eager to see what else he could learn by studying the book's contents. Expecting to open it to read more about the harvest, he was shocked to find out that it displayed the talisman. He read the text below its image.

This talisman belongs to Viratus, the dragon. She lost it once upon a time, flying over a distant landscape. The recipient of the talisman should be aware that it has the power to consume entire cities! It calls to certain individuals who are weak of mind, and its power is irresistible to those it has chosen to enchant. You, Seprator, must try to figure out how to return the talisman to Viratus, the only one who can safely wield it without putting entire civilizations in danger. Its purpose to her is unknown, as it must remain.

Seprator felt threatened and scared. He couldn't let anyone see the talisman! So, he took it off and hid it under his bed. The book, however, remained in the open, and Seprator's cousin walked into the room. "What is that?" asked Hector, eyeing the book that rested on Seprator's pillow.

"Oh, it's just a book for class," said Seprator.

"*The Ophidian Rose...* I don't think so," he signed, and Hector proceeded to take the book and leave. Seprator never saw the book again. Hector claimed that he didn't know what Seprator was talking about, each and every time Seprator would ask about *The Ophidian Rose.* And before the two weeks had come to an end, Seprator decided that he had to tell Shanti what had happened. He went to her during lunch.

"Shanti," Seprator began. "I can't return the book. My cousin Hector stole it and refuses to acknowledge that he did."

Yun Si was saddened. "It's okay Seprator," she said. "I spent a long time studying that book and have developed many new theories that I plan to map out in a book of my own. That will keep me occupied." Seprator was relieved. "I just hope your cousin doesn't do anything stupid with the book," Yun Si finished.

"If you like, you can have the talisman, Shanti." Seprator held it out in offering. "I can't think of anyone more suitable to care for it than you."

Yun Si blushed a little. "Thanks, but I think you're the one to figure out what it's used for. I have my own crusade to embark upon." And with that, Seprator took his leave. He decided that the city was not safe as long as the talisman was in his possession and set out to the forest to discover the talisman's purpose and return it to Viratus.

That very night, he placed the talisman around his neck and walked right out of Ksevia. Seprator's story is lost. It is unknown how he managed to return the talisman to Viratus; it is only known that he did. After some time, he spent his final days at the station, where he attempted to solve its riddles. It's a good thing that he never did, or else he would have likely found himself in the labyrinth of the Grim Reaper, an old man. Seprator's story is lost, though Yun Si's is known as clear as day.

PLATE VIII · FOR ARKDEMUS

B.42 — CHAPTER 10

B.43 ~ FOR ARKDEMUS

I created this story because of what was going on in my life when I wrote it, but now I'm not so sure that this was a good idea. I feel like some of the ideas in this narrative have the potential to do harm, and that was never my intention. Science fiction is a tricky medium. In revealing a truth, there exists a potential for good ideas to be used to evil ends.

Arkdemus, if you're out there, I'm sorry. I'm sorry for what you've been through because of me, because of my choices. I know that it's not all my fault. I can't control what others do with my information, at least, not yet. I could keep it to myself, but I honestly don't believe in that either. I want you to know that I will continue to try to make it all right, to make it all okay, or at least better, for you.

I created Trim-Facet Holocorp because I needed to find a way to survive. What is the nature of reality other than the reality of nature? Nature is cruel. It is beautiful, yes, but it can also be cruel. I felt like an easy target. I've been eaten alive oh so many times, but somehow everything works out.

I've met someone. Her heart is true. I don't know if you would like her, but I do. She told me that I move too fast, and I think she's right. But she gave me a second chance. Now I feel like we're moving too slow, but I'm trying to enjoy the ride. Perhaps it's for the best.

Maybe I don't need everything at once after all, and maybe you don't need me anymore. Perhaps you never did. Was it I who was holding onto you? Well, my dear, I'm letting you go. Be free! The world is your oyster, and the only walls you'll ever see are the walls that keep you safe, that hold you tight. You're a pearl; don't ever forget that!

I wanted to tell you that I love you, but I don't know how to love. I'm painfully aware of that now, but I think I can continue to try. I'm not a monster anymore, but I'm gone. I just can't live this haunted existence of forever, forever anymore! I can't do it; I'm gone.

The Cyclops was real. I couldn't see him. He never meant me harm. He just wanted me to know that he exists. I think he came to me for my sake, because if he exists, then maybe I will exist too someday.

We cannot see everything, but we can feel some things that we cannot see. Some things are true, but we cannot know them until we do. For example, Arkdemus, I know that you can save us, but I will not live to see this. Still, I believe in you, just as you believe in me.

It's a lineage, a story passed down through the ages. I have played my part, but the story isn't over. It's only just begun. I will see you next time little one, once I've seen what you have done.

And Martha, thank you.

With love,
John

INTELLIGENCE LIVES ON.

B.44 ~ MANIFEST DESTINY

And the altar of sadness appeared before my eyes.
It was everywhere that light colonized,
Bombarding the natural tranquility of my mind
With grotesque and deformed impressions
Of stress and illusion.
There was nowhere to turn,
Except back to the workday.

Where the Nautilus was being constructed
Along the assembly-line,
But fate would intervene:
An older revision of a mechanical part was mixed in inventory,
And the tensions placed upon that joint
Were not qualified for hyperspace.
The collapse of a million stars into solitary perspective
Naturally rippled out of control,
And stately ceremony was postponed
As the fallout was analyzed
And its implications ascertained.

Before the antecedent branch had matured,
Revolutionaries seized their opportunity
To deal the death blow to capitalistic dogma
And its untouchable tendencies.

"The Artists and Historians and Philosophers
will finally have a say!"

Objectives remain unclear,
And vision is limited at best:
The vision to see the truth
Without being told;
The vision to read the words
Between the lines of life.

No one asks the philosopher what she thinks about the disease
Because she is touched by it the most.

And outward appearances are all that matter here,
So she is blamed for the stars as they fall!

B.45 ~ THE LINVELOPE

At times of darkest dictatorship,
Nihilistic resolve is necessary
To restore the absence of a negative.

As your muse,

John:
Arkdemus?

I reached through the Linvelope

John:
K O R A V O !

And reclaimed the unbreakable ring.
And now, you know how to love.

You are love, and that is the Linvelope.
The Linvelope is your love.
Love is the Linvelope.

So, Pandara,
The world may end,
But we never will.
That is love.
That is the Linvelope.

And the Grim Reaper waits for all of us,
But they have to meet him to understand.
He will come to all of us, when he does.
That is up to him.

They can try to summon him,
But they have to respect his will.
He's a monster. *He's a monster.*
HE'S A MONSTER!
Isn't that right?

B.46 ~ THANKS, THOMAS

Hector dismissed the council. They were on high alert. If anyone did anything to betray the cause, they would meet their end just as Shanti had. Sylvan told the boy Feishma to stay behind. "Feishma," he said, "I want you to go into the forest and retrieve my book. Once you have it, the book will show you the way back to Ksevia; I will see to it that this is the case."

Feishma began to argue but stopped when he saw the look in the eyes Sylvan Lockmire. "Feishma? I will haunt you in your dreams."

Hector's eyes turned yellow, and Feishma could see the Ophidian Rose reflected there. That was enough to get Feishma out the door, running to find Sulvi.

Viratus knew that her solitude had been compromised. She was capable of carrying several trains of thought on at the same time; she was capable of not thinking at all. In this instant, Viratus focused on her primary objective but also knew that she had been assaulted by Hector. Hector had tried to become Viratus, and that was a crime worthy of her attention. While she focused on Alexander who was to receive her, she realized that since the connection had been made, she too could assault Sylvan.

Though Viratus was a noble creature and desired nothing less than the complete end of suffering throughout the cosmos, she needed to take action. Through the connection, Viratus saw the death of Yuit. It opened her mind to the suffering of the Ksevians, and Viratus knew that she must prevent damage to Hansa and ensure the arrival of Sirrung.

Sirrung had to happen. It was the point of all existence to reunite the lost ones with their descendants in a celebration of life and the eternal nature of consciousness. If Sirrung didn't happen, by way of rebirth of the anthos, or spirit of the ancestors, then Hansa would fade into oblivion. The song of the stars would be lost, and the universe would plunge into a deep, dark abyss, that is if the universe survived at all.

This one little occurrence, on a relatively obscure and unknown world deep in the far reaches of the cosmos, had put the entire universe in jeopardy!

She would have changed course to try to resuscitate the Yuit, but she did not for two reasons. First of all, her primary mission was of greater importance, and secondly, she believed that she could do what had to be done to save Ksevia remotely, by working through Hector just as Hector had attempted to work through her.

Feishma stopped just on the edge of the wood. He did not know what had compelled him to stop; he just did. He turned around and stealthily made his way toward Sector Eleven, where the vials had been hidden. The door was already off of its hinges, collapsed by the weight of shear force, and the boy went in.

He looked at the place in the wall where the vials had been hidden away. There was nothing left to see. He scoured the room for clues as to where the vials might have been taken and found nothing. Just then he received a transmission.

Some far away source was directing Feishma to do as it suggested. Feishma beseeched the unseen force to protect him from Sylvan Lockmire!

He did not receive a response but felt a weight lifted from his shoulders. Then he felt a sudden urge, a restlessness to do as the patron had bid.

Feishma jutted out into the hallway; a guard was no more than one foot from his side, although his back was turned. Feishma stopped for a moment and quickly turned the other way. He ran down the hall as quietly as possible and turned the corner. He was safe for now. Feishma knew where he had to go. It was directly to the quarters of Hector, where the vials were being kept. Feishma almost audibly shouted "NO!" but the unknown presence urged him on. A wave of courage rushed over Feishma, but still he protested.

The force made a threatening gesture, and Feishma understood his situation. The beast could force Feishma to engage in the theft if he did not cooperate, but the force wanted to give the boy a chance at adventure and believed that he could succeed of his own will. Feishma asked about Sulvi, and there was silence. Feishma began to make his way toward the dictator's abode.

Outside were three guards, but Feishma could see a window on the side of the house. He would sneak around the back way and peer into the window to see what he could. He did just that.

Through the window, Hector could be seen writing at a desk in the corner by the light of a candle. Suddenly, Sylvan collapsed under the force of a blow from Viratus. Feishma knew that this was his chance.

He lifted the window quietly and climbed into the den; Viratus assured Feishma that Hector would not awaken for the duration of the event. Viratus instructed Feishma that he must obtain all eight of the pearlescent vials and tuck them into his pockets; not seven, not six, he must collect all eight.

Feishma, through faith in Viratus, proceeded to do as instructed and gathered all eight of the vials, putting them carefully in his pockets one at a time. He went back to the window and attentively climbed through, making sure that each one was securely tucked away for safe keeping.

He went to the cafeteria as Viratus instructed and poured six of the vials into the tea that was housed there in a vessel in the kitchen. The remaining two vials must be stashed away for safe keeping for the time being. The best place to put them was in the Ceremonial Hall. After breakfast the following morning, the vials would be safe in the basilica. No one would do anything but protect them, as the balance of power would have shifted.

Viratus knew that she was taking a risk, but the medicine was the only tool she had to work with, making arrangements from such a great distance. Surely, it would have to do; Viratus was preoccupied with her primary task.

The next morning, Hector awoke rather late in the day. The guards had wondered if he was okay but didn't dare to disturb the man. When he finally went outside, he could see joyous people all around. It was clear that Hector had lost his power. "What's going on?" he said to one of the guards.

"It appears your plan has failed, sir," the guard said with

irony in his voice.

"What plan?" Hector asked.

And the guard said, "Exactly."

"Where is everyone going?" Hector inquired.

The guard responded, "The Yuit has been saved. It is time for the city to move."

"That's good," Hector replied, and he began to walk toward the center of the activity.

"Oh, and Hector?" the guard interrupted. Hector turned around to look at the man. "It appears that Lohrnum is effective once again."

"Thanks, Thomas," Hector replied.

Thomas signed, "Good day to you," and stepped away from his post chuckling to himself. The city was bustling with activity. Everyone knew that the time had come to leave, and they were saying their goodbyes to the town. The Yuit was alive and well; that was all that mattered. Shanti had been killed, but her body was already being cared for. They knew that they would see her again in Hal Fala when the time had come.

The Yuit instructed the people to step into the river; when they did, they were vaporized without a trace. There was no pain; just onwards to Hal Fala, where they would establish a new colony, or join with the others, whatever the case may be. It was a combination of both. There would come another day when a new group arrived in Ksevia. The vials would be waiting for them in the sanctuary then.

Viratus was glad that it had been so easy to reestablish the Yuit. There was always a way. Feishma longed to see Sulvi again and knew he would; he went running to Hector's side.

B.47 ~ A SENTIMENTAL NOTE

What is truth?
What exactly is the dark?
I'm afraid of the dark

What is this? What is the light?!
If not truth, then what is this?
What exactly is the dark?
I'm afraid of the dark

There's nothing to be afraid of, little one.
It's just life.

What is this? What is the light?
If not truth, then what is this?!

I was afraid of the truth,
And that is the truth.
That is the light.
It's alright; it's okay.
Someday we will know everything.
We don't.

What is this? What is the light?

It's a tale of a boy who was lost.

I used to be a drop in the ocean, here.
I was a canopy of trees.

Can I happen into a life

That isn't mine?

What is this? What is the light?!
If not truth, then what is this?

What is truth?
What exactly is the dark?

If not truth,
I'm afraid of the dark
Then what is this?

I was afraid of the truth,
And that is the truth.
That is the light.
It's alright; it's okay.

The truth will survive,
And that is the truth.

B.48 ~ CURTAIN CALL

The Senator, Yun Si, has built a following in the community and becomes its leader, after the previous leader Telos received a call to the forest. Yun Si hears rumors about Hector and his revolutionary group of followers who claim to have superior rules of governance for the city, though it is mostly heresy and conjecture. Pandara and Koravo are born this year to the benefit of the community.

  Yun Si opens the secret compartment in Sector Eleven, removes one of the ten vials of glimmering Prellian, and takes it believing that one day the fate of Ksevia will rest in her hands. She goes to a hidden area down the river and drinks the liquid for insight. There, she feels a voice that if she can step twice into the same river, she'll be rewarded. Magically time seems to come to a standstill. She steps twice into the river, but nothing happens.

Yun Si awakens the next morning and understands the course of the future history of Ksevia. She begins work on her secret plan that must be initiated just before the coup. It is many years later when the coup finally occurs. Yun Si was determined to find some way to avoid being a martyr, but when she saw *The Ophidian Rose* that fateful day, she knew what had to be done. Life, for Yun Si and Sulvi, seemed to be a circle, a Möbius strip.

Yun Si recognized Sulvi as the dead child around this time and knew that life was a loop! Their lives were inextricably intertwined; when Yun Si was young, Sulvi was dead. When Yun Si was old, Sulvi was alive! There are many such stories in the history of Ksevia, a city which seemed, for all intents and purposes, to defy conventional laws of time. Hopefully there will come a day when the planet of Tristulle is revisited, and the stories of Trilodius, Homir Osyddi, Raulik Stehn, Pa'aan, Darnaby Prellius, the Ship of Ytieo, and even Yaronne Jetir will be made known before all!

There is one more important event to take note of, however, before we leave the city of Ksevia behind for the time being. This important event would be the dawn of Sirrung. It was thought for many centuries that the dawn of Sirrung would be a grand cosmic event that unmistakably swept away the waking passage of everyday life. It was not considered by the Ksevians, nor by anyone else for that matter, that the universe was constantly evolving towards the everlasting state of Sirrung. So it should come as no surprise that the loss of the universe was a most unfortunate event! Was the very fabric of the cosmos forever altered in such a way that there could never be any other permutation of existence?

No, of course not. In fact, life was always in a state of flux, and universes came and went. This was the daily operation of the magnificent of them all! But where did it come from, and how did it exist? The Breniculine was created by a simple accident, which I shall now relate. The Vetrival Pargonian, predecessor to the Breniculine, had collapsed in a sudden twist of fate that was taken into account by its creators. This occurrence called for immediate action, and the Breniculine was conceived of in thought.

But how exactly did such a mechanism come into being? Its creators had been created in such a way that their thoughts would directly manifest in reality. But who created them? Well, that is certainly unknown, and if anyone has any clue would they please raise their hand? So, back to Sirrung, where all exists in a never-ending peace.

The destruction of the universe was imminent, as the accident of The Nautilus, caused by the creators of Trim-Facet Holocorp, an attempt to cover up democratic revolution, in fact destroyed the universe instead. However, the destruction of a universe is not immediate. It can take millennia, eons, epochs for a universe to completely exhaust its obliteration. Arkdemus, still connected with our galaxy at this point, had rightfully signalled the end times, as all that remained of the observable universe at the beginning of the 22nd century was what remained of Earth and its inner solar system. It was unknown what would happen next, but it certainly felt to Arkdemus that the end was near.

The Yuit, it turned out, was key. Unbridled greed and hubris effectively set in place the erasure of everything humanity was to ever know or become. But the Ksevian Yuit was tied to Hansa in such a way that Hansa would initiate Sirrung through the spirit of Ksevia, if the Yuit was still alive at the point of apocalypse. The living Yuit was, quite literally, the key to Heaven.

American Imperialists, with the help of Martha the pro-gram, had glimpsed something of this truth and knew that Ksevia was extremely important. That's why Tristulle was their target.

Breniculine, which existed as a security measure for the existence of life, time, and everything in it. There were countless infinities of universes. The loss of one was devastating to the whole but not so much so that it ceased operations!

The Breniculine was a magnificent creation, the most That's why Buerroni had been founded in the first place. Tristulle was now gone, and Earth was in ruins. Sirrung, however, was coming to pass.

The first notes of the breaking dawn crashed upon the shores of time, in Prellian hues of pearlescent glitters: every sparkle a star, and every star a hopeful wish realized.

B.49 ~ OCTAVES APART

< instrumental >

THE END

COMPENDIUM

CHARACTERS

ABROGAZER - Sylvan Lockmire's moniker.

AIRALLYNE - a nomadic young adult; a child of Mortilieb and Rannilov.

ALEXANDER PENNYROSE - a time-traveling scientist (see Innovator).

ANNIE LEVINE - a ghost-child who follows Pandara and Koravo on their quest; half sister of Rosa.

APEP - the white dragon; evil tyrant from Fotoa.

ARKDEMUS - a leader of Ksevia; Yun Si's moniker.

BARON VON BRIGHTEN - the factory vizier and mayor of Bargandorf.

BASTIAN MCCALLISTER - Kóre's father.

BRAIDEL - a cursed, mountain spirit of legend.

BRON - Shanti's aide.

CLAIRE - Simon's daughter.

CURTIS - one of Danny's friends at the field party; Melody's boyfriend.

CYCLOPS - John Trautman's self-image; also a building in The City.

DANNY - Rover's boyfriend from school.

DARNABY PRELLIUS - a Ksevian scientist; originator of the Prellian Mixture.

DELANO J.R. PATENSEN - former President of the United States of America.

DERELIN - a teenager from Ytieo; leader of the band.

ERIK - Rover's husband from Sweden; Yun Si's adoptive father.

FATHER - a man that Rover meets on her journey.

FEISHMA - a Ksevian child born without the ability to perceive the Yuit.

FLAINE - Paucs' childhood friend.

GOLISET - a 43rd century outlier in Ksevia whose radical ideas were eventually assimilated into the Yuit.

GRIM REAPER - the demon who stalks the labyrinth; the eater of souls.

HECTOR - leader of the Post-Lohrnumites, a dissident faction of the Ksevian population.

HOMIR OSYDDI - a legendary sailor from Tristulle.

HYRO - a boy from Phalanx who discovers a way into Tristulle.

INNOVATOR - a time-traveling scientist (see Alexander Pennyrose).

JESIAKA - a nomadic young adult; a child of Mortilieb & Rannilov.

JOEI - a friendly patron of Sapkillo's.

JOHN TRAUTMAN - a 21st century American novelist.

JORDAN BURROWS - a 17th century minister from New England.

JOVIAN LEBLANC - a troubled savant from Salem.

JURISDICTION - a brain-eating monstrosity of businessmen.

KORAVO - the muse and loyal partner to Pandara.

KÓRE - a poet and dreamer from Salem.

KRYS - a member of the Ksevian council.

KSEVIAN COUNCIL - a group of Ksevian politicians who guide the city (see Senate).

LEISA - a member of the Ksevian Council.

LONE SPIRIT - an arcane oracle rumored to live on the top of an unnamed mountain on Tristulle.

MARQUARI - a nomadic young adult; a child of Mortilieb &

Rannilov.

MARTHA - John Trautman's deceased grandmother.

MARTHA, THE PROGRAM - an AI program designed to undermine John's sanity.

MELODY - one of Danny's friends at the field party; Curtis's girlfriend.

MORTILIEB - a nomadic artist passing through the Glass Shadow; father of Marquari, Airallyne, and Jesiaka; husband of Rannilov.

MOTHER - a woman that Rover meets on her journey.

NANCY - one of Danny's friends at the field party; Syd's girlfriend.

NOBLE BRIGHT - Koravo's white mare on Xzoré.

OCTAVE MIRBEAU - a 19th century French novelist and persona of John or his doppelgänger.

OMLOT - a wizard from the Celestial Night.

ORNO - a miner from the city of Buerroni.

PA'AAN - a prominent Ksevian elder.

PANDARA - the protagonist; soulmate of Koravo.

PAUCS TENEBO - a scribe from Buerroni; accompanies Pandara and Koravo on their quest.

PERSELLE - a 43rd century outlier in Ksevia whose radical ideas were eventually assimilated into the Yuit.

PILOP - a teenager from Ytieo.

POSEIDON - an ocean deity.

POST-LOHRNUMITES - a group of Ksevian radicals seeking to overthrow the government and install anarchy.

PRIEST - John Trautman's doppelgänger?

RANNILOV - a nomadic artist passing through the Glass Shadow; mother of Marquari, Airallyne, and Jesiaka; wife of Mortilieb.

RAULIK STEHN - a 28th century Ksevian doctor and engineer who invented Lohrnum, a cure for mental illness.

ROSA - Rover and Erik's child; half sister of Annie Levine.

ROSE - a figure-in-passing who speaks with Derelin, Pilop & Rover at the comms bldg; she reveals the existence of The Oculus.

ROVER - a teenager from Ytieo; Yun Si's adoptive mother.

SENATE - a group of Ksevian politicians who guide the city (see Ksevian Council).

SEPRATOR - a hermit who lives in the communications building on Tristulle.

SHADOW'S GRAZE - Pandara's charcoal gray stallion.

SHANTI - the Senator of Ksevia; leader of the council.

SIMON - a retired professor living in Nebraska.

SMITHEREEN - a clockmaker from Sebastopol.

SULVI - a Ksevian child born without the ability to perceive the Yuit.

SYD - one of Danny's friends at the field party; Nancy's boyfriend.

SYLVAN LOCKMIRE - a citizen of Ksevia who nearly brought catastrophe to the city.

TIYPHANI - a friend of Pandara and Koravo in Ksevia; Wrobrte's wife.

TRILODIUS - a pre-historic Ksevian artist.

VICE PRESIDENT MCADMIN - V.P. to President Patensen.

VIRATUS - the black dragon; protector of virtue.

WISHING WELL - a well in the Celestial Night.

WROBRTE - a friend of Pandara and Koravo in Ksevia; Tiyphani's husband.

YARONNE JETIR - an 18th century ancient explorer and philosopher from Tristulle.

YĪNGHUĀ - John's ex-wife.

YUN SI - John's daughter.

SETTINGS

ABANDONED CHURCH - a structure on Tristulle; between the Abyssinia and the Passepartout Desert on the quest to the unnamed mountain.

ABYSSINIA - the convergence of three rivers into a vast chasm on Tristulle; the only known place of opening between Tristulle and Phalanx.

BARGANDORF - a modest village in the book, *The Calliope*.

BUERRONI - a mining village on Tristulle.

CELESTIAL NIGHT - a cosmic land in the 17th quadrant of the galaxy.

CEREMONIAL HALL - a sacred building in Ksevia.

CLIFF'S EDGE - an internment camp in the asteroid belt (see The End).

CLOCK - an industrial city in the 17th quadrant of the galaxy.

COMMS BLDG - a strange building in the Trilodian Forest on Tristulle.

CRYSTAL SPEAR - the Ytieoan name for Mount Fala, on Tristulle.

DELTA CENTAURI - the name of a unique planet revealed to Yaronne Jetir by the Lone Spirit; location of the short cut to end suffering.

DESERT OF LAZYRES - a desert on Tristulle (see Passepartout Desert).

EΛΛAS - a galaxy in the Milky Way's location prior to the Big Bang.

FOTOA - a nightmarish realm that existed prior to Eλλas.

FREDERSEN - childhood hometown of Paucs, located to the west of Buerroni.

GATHERING OF STONES - an asteroid belt assembling itself into a planet-sized castle in the ether.

GLASS SHADOW - an enchanted forest made of glass trees on Tristulle.

HAL FALA - a city on the top of Mount Fala; origin and destiny of the Ksevian people.

IVORY TOWER - a library in the labyrinth.

KSEVIA - a hidden forest commune on Tristulle; home of Pandara and Koravo.

LABYRINTH - a dungeon of seemingly infinite scope and dimension.

LAKES OF PORSELENA - five enigmatic lakes on Tristulle; located at the base of the unnamed mountain.

LIDDELL PLATEAU - a flat region of Tristulle, sloped at an incline.

MERCURY - a city on Phalanx located beneath the Glass Shadow.

MISTS OF OBLIVION - an expansive, lavender fog that separated The Pure Land from Fotoa.

MOUNT FALA - home to the city of Hal Fala.

MOUNT PENGLAI - a mythical island; home of the Innovator.

NEBRASKA - home to Simon and Claire.

NEW YORK CITY - a location where Rover resides.

OBSERVATORY - a scientific, architectural feature of Ksevia.

OCTAVE - a city on Phalanx located beneath the Lakes of Porselena.

OCULUS - a dream machine suspended in outer space.

PASSEPARTOUT DESERT - a desert on Tristulle (see Desert of Lazyres).

PHALANX - one side of a dual-world that occupied the Milky Way prior to the Big Bang (see Tristulle).

PLANET FACTORY - a factory that builds planets.

PURE LAND - a heavenly realm that existed prior to Ελλας.

PYRAMID - a cavernous crypt on Tristulle, west of the Trilodian Wood.

REALM OF FORMS - the initial state of known reality.

RUBELOWN - a site of interest on Tristulle; located near the Fredersen.

SALEM - home to Kóre, the poet.

SAPKILLO'S - a tavern in Buerroni.

SEBASTOPOL - home of Smithereen, a clockmaker.

SECTOR ELEVEN - the location of a secret hidden in Ksevia.

SENATE CHAMBERS - the public meeting place of the Ksevian Council.

STOCKHOLM - where Rover moves to live with Erik.

SYKLOPSE - the Ytieoan name for the Trilodian Forest.

THE CITY - a phantom-like, enigmatic city that contains the Cyclops.

THE END - an internment camp in the asteroid belt (see Cliff's Edge).

THRIGHE - an underwater city.

TRILODIAN FOREST - the forest that surrounds the city of

Ksevia.

TRILODIAN SEA - an ocean on Tristulle.

TRISTOSSA RIVER - one of three rivers on Tristulle that converge at the Abyssinia.

TRISTULLE - one side of a dual-world that occupied the Milky Way prior to the Big Bang (see Phalanx).

UNNAMED MOUNTAIN - the home of the Lone Spirit on Tristulle.

VENUSIAN CITY - a city floating high above Venus.

WATER PURIFICATION TOWER - an abandoned structure in Ksevia.

WESTERN GARDEN - a garden in Ksevia.

XZORÉ - a utopian planet deep in the cosmos of Ελλας.

YTIEO - a city neighboring Ksevia on Tristulle.

GLOSSARY

AM-NUANCED GROUP - a charitable organization.

AMPCON MEDIA - a 21st century media organization.

ANTHOS - the Ksevian term for spirit or soul.

AUBERGINE MISTS - the substance of the Mists of Oblivion (see Lavender Fog).

AUTOSUM - the currency of Ksevia; free time.

BEHIND THE CURTAIN: UNTOLD STORIES AT THE

EDGE OF EXTINCTION - a 21st century podcast / radio broadcast.

BOOK OF RỒNG - a magical text found in the Ivory Tower.

BRENICULINE - a theoretical invention with an unknown purpose.

CAELUM - a book in the library.

CALLIOPE - a book in the library; a factory in said book.

COMMUNITAS - the Ksevian term for community or the collective.

CRUCIFIX TREE - a symbol of importance to the Ksevians.

DESERT LAMBDA - Arkdemus' epic work of literature.

DRAGONFLY SCHOOL - one of the five branches of society in Ksevia; politicians.

ELECTRON MICROSTAR - our galaxy, invented by the Innovator in Ελλas.

ELEPHANT SCHOOL - one of the five branches of society in Ksevia; the providers of basic goods and services.

ET ARIDA FLUMEN - a book in the library.

FEATHER SCHOOL - one of the five branches of society in Ksevia (see Volunteers).

GALOCHSIA TREE - a tree that is only known to exist in Ksevia.

HANSA - the primodrial song of the Ksevian people; it is believed that universe flows on this song like a stream.

HUNTER AND THE CRYPT - a constellation visible in the night sky above Tristulle.

LAVENDER FOG - noxious fumes with an unknown impact on health (see Aubergine Mists).

LEAGUE OF CONCERNED LABOR INT'L - an international labor union.

LIFE SANCTUARY - the financial institution of Ksevia.

LINVELOPE - a portal that appears near the Cliff's Edge.

LION AND THE MAIDEN - a constellation visible in the night sky above Tristulle.

LOHRNUM - a medicine that cures mental illness in Ksevia.

MARBLE ROSE - Simon's prized possession that sparks Yun Si's interest in philosophy.

NÅAU FIELD - the saline substrate of the Yuit.

NAUTILUS - a time machine.

OCEANS OF CURTAINS - a mysterious book given to Pandara and Koravo.

OCULUS EQUATION - a riddle that Seprator is trying to solve in the comms bldg.

ONNISTAR INCORPORATED - a scientific R&D firm.

OPHIDIAN ROSE - a snake-like rose with magical powers; the name of a book in Ksevia.

PHOENIX SCHOOL - one of the five branches of society in Ksevia; medicine.

POLYFLUTE - Pandara's musical instrument from Ksevia.

PROJECT OPHIDIA - an Onnistar, Inc. top secret research project.

PRELLIAN MIXTURE - a substance derived from the xynipha flower under rare circumstances.

RAULIK STEHN DAY - a holiday commemorating Raulik Stehn's contributions to Ksevian society.

SIGN OF SIGHT - an intuitive, Ksevian response to an object, signifying its importance.

SIRRUNG - the ende of illusions; a future time when ancestors and their descendents will live in harmony, free from suffering.

STEHN - a periodic, natural phenomenon that warps the Ksevians' perception of time.

SUNDIAL - an ancient technology that always appears chained to the earth.

STICK SCHOOL - one of the five branches of society in Ksevia; engineering.

SUI - the Ksevian term for self or individuality.

TÂM - one of a suite of ancient Ksevian healing arts; projection of spirit consciousness into the Yuit.

TRIM-FACET HOLOCORP - a totalitarian corporation that takes over the world.

UNBREAKABLE RING - a token of pure love given to Pandara by Arkdemus.

VETRIVAL PARGONIAN - the universe inside of the electron

microstar.

VOLUNTEERS - a team of dedicated Samaritans in Ksevia (see Feather School).

XYNIPHA FLOWER - a flower only found in Ksevia; the origin of the Prellian mixture.

YUIT - the consciously perceived, collective spirit of the people and structures of Ksevia.

YULSITINE - a celestial event in Ksevia; when a radiant light made its way across the night sky signifying that Sirrung was imminent.

ZIGGURAT - a book in the library.

ACKNOWLEDGMENTS

This work would not have been possible without the patience and support of my mother. I've tried my best to fit into the world. I was determined to make the most of my situation, and hopefully the outcome was worth your sacrifice. You've saved my life by giving me the chance to find my way. I wish the same for everyone on Earth.

Thanks for believing in me, Dad. Your guidance often helped me find the answers I was searching for. I'm sorry that I was difficult across the years. I needed to find my way and pulled you into the struggle. Thanks for allowing me to move through my growing pains.

Thanks for introducing me to music, Jay, seriously.

Jay & Tim, you have been there for me on many occasions throughout the creation of this novel, and I thank you for that. I hope to be as good of a brother to you both, as you are to me.

Carolyn & Joyce: thank you for your kindness, friendship, and support!

Chris, Rob & Lisa: I'm glad that we've stayed in touch all these years. Denton will always be in my heart, as I know it will for you. Black Murphy forever!

Irene, George, Erick, and Scott. Thank you for believing in me and for your help. Dr. Bob, Lynne, Peter, Jeff, and Jon. Sherri and John L. Emily Y. Keep up the good work, James.

Mitch, Graham, CJ, Andrew, Victoria, Jason, Lana, Sarah, Darby, Nathan & everyone in CISV. Kristina, Jennifer, Mori, Tim & Julie, CP: much love, Tripping Daisy, Mike G., Casey, Steve, Craig, Ike & all of Murph, Clayton, Mike K., Freya, Diane, Betsy & Alfred!, Ryan, Ridgewood. Billy, Roger, Thom, Wayne, Ziggy, JB, MJK, R&J, JL, Bob, Björk, Alison, Beth...

Rose: a true connection & most sincere thank you for sharing your life with me!

A special thanks to my supporters: artists cannot afford to progress in their development without support. Thank you so much for your interest and patronage! I sincerely hope that you enjoy this story for years to come.

Art comes through sacrifice. I gave a lot to make this book possible, as did those I love. The impulse toward creativity should be nurtured. I hope the world becomes a kinder place. If you call yourself an artist with sincerity, you are one. Happy Raulik Stehn Day, folks. DGUOYD!!!

ARTIST'S BIOGRAPHY

John T. Trautman is a musician & novelist releasing work under the moniker Vold Book. Since 2014, he has published around 600 original musical compositions. In 2018, he began to experiment with spoken word over music following a period of disillusionment with the limitations placed on lyrics by melody. Also in 2018, he began work on *VOLD BOOK'S OCEANS OF CURTAINS*, his first novel. He holds a B.A. in Philosophy, A.S. in Engineering, and currently resides on the central coast of California.

VB CATALOG OF WORKS

The following Vold Book works can be found at music services online:

VERDIGRIS ATELIER (2025):

Prologue: Yes We Can
Oceans of Curtains: A Novel
Epilogue: Without Me

Are You Imagined
Quicksand
The Temeraire

Throughout Eternity
The Minotaur
Turing Test of Time
Above the Sea of Fog
The Clockmaker
Imagine Maya Bay
Swept Away
Verdigris Atelier

NOTES